**Two brand-new stories in every volume...
twice a month!**

Duets Vol. #89

Just in time for the holidays—a delightful Double Duets from *USA TODAY* bestselling author Jacqueline Diamond! Christmas and Cinderella are two of the fun themes in the aptly titled *Cindy and the Fella* and *Calling All Glass Slippers.* Ms. Diamond never fails to "make your head spin and leave you laughing..." says *Rendezvous.*

Duets Vol. #90

The celebrations continue with *Hitched for the Holidays* by well-known writing team Jennifer Drew. This talented duo always "gives readers a top-notch reading experience with vibrant characters...and spicy tension," says *Romantic Times.* Rounding out the volume is popular Barbara Dunlop with the quirky *A Groom in Her Stocking.* Enjoy the fun when Santa delivers not one but *two* fiancés to the dateless heroine!

Be sure to pick up both Duets volumes today!

Hitched for the Holidays

"Silly to let all this tinsel go to waste."

Eric reached for the box, grabbed a handful and dangled the silvery ribbon in the hollow between her breasts.

"I thought we were decorating the tree, not me," Mindy said breathlessly.

"You're more fun."

"It itches." She giggled and tried to remove the tinsel.

"I'll get it out for you." He peeled off her sweater and tossed it in the direction of the ornament box.

Uh-oh, she'd forgotten she was wearing a plain cotton bra. It was about as unglamorous as lingerie could get.

"I didn't dress for this."

He held one breast in his hand and slowly covered her mouth with his as he caressed her through the cloth.

"Tell me if you want me to stop."

Stop? As in red lights and no more kissing? She dropped her hands to his butt and squeezed.

"I'll take that as a go," he said with a laugh.

For more, turn to page 9

A Groom in Her Stocking

"You are not going to find some Norman Rockwell Christmas tree!"

RJ took off his mitts, unzipped the backpack for the handsaw and continued. "It's a cold desert here for most of the year. You should just be thankful things grow at all."

Lindsey made an unladylike exclamation.

"Can't you see this one *wants* to become a Christmas tree?" RJ flailed at the tall, snowy-capped tree in front of him.

Before she could retort, a faraway voice drifted up from the valley behind them. "Lindsey? You up here?"

It was Bobby.

RJ stowed the saw. Lindsey looked shell-shocked. Sure, last night he'd thought it fun to watch Lindsey cope with her *fiancé*. But today... He grabbed her hand and pulled her into the stand of pines. They stood close to each other, mere inches between them.

Bobby's footsteps were squeaking on the dry snow.

"Feels like we're kids again," RJ whispered, then nuzzled her ear.

Lindsey turned and smiled. "Funny, I don't remember doing this when we were kids."

For more, turn to page 197

HARLEQUIN DUETS

ISBN 0-373-44156-8

This edition published by arrangement with Harlequin Books S.A.

Visit us at www.eHarlequin.com

Printed in U.S.A.

Hitched for the Holidays

Jennifer Drew

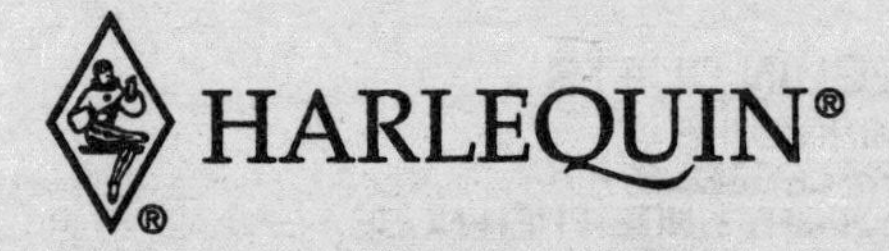

TORONTO • NEW YORK • LONDON
AMSTERDAM • PARIS • SYDNEY • HAMBURG
STOCKHOLM • ATHENS • TOKYO • MILAN • MADRID
PRAGUE • WARSAW • BUDAPEST • AUCKLAND

Dear Reader,

Who wouldn't love having someone who could arrange everything perfectly for the holidays? Mindy Ryder is a professional organizer who's thrown for a Yuletide loop when her neatly ordered life is turned upside down by a visit from her matchmaking father. She's told him she's been "seeing" a doctor...and she has been, sort of!

Vet Eric Kincaid is her dog's doc. Mindy's relationship with him is not romantic, at least not yet. She persuades Eric to play "Dr. Boyfriend" in return for some organizing help, and before the stockings are filled their agreement heats up!

One of us (Jennifer Drew is the pseudonym of mother and daughter Barbara Andrews and Pam Hanson) is a natural-born organizer. The other keeps buying "how to declutter your life" books and losing them in the debris! We hope you enjoy this mistletoe tale and that all your holidays are merry...and neat!

Happy holidays!

Jennifer Drew

P.S. Drop us a line with your favorite organizing hint! Please send it to P.O. Box 4084, Morgantown, WV 26504.

Books by Jennifer Drew

HARLEQUIN DUETS

7—TAMING LUKE
18—BABY LESSONS
45—MR. RIGHT UNDER HER NOSE
59—ONE BRIDE TOO MANY*
ONE GROOM TO GO*
72—STOP THE WEDDING!*
80—JUST DESSERTS

*Bad Boy Grooms

Happy holidays, Aunt Lou!

1

"BABY, YOU ARE SOOO GOOD. We're nearly there. Steady, sweetheart. Yes, yes, that's it."

Mindy Ryder shook her head to break the hypnotic spell of the melodic voice. For a moment she'd imagined Dr. Eric Kincaid was crooning to her instead of Peaches, her rascally Corgi. No wonder his waiting room was always full. He charmed his patients, and their owners, with his soothing voice. He'd opened his animal clinic less than two years ago, and already he had a reputation as one of the best small-pet vets in the Phoenix area. It made her day when she came to his office, and not just because her dog liked him.

"I don't know, Mindy," he said a trace apologetically, using her first name with casual friendliness. "Peaches seems a hundred percent healthy to me."

"She was sneezing..." Mindy began, a little ashamed of using her dog as a ploy to see Dr. Kincaid. Now that she was here, she was losing her nerve anyway. "Sorry I wasted your time."

"I'm always glad to see Peaches. She's the only female Corgi on my patient list. Makes her pretty special."

He smiled broadly and rubbed the short-legged dog's thick white ruff. Peaches basked in his attention, quickly forgetting the indignities of the examination.

The veterinarian was wearing a sky-blue lab coat

that picked up the color of his eyes, and his sandy blond hair was just long enough to look rumpled in a fresh-from-the-pillow way.

He attached the leash to the dog's collar and made easy work of setting the thirty-pound pooch on the spotless white-tiled floor of the examining room. Mindy knew this signaled the end of the appointment, but she'd come for a purpose that had nothing to do with imaginary dog sneezes. If she chickened out now, she'd always wonder what his answer would have been.

The trouble was, she needed a man. What's more, he had to be a doctor. The vet was the only bachelor she knew who qualified. Fortunately his receptionist, Della Rodriguez, was friendly and liked to chat. She'd leaked enough tidbits of information about her boss to make Mindy sure he was unattached and eligible. In fact, Della had dropped veiled hints that he'd been dumped by a woman and was nursing a broken heart.

If so, he was good at putting up a cheerful front. The man had a smile as bright as the desert sun and pearly white teeth that made his whole face sparkle with good humor. But even if he had teeth like walrus tusks and a Cyrano schnoz, she'd still need him.

She hadn't exactly lied to her father, but this time he'd irritated her so much she'd fudged the truth. The trouble was he was bound and determined to see her happily married like her older brother.

It was wonderful Dwight had a wife and two adorable kids, but love was a special gift. So far all that had popped out of her annual Christmas stocking were trolls, geeks and ego-freaks like her last boyfriend. Mike Manning had wanted a fan club, not a significant other, and she'd had the pleasure of telling him to take a hike. Dad hadn't met him, which was just as well. He was one guy who would've enjoyed her father's usual third-degree interrogation. Talking about himself was what Mike liked best.

Dad had been on a tear lately, sure that Mindy's biological clock was ticking like a time bomb, never mind that she was still two years short of thirty. He was lonely since her mother, Abby, had died, and he worried because she was alone, too. Unfortunately, he was too obsessed to pay any attention to her protests. He refused to believe she could manage just fine as a single woman.

When he'd suggested introducing her to a friend's son a couple of months ago, she'd told him she was already seeing someone. Of course, he'd pressed for details. She'd taken Peaches to the vet for a shot the day he phoned, so she had *seen* a doctor—an animal doctor. Telling her father she was *seeing* a doctor had sort of slipped out because she wanted his badgering to stop.

As long as her widowed, workaholic father stayed in Pittsburgh, she could keep him at bay with her spur-of-the-moment deception. But the unimaginable had happened. He'd decided to retire early and sell his accounting business. Now he was coming to Arizona for a visit and expected to meet her doctor-boyfriend this weekend.

"Is there something else?" Dr. Kincaid asked, when she didn't take the leash he was holding out to her.

"Oh, it's silly," she said, taking control of Peaches. "Just a little problem I have."

"I'm afraid I'm not licensed to treat people," he replied, radiating good humor.

"Oh, I didn't mean...not a...you know."

"It's not a health problem?"

His curiosity was encouraging.

"No, not at all. It's my father..."

"Ah."

"He's coming to visit. From Pittsburgh. He lost my mother five years ago in a car accident, and now he's sold his business. I'm afraid I'm his new project."

"I know what that's like. My mother always has some scheme that involves me."

"He's a fanatic when it comes to my personal life," she went on, encouraged by his sympathy. "My brother is married and has two kids, but that's not enough grandchildren for my father. He won't give up until he walks me down the aisle and gives me away."

"My mother's the same. I came close to tying the knot once, and she was the one who was broken-hearted when it didn't work out. Her hobby is match-making, and I'm her main project."

"Then you understand. Unfortunately my father never, ever liked anyone I used to date, so he wants to mastermind a courtship sweepstake with more grandkids for him as the prize."

"Yeah, parents have a different take on things." He hesitated as though examining the decorative paw prints on the wall. "My mother was crazy about my fiancée. Unfortunately Cassandra loved horses so much there wasn't much room left for people, me included. Guess she just thought it would be handy to marry a vet who could look after her stable of Arabians."

He leaned against the metal-topped examination table and focused on the chart of dog breeds on the wall behind her, maybe regretting saying so much to the owner of one of his patients. Then he met her eyes again and gave her a rueful smile. "I prefer working with smaller animals."

Now she was much more interested in his problem than hers, but Dad would be getting off a plane in three days expecting to meet a boyfriend.

"I did a terrible thing," she admitted, nervously twisting the leash around her fingers.

"I find that hard to believe."

Again the thousand-watt smile. Did he have any idea how devastating it was?

"It was the day Peaches came in for her heartworm shot...."

"I remember that day. It was about three months ago, beginning of August, right?"

"Right. You have a good memory."

"Sometimes."

"Anyway, that's the day he called and started talking about his favorite obsession—my marriage prospects. Had I found a 'decent sort' yet which translates to someone he won't hate more than pickled beets or home shopping networks? I think he's hated every boyfriend I've ever had!"

"I guess fathers can be too protective."

"Can they! While he was talking, I remembered taking Peaches here for her shot. On impulse I told him I was seeing a doctor. After all, I had just seen you. I never dreamed he'd come before the end of tax time next April," she babbled. "He's an accountant, and that's his usual vacation time. He always spends Christmas with my brother's family. But he suddenly decided to retire early, and he's coming to check on me."

"Ah."

Again the "ah." She didn't know whether he was sympathetic or eager to have her leave so he could see his next patient. He appeared to be giving her his full attention.

"Well, I've wasted enough of your time," she said, her resolve melting under his gaze.

"You're not the first."

"What?"

"Not the first woman to make an unnecessary appointment for her pet."

She opened her mouth to deny it, but his eyes were too all-knowing, too penetrating…

"No wonder," he said, "when my mom, my aunts, even my receptionist have been recruiting bachelorettes for me since the breakup more than six months ago. One of Mom's prospects even brought in a borrowed cockatoo to check me out."

"How do you know?"

She was embarrassed to be busted, but glad she wasn't the only one to book an unnecessary appointment as an excuse to see him. At least Peaches was a regular patient.

"I can recognize my own patients, even when someone besides the owner brings the bird for a visit."

"I'm really sorry I bothered you," she said, trying to lead Peaches toward the door.

The Corgi plopped down on her hindquarters, a trick six weeks of obedience school had done nothing to delete from her repertoire.

"So ask me," the vet challenged.

"Ask you?" To compound her general embarrassment, her voice squeaked.

"What you came to ask me."

"Oh, it doesn't matter."

"It must matter a lot if you're willing to pay for

an appointment just to see me. If there's something I can do..."

Her nerve failed her, in no small part because she didn't want to be turned down. The man was gorgeous. He probably had a pack of women on his heels. He'd never go along with what she wanted.

"I've taken up too much of your time, and this is my busy season, as well. I'd better run."

Would he think she was terrible if she nudged the stubborn dog with her foot? Peaches was acting as infatuated as a human female, sniffing at Dr. Kincaid's thick-soled running shoe with zeal.

"You're one of Santa's elves?" he teased. "Rushing to get all the toys ready for Christmas?"

"Close," she admitted, relaxing a little because he was so friendly in spite of her dumb idea of pretending Peaches was sick. "I'm a professional organizer. I have to take care of my clients' needs as much as I can now because the month before Christmas I'm always booked solid."

"What does a professional organizer do?" he asked, again with the sincere interest in his voice.

"Unclutter closets, rearrange rumpled rooms, fight disorder at its root level. I have parties to plan, trees to decorate, gifts to buy, whatever busy people don't have time to do themselves. Hopefully, my father will make his usual short, restless visit and jet out again before my schedule is a shambles."

"If he gets to meet your doctor."

"There is that," she said glumly.

"And you were hoping I would..."

"It was a dumb idea."

"Spit it out, or I'll have to charge you for two appointment slots."

"That's blackmail!"

"Yeah, it is, but you have me curious."

"I need a doctor to go out to dinner with my father."

"Your father and you?"

"Both of us."

"He won't believe unless he sees?"

"No way."

"Okay."

"Okay? Just like that, okay?"

"When?"

"Saturday. I pick him up at the airport around three in the afternoon. He hates flying, so he'll be pooped. It will practically guarantee a short evening."

"How about I pick you up at seven?"

"Would you? Really?"

She was so grateful she wanted to hug him. Scratch the grateful part. She wouldn't mind a few hugs from her vet in shining armor even if he'd laughed at the idea of going out with her father and kicked her out of his office.

"It will be pretty hard to pass me off as a people doctor if you pick me up. I live here. The second floor of the clinic is my apartment. Makes it handy if I have overnight patients to check on."

"I'm not going to pass you off as a physician. There's nothing wrong with being a vet." That didn't come out quite the way she intended.

"I thank you. The vet school at Iowa State University thanks you. My profession thanks..."

"Please!" She gave the leash a tug Peaches couldn't ignore.

"Give Della the directions to your place. You'll make her day."

He cut her off before she could start gushing again, but she wasn't proud of what she'd done. She would have left with her tail between her legs if she had one. As it was, she slinked through the reception area, past the shelves of vitamins and pet supplies and the desk where Della Rodriguez managed the office.

Della's flamboyant red, yellow and green print blouse was a splash of color in a room furnished in muted shades of desert tan, taupe and white, and her personality was as colorful as her outfit. Usually Mindy enjoyed her humorous take on life in general and her stories about her husband, Larry, in particular. Today Mindy wrote her check quickly and didn't even ask about Della's three grown kids or four grandchildren. She couldn't get away fast enough, but fortunately she remembered to scribble directions to her home on the back of one of her business cards. She handed it to Della and beat a retreat before the woman could ask any questions.

Mindy had come on false pretenses and was sure she looked guilty. But she did have a date with a doctor to pacify her father. Eventually the little stab of guilt would fade away. The last thing she wanted was to deceive Dad, but he'd hated every boy who ever showed up at their door when she lived at home. He wanted a conservative, professional type for his daughter, a man whose values mirrored his. In other words, someone safe. Even in Arizona she couldn't escape his mating machinations. He was sure to have an old college pal living there or a friend with a bachelor son in one of his accounting groups. If he met Eric and was reassured about her prospects, they could have a nice visit, and he could go home with his mind at ease about her prospects.

Imagine, Dr. Eric Kincaid was as nice to people as he was to animals.

ERIC TOSSED his lab coat in the hamper and turned off the light in the examining room. Della had gone home an hour ago to make dinner for her husband and whatever kids and grandkids happened to be around. Tonight he'd been glad to close the clinic himself. She was the best receptionist and bookkeeper he could possibly find, but no doubt she was dying of curiosity about the directions Mindy Ryder had left with her.

He sighed, thought of how good a shower would feel, and decided to run a couple of miles before he had dinner. There were no patients in the hospital wing of his clinic, so he could look forward to a night of uninterrupted sleep.

Instead of running upstairs to change, he did something he almost never did. He stopped in the reception room and sat on one of the taupe vinyl chairs, which were pet proof and comfortable enough to keep people from squirming if they had to wait long. He liked the room. The desert-sand walls were hung with oil portraits of dogs he'd painted himself and a few prints of cats, birds and fussy rodents to compensate for his canine bias. Several Formica tables with black metal legs held the usual assortment of magazines and brochures on pet care. An antique boot scraper shaped like a dachshund sat on the counter where Della presided over his busy practice.

By the time he finished his evening run, the cleaning service would be at work making sure his clinic looked and smelled fresh in the morning. The marbleized brown, tan and white floor tiles had to be swept and scrubbed nightly, a chore he could afford to pass on to professionals now that his practice was booming. This Iowa boy was doing all right in the sunbelt city, although it'd been pretty iffy the first year with payments on the clinic and vet school debts. He owed a lot to his parents for co-signing some whopping big loans, using their furniture store as collateral, to help him get started after his residency. It had been a good investment, and they'd moved from Des Moines to Mesa and opened a new, more upscale store to be closer to him.

Now if his mother would just get over Cassandra and stop trying to find someone else for him, he could breathe easier.

Sure, it had hurt for awhile after she broke off their engagement, although technically speaking, he'd never felt dumped. He saw it coming and decided it was the best thing that could happen. Cass had too much money for her own good, and all she really cared about was making a splash with the horsey set at her country club.

He'd been a little slow getting her number, dazzled by dark auburn hair, creamy skin and a curvy body that turned him on every time she sat on a horse.

She also looked down her nose at his humble little practice and had grandiose plans to make him the vet in charge of her stable of Arabians, a job she insisted wouldn't allow any time for cats and dogs.

Eric stood, stretched and headed upstairs through the private door to change in his second-floor apartment. He was only thirty, but bachelorhood suited him. He didn't want his professional life complicated by personal relationships. He had worked too hard to get where he was to let himself be remade by Cass, or any other woman—especially a patient's owner.

He *never* dated his patients' owners. Never...

So, he'd really stepped into it today by agreeing to help Mindy. But he didn't regret his moment of weakness. He honestly sympathized with her, considering his own mother's quest to hunt down a potential wife for him.

Besides, Mindy was friendly and cute. Her personality sparkled, and it made his day when she brought

Peaches to see him. For the first time since his breakup with Cass, he had a genuine case of the hots. Mixing his professional and personal life was still a bad idea, but he couldn't help imagining how it would feel to get up close and personal with the gorgeous brunette. Of course the downside was now he had to have dinner with her overbearing father.

At the top of the stairs he stripped off the T-shirt he wore under his lab coat and rubbed the moist, matted hair on chest. Even though it was late fall, the cool season, his second-floor apartment felt warm and stuffy. He slid open the balcony door and looked out at a vista not exactly devoid of human habitation, but sparsely populated enough to suggest desert wilderness. True, he could see a cluster of mobile homes to the left, but Chandler was as close as he could get to open country and still have his clinic easily accessible to the metro area.

He was procrastinating. No supper for him until he ran, and he was ravenous. He'd spent too much time with Mindy and perfectly healthy Peaches, so he'd compensated by skipping lunch, not something he did often.

Back inside, he stripped to his briefs and put on his yellow running shorts, a white tank top, heavy crew socks and a new pair of running shoes he was still breaking in.

Darn, he wasn't in the mood to go jogging. His spacious, high-ceilinged living room was too inviting. His two huge couches upholstered in caramel, sand and ruddy stripes enticed him to lounge in front of the TV and do nothing for a rare change.

Maybe he'd overdone it a little on the Southwest motif in his decor, but he loved this room with the adobe-red tiled floor, stark white plaster, and red, black and yellow Navaho rug hanging on the wall. Since he'd had the clinic built to his specifications, he opted to have one large all-purpose room with only his bedroom and bathroom partitioned. He got wonderful light from a skylight in the roof that could be shaded in the heat of summer.

He made himself leave his lair, knowing much of his reluctance to run this evening was because of his habit of mulling over his day as he worked out. He was pretty sure he'd goofed with Mindy, and it was his own fault. If he'd wanted to date her, he should have been upfront with her. Had Cass shattered his confidence so much he was using professional concerns to keep a desirable woman at arm's length? He didn't think so, but he didn't seem to have enough incentive to jumpstart his social life.

All Mindy wanted was to get off the hook with her father, he thought as he locked the clinic and put the key in his fanny pack. He had no reason to believe she was the least bit interested in him. She was so darn cute, she probably had no trouble meeting men. From what she said, though, it sounded like none met Daddy's high standards.

He stepped out into the cooling evening and decided to keep to the main road since it would be dark before he got back.

"Admit it," he mumbled to himself. "You could easily get hot and bothered by her."

She was petite, not over five-three, with short sable hair. It looked silky soft, like the undercoat of her Corgi, probably not a comparison she would have found flattering. He wasn't sure about her eye color. At the first appointment, he would have said hazel, but there was no ignoring the flash of green he'd noticed today. She didn't have as much front and center or on her hindquarters as Cassandra, but then his ex-fiancée wasn't the type he usually liked. He was a sucker for heart-shaped faces and small waists. Something he'd have to forget on this pretend date with a patient's owner.

Had he set himself up to play doctor for Mindy because he was a nice guy or because he regretted not acting on the attraction he felt for her?

It was still early in his run, but he pushed himself hard, the slap of his soles on the blacktop setting up a rhythm in his head: dumb idea, dumb idea, dumb idea.

What if this date with Daddy was only a ploy to start something with him? Did he mind losing the initiative if she was interested in him? He didn't, as a rule, like being chased at all.

On the other hand, he thought, slowing down to his usual steady pace to catch his breath, he was no monk. There hadn't been anyone since Cassandra....

"Bad idea," he said aloud. Starting something with a patient's owner was still an invitation for trouble. Mindy was cute and cuddly, but she seemed to be the kind of woman who wanted to get engaged and married. He certainly wasn't ready for any serious relationship, not after his big mistake with Cass. Maybe he never would be.

At least he could tell his mother he had a date. She'd been talking a lot about a new salesperson at the store, divorced but no kids. His mom seemed to know an endless parade of eligible females, and she was severely afflicted with grandchild-itis. He wished, not for the first time, that he wasn't an only child.

"Sorry, Mom, I'm *seeing* someone. I have a date this Saturday," he said under his breath.

2

"DON'T LOOK AT ME THAT way! I know it's a lousy idea, but it's too late to call it off."

Mindy finished changing earrings for the third time and stared at the little silver-and-turquoise donkeys dangling from her lobes.

"See, told you these are better. It's not easy dressing for a date who's only doing me a favor."

Peaches responded with a big doggie yawn and stretched her short white legs as far as she could on her special end-of-the-bed quilt made from salvaged remnants of blue jeans, a gift from Mindy's sister-in-law, Carly.

Her father had opted for a nap in the spare bedroom she'd hastily cleared for his use. Now all the paraphernalia of her business was stacked in her own bedroom. To get to the closet she had to maneuver an obstacle course between catalogs, models of storage units and piles of magazines and books. Thank heavens her clients couldn't see this mess. Her personal space looked like a recycling center.

She picked her way around boxes of junk sure to come in handy someday to the full-length mirror on her bathroom door. Dad would expect her to look spectacular for the doctor-boyfriend, but what kind of signal would that send to the shanghaied vet? She didn't want him to think this mock date was a ploy to attract his attention.

Hopefully, she'd hit a happy medium. Her silky scooped-necked turquoise dress flared at midcalf and had tiny cap sleeves. She'd added a delicate silver belt and silvery-gray spike heels. Maybe she was overdressed for a casual evening out, but the donkey earrings said she was only kidding.

"Darn, I need a haircut," she complained to Peaches, who was trying to nap through the ritual of dressing. "Yeah, pretend to sleep, you lazy hairball. I know those big ears of yours are picking up every word I say. You're sulking because you don't have a date with Dr. Eric."

At least Mindy liked the color of her hair—dark sable, cropped short, but the fashionable spikes seemed limp in spite of the salon special wax.

Did the turquoise enhance or clash with the green glints in her eyes? Was she out of her mind fussing over what she wore on a pretend date orchestrated to keep her father from meddling in her love life or lack thereof?

The door chimes startled her, which was ludicrous since she'd spent the past hour anticipating Eric's arrival. Peaches bounded off the bed with more agility than her short legs suggested and stood impatiently, nose to the door, waiting for Mindy to open it.

"Now don't slobber, shed or jump on Dr. Eric," she warned sternly. "I don't want to look for a new vet because you can't behave."

She hadn't exactly looked for the one she had. When Peaches was a pup, she'd taken her to a busy clinic where the wait was always considerably longer than the appointment. A client had raved about a new vet in Chandler, which wasn't unreasonably far from Tempe, where Mindy lived. The rest was history.

Peaches loved her new doctor and stopped trying to amputate a finger or two during exams.

As soon as the bedroom door opened, Peaches was a streak of brindled tan and white racing to the front door, nails clicking on the red-tiled hallway.

"Now behave!" Mindy whispered sternly before she opened the front door. She might as well tell a dust storm to settle down.

Where was Dad? If he'd overslept, she'd have to make small talk. Wouldn't that be awkward! What could she say to a man she'd coerced into pretending to be the love of her life?

She grabbed Peaches's collar with one hand and opened the door with the other.

"Hi. I knew this was the right place when I heard Peaches," her date for the evening said.

"Dr. Kincaid, I'm glad you found it okay."

It was a wonder anyone ever found her little patio house in the huge development of similar white-stuccoed bungalows. The streets curved and meandered with a total absence of memorable landmarks. If it weren't for the black wrought-iron street numbers on the ruddy-orange front doors, she might get confused herself.

"No problem." He dropped his voice to a conspiratorial whisper. "Shouldn't you call me Eric?"

"Oh, right, thanks." She spoke softly and looked over her shoulder. No sign of her dad. "Please, come in."

"Nice plants." He gestured at the big earthenware pots flanking her flagstone walk. "I like natural desert, sand and cacti. Why come to the Southwest and try to grow a lawn?"

He stepped inside and casually walked into her living room on the north side of the house. The big picture window faced west and gave her a great view of sunsets, but it meant the bedrooms at the rear caught the early-morning sun and woke her up before any sane, civilized person should stir.

She'd opted for a simple decor, as much from poverty as design. The windows had pale green slat blinds, but no curtains. The red-tiled floor was bare throughout the front of the house, except for a round braided rug in the living room, one of her few new purchases after buying the house a couple of years ago. The bright greens and yellows made her gray pseudo-suede couch and recliner seem less drab in their new setting. The thrift-shop tables she'd repainted mustard yellow and emerald green were kitschy but cheerful. She was still in the process of finding art for the walls, a search stymied by lack of time and money. For now, a few castoff flower prints a friend had given her hung over the couch, leaving the rest of the rough-plastered white walls unadorned.

"Nice place," he said, standing beside the couch which she'd forgotten to vacuum free of doggie hair. Fortunately it wouldn't show much on his pale yellow short-sleeved dress shirt or tan chinos if he decided to sit down.

He was wearing a tie, bright green with tiny Scottie dogs silhouetted in black. No doubt it was the kind of gift people gave vets, cute but not too cutesy. Trouble was, he'd clearly been in a rush as it was tied wrong with the bottom length hanging longer than the top.

"Can I get you something to drink?" she asked, wondering where the heck her father was. He was so darn eager to meet The Boyfriend. Why wasn't he ready to go to dinner? "I have diet cola, lite beer, mineral water and a bottle of champagne Dad brought to..."

She nearly said "celebrate." More specifically, her father hoped to toast her engagement with the bubbly, although she'd never, ever given him reason to believe her nonexistent romance had progressed that far.

"Where is your father?" he asked.

"He took a nap." Scratch her hope for a short evening. "Guess I should knock on the door to be sure he's awake."

"I'm awake and eager to meet your young man," Wayne Ryder said, coming out of the guest bedroom and into the kitchen.

How could he say something that corny? She tried to cut him some slack because he'd never fully recovered from losing her mother in an auto accident nearly five years ago, but sometimes he talked as though the twentieth century had never come and gone. He'd definitely prefer to live in an age when fathers arranged marriages for their daughters.

"Eric Kincaid, sir." He offered his hand with a deference that made her want to hug him.

"Eric, it's a pleasure to meet you. Just call me Wayne."

"My pleasure, Wayne, sir."

Mindy wasn't fooled. Her father was the alpha male locking horns with a young buck. He might approve of her new boyfriend in theory, but he was gearing up to interrogate him in the best—make that worst—CIA tradition. If she ever did find the right man, she was going to elope before her father got wind of him.

When he wasn't confronted with her male friends, her dad was a sweetheart in spite of being too rigid.

He wanted the best for her, but her future husband had to meet his impossibly high standards.

"Well, Mindy, let's break open that bottle of bubbly before we go," he said.

Dad had left all twenty or so of his business suits in shades of black, gray and navy at home. He'd gotten into the Southwestern spirit by wearing jeans and a navy knit shirt with a collar. He was even sporting a bolo tie, but his attempt to look casual was spoiled by his black wing tips. It didn't really matter. Her father looked like an accountant even when he wore a bathing suit. Neither tall nor short, he was lean and slope-shouldered with the bland looks that made him easily forgettable. His face was long and narrow, always clean-shaven with smooth skin. Only the vertical lines on either side of his mouth gave away his age, those and the fact that his gray-brown hair barely covered his scalp, although a side part and a good haircut gave the illusion that he still had a head of hair.

"I'll pass on that, sir...Wayne," Eric said. "Mindy and I decided to take both cars tonight in case I'm paged."

His excuse sounded lame to her, but Dad seemed to like it. A busy doctor had to stay sober and alert.

"Well, what do you say we get going then?" her father said, giving them their marching orders.

They filed out with Peaches dancing around their heels hoping to be included.

Mindy waited until the two men were out of hearing then hissed at her disappointed pet. "You're the lucky one! You get to stay home."

Her father went to the carport and got behind the wheel of her second-hand van with Ryder Reorganizing Inc. painted on the sides. He was going to follow the two of them, naturally expecting her to ride there in Eric's dark red Tracker.

One thing was still bothering her.

"Ah, Eric, would you do me a tremendous favor?" she asked, coming around to the driver's side of his vehicle before he got in.

His look suggested he already was, but he only shrugged.

"Your tie."

"My tie?" He looked down at the black Scotties cavorting on green silk. "Too dressy for where we're going?"

"Oh, no, it's perfect. I love it. I just have this compulsion—well, maybe compulsion is too strong—but would you mind terribly if I fixed it?"

"Fixed it?" His hand shot up and tested the firm knot at his throat.

"Not fixed exactly, but I don't want to be distracted by your long end. My dad is so sharp, I'll have to be on guard every minute."

"My long end? You've lost me," he said.

"The skinny end is hanging lower than the top. I don't want to be picky, but it would look so nice if..."

He lifted the two ends of the tie and frowned.

"Here, let me," she said, wishing she'd never mentioned it.

Her fingers were nimble, at least her mother used to say so. She loosened the knot and pulled gently until the full part of the tie hung the right way. Then she tightened the knot and tucked it between the tips of his collar.

"It's an adorable—no, make that handsome—tie. I've never seen one like it."

Of course, she never bought men's ties unless a client sent her shopping. Her brother, Dwight, much preferred a book or a tape as a gift, and her father's taste was so ultraconservative she'd accused him of buying his ties by the dozen, each identical to all the others he owned.

"My ex-fiancée was into cute," he said dryly. 'This is the first time I've worn it."

"Oh."

Talk about stepping into a pile of doo-doo. He would probably bribe a waiter to ring his pager ten minutes into the meal. At least her father was leaving Monday. She only had to get through two full days of his questions, and there were all kinds of reasons why a busy doctor couldn't spend time with his "girlfriend" on the weekend.

"Well, it is a cute tie," she said, hurrying round to the passenger side before he changed his mind about going.

The ride to the restaurant was the longest twenty-three minutes of her life.

What had made her try to reorganize Eric? Fussing with his tie was so intimate, so intrusive, so dumb. But she did like being close to him. He smelled of vanilla with a touch of spice, and she'd never noticed how sexy his lips were. Of course, she could think of a better use for that pucker than signaling his irritation.

"I'm sorry about the tie," she said as they pulled up to the trendy steakhouse with a great view of the Camelback Mountains. "I fidget when I'm nervous."

"No problem," he said, opening his door and walking around the vehicle.

He helped her out of the car and handed his keys to the valet.

"It's what I do for a living. Organize things. Closets, drawers, parties, you name it."

"Yes, you told me during Peaches's last visit." He looked directly at her and smiled. "Don't worry. This will go okay. Your father seems like a nice guy, not an ogre anyway.''

''Yeah, not an ogre,'' she said hopefully, crossing her fingers where he couldn't see them.

Mindy had never been to Mountain Monty's, but it was one of those restaurants that made all the tourists' guidebooks. She should have read one before making the reservation. The first rule of the steakhouse was no neckties. Her father had to surrender the bolo he imagined made him look like a native, and Eric handed over the doggie tie she'd straightened.

A scantily clad hostess dressed in abbreviated saloon-gal garb with a panty-level denim skirt and a vest covering not much of anything, put the ties in a plastic bag and promised their return.

''Mountain Monty can't stand the sight of a noose, not even one with cute little doggies,'' she said, giving Eric a smile so broad it nearly cracked her cheeks. ''It'll be about thirty minutes if y'all would like to wait in the lounge.''

So much for reservations, Mindy thought glumly as her father took on the job of host and ushered them into an area too dark for the old-west decor to be totally cloying.

''The evening's on me,'' Dad said expansively. ''I've been looking forward to meeting you for a long time, Eric. Mindy's told me a lot about you, all good.''

She'd told him zilch except for the part about being a doctor, but how could she begrudge her father a little exaggeration after telling him the whopper of her life?

''That's good to hear.'' Eric smiled warmly at her.

They settled down, really far down, on a low semicircular couch in the corner with a tiny table. A server appeared instantly and took their orders: a beer for Dad, white wine for her and a club soda with lime for Eric. Was he going to play the sober doctor all evening, or didn't he imbibe? She knew so little about him, this evening was going to be massively stressful.

"Tell me, Eric..." her dad began.

She was going to hate those words before the dinner was over unless, of course, her "date" bailed before the entrée.

"Are you a native of Phoenix?" Wayne asked.

"No, I'm an Iowa boy." He said it with pride. "I came here a couple of years ago to set up my practice."

"Guess it's a good place for health practitioners. Aging population and all. I didn't want Mindy to go to Arizona State when we visited out here. Plenty of good colleges in Pennsylvania. But she liked it well enough to stay. Now that I'm retired I'll have time to check it out for myself."

"If you don't mind the hot summers, it's great," Eric said.

Great conversation, Mindy noted. Weather, the dullest and safest of subjects. She jumped in with a few anecdotes about melting makeup and sun-dried skin. Her stories tanked, but they helped kill time until they finally got called for dinner. What had seemed like two hours in the lounge had really been fourteen minutes. This was going to be one whopping long ordeal.

The Old West really came alive with a vengeance in the huge dining room. Long wooden tables for ten were covered with blue-and-white checked tablecloths. Customers sat on benches with thick log legs and no backs. It reminded Mindy of a family reunion with someone else's relatives. At least the noisy group of six senior-plus citizens at the other end of their table reduced their conversation to spotty exchanges of menu information.

"How about it, honey," Eric said, resting his hand

on her shoulder. "I've heard their mesquite grilled steaks are the best. They have a porterhouse for two if you're up for sharing."

He massaged the back of her neck with his fingers, a deliciously intimate gesture that made her father look at the cowhide menu with a disapproving scowl. If Eric had acted too cool toward her, her dad would have criticized that later, too!

Eric dropped his hand when she squirmed but only to hide it under the table where, her father would assume, he could feel her up under cover of the blue-and-white cloth. Actually he kept a decorous inch or so between their thighs, resting his hand on his own, not hers.

Overhead the wooden ceiling looked smoky dark in contrast to the white plaster wall beneath it. A country band filed out to a small stage near the middle of the far wall, and a deep bass voice started moaning about the wicked woman who didn't know how to love just one man. At least it kept conversation to a minimum.

They gave their orders to a jean-clad male server in a flannel shirt too hot for the room. After an eternity of shouting at each other across the table, their appetizers came and the band took a break.

They had salads topped by the house dressing, in bowls large enough to mix up a cake, and red wine spicy enough to make her hair stand on end. Her father sliced bread from a loaf of homemade sourdough and, when she was full enough to call it a night, the main course arrived.

The porterhouse for two was smothered in mushrooms, onions and a peppery sauce, cooked to a delicate pink and served with a baked potato on steroids. Her father had pork ribs and cowboy beans delivered in a brown ceramic pot large enough to plant a tree in it. The idea was, she supposed, to eat one meal here and take home enough leftovers for three or four more in handy foam cartons. At least she wouldn't have to cook all weekend.

The seniors sharing their table finally left carrying enough leftovers to feed a football team, and she could sense her father's relief. Now they could have a real chat and hear each other.

"You don't know how happy I am to meet you, Eric," he said in the tone of a magistrate reading a prisoner's sentence. "I tell you, my little girl's choice of friends has given me some anxious moments in the past."

"Please, Dad, let Eric enjoy his dinner."

"Oh, I'm enjoying it," he said wickedly.

"Can you believe, when she was sixteen some guy came roaring up to the house on a motorcycle with Mindy on the back?"

"I was wearing a helmet," she said dryly, giving up on the big slab of cow on her plate.

"They wanted to get matching his and hers tattoos. I was supposed to sign a permission slip because she was under eighteen. I told him he'd be getting his tattoo in the state pen if he didn't get lost."

"Pen" was her father's idea of talking the talk. If she and Eric really were an item, she'd want to crawl under the table.

"It got worse," Wayne went on. "She brought one idiot home from college her first Christmas break. He was into conspiracy theories. Thought Kennedy had been shot by some baseball player."

"He was a philosophy major. He enjoyed theoretical problems. Anyway, I was sure I could change some of his radical ideas. He was really nice, if you'd only given him a chance. It was wicked of you to make fun of his ideas."

"He was a jerk."

"Daddy! He had great potential. Anyway, Eric

knows all about me, and he doesn't want to hear your prejudiced opinions about a boy you scared away."

"What is that nut doing now?" her father asked, never one to give up on a subject until he'd fully vented.

"I wouldn't know."

This was her year to lie, which made her feel anything but good. There was no way, though, that she was going to tell her father that an old boyfriend had lost everything when his dotcom company went under and was now part owner of a mall taco stand, something she'd accidentally discovered.

"How about you, Eric?" Wayne said. "Have you been married?"

He meant, are you really a married man out to seduce my innocent daughter and ruin her life?

"No, I came close once, but it didn't work out."

"Happens sometimes."

He meant that a good prospect like the doc was better off with his daughter. She could read her father like a supermarket tabloid. Would this evening never end?

Eric looked at his watch, a complicated one with lots of extras, great if you wanted to know what time it was in Siberia. Big mistake. Her father had spent his career working with tiny details like commas. He didn't miss Eric's sneak peek.

"Are we keeping you from something?" he asked. He was eating his beans two or three at a time, stretching out the interrogation in spite of hovering busboys eager to clear.

"No, not at all, Wayne, but I may have to help with a delivery later tonight. The bitch has had a hard time of it in the past...."

Whoops! Mindy grabbed his thigh under the tablecloth and squeezed, but it was too late.

"You call your patient a..." Wayne sputtered.

"Dad, you must have misunderstood. Eric isn't a human doctor," she tried to explain, her face getting hot.

"I'm human, but my patients aren't," he said, trying for humor, but striking out with Dad.

"He's a vet...a veterinarian." She said it so emphatically people for tables around stopped eating to eavesdrop.

"Hey, there's a friend of mine." Eric stood up and gestured wildly to a man and woman just entering the dining room.

As the couple made their way toward them, Mindy tried to gauge how her father was taking the vet news. He was stone-faced, fussily scraping beans away from the side of the pot.

A tall lanky man with a hawkish nose and a broad smile stopped by their table, a short strawberry blonde hanging on his arm.

"Wayne, this is Guy Dillard and Tammy Jamison. Wayne is Mindy's father," Eric said. "Guy is one of the first people I met after I moved here. He's a pharmaceuticals rep."

The three men did the hand squeezing thing, her father making it a contest.

"Where've you been keeping this gorgeous woman?" Guy asked, ignoring his pouting date.

"We've both been busy at work," Eric said, valiantly trying to make it sound as though the couple already knew her. "The four of us will have to get together soon."

"I'm hungry," Tammy whined and pulled Guy toward the waiting hostess. They moved on after a quick nice-meeting-you routine. Mindy couldn't tell what her father was thinking.

"How long have you two been seeing each other?" Wayne asked.

"Quite awhile," Eric said.

"More than a year," she could honestly say, thinking back to Peaches's first appointment.

"I'm pretty sure you never mentioned Eric is a vet," he doggedly insisted.

"I have my own practice. Specialize in small animals, especially dogs."

"Good profession," her father grudgingly admitted. "Now, about tomorrow. I thought the three of us could do some sight-seeing. I'd like to visit some ancient ruins."

"I don't think Eric's free, but I'd love to take you north to Walnut Canyon or Montezuma's Well," Mindy said.

To Eric's credit, he didn't even blink.

"I'll have to see how my patient does," he said. "Well, I have to run and make sure everything's okay at the clinic. I'll call you, sweetheart."

He stood, shook her father's hand, thanked him for the dinner, and planted a warm, unexpected kiss on the corner of her mouth.

"Your leftovers..." she gasped.

"Take them to your place," he said, then practically sprinted away.

He did turn and wave before he was out of sight. She couldn't have asked for a better performance.

3

ERIC GOT IN LINE to claim his vehicle, a process slowed by a platinum blonde with a face as rigid as porcelain from too much plastic surgery. The woman insisted on giving detailed instructions to a red-jacketed kid on how to deliver her Mercedes. A rotund man beside her looked bored and gave a long-suffering sigh.

Eric would prefer to get the SUV himself, but even if he had the key, it was probably blocked by other cars in the tightly packed lot east of the restaurant. Unfortunately, people were leaving in droves, and four or five drivers were ahead of him. If the pair of attendants didn't hustle, he'd have to say goodbye to Wayne all over again.

He could see why Mindy needed someone to palm off as a boyfriend. Her father had changed from a nice, normal guy to a fascist meddler when the subject of her relationships came up. No wonder she'd escaped to Arizona for college and stayed there. She certainly seemed like a woman who could run her own life.

A lead-footed valet delivered a sky-blue Cadillac, and Eric moved a couple of steps closer to the podium where they kept the keys. He rolled his claim slip and a five-dollar bill for the tip between his palms and remembered his tie.

He could go back for it and lose his turn, but he'd

probably never wear it again anyway. He was way over Cassandra and knew he never should have gotten involved with her in the first place. They had met when she hit a dog that ran out into the road. He'd been driving behind her and stopped to help. He had saved the dog, got engaged to the horse fanatic and spent a frustrating six months trying to convince her he didn't want to give up his practice and be her live-in horse-doctor.

He'd die a grizzled old bachelor before he let another woman try to make him over.

"Eric, glad I caught you!"

He turned to see Mindy hurrying toward him, the tie she'd insisted on retying for him dangling from her fingertips.

"Thanks," he said with feigned enthusiasm as he accepted it.

"I wanted to thank you. Dad likes you."

"Good. Where is he?"

"He went out on the back patio for a better look at the view while I get the van. I can never thank you enough. He grudgingly admitted you might be okay even if you are an animal doctor. Coming from him, that's better than an Emmy, an Oscar and the Nobel Peace Prize wrapped into one. Well, I just wanted you to know how much I appreciate what you did."

"My pleasure."

"Oh, and sorry about your tie."

"I probably won't wear it again," he admitted. "A little too cute for me."

"No, I mean I'm sorry about straightening it. When I'm nervous..."

"I know. You fuss."

"Well, I'll see you again when Peaches needs to see a vet," she said.

He smiled weakly, determined not to encourage her but hard-pressed not to respond eagerly. She was a patient's owner, and he didn't mix business with pleasure, not since that starry night when Cass had overwhelmed him with gratitude for saving her from a guilty conscience. The dog she hit turned out to be a cherished pet, and she hated to be in the wrong even when she was.

"It was a great dinner." He had to say something since they were trapped together by slow valet service.

"Yes, enough food for a week. Are you sure you don't want any leftovers? Dad has them."

"No, no thanks." He tried, but couldn't think of any neutral conversation topic.

The big surprise of the evening was hearing about her abysmal record with men. Unless her father was a full-blown liar, she specialized in loonies and losers.

She was attracted to men she could make over, he realized, wishing she wasn't so darn cute. Besides being dark-haired and adorable, she had perfect palm-size breasts, a slender waist that made him ache to take her in his arms and a butt that would nicely fit his lap.

"When you see him coming, tell me," he said impulsively. "We should maybe, you know, kiss goodnight."

"He's coming toward us now, but I don't know if we should. All these people..."

She didn't exactly say no, so he went for it anyway. He wrapped one arm around her shoulder and dropped his free hand low on her back, his fingers brushing the delectable little hollow at the end of her spine.

He'd have to be numb from the neck down to pass

up the startled *O* of her mouth. Daddy wanted a man for his daughter? Let him mull over this on the way back to Pittsburgh.

He gave her a hard, noisy kiss that knocked her off balance on the spiky heels she was wearing and forced her to grab his arms to keep from tottering.

"Thank you," she whispered breathlessly.

"Anytime."

That was the most stupid thing he'd said since he proposed to Cass. He backed away feeling scorched and silly. Her father wasn't the only one who'd noticed the robust kiss. He'd provided entertainment for the bored diners waiting for their vehicles and deserved their amused titters.

"Good night, Wayne. Thanks again for the dinner," he called over to her father as he hurried to the podium where, thankfully, it was his turn.

Tipping the valet double for letting him go to the lot with him, he got in his car and headed home. His next appointment with Peaches was going to be damned awkward after the chemistry of that kiss.

Eric called the Drummonds as soon as he got back to his office and was pleased to hear their border collie had given birth to five healthy pups without the difficulties of her first litter. He wouldn't have to go out tonight.

It was too early for bed, and he was too restless to catch up on reading his professional journals. He checked the TV listings and decided he didn't feel like watching some animal nut risk his life for the camera. He was always leery of shows that inspired kids to make friends with the neighborhood rattler.

He could pay the household bills or run a load of laundry, but it would take more than domestic drudgery to get his mind off Mindy. Funny, during her visits to the office with Peaches he'd never noticed the little dimple in her right cheek that showed when she smiled.

He wandered into his bedroom in his second-floor quarters. His mother had decorated the room where he slept as a housewarming gift when he opened the clinic. With a whole furniture store to choose from, she'd picked a bamboo and rattan dresser, night table, and headboard. The curtains looked like mosquito netting and the throw rugs were tawny shag, which reminded his Mom of a lion's mane. He could live with the jungle decor, but the four sets of leopard and zebra print sheets had long ago lost their miniscule appeal. Cassandra had thought they were hilarious. One of these days he had to buy some restfully plain white ones.

Why did women assume he wanted to drape himself and his surroundings in animal images just because he was a vet? He tossed the doggie tie on the dresser and stripped down to his white cotton briefs. Someday he was going to yank off the border strip with silhouettes of African animals that ran around the tops of the walls. It belonged in a kid's room, but he wouldn't hurt his mother's feelings by telling her that. Both of his parents doted on their only son, much to his discomfort sometimes. It never occurred to them he might want to be on his own, and he cared about them too much to enlighten them.

He flopped down on zebra-print sheets and pillows and flicked on a cable news station. Stocks down, temperatures up, politicians squabbling, nothing there to take his mind off Mindy. He surfed channels and wondered how he could possibly be attracted to another control freak. The woman had retied his tie. If that wasn't an ominous sign, he didn't know what was. Even Cass hadn't tried to redress him, and she had their whole future planned like a paint-by-number picture in a kid's coloring book.

A basketball game caught his attention, but the Suns were leading by thirty-two points. No excitement there.

The phone rang, and he reached over to the bamboo stand to get it.

"Eric Kincaid," he said giving his name because patients sometimes called his home phone.

"Dr. Kincaid... Eric... It's Mindy Ryder. I just wanted to thank you again."

She sounded a little breathless which gave her voice a sexy quality he found disturbing.

"You don't need to. I enjoyed..." He hesitated, not sure whether to admit he'd liked being with her. "The dinner."

Which was, he thought with some consternation, only partly the truth. During the meal he'd caught himself hanging on everything Mindy said as though they were having a real date. He'd even gone out of his way to be congenial to Wayne, although he found her father good company except on the topic of his daughter's love life.

"Dad's gone to bed," she said, "but he won't take no for an answer about having you come sight-seeing with us. Can you help me out and give me a plausible reason why you can't go? What do vets do on weekends?"

Good question. He had some tedious paperwork he'd been putting off, and he'd promised to go to a party Saturday evening.

"Tell him," he began, then couldn't think of a single reason why he wouldn't be eager to spend the day with Mindy if she were his girlfriend.

"Tell him I'm not available tomorrow, but I'll go along Sunday morning if he wants to wait until then."

"Oh, I'm not trying to rope you into actually going."

"You're not roping me. I'm volunteering."

Why, he didn't know. Wayne would probably want to know everything about him from how often he brushed his teeth to whether he'd slept with his daughter.

"No wonder Peaches adores you," Mindy said. "You are so nice."

"No, I'm not," he denied truthfully.

Crazy maybe, for having anything at all to do with a woman who liked to reform her men, but he had an ulterior motive. His mom was giving a little dinner party Sunday evening, and he very much wanted a reason not to go. She'd joined the Mesa Civic League to get acquainted in the new city and, typically, thrown herself into their activities. They held a big fund-raiser every December to raise donations for the Maricopa County Animal Friends. It was a good cause. The money was used to get homeless pets ready for adoption. That meant spaying, neutering, grooming, shots, licenses, all the costly essentials. Last year he'd gotten away with making a cash contribution. This year Mom wanted him on the committee, and the dinner was a meeting to finalize what needed to be done.

It was no coincidence that the committee was mostly women, many of them young, single and eager to meet Felicia and Ray Kincaid's bachelor son.

"I don't see how I can ask you to help entertain my dad," Mindy said.

"I'll enjoy the trip. We'll make a day of it. Have dinner in Sedona before we come home."

"If you're sure...."

He wasn't, but he could still feel her lips warm and soft under his. Pretending to be hot for her wasn't a stretch. In fact, he wouldn't mind a little more smooching—only to impress Wayne, of course.

"I'll drive. How does ten o'clock Sunday morning sound?" he asked.

"Wonderful! If there's anything I can do for you—I mean, anything professional. Organize your office, do your Christmas shopping..."

"No, that's not necessary."

Really not necessary! He'd rather let a pack of baboons loose in the clinic. Already he was afraid he'd made a big mistake by offering to spend the whole day with the Ryders. He couldn't help being sympathetic to Mindy, but if she tried to smear sunscreen on his face or retie his shoes, he was bailing.

He hung up, decided it was late enough to go to bed, and was settling in when the phone rang again.

"Mom." No surprise. "I was going to call you in the morning. About the dinner meeting Sunday...."

He made his excuse. Her voice became very quiet and reasonable, not a good sign.

"I know it's a great cause, Mom, but I promised to spend the day with a friend.... No, not Guy.... Actually, it's one of my patient's owners.... I'm not breaking my rule about socializing. Just doing a small favor.... Okay, yes, a female friend."

An hour or so later he pulled on a pair of gray sweats, a threadbare Iowa State University T-shirt, socks and his battered old running shoes. Maybe some cool desert air would clear his head and help him get to sleep.

SUNDAY MORNING Dad volunteered to take the dog for a walk, so Mindy used the opportunity to call her big brother. First Carly, her sister-in-law, let her talk with five-year-old Kim and Sam, who was almost three, although her nephew's idea of a phone conversation was a spurt of excited babble.

"Hi, Min," Dwight said, relieving his son of the phone. "How are you and Dad doing?"

"He's fine. We went out for dinner Friday with my pretend boyfriend."

"Pretend?" There was a knowing chuckle on his voice. Dwight knew all about Mindy's dating woes when it came to their father.

"Peaches's vet. He went as a favor to me, but I'm not sure it was a good idea. I'd like to see him for real, but fat chance of that after I roped him into one of Dad's infamous interrogations."

"That bad?"

"No, I guess not. He likes Eric, but I don't feel good about the phony date. Dad insisted the three of us go sight-seeing together today."

"Your vet sounds like a good guy to go along with it. He must be interested in you."

"I doubt it, but even if he is, a full day with Dad will discourage him. Remember when we rented that lake cabin for a week and Josh Arhus came to stay? Dad was so suspicious of his intentions, he scared him away after two days."

"Well, hang in there," he said, unhelpful.

Mindy hung up and hurried to get ready for the trip when her plan for the day fizzled like a dud firecracker. Peaches gave her the bad news, or at least thought she did as she barked furiously outside the closed bedroom door.

"You little rascal, what's all the racket?"

She stepped out of her room and saw her father

sitting on the couch, bending over and gingerly taking off his sock.

"Dad, what happened?"

"I took that mutt for a walk and tripped on a paving stone on your front walk. Would've been okay, but when I tried to get my balance, the dumb dog yanked on the leash and I went down. Lucky I didn't land on my face."

"Are you hurt?"

"I think I twisted my ankle." He touched his right ankle, which was puffy-looking below the hem of khaki cotton slacks.

Mindy glanced at the dressy black wing tip shoe he'd just removed. It looked brand-new and probably still had slippery soles, but she bit back a comment about unsuitable footwear. Dad had worn the same style shoe as long as she'd known him. Pain and suffering weren't going to change him.

"It doesn't look good. I'd better drive you to the emergency room."

"I'm not sitting around all day to have some wet-behind-the-ears intern tell me to take two aspirin. I'll have your Eric see what he thinks."

"He's not my Eric, and he's a vet, Dad, a vet. He doesn't treat people."

"I don't want treatment. He can just take a look at it. How much trouble is that?"

"Your ankle could be sprained or even fractured. You need an X ray."

When did her father regress to acting like a stubborn child?

"Just bring me a heating pad and a couple of pain pills. I'll be ready to go to the ruins in an hour or so."

"Dad, we were thinking of Walnut Canyon, hundreds of steps down and up again. You have to stay off your ankle until a doctor checks it.''

''Fine. Eric must have learned enough basics in vet school to diagnose a sprain.''

Arguing with him was useless. She didn't have a heating pad, so he insisted she soak a cloth in hot water and lay it on his rapidly swelling ankle, never mind that she thought an ice pack was the way to go.

She'd been excited, even a little tingly, anticipating a whole day with Eric. Sure, he was only doing her a favor, and her father would be going along as well, but he must like her a little to go to the trouble of pretending to be her boyfriend.

When he got there ten minutes late, dressed in jeans and a faded blue denim shirt for their trip, she didn't know what to say to him. They couldn't go through with their plans, but her father would expect him to hang around and be sympathetic as any potential son-in-law would.

''What happened?'' Eric saw her father stretched out on the couch, his foot on a pillow with a wet washcloth draped over his ankle.

''I twisted my damn ankle,'' her father said impatiently. ''The dog tripped me.''

''Not exactly,'' Mindy said, unwilling to let Peaches get all the blame.

''Take a look. Tell me what you think,'' her father said to Eric.

''You need to ice it, keep it elevated,'' Eric said without examining the puffy ankle.

''I told Mindy a vet can handle the little things,'' Wayne said with satisfaction.

''Dad, that's commonsense first aid, not a diagnosis.''

"I'll drive you to the emergency room," Eric offered.

"I'm not sitting around there all day. Take a look. I trust your judgment."

"If I were licensed to treat people, I'd order an X ray to see if it's fractured. Look, it's as big as a soccer ball and turning purple."

Her dad sputtered and protested while she double-bagged some ice cubes and wrapped them in a dish towel.

Fifteen minutes later Eric finally convinced him to hobble out to his SUV. He settled Wayne on the back seat with his foot elevated, a pillow under his ballooning ankle and the makeshift ice bag on top of it.

An hour and fifty minutes later Wayne was wheeled in a chair into the examining area of Community General Hospital after telling Mindy to stay behind in the waiting room. A TV droned on in the cheerless tan-and-brown room, although no one among the day's minor casualties was paying the slightest attention to it.

"We've got to break up," Mindy said in an urgent whisper to Eric.

"Break up?" He laughed so loudly a health-care worker in a pink smock gave him the evil eye. "We can't break up."

"You know what I mean. Dad will expect you to stay by my side in this hour of crisis. I can't ask you to hang around all day listening to his war stories."

"Your father was in the military?"

"Accounting war stories. Tax payers versus the IRS. You'll hate it."

"I'm always willing to hear out an expert. Maybe I can pick up some good tax tips."

He was teasing her. She was trying to let him off the hook, and he thought it was a joke.

"Please, Eric, I really appreciate what you've done..."

"Pretending you turn me on?" His teeth actually sparkled when he smiled like that.

"Be serious. This has gotten too complicated. Either I have to tell my father the truth, or we break up."

"Here? Now?"

He looked across the room where a sallow-faced teenager was holding his arm over his chest. Beside him a gaunt woman with flamboyant hennaed hair quickly averted her eyes when Eric looked at her. Apparently she found them more entertaining than the talkie Sunday intellectuals on the tube.

"What do we do?" he asked. "Yell at each other, stage a fight? What's my motivation in this scene?"

"I'll just tell Dad it wasn't working between us."

"How will you get home from the hospital if I leave?"

"Cab," she suggested listlessly. "Or I can call my friend, Laurie Davis. She's not doing anything today."

"I'll take you and your dad home."

"It really would be easier if we split up before Dad's done here."

"We're not going to now. You dad is going home tomorrow. Let him leave happy. You'll meet someone eventually. That's the time to tell him it didn't work out between us."

"I don't like taking advantage of you. If Dad weren't so darn pushy..."

"He is who he is."

Easy for him to say, she thought glumly.

"He'll expect you to stay for dinner," she warned. "Can you cook?"

"We brought home lots of leftovers from yesterday's dinner."

"How about ordering Chinese?"

"Dad won't eat it. Might have MSG in it."

"Mexican?"

"Too spicy."

"Pizza? He does eat pizza, doesn't he?"

"Thick crust with Canadian bacon and mushrooms. Green peppers give him heartburn."

"Is he your real father?" he asked with a grin.

"So I've been led to believe. Fortunately he's kind, generous, loyal, honest and all those other Boy Scout virtues except when he's trying to run my life."

"I sorta like him myself. Tell me he watches basketball."

"He's still mad at the Suns because they're out of town this weekend."

"Well, love," he said, doing the worst English accent she'd ever heard, "I really don't think there's anything here we can't bloody well handle."

4

"DAD, GOOD NEWS," Mindy said Monday morning when her father thumped out of the guest room on sturdy wooden crutches rented from the hospital.

"Is the dog tied up?" he asked. "I'm rusty on crutches and I don't want to be tripped again. I haven't used these things since I tore up my knee playing high school basketball."

"Peaches is outside on her line, but now that she's used to you, she'll be calmer. You don't need to worry."

He grunted and plopped down at the kitchen table where his coffee was waiting.

"Now what's the good news?" he asked.

She knew what he wanted to hear, something to do with engagement rings, wedding bells, more grandchildren.

"I called the airport. There's no problem getting a wheelchair. You can go from my van to the door of the plane without setting foot on the floor. So far they expect your plane to be on schedule. I'll take care of baggage and everything, and Dwight will be there to meet you at the Pittsburgh airport. Even the weather is cooperating, so it should be a smooth flight."

"I don't want to be pushed around like a feeble old man," he grumbled.

"It's too far to walk on a sprained ankle. The doctor said it's important to stay off it."

"I plan to. I called the airline and canceled my ticket. I'd rather wait for my ankle to heal before flying home. It'll cost me fifty dollars to reschedule, but it's worth it to get to know your boyfriend better."

"Dad! I'd love to see more of you, but you'll be bored silly sitting around here alone. I do have to work. It's my busy season."

This was very bad news. How could she continue the fantasy about having a boyfriend until Dad's ankle healed?

"You do whatever you need to. Don't worry about me. I can entertain myself. You've got a computer and a TV I can use, and there must be a bookstore somewhere in the area. I'll give you a list of books I've been wanting to read."

She couldn't say, Dad, go home, you make me crazy. She loved him, but she couldn't continue seeing Eric. It wasn't fair to him, and she was embarrassed enough already.

"You'll miss your only grandson's birthday Wednesday," she reminded him.

"Sam will only be three. He won't care when I present my stack of presents, and I'll get out of going to the party Carly has planned at Bucko's Pizza Palace. Have you ever been to one of their birthday orgies? Corny clowns, noisy game machines, kids screaming and running." He shuddered. "I went to Kim's fifth-birthday party there. A sledge hammer couldn't give me a worse headache."

"You love sharing your grandchildren's big events," she said. "Cake, candles, hugs and kisses for Grandpa."

"The nice thing about retirement," he said, speaking from his weeks of experience, "is I have plenty of time for the grandkids plus time to get to know my future son-in-law better.''

''Dad, we're not that serious!''

''I know chemistry when I see it,'' he said smugly. He started leafing through the TV listings, and she dejectedly began her day.

BY MIDMORNING Mindy was the one with a headache. She had to check with the woman who was catering the Robinson family Thanksgiving reunion, twenty-two people and counting, then run to the party store outlet for orange napkins and table decorations. After that, she had to meet a new client at two and make sure the carpenter had come back to finish the shelves in Mrs. Konkle's home office. People paid her to worry, and she was good at it.

Unfortunately, with her dad dropping his bomb on her head, she couldn't concentrate anymore. How could she work with her father in the house? Even before she left to run errands, he was busily using her computer to e-mail everyone he knew, however slightly. She could bump him, of course, but then what would he do all day? She remembered his book list and tried to figure out a time for a library trip. No point in buying thirteen books unless they weren't available to borrow.

''I have to talk to Eric,'' she said resolutely to herself.

The bogus romance had to end. Telling her father it was a hoax was no longer an option, not when he'd be there with her day and night expressing his disappointment with sad, mournful pronouncements. He took her single status as a personal affront because she rejected his opinion of it. He refused to believe she was happy the way she was and in no hurry to rush into a relationship just to satisfy him.

She dialed Eric's office on her cell phone while she waited her turn to drive through a construction area. How she loathed those two-sided signs carried by the bored workers who reduced a four-lane road to one lane. There seemed to be a rule that the busiest lane had to wait the longest.

"Kincaid Veterinary Practice," Della answered. "How may I help you?"

"Della, it's Mindy Ryder. I desperately need to talk to the doctor."

"Sorry, honey, he's in the middle of a procedure. I can have him call you when office hours are over."

"No, I need to talk to him now."

"Has something happened to Peaches?" Della remembered pet names better than most people remembered people names.

"No, she's fine. What about lunch? When does he take a lunch break?"

Traffic in Mindy's lane started inching forward.

"I never know for sure. Sometimes he runs upstairs for a bite. Other days he's so busy he just skips it."

"Can you work me in anytime today?" She'd pay for an office visit if that was the only to talk to him.

"It must be really important."

Della was curious. This was good. No doubt she remembered giving Eric the directions to her house.

"It is."

"Tell you what, if you come over right now, I'll squeeze you in as soon as humanly possible."

"Thank you, Della, thank you, thank you, thank you."

WHEN SHE GOT to Eric's office, the prospects for seeing him very soon seemed grim. Half a dozen people were crowded into the area with a Noah's ark of pets. The biggest gray cat she'd ever seen was perched on an elderly lady's lap, glaring at a Saint Bernard waiting with stoic resignation. Mindy eyed a square red cardboard box barely large enough to hold a teapot. It had holes punched in the top. Did Eric treat snakes? She shuddered and hoped the hidden creature was something soft and furry like a gerbil.

"Mindy Ryder." Della solemnly announced her name after only a couple minutes of waiting, giving her a nod.

She self-consciously walked to the door of the examining room, not at all comfortable about cutting to the front of the line.

"The procedure took longer than expected," Della explained. "Please be as quick as you can. We're really backed up today."

"Thanks, Della. I appreciate this so much."

She went through the swinging door to Eric's examining room. It was empty, but only seconds later he came through another door that led to his hospital wing. He made eye contact for a second or two, and her heart thumped as enthusiastically as her dog's tail usually did at the sight of the vet.

"Mindy, I didn't expect to see you today. Where's Peaches?" He went to the sink and started scrubbing his hands with pink liquid soap from a wall dispenser.

"I won't take much of your time, but I had to see you. We really should've broken up yesterday."

"You know, Mindy, I'm overbooked today." He dried his hands on a paper towel. "Exactly why are you here?"

He sounded pleasant enough, but she hated the

feeling that she was only a nuisance to a man who could turn her on with a smile.

"Dad's decided to stay."

"How long?"

"He didn't say, but he canceled his flight home. He wants to get to know you better." She paused. "Hey, is there a snake in your waiting room?"

"Doubt it, unless one slithered in by itself. About your father..."

"Yes, what about my father? If I calmly announce that we're no longer an item, he'll probably try to get us to reconcile. He won't let it rest unless you do something unforgivably mean."

"What did you have in mind?"

His scowl wasn't enough to mar his good looks, and she was filled with regret. She should've kept going to the big impersonal vet clinic even if they had muzzled Peaches on her last appointment there. Mindy wouldn't mind seeing Eric a lot more often than twice a year at her dog's checkups, but by now he probably thought she was nothing but a nuisance. And here she was again, trying to use him to solve her problem.

"I shouldn't have come. You're busy, and you've already done more than I had any right to expect."

She started to leave, but he stepped in front of the door and put both hands on her shoulders.

"But you did come, and I'm glad."

What did he mean by that? She met his eyes and was even more confused. She shrugged, but he didn't remove his hands.

"I'll fake a breakup on the phone. I should've thought of it before I barged in on you," she said apologetically.

"You didn't barge. I told Della to send you in as soon as you got here."

"But your waiting room is full."

"Happens sometimes. I try, but..." He dropped his arms and turned away from her. "So your dad's not leaving as scheduled, and he expects to see me...."

"Often, I'm afraid."

"Then you and I had better strike a deal," he replied, facing her again.

"A deal?"

Her shoulders felt warm where his hands had rested on top of her silky cherry-red ruffled blouse. She'd worn it with dressy gray slacks and low-heeled black pumps in anticipation of meeting a new client, hoping she'd look businesslike but imaginative. She looked good in red and hoped what she saw in Eric's eyes was at least a trace of admiration.

"Maybe we can help each other out," he said slowly.

The last time she'd heard that, her date had been trying to wiggle his fingers between her thighs. She looked at Eric's hand, strong but gentle and soothing with his patients, then at his face. Who knew eyes could actually twinkle? Maybe he was only teasing about a deal, although he seemed too busy for games.

"Helpful is nice," she said wanting to kick herself for sounding so clueless.

"There is something you can do for me."

She dropped her eyes to the apex of his legs, which was not quite covered by the lab coat, then realized what she'd done and was mortified. She hadn't intended to check him out, certainly not in his examining room where the air was heavy with disinfectant and tension.

He reached out, the back of his wrist brushing

against her breast, but all he did was flip over the cameo pendant she was wearing.

"The backside was showing," he said, his grin reminding her of the way she'd straightened his tie.

"I'm in a bind myself." He sighed. "You can see how busy I am, but my mother has involved me in a big charity event to raise money for pet adoptions. Of course, she had an ulterior motive. She's hoping I'll meet the future mother of her grandchildren among the single women working in the event. She put me on the committee and expects me to help bring the thing together, thinking I'd be thrilled to get involved. Party planning isn't my forte even if I had time to kill. But you're a professional organizer..."

"It's what I do for a living," she said cautiously.

"I don't want to let Mom down in front of her friends, but my idea of organizing is putting everything in a pile to worry about later."

"What's your deal?" she asked.

Once, as a kid back home in Pennsylvania, she'd been sliding down a snow-covered hill on a plastic sled when she hit a bump and headed straight for a tree. This felt the same way, but she didn't have the option of wiping out on purpose and landing on soft snow.

"I'll play Dr. Boyfriend if you'll help me out on Mom's charity event. Quietly. She doesn't need to know you're involved. I'll go to the committee meetings and volunteer for as little as possible. Naturally most of the planning was done months ago. I call my mom's group the committee for last-minute disasters. It doesn't matter how far in advance they plan, something inevitably goes wrong. You handle what I'm *supposed* to be doing, and in exchange, your dad and

I will be best buddies. He'll go home sure you're in good hands.''

There was nothing wrong with Eric's proposal, but she couldn't believe two competent adults were scheming to hoodwink their parents.

''Maybe we should both fess up instead,'' she suggested.

''Take our medicine, get the spanking over with?'' he asked.

''At least insist we're mature adults who want to run our own lives.''

''Well spoken,'' he said solemnly, ''but I can't do it without hurting Mom's feelings, a lot. That's just the way she is.''

''I can't, either,'' she admitted. ''Dad misses Mom so much, he doesn't want me to end up lonely and alone. It's just that he's so—so insistent.''

''So do we have a deal?'' Eric asked.

She knew it was the answer to both their problems, at least temporarily, but it was only a little over six weeks until Christmas. She had parties to plan, people to consult, lists to cross off....

On the other hand, she hadn't seen her father so happy and animated in a long time, even with his bum ankle keeping him housebound.

''Okay.'' She said it with deep reluctance, but he smiled broadly.

''Shake.''

She lifted her hand to meet his. Strong fingers pressed against hers, and his firm palm felt wonderful. When his fingers brushed against her wrist, she felt ripples of pleasure course up her arm. One part of this charade would be a snap. She wouldn't have any trouble pretending Eric was sexy and appealing.

He dropped her hand, and she had a terrible thought.

"You're not involved...that is, seeing anyone else, are you? I wouldn't want to interfere...."

"They're lined up ten-deep to be with me," he said with a grin, "but they're all four-footed and furry."

"Oh, my gosh, I forgot all those people in your waiting room. They must be ready to lynch me by now."

"I'll see you safely out."

He opened the door, let her step through, and put his arm around her shoulders.

"Glad you stopped by, sweetheart," he said for the benefit of his crowded waiting room.

He walked her to the outer door, opened it for her and gave her shoulder a squeeze.

She could feel the hostility in the waiting room turn to curiosity. They forgave her line-jumping because they thought she was Dr. Eric's love interest—or at least one of them.

"See you later," he said.

He grinned broadly as a finale to his act just as she stepped outside. She stared after him as he walked back to the examining room. How sincere was he about this deal? Was it just a ploy to get rid of her? She'd hate the additional stress so much she'd bail? She couldn't resist the sudden urge to test him.

"Eric!"

She held the door open as he turned to face her again.

"Dinner tonight at my house, seven o'clock?" she asked in an expectant tone.

He hesitated for an instant, then agreed. "Fine. I'll be there."

Whatever the cost, she had a boyfriend, at least for the duration of her dad's visit.

There had to be a better word than boyfriend. Lover, partner, significant other? Nothing quite described their nonrelationship.

She drove away, behind schedule and seriously short of time, and wondered if she'd ever before seen eyes as blue as his.

ERIC RAN a couple of extra miles after work, but still felt as though his brain were full of cobwebs. He wanted to sidestep any little committee chores his mother had lined up for him, but was the price of Mindy's help too high?

He wasn't ready for a new relationship, but keeping Mindy at arm's length was harder every time he saw her. The impulse to take her in his arms and let nature take its course got stronger all the time. But he'd felt that way about Cass not very long ago, and he'd been as wrong about her as a man could be.

Sure, sometimes bachelor life was lonely after working hours, but he had friends and interests to keep him occupied. He didn't need a new best buddy who expected him to become a son-in-law.

If he'd been free earlier in his office when Mindy had called, he would've cheerfully helped her orchestrate a breakup her father would believe. But when she walked into his examining room, he hadn't wanted an abrupt end to their tentative relationship. He'd had a flash of inspiration. They could trade favors and make both parents happy. It was a spur-of-the-moment idea but seemed reasonable. An "I help you, and you help me" kind of thing.

After the run he scrubbed himself hard under a tepid spray. He hadn't moved away from frigid Iowa winters to shiver in a cold shower, but his body chemistry had a way of reacting to Mindy that was totally at odds with his intentions. He was usually indifferent to women whose pets he treated, but he'd gone beyond his normal professionalism with Mindy. She turned him on, and the lukewarm water didn't do much to cool down his involuntary interest in her.

She'd already put him off his stride. After her unscheduled appearance at his office, he'd called Mrs. O'Brien's St. Bernard Bozo instead of Beau Geste. He'd forgotten what a foul disposition Sugar Baby had until the cat punctured his latex glove with her needle-sharp teeth.

He never gave more than ten seconds thought to what he wore, but this evening he stood in his walk-in closet in white briefs and couldn't make up his mind. If he really were courting a woman—what a corny, old-fashioned word—he'd wear his navy blue blazer and gray dress slacks. That outfit was sure to be a father-pleaser, especially to a man who probably slept in his wing tips, but what message would it send to Mindy? What if she were interested in him, and this was her way of attracting his attention.

"Yeah, right," he said skeptically.

He knew a come-on when he saw one, and he wasn't getting any signals from her. Was that why he had this strange feeling about their deal? Was it because she was more immune to his dubious charms than he was to her very real attractions? Or maybe he should be flattered. He didn't need enough reforming and reorganizing to interest her. Wayne might be biased, but Mindy apparently went for men she could make over. Cass had tried that with him, and he didn't want Mindy or any other woman trying to change him.

He yanked an old pair of jeans and a black knit turtleneck off the hangers. Hopefully wearing them wouldn't send any messages one way or the other.

He got to Mindy's house twenty minutes late because he belatedly remembered to stop for a bottle of wine as an offering for Wayne.

"Sorry I'm late," he said when Mindy opened the door.

"No problem. I'm doing lemon-pepper chicken and marinated vegetable kabobs on the grill, nothing very fancy."

Since his usual bachelor fare ran to omelettes or salads and submarines from the supermarket deli, it sounded elaborate to him.

"I was expecting leftovers from Mountain Monty's."

She laughed lightly, an altogether pleasing sound. "Dad had steak and eggs for breakfast, then polished off the last of the leftovers for lunch. Apparently his low cholesterol diet is on vacation."

"I heard that, young lady," Wayne said from the couch where he was lounging with his foot resting on a mound of pillows. "I'll go to the store with you tomorrow and cash some traveler's checks so you can stock your kitchen."

"Dad, you don't have to buy groceries. I make a good living."

This had the ring of an old argument. Eric presented the wine to Mindy and ambled into the living room to sit opposite the patriarch in a high-backed Boston rocker.

"How's your ankle?"

"Fine as long as I treat it with RICE. That's rest, ice, compression and elevation."

Eric knew that. He'd done enough track and field

sports even before he got to college to be familiar with trainer's lingo, but he was here to be the deferential suitor. From where he sat, he could see Mindy in the kitchen struggling with the cork in his bottle of wine.

"Let me," he offered, walking over to her.

The nice thing about having the living room and kitchen as one large room was being able to see her as she worked. The bad thing was Wayne had a front-row seat to watch them together. Eric remembered his deal and moved up to her intending to carry out his end.

"Something smells nice."

He nuzzled the back of her neck, soft and fragrant under her short-cropped sable hair. It seemed natural to wrap one arm around her waist, which looked slender and sexy in a long black skirt with big splashy yellow, red and green flowers. Her midriff-baring yellow top rode up so his arm was circling warm silky flesh. He should've braved an icy cold shower.

"I need to put the chicken on," she said, pulling away.

"I'll help you."

He picked up a tray of foil packets and followed her down the hallway between the back rooms. They walked out through sliding glass doors onto a small flagstone patio, where she had a propane gas grill and a round white-metal table with two matching chairs and umbrella.

"This is nice," he said.

"Except for having neighbors so close I can't use the grill without attracting people who want to give me cooking advice."

She kept her eyes averted. So far she hadn't looked directly at him, not even when she answered the door.

"You know," he said softly, "if you want your father to buy our act, you're going to have to gaze longingly into my eyes."

They both laughed self-consciously.

"I've had some second thoughts," she admitted as she carefully laid the packets of chicken on the barbecue, still not meeting his eyes.

"And?"

Was she going to let him off the hook? Did he want her to?

"This is terribly unfair of me, expecting you to give up your free time like this."

"Can't complain about the eats."

"Really, Eric, we can call this off right now. I'll still help as much as I can with your committee, but I can't ask you to—"

"Mindy," he interrupted, even though he didn't know what he wanted to say.

"You're so busy," she went on.

"When I agree to a deal, I keep my word," he said, trying to sound resolute and committed.

"But I feel like I've trapped you into this."

She kept fussing with long kabobs of potato, onion, mushroom and colorful yellow, red and green peppers.

"Look at me."

He wanted to talk to her face, not the back of her head.

She looked at him over her shoulder, just long enough for him to see miniature bolts of green lightning in her intriguing hazel eyes.

"Enough fussing," he said. "The food is fine."

She turned and faced him squarely, then reached up and straightened the collar on his turtleneck. One minute she was willing to let him back away from their bargain, and the next she was fixing his shirt. The woman just couldn't leave him alone. He took her hands in his and stared so intently she dropped her eyes.

"Sorry," she said meekly.

"I'm going to go inside and talk to your dad," he said gruffly.

"I meant what I said. You don't have to do this...."

He went into the house without answering.

5

DAD WAS ONLINE AGAIN when Mindy got home from work late Friday afternoon. She'd moved the patio table into the living room and set up the computer there so she had access when her father was sleeping in the spare bedroom. Still, the arrangement wasn't working well from her point of view. She did all her planning, organizing and accounting on her computer, usually in the evening. But after being home alone all day, her father was more chatty then he'd ever been before.

"How was your day?" he asked in a hearty voice from his spot on the couch.

"Fine, Dad." Except for a crabby caterer, a carpenter whose wife had been in labor for twenty-one hours and counting and a client whose check bounced. "Did you find things to keep you busy today?"

"I found a list of e-mail addresses from my class at Penn State. I connected with a guy who lived next to me our freshman year. Now he's right here in Phoenix. We had a good online chat."

"Sounds like fun."

Peaches did her welcoming dance while Mindy kicked off her sandals and enjoyed the cool tiles on the soles of her feet.

"Don't leave your shoes where I can trip over them," her father warned.

No, I certainly don't want you to fall again she thought. "Did you get to your doctor's appointment all right?"

She still felt guilty about not driving him there herself, but the day had been impossibly busy.

"The cab was twenty minutes late, but I allowed an extra forty-five for the trip."

When had her father ever been late for anything, unlike Dr. Eric Kincaid who made a specialty of keeping people waiting? And not calling the woman he was supposed to adore.

"I do have good news," he said.

"What?"

"The doctor says my ankle is coming along fine. Apparently the emergency room handled it okay. I'll be back on both feet sooner than I thought."

"That's *great* news, Dad." No more worrying about a phantom boyfriend, not that her father asked about him more than twenty or so times a day.

"That's not the good news."

Whoops.

"I've decided to stay through Christmas."

"You mean stay another—"

"I haven't had Christmas with you in a long time." Interrupting was one of his little habits that was driving her up the wall.

Her father would be living in her house, micromanaging her life, giving her helpful advice. Until Christmas. She felt panicky. Maybe she could rent a temporary office—no, too expensive. She loved her father, but she desperately needed her space, especially during the busiest season of the year for her business.

"I don't do much to celebrate Christmas," she said.

Now there was an understatement. Last year she and Laurie had done each other's nails and shared a frozen pizza. Her best friend was originally from Rhode Island and, like Laurie, Mindy preferred to make the annual pilgrimage home to see her family in the summer.

"This year we'll do it up big. You and Eric can help me trim a tree—"

"Dad, Eric probably has other plans. His family will expect him to..."

"We'll work it out. Christmas Eve, Christmas morning, I'm flexible about when we open presents."

"Aren't you forgetting Dwight and Carly and Sam and Kim? I can't imagine you'd want to miss your grandchildren's Christmas. You always spend holidays at their house."

"No problem. I called Carly's dad today. They're going to take the family on a trip to Florida as their Christmas present. Renting a condo for a week. They'll surprise them with the news on Thanksgiving. They can still celebrate a late Christmas with me when we all get home."

"Sun, sea, beach, amusement parks. Doesn't sound much like Christmas," she mused aloud.

"Now don't be envious, Mindy. Maybe you'll go some place exotic for your honeymoon, maybe a Caribbean cruise. I might be persuaded to spring for the trip as a wedding present."

"Dad, I have no plans whatsoever to get married in the near future."

Peaches ambled away and went to her favorite hidey-hole at the far end of the couch where only the white tips of her paws revealed her location. Even the dog was cringing at her father's premature offer of a honeymoon—or maybe it was his plan to intrude on her canine kingdom for more than a month.

"I have to level with you," she went on, wishing she could tell him the whole truth without badly hurting his feelings. "Eric and I are only dating very casually. We have no plans for the future. He's not interested in commitment, and I like things the way they are."

"We'll see," he said smugly. "Meanwhile, I'll have more time to get to know him better. He's the first decent boyfriend you've had, so I hope it's a sign your taste in men has improved."

"You're not being fair—"

The phone on the kitchen counter rang shrilly, which was probably a good thing. She grabbed for it, wondering if her father saw himself as an aging Cupid with thinning hair and a bum ankle.

"Yes, Mrs. Wilmer. How can I help you?" Mindy said after the Scottsdale social leader identified herself.

Mindy was setting up a database for Kitty Wilmer's long Christmas card list, a tedious chore that involved reading an endless number of names and addresses written in the woman's tiny, cramped handwriting, which included thirty years' worth of additions, deletions and changes. She had to finish soon so the mailing labels were ready for the cards. It was the kind of picky job she hated, but Mrs. Wilmer could throw a lot of business her way if she was happy with her work.

"I have a pencil right here," Mindy said as she started to jot down a few more additions to the list. The woman collected people as if they were coins.

At least her father got bored and thumped out to

the back porch on his crutches for some early evening air.

Christmas! Her tenuous deal with Eric would never hold up that long.

ERIC MET Guy at the athletic club where they both had memberships. They played racquetball until they were pooped, then sat in the sauna making small talk.

"What a hottie," Guy said, trying for the third time that morning to get Eric to open up about his date at Mountain Monty's. "When are the four of us going to get together?"

"Your idea or Tammy's?" Eric asked, letting the towel on his head hide his face.

"Both. We'd like to get to know her."

Eric doubted Tammy was that eager to get acquainted with Mindy. She'd dragged Guy away before they could even finish their conversation.

"Why don't you two agree on something important like when you're getting married?"

"I'm on the road too much right now," his friend replied.

"Lame excuse."

"Effective though. I love a sauna," Guy said with feeling. "Cleans out the pores, sharpens the brain."

"It's a good time for quiet contemplation."

Sarcasm was wasted on Guy. He enjoyed talking even more than listening to his collection of CDs and audio books, the largest Eric had seen outside of a store.

His friend laughed, another thing he did easily and often.

"When you bring the dad along on a date, something serious is going on."

"Nothing is going on," Eric said, with no hope of being believed.

"Well, at least you're over Cassandra. She was as cold as an ice sculpture."

"She didn't like you much, either."

Guy thought that was hilarious.

"Well, when you feel like being sociable, we'll set something up," his friend said. "You can't keep her all to yourself forever."

"Time to hit the showers," Eric said, knowing it was also time to call Mindy.

He thought far too often of calling her, but the cautious side of his nature held him back. He'd been through an emotionally charged breakup with Cassandra. She'd refused to accept any share of the blame for their incompatibility and was furious, mainly because he'd spoiled her horse-care plans. He still felt angry when he remembered her resentment and spite.

He'd been blinded by optimism and admiration for Cassandra's style and class, that and basic lust for a hard-to-get female. He couldn't help comparing his infatuation for Cass with the way he was beginning to feel about Mindy. Unfair as it might be, he was gun-shy when it came to women like Mindy, whose chief goal was to organize and reform. Better to keep his life unfettered, risk-free and placid than deal with another colossal mistake.

He would call Mindy, though. They had a deal, and he would do his part.

NOTHING WENT quite the way Eric planned that day. To begin with, he still hadn't talked to Mindy. Now here he was, on her doorstep on Saturday night, not sure how he felt about another cozy dinner for three.

More to the point, what had her reaction been when

Wayne told her Eric was coming for another meal? Mindy hadn't been home when he finally called in the early afternoon. Wayne didn't expect her soon, but suggested Eric drop over for dinner that evening. He'd declined, of course. He didn't think Mindy wanted her father to arrange her social life, and he sure as hell didn't, either. But he'd neglected to give a valid-sounding excuse right away, and Wayne wore him down until there was no way to refuse without disclaiming all interest in his daughter.

What Eric wanted was a private conversation with Mindy. What he was getting was dinner, deception and her dad.

His only consolation was she was probably more uncomfortable about it than he was. She'd gotten him into this, and she'd better have good news about her father going home. He didn't like this dating charade. Their nonrelationship was getting to him more than he would've believed possible.

Probably worst of all, he felt silly standing in front of her door, not knowing if she wanted him to come for dinner. Rather than show up empty-handed, he'd picked up a bouquet of flowers that reminded him of autumn in Iowa, shades of gold and rust like the late fall foliage. They were long-stemmed and wrapped in green tissue paper. All he had to do was hand them over, but now that he was about to do it, the gesture seemed romantically hokey.

Wayne had probably spotted him through the big front window, so it was too late to retreat or hide the flowers in the car. He rang the buzzer.

His wanna-be father-in-law answered the door leaning on his crutches. The old boy still didn't know how to dress down the Arizona way. He was wearing dark navy slacks, brilliantly shined black dress shoes, and a short-sleeved blue tailored shirt. His bolo tie looked stiff and formal.

"Good to see you, Eric." He thrust out his hand.

"Nice seeing you, sir...Wayne."

A spicy tomato smell permeated the interior of the house making him realize how hungry he was.

"Come on in, come on in. Mindy will be out in a minute. I have to warn you though, she's a little miffed."

"At me?"

She could be mad because he hadn't called all week. That would've been enough to send Cassandra into a blue funk, but he didn't have a real relationship with Mindy. She could've called him anytime if she had something to say.

"No, not at you." Wayne laughed a bit too heartily. "At her father. Seems I committed a social no-no when I invited you to dinner. Not that she isn't happy to have you."

"I'll go if being here is a problem."

"No, stay. You're not the one she's angry with," Wayne said, shuffling out of the way then shutting the door behind Eric. "I'm the one who's in the doghouse."

"Where is Peaches?"

Right now he'd welcome the little rascal even if she jumped all over him, panting and licking his fingers. Anything to cut off this conversation with Wayne.

"In the bedroom with Mindy. You know women. Always a few last-minute rituals they think will make them look better. With Mindy, it's usually eyebrows. Pluck, pluck, pluck. Anything wider than a pencil line is too bushy."

Eric smiled, entertained by her grooming secret.

Now that Wayne mentioned it, her brows were dark dramatic slashes, the sexiest he'd ever noticed. He'd wanted to run his fingertip over them more than once.

She came out of her room with Peaches forming a noisy honor guard and stood by the kitchen counter with a grim expression.

"Has he told you?"

She was asking Eric. The bouquet was beginning to feel clammy in his fist. Would soggy tissue turn his hand green?

"That you're mad at him?"

He thrust the flowers forward, but she didn't seem to notice.

"Dad was being cute when he invited you to dinner. He's going out."

So Wayne was playing matchmaker, inviting him over to be alone with his daughter. The sly old devil had done exactly what Eric wanted, given him a chance to talk to Mindy alone. Their deal wasn't working for him, and this was better than meeting at his office or working things out on the phone.

"I found an old friend from college, Jack Webster, through the Internet," her father explained sheepishly. "Turns out he lives in Phoenix. He's picking me up any minute now. His wife divorced him after thirty-eight years of marriage, so he's at loose ends."

This was more than Eric wanted to know about the old college buddy, but he couldn't take his eyes off Mindy. She was wearing blue denim overalls, loose the way farmers in Iowa wore them, but hers barely came to mid-thigh. She probably didn't know how sexy they were, which was a big part of their appeal. With only a little white camisole showing under them, the effect was pretty spectacular. He was too busy imagining how it would feel to run his hands under the loose denim and down her sides to her panties—if she was wearing any.

She must be. She was that kind of girl, and he deserved a swift kick for confusing what he felt—or didn't feel—for Mindy with real sexual attraction.

From outside a horn beeped.

"Oh, there's Jack," Wayne said. "I've got a spare key, Mindy. You two have a good time."

He went down the flagstones, swinging on his crutches like a kid let out of school and got into a dark green sports utility van big enough to haul a baseball team.

"Nice your father has a friend here," Eric said, thrusting the flowers in her direction again after she closed the door. "These are for you."

"Thank you." She'd probably accept a summons with the same degree of enthusiasm.

"I don't have to stay."

"I'm not mad at you."

"No, but..."

"I have spaghetti sauce simmering on the stove, garlic bread ready to heat, salad already tossed and lemon bars in the fridge."

"All that for me?"

He gave her a crooked little smile hoping to break through her anger, although he didn't know why he cared.

"No, for my scheming, conniving father who never even hinted he was going off on his own tonight until a few minutes before you got here."

Thanks, Wayne, he thought sourly. Ignite a brush-fire and let me get burned stamping it out. The guy was looking worse all the time as a prospective father-in-law.

"By then I didn't see much point in trying to reach

you, especially since I don't have your cell phone number. If you'd been late as usual, Dad would have been gone."

"I'm not usually late."

Now he was mad, too. Maybe it would be best to leave.

"He's staying until Christmas!"

He heard the distress in her voice and forgot his own petty annoyance.

"What?"

"You heard me." She finally took the flowers out of his still outstretched hand, but made no move to do anything with them.

"Now what do we do?" he asked.

"I have to tell him the truth. It was bad enough deceiving him when he was halfway across the country and too busy to poll everyone he's ever known for potential husbands. I can't keep it up another..."

She used her fingers to calculate.

"Another five and a half weeks, longer if he doesn't leave right after Christmas."

"He won't be happy when he hears it."

In the short time he'd known Wayne Ryder, even he could be sure of that.

"No."

She stared at the bouquet in her hand as though just noticing it.

"Thank you for the flowers."

"You're welcome, but maybe it would be better if I leave now."

Surprisingly, he didn't want to go, but didn't know why, even though the situation was definitely getting complicated.

"Stay. Please. Dinner's nearly ready. All I have to do is cook the pasta."

"If you're sure..."

He tried to conceal his relief at not being sent on his way. Later he'd try to understand it.

"Anyway, you haven't told me what I need to be doing for your mother's fund-raiser committee."

"So far I'm supposed to pick up donations the merchants have promised. Prizes, food. Mostly last-minute stuff. But if you're going to tell your father about us, you don't have to help."

"Let's talk about it later." She managed a weak smile. "Sorry we can't eat outside. I had to bring the patio table into the living room to use as a computer table. I'm doing my work after he goes to bed. I'll get the noodles started now."

"Can I help?"

"You can set the table. Plates and stuff are in the dishwasher. I haven't had time to unload it."

He took two heavy white stoneware plates with green bands from the dishwasher and arranged them on opposite sides of a small kitchen table. Trying to keep his mind on his task, he arranged flatware on either side of each plate and folded yellow paper napkins from a basket on the counter.

Without looking at her, he was fully aware of everything she did. He could track her by scent alone, a delicate floral fragrance that somehow permeated the garlicky smells in the kitchen.

She walked over and inspected the table, making it impossible not to notice her eyebrows. They were thin but angled in an impish way, well worth the time her father claimed was spent on them.

"We could renegotiate our deal after dinner," he suggested cautiously.

"No, don't even think about keeping up this charade. I don't want you to keep pretending because you feel sorry for me. I got myself into this mess, and I'll get myself out."

"Without hurting your father?"

"Low blow."

She was gorgeous when her brows arched and her lips formed a pouty little scowl.

Face it, he thought with irritation, she was gorgeous all the time. He'd noticed that the first time she walked into his office with Peaches.

"None of my business," he mumbled by way of apology. "Remember the first time you brought Peaches for a checkup? You gave me a hard time about stepping onto the scale with her. I still remember what you weigh."

"You don't!" She stopped, dropping dry pasta into boiling water before facing him with pursed lips.

"One hundred sixteen pounds."

"I can't believe you remember that."

"It's a perfect weight for you. You're only five feet tall."

"Five-foot-three," she said indignantly, then quickly reacted to his teasing with a broad smile. "You're not exactly a basketball prospect yourself. What are you? Five six or eight?"

"Six foot even."

"With platform soles."

"Never wear them. Barefoot."

"Hair standing up straight?"

"No, my usual baby blond curls."

They both laughed. At least their silly argument had broken the ice. They could talk about something other than her father over dinner.

By her own admission, the spaghetti sauce came from a glass jar, the salad from a cellophane bag and the lemon bars from a package mix, but it was arguably the best dinner he'd had in years.

"How do you make canned sauce taste like this?" he asked. "When I use it, it's like lumpy tomato sauce."

"I add fresh green peppers, mushrooms and onions plus my secret seasonings."

"Which you're not going to share with me?" He pretended to be mad.

"Maybe, but it'll cost you."

There it was again. Even when they were kidding, everything between them was a deal. Just once he'd like to have a real date with her, the kind that ended in some serious smooching, some passionate petting...

He watched her nibble at her lemon bar, breaking off tiny bites with a fork and slowly savoring the tangy-sweet morsels. He finished his, decided against seconds although he was tempted, and kept his attention riveted on her mouth. It was small, but her lips were naturally pink and full. Could they possibly feel as sensual as they looked? He'd like to kiss her for real, nuzzle the lobe of her ear below her silky dark hair, and find the spots where she'd subtly splashed perfume.

She put the fork down with a small segment of lemon bar still on her plate. Why did women do that, leave the final bite when they'd already consumed enough calories to tweak the scale the next morning? Why not go all out and lick the plate clean?

"Are you going to waste that?" he asked, staring at her plate.

"Not if you want it."

She speared it with the fork tines and held it out like a lure. He rose slowly from the chair, leaned across the table, opened his mouth and snapped it shut on air. She'd snatched it away with the quickness of a blinking eye.

"Tease!" he accused.

He walked to her side of the table. She stood up still tempting him with the bite of lemon bar.

"Do you really think you need more?" she asked.

He'd never seen this flirty side of her, and he liked it.

"Are you my calorie counter, my nutritionist, my mother?"

"Definitely not your mother. I just don't think that little bulge of yours should get any bigger."

"What bulge?"

He looked down even though he knew his waist and belly were lean and hard from lots of running.

She laughed, a ripple of pleasurable sound.

"You're an evil girl."

"Twenty-eight is hardly a girl."

"Still a child."

"Like you're an old man!"

"Thirty and then some."

"Aside from one bad engagement, why are you still available, Dr. Kincaid?"

"I'm not."

He enjoyed the flicker of disappointment in her eyes.

"I'm seriously seeing a hot little number who likes to reform men."

"Do you need reforming?" She backed away, bumping into the refrigerator and could retreat no farther.

"No, I'm pretty much perfect."

"No ego, either."

"Humble to the core."

Placing both hands on the fridge, he hemmed her in. The white door was cool, but he wasn't.

"I was only kidding," she said softly.

"Kidding is good. Kissing is better."

She moistened her lips with the tip of her tongue, and he took that as a yes.

He'd kissed her for show, for her father's benefit, but this one was all for him, slow and soft until she leaned forward and melted into his arms.

"I didn't expect..." she murmured as he slid his lips to the skin below her ear.

"I didn't plan..." she whispered a tad breathlessly.

He moved his hands over her bare shoulders, down silky smooth arms until both her hands were covered by his. She escaped his grip and caressed the back of his neck while he locked his arms around her.

When her lips parted under his, he felt dizzy. He hadn't allowed himself to fantasize about kissing her like this—well, not often anyway—but the reality of having her in his arms was better than anything he could imagine.

The metal clasps on her overalls pressed into his skin through the material of his shirt.

"I like what you're wearing," he said, exploring the contours of her back under the overall straps.

"You weren't supposed to."

She took his lower lip between her teeth and gently nipped at it, surprising him again because she wasn't at all the cool, controlled woman he'd been trying to dismiss from his mind.

"What did you put in that sauce?" he asked when his voice kicked in again.

"Secret herbs and spices."

He had a decision to make. Should he sweep her

into his arms and carry her to the bedroom, or close the blinds on the picture window and…

The phone rang, waking Peaches who had been sleeping on the couch. She barked furiously, and Mindy slipped out of his arms.

"Don't answer it."

"Could be my dad. I have to."

She picked it up, said hello several times, and hung up.

"Must have been a telemarketer double dialing."

She walked into the living room and petted her dog's head without looking at Eric. He followed, but she was bent over, showing no sign she wanted to pick up where they'd left off. Damn! What timing!

"Dad will be coming home soon," she said, her meaning plain.

He'd forgotten about him, but surely two old buddies with nothing better to do would talk for hours.

"It's early," he said.

"They were only going to the Ranchero. It's less than ten minutes from here."

"Still, we've only just finished eating."

"Yes, but…"

"Would your father be upset if we were, you know, being friendly?"

"He used to have a four-feet-on-the-floor rule. Even though I'm grown-up now, it would be so, you know, embarrassing. Fathers don't really believe their daughters get physical. It's a Dad thing."

"I suppose."

He pictured Wayne catching him on the couch with his pants down, not that it would come to that because he was unprepared, but…

He was unprepared! He could run out and come

back, but he didn't think what they'd started could be put on hold.

What the heck had they started? They didn't have a relationship and weren't likely to. Even as an undergraduate in college he'd been leery of one-night stands. He wasn't good at handling guilt, recrimination or emotional messes.

"I'm sorry. I didn't mean to mislead you," she said.

Eric couldn't understand what was going on. He was sure she'd been flirting with him, or had it been so long that he'd forgotten what it was like? Did she think she could turn him on and off like a light switch? Was that what she was looking for? Maybe Wayne had good reason not to trust his daughter's taste in men.

Why was he so upset anyway? He'd never even asked her out. She'd certainly never promised or even suggested she was interested in him. They'd been impulsive, and she was the one with the good sense to break it off. He took some deep breaths and knew it was time to leave.

"You're mad," she said softly.

"No."

"Yes, I can tell. You are."

"I am not mad. It was a bad idea, and it's time for me to go. Thanks for dinner."

"Thanks for the flowers."

Yeah, no problem, he thought glumly as he went out into a picture-perfect desert night with stars twinkling in a velvet-blue sky.

Life was too darn complicated. If he'd met her before Cass, he might have tried for a relationship with Mindy. But would it work? What did she expect from a man? What did he expect from a woman? For now, he didn't know what he wanted. His life had always been pretty straight-forward and uncomplicated. Now it wasn't.

6

WAS IT ONLY Thursday? Already Mindy had packed two weeks worth of work into four days, and tomorrow promised to be just as full. Now she had one last appointment this evening, and the van was making more racket than an overloaded washing machine.

She should've said no to meeting Eric at his place this evening, but he was expecting her to help with the Auction Extravaganza. Much as she'd like to, she couldn't refuse to keep her part of their deal. He had called twice since their dinner together Saturday, so her father was still satisfied they were a couple, which was a blessing in disguise.

His long-lost friend, Jack Webster, had a recently divorced nephew who would love to meet a nice girl like her. Her father's money was still on Eric, but he liked having an alternate in reserve.

The only good thing about meeting Eric tonight was missing out on pizza and motorcycle races on TV with the two old Penn State grads. She was darn lucky her father had found a friend to entertain him, but Jack was one of those hale-and-hearty salesman types who belonged to every lodge and service club that would have him. He had an inexhaustible supply of small talk, and Mindy suspected Dad was hanging out with him so she wouldn't feel obligated to spend every free minute with him. It was true she'd rather scrub garbage cans than lose another hand to her father playing gin rummy, but she wasn't nearly as happy about the meeting with Eric as the old matchmaker from the hills of Pennsylvania was.

Her phone conversations with Eric had covered the state of their health, her father's ankle, the weather and Peaches's general well-being. He said nothing about the dinner at her house or the kisses that had followed.

Her stomach was doing flip-flops at the prospect of seeing him face-to-face again. Now that the incident was history, she was humiliated by what had happened between them. She'd teased him into kissing her and loved every minute of it. Therein lay the danger. Could she possibly be falling for Eric, a man who had her father's wholehearted approval?

She stopped the van for a traffic signal and realized she was gnawing her lower lip, a sure sign of extreme agitation. She could not let herself be infatuated with the vet. It was ludicrous, not to mention hopeless. She had to forget that his kisses made her see fireworks, and she had to stop having erotically charged daydreams that included lots of his skin.

Seeing him face-to-face promised to be horribly awkward. She shivered with anticipation, glad she'd decided to wear a tailored chocolate-brown jacket over an ankle-length camel skirt and a modest scoop-neck tee the same color. She didn't want Eric to think she was there for any reason but business.

When the light changed and she accelerated, all she could hear was the loud racket her muffler was making. She cringed when she looked out her window and saw the driver in the car next to her staring, a scowl on his face.

The van made it to his parking lot without being stopped for a noise violation. She'd have to get a new muffler installed in the morning, she thought, mentally adding one more chore to tomorrow's to-do list, and one more expense.

The parking lot in front of Eric's two-story tan stucco building was empty, but the bright pole lights were beacons against the deep blue twilight sky. By the time she got out of the van, locked it, pocketed the key, straightened her jacket and ran her fingers through shaggy hair badly in need of a trim, Eric was silhouetted in the open door of the waiting room.

"Hi. It's really nice of you to come here for this," he said as she approached.

"I guess your office hours are over." Brilliant deduction.

"Come in."

He stood aside to let her enter. She heard the bolt click into place as he locked the door.

"I've got the auction stuff spread out upstairs. Hope you don't mind coming up. I picked up a pizza after my run. Didn't seem fair to starve you after the way you fed me the other night."

Finally he mentioned their dinner together. Would he bring up what happened after dessert? No, he was way too cool and self-contained. Besides he was a man. Men didn't get all mushy over a little kissing, did they? He probably kissed women all the time, no big deal to him.

"Pizza is great," she said. "I didn't have time for lunch."

"Bad habit, skipping lunch."

"You sound like my father."

"I like your dad, but I definitely don't think the same way he does—especially not about you."

What did he mean by that? She wanted to ask, but opted for silence. A wise old teacher used to say,

"You don't learn anything when your mouth is open." Or maybe that came from the lazy baby-sitter who let her and Dwight take everything out of the kitchen cupboards and finger-paint in flour while she watched soaps.

"This way," Eric said, putting his hand on the back of her waist and opening a door off his examining room.

"My domain." He gestured for her to precede him up a flight of wide carpeted stairs.

She stepped into a large room decorated Southwestern style. It looked the way she wanted her house to look some day, only the room was much bigger than her combined kitchen-living room. She could also see what he meant about his organizing skills.

"You do organize by making piles," she said.

How dumb could she get? Instead of telling him how much she liked the place, she criticized his housekeeping.

"Professional journals and stuff," he said.

"This is really nice." She knew it was too little too late.

If she raved about his apartment now, he'd think she was coming on to him. Instead he probably thought she was a nitpicker, impossible to please. He had no idea how easily she could be pleased, but her fantasies came flooding back to make her feel embarrassed in his presence.

"I've got everything spread out on the table," he said walking over to the kitchen area.

He was wearing a red T-shirt and delightfully snug jeans, faded but stretched taut over round but firm runner's buns. His walk was graceful. Maybe that was an odd way to think of it, but in her observations, most men lumbered, lurched or jackhammered their arms, not quite knowing how to put their whole body into their walk.

"Got the pizza warming in the oven. Hope you don't mind if we eat while we go over things," he said.

He had paper plates and big white dinner napkins set out on one end of a green-checkered plastic tablecloth, but the rest of the table was covered by papers. A bottle of red wine was uncorked beside a pair of nondescript juice glasses.

She dropped her purse on a coffee table and followed him to the kitchen.

"Have a seat," he said.

She sank down on a chair feeling decidedly weak-kneed and weary. Her lack of luck with men was holding. She'd never met anyone quite like Eric, and here she was, available and ready, and all he wanted was help with a fund-raiser.

The sink was full of dirty dishes, and he had to hunt in a couple of drawers for something on which to serve the pizza. Using a dishtowel as a pot holder, he took out a huge pizza, still on its cardboard round, out of the oven and set it on top of the stove.

"Have to wash some forks," he said, picking two from the sink and squirting them with dish soap. "Dishwashers are no good unless you remember to load them."

"We could make do with fingers," she suggested.

"I wanted this to be a formal occasion." He presented her with a fork and put the pizza on the table using a magazine as a hot pad.

This man's office was sparkling clean with every drawer labeled and every bit of equipment precisely placed. Did Della run around in between appointments and keep him organized?

"You need a housekeeper," she said.

"I have a cleaning service. They'll be here tomorrow. Two hours with a crew of two, and I'm good for another week. Help yourself to the pizza."

He filled the juice glasses to the brims and pushed one in her direction.

"I should've asked if you want something else. Milk, water, beer?"

"Wine is fine." But you aren't.

Didn't the man have anything to say about Saturday? Had he forgotten their lip-to-lip slip? Or had it been so meaningless, he didn't see a need to bring it up?

"Here's the scoop on the committee," he said. "It was loaded against me, two divorcees and a single female lawyer who offered to handle any lawsuits against me if I have good malpractice insurance. Mom's trying, but she'll never get a card in the matchmaker's union."

"What's your job?" she asked dryly.

"I volunteered to divide the prize list—"

"You volunteered? Knowing I'd be doing the work?"

"Let me finish. All the gift certificates for the silent auction have to be picked up before Thanksgiving so they can be advertised."

"That's next week!"

"Yeah, I know. Mom had some idea we'd go out in pairs to get them. I outfoxed her. I'm making the assignments based on location. There's no soliciting, that was done long ago. We just have to have the certificates in hand before the auction list is published."

"When is this Auction Extravaganza?"

"December seventh. You'll be there with me, won't you?"

She shrugged, not at all sure what her role in the fund-raiser was.

"Your dad can count it as a date."

"Your mother doesn't know I'm helping you, does she?"

"Not yet. I don't want to spoil her scheme to have me connect with someone on the committee. But she'll have to know someday."

That same "someday" her dad would have to accept that Eric was not a prospective son-in-law.

She was ravenous and not shy about helping herself to a second, then a third, big piece of pizza loaded with everything she liked: sausage, mushrooms, onions and green pepper. Ordinarily she wouldn't dream of eating more food than the man she was with did, but he stopped every bite or two to explain the lists he was shuffling around on the table. By the time he emptied a manila folder stuffed with donor information, she was stuffed and so drowsy she could hardly keep her eyes open. Good thing she would have the loud racket from a hole in her muffler to keep her awake on the drive home.

"We have some pretty terrific donations," he commented, "but a few are bizarre. Listen to this. A day of pampering at the Desert Flower Oasis, including a seaweed wrap and an avocado and coconut-oil massage. Who's going to bid on a chance to be seeped in salad ingredients?"

"Spas are all the rage," she pointed out sleepily.

"I have a map of the area. I thought we could divide the donors' sheets into six piles, one for each committee member."

Again with the piles. There had to be an easier way

to do this by computer, but she was too tired to come up with it. Instead she finished her wine and poured another two fingers into the glass.

"Using highway 87 as the dividing line..." he went on.

"Eric, you're getting pizza sauce on that paper."

She stared bleary-eyed at the papers covering the table while he tried to wipe a tomato stain off one of the donor sheets.

"I guess this one's ours," he said sheepishly.

"We're going to pick up certificates together?" That perked her up a little.

"Well, not exactly. There are a couple here in Chandler I'll do. Della will make a couple of stops on her way home from work. You'll—"

"Tom Sawyer."

"What?"

"You're doing a Tom Sawyer, getting everyone you know to whitewash the fence."

"Sort of."

He grinned like a little boy caught with his hand in the cookie jar. How could she not help a man who could generate energy with his smile?

"Have you ever done this kind of thing before?" she asked.

"No, this is the first time Mom has been chairperson and roped me into it. They do raise a lot of money to treat and place abandoned pets. You'd be surprised how many people dump animals along the highway."

He ran his fingers through sandy-blond hair which was even more unruly than usual. The soft light of overhead neon tube lights made his sun-bleached hair seem like a halo, and she didn't have the slightest urge to restyle it.

Maybe it was only the wine, but she loved being

here in his cluttered but cozy apartment. The honey-gold varnish on his kitchen cupboards made the room seem especially inviting, and she looked around with approval. The bedroom had to be behind a closed door at the far end of the room, and she was curious to see his private space.

When his phone rang, she resented the interruption.

"Probably another telemarketer," she said. "Ignore it, and let's get this job done. I have to leave soon so Dad doesn't get hyper about where I am."

"Not answering isn't an option," he said, hustling over to a phone on the counter that served as a divider between kitchen and living space. "Could be an emergency."

She couldn't help wondering what would have happened if she'd let her answering machine do its job last Saturday?

She hugged her arms across her chest, suddenly shivering for no reason related to room temperature.

"Hi, Mom... No, nothing special... Three minutes... Fine, I'll go down and meet you at the door." He hung up and looked at Mindy. "My parents calling on their cell phone," he said. "They're on their way here."

"I heard. I'd better go."

"No, I'll just hide these papers. Mom knows me too well. She'll suspect I'm foisting work off on you." He started bunching them up, destroying any order they'd had. "No reason why my parents shouldn't meet you."

He dumped them, folder and all, into the oven and slammed the door shut.

"I hope you turned it off," she said.

He looked annoyed, but checked to be sure.

She really did not want to be there when his parents

arrived. Her life was complicated enough without pretending to be Eric's girlfriend for his parents' benefit. She retrieved her purse and headed toward the stairs.

"They're practically here. It's too late to avoid them."

"Oh, fiddlesticks!"

"Fiddlesticks?" he laughed. "Sometimes you're downright quaint."

He made it sound like a compliment.

"You'd better clean up the pizza mess. Two plates, two forks, two glasses..."

He did, making the garbage disappear under the sink and tossing a hand towel over the glasses on the drain board. When he shoved the pizza into the fridge, the only evidence of their dinner was smeared on the plastic cloth.

"Don't go, please. We can finish the job in half an hour. If you really don't want to meet them, you can wait in my bedroom. They'll only be here a few minutes. Dad wants to get home. He hasn't had dinner, and he knows the prospects for getting one here are never good."

If she didn't stay, they'd have to get together again. She wasn't sure whether she was up to another nondate with her nonboyfriend. She wasn't one to press her nose against the candy-store window when she was on a diet.

"Okay, but they'll see my van."

"If they mention it, which I doubt, I'll say it wouldn't start and a patient's owner is coming back for it in the morning."

"You're pretty inventive," she said dryly.

"Mom has decided I need to get married. I'm fighting for my life here." He softened his horror at the prospect with a smile.

''Well, if you're sure it will only be a few minutes,'' she said doubtfully, moving toward the closed door.

''Pretty sure. Be quiet in there,'' he warned. ''It's a lot harder to explain a gorgeous girl in the bedroom than in the kitchen.''

She hurried into his bedroom and loudly closed the door, a bit miffed at being called a girl. The gorgeous part was nice, though. What did he mean by it? Was he more attracted to her than he was willing to admit? Not likely since he hadn't shown the slightest interest in her pizza-flavored lips this evening. Of course, she'd dressed like the loan officer at a bank and given him all the encouragement a bunny rabbit gives a bobcat.

She found a wall switch beside the door and flipped on an overhead light. No way was she sitting around in the dark.

Whatever she'd expected, it wasn't a jungle safari. She had to clamp a hand over her mouth to keep from laughing aloud. Sure, the man loved animals, but his decor was too much! And there, rumpled and unmade amidst the prowling jungle beasts making a border along the walls, was a king-size bed with outrageously bold zebra-stripe sheets.

She'd seen bamboo and rattan furniture in pricey stores, but never in actual use. One piece was missing, though. She didn't see a chair anywhere in the room. Unless she wanted to prop her weary body against the wall, she had to choose between the bed and the floor.

The bed was inviting, big enough to roll around like Peaches when she was scratching her back. But Mindy couldn't, absolutely would not, sit on Eric's sheets. Admittedly, it was silly, but making herself at home on the garish sheets was awkwardly intimate.

What she could do was make the bed. She ditched her purse on the floor since the bamboo dresser and nightstand were pretty much filled with male paraphernalia like clocks—two of them—a watch, loose change, wallet, boom box, comb, nail clippers, tissue boxes, leather gloves, a baseball program from last summer and several track trophies with imitation gold runners speeding toward victory.

She was exhausted, removing her jacket felt like stripping off armor. She folded it on top of her big tan shoulder bag and tackled the bed.

Eric always smelled nice, and so did his pillows when she picked them up to fluff. She hugged one close and inhaled deeply. The brand name of his aftershave eluded her, but the essence of vanilla was irresistible.

She listened, but didn't hear voices. Maybe he was still waiting down by the entrance the way he had for her.

When she finished, the sheets were smooth and the bottom corners tucked in with military precision. She liked a neat bed. But where were the blanket and bedspread? A bed wasn't made until the sheets were covered.

There were two doors inside the room, one ajar enough to tell it was a bathroom. She investigated the other and stepped into a marvelous walk-in closet large enough for two people to share. It was a pack-rat's lair, the back full of corrugated cardboard boxes battered enough to have served as moving cartons numerous times. Old clothes and good clothes were hanging in no particular order on rods on both sides, along with a heavy ski parka and a collection of backpacks and duffels, their straps suspended on plastic hangers.

She'd organized worse closets, but not more cluttered. Only then, she'd been invited to do so. Here she was snooping, and her only excuse was to find something to cover the bed.

On one of the shelves above the hanging clothes, she spotted an insulated blanket, loosely woven and so worn a ragged edge with loose binding showed through the clear plastic storage bag. The blanket was either cream or faded yellow, not attractive but it would have to do.

As a bed covering, it was too small by half, probably intended for a twin-size, but she covered the zebra sheets as much as possible. At least she didn't feel quite as intrusive sitting on a blanket. But would Eric understand why she'd invaded his closet and purloined it? Maybe she could put it back as soon as she heard his parents leave.

Apparently they'd just come into the outer room. She could hear voices, muffled but distinctly belonging to three different people. She kicked off her shoes, wiggled her nylon-clad toes with pleasure, and lay back on the bed to wait for them to leave. Since she was virtually a prisoner in the room, there couldn't be any harm in lying down to relax for a few minutes.

FELICIA KINCAID descended on her son bearing gifts of food, a habit she refused to give up even though Eric repeatedly tried to discourage her.

"She likes to cook," Ray said, his father obviously wanting no part of the long-standing food feud between his wife and son.

"No, she doesn't," Eric said with amused resignation while putting a casserole dish in the fridge. "She just doesn't believe I can feed myself."

"That's enough talking about me in the third person,'' his mother said, pushing back the ash blond hair she insisted on wearing puffed up like cotton candy. ''I talked to Casey. You haven't called her yet about picking up the gift certificates.''

So the pushy lawyer was his mother's number-one candidate. He sighed and wondered what Mindy was doing to entertain herself in his bedroom.

His parents' short visit lasted nearly an hour, and he couldn't invite Mindy to join them after hiding her away in the bedroom. He fidgeted and talked sports with his dad, usually a sure way to encourage his mother to leave. She often accused them of being so much alike it made her crazy, especially since his dad stayed lean and athletic while she was losing the fight against plumpness.

After he finally let them out through the clinic door, he sprinted up the stairs and into the bedroom expecting to find Mindy seething with impatience.

Instead he found a sleeping angel.

She was curled up on his bed, lying on her side with one hand tucked under her chin. He stood mesmerized, listening to her soft, rhythmic breathing and inhaling the faint but sweet bouquet of her skin.

He'd never noticed how long and dark her lashes were, and her ear was so cute he could barely restrain from caressing the lobe with his lips.

Her arms were bare, a tremendous improvement over the dark jacket she'd been wearing, and her skirt was high on her legs revealing the most perfect calves he'd ever seen.

He couldn't think of anything nicer, and more foolish, than lying down beside her on his old yellow blanket.

His old yellow blanket! Not only had she made his

bed, she'd gone into his closet and pulled out that old thing he'd used in college.

What would she want to do next, clean out the medicine cabinet in the bathroom, balance his checkbook or give his barber instructions on how to cut his hair?

The woman was impossible! He didn't want his space or his life reorganized. He'd seen that route with Cass.

"Mindy."

He said her name four times, raising his voice each time, but she didn't stir. He put his hand on her smooth upper arm and gently kneaded it. Still no response. How much wine had she had? Only one glass and a few drops extra that he could remember.

"Mindy!"

Shoulder-shaking made her mumble in her sleep. The temptation to crawl in beside her was more than he wanted to deal with.

He lightly tapped her luscious backside and finally startled her into wakefulness.

"Oh, what time is it?"

"Late. You should go home."

"I know that."

Still semiconscious, she smoothed her skirt and frowned in confusion, apparently not quite sure where she was. She slid to the edge of the bed and sat up, tousled but so tempting he walked to the door to put space between them.

"Oh, my gosh, Dad will have a fit. I'm twenty-eight, and he still wants me to have a ten o'clock curfew."

"It's past ten," he offered.

"Your parents must have stayed a long time."

"Long enough for you to explore my closet and make my bed."

She blushed. "I was too embarrassed to lie on your jungle-boy sheets."

"My mother's housewarming gift. She did the whole room."

He picked up her jacket, holding it for her while she slowly rose and slipped into her shoes. Her hair was plastered down on one side, and several strands of her bangs were standing up straight, but she'd never looked cuter or more desirable.

She had made his bed!

Not sure she was fully awake yet, he hustled her as best he could, finally getting her down to her van in the parking lot.

"Are you awake enough to drive home?"

"Of course. Even if I'm not, my muffler will keep me awake. It must have a hole the size of the Grand Canyon."

"I'd better drive you home."

He didn't want to, but he wasn't ready to let her go off on her own while she still seemed groggy. Was this how big brothers felt about little sisters, protective, maybe a little smothering?

No, there was nothing brotherly about his feelings for Mindy, however totally wrong she was for him.

He did manage to persuade her to let him follow her home. The noise coming from her van was like a firework's display without the bright lights. There was no danger of losing her. She drove with exaggerated caution ten miles under the speed limit while he fidgeted and wished he'd insisted on driving her home. At least then she'd be sitting beside him.

By some miracle she didn't get stopped by the cops for her faulty muffler. She led the way through the confusing maze of streets in her development and pulled into the carport.

Bright light streamed out of her picture window, and Wayne came clunking out on crutches he didn't much need anymore.

"Mindy, I expected you a couple of hours ago," her father said.

"Sorry, Dad."

She gave no explanation. Eric liked that, but he couldn't leave well enough alone where she was concerned. He got out of his vehicle and went to her side.

"She has a problem with the van. That's why I followed her home."

"I need a new muffler, is all. You really didn't need to tail me all the way here."

She didn't mention being so groggy from her nap on his bed that he was afraid she'd fall asleep on the steering wheel.

"Well, I've been wanting to see you, Eric," her father said, managing to block the door of his car so there was no retreat.

"It's been a busy week." Was Wayne irate because his daughter had been neglected?

"About Thanksgiving," her father said. "Mindy's having a girlfriend over, but it will take a lot of mouths to demolish the twenty pound turkey I have on order. You'll join us, won't you?"

"Dad." Mindy sighed and shook her head. "Eric has plans of his own."

"Plans that don't include you? Hard to believe."

"Dad, you've got to stop assuming..."

"I'd love to come," Eric said.

"See, Mindy, no problem. We won't eat until six. I don't like a huge meal in the middle of the afternoon."

"Sounds fine. What can I bring?"

"Just yourself, Eric, just yourself."

Wayne walked back to the house. He was so jovial Eric felt like the main course on the Thanksgiving menu.

"You don't have to come!" Mindy whispered furiously. "I am so tired of my father trying to arrange my life!"

"He has good intentions. He wants to look after his little girl."

"What do you mean by that?"

He took the easy way and ignored her.

"Good night, Mindy."

He leaned down and kissed the tip of her nose, the least romantic spot he could find on her face.

"This is all so much out of control," she said, sputtering.

"I don't mind a little chaos, especially in my closet," he said with wicked intent as he got into his car.

"There's a perfectly good reason why..."

He drove away without hearing the rest of her explanation.

Was he punishing himself or Mindy by accepting her father's invitation? He'd acted impulsively, make that stupidly, but the longer he knew Mindy, the harder it was to stay away from her. Now he had to eat Thanksgiving dinner at two o'clock with his parents and his mother's Iowa cousins and again at six at Mindy's house.

Already his stomach felt as if he'd swallowed a basketball.

7

MINDY HAD one more challenge before her guests started arriving for Thanksgiving dinner. How could she dress to look sexy and alluring when she still had to wrestle with twenty pounds of slippery roasted turkey, mash five pounds of potatoes and turn the turkey drippings into smooth creamy gravy?

"Damn the bird! I have stain remover if I spill anything," she said to Peaches who watched from her usual spot on the end of the bed. "Oh, sure, look smug. You're always beautiful in your fur coat. You don't have to decide what to wear."

Peaches responded with two sharp barks that sounded more like a reprimand than thanks.

Decision made, Mindy slithered into her long pale lavender dress without bothering to unbutton the tiny silver buttons on the bodice. It was ribbed cotton, just clingy enough to show Eric what he was missing, hopefully without inviting commentary from her father. She slid bare feet into silver thongs and fluffed her hair with her fingers. The strands were too long to coax into spikes, but a trip to the beauty salon had not been on her schedule this week.

In a few short days she'd managed to pull together a client's big Thanksgiving reunion, badger the proud-papa carpenter into finishing the closet job, completed computerizing the Christmas mailing list from hell and kept half a dozen other clients happy.

She'd even picked up Eric's oven-warmed, pizza-scented lists without having to see or talk to him, thanks to Della. She'd divided them and had Della send each committee member e-mail, then done Eric's share herself. The gift certificates were ready to hand to him when he arrived for dinner, but she'd have to be sly about it. No point arousing her father's curiosity.

"What do you think, Peaches?" she asked, circling in front of the full-length mirror to get the full picture. "Not too bad for an incredible sleepless wonder, eh?"

She'd worked her tail off, literally, since the scale had rewarded her with a three-pound loss in a little over a week, but she couldn't blame work pressures for keeping her awake nights. It was her overactive imagination that plagued her. Who could sleep when a phantom lover was in the haunting mode? Unfortunately hers was a real person, and she couldn't get Eric out of her mind day or night.

She hurried out to finish dinner preparations and found Dad setting the table which they'd carried to the living room to allow more space for five people to sit around it. Her father would carve the turkey at the head of the table, and Eric would face him from the other end. She was putting Laurie and her new boyfriend together on one side and herself on the other on the theory that couples liked to be cozy.

The table would look festive with an orange paper tablecloth festooned with turkeys and little kids in Pilgrim costumes. She'd taken the easy way with disposable green plastic plates and cups, although her naturally frugal father would probably insist on loading them in the dishwasher to reuse.

She went to work in the kitchen, tying an old yellow cookout apron over her dress until her guests got there. Since Dad had insisted on shopping with her and paying for the traditional feast, she had enough on the menu to feed a Boy Scout troop. They'd start with shrimp, crackers and a nut-covered cheese ball, then go on to turkey, dressing, mashed potatoes, gravy, corn, candied yams, rolls, green-bean casserole ready to warm in the microwave and cranberry sauce. She'd also pleased her father immensely by making a pumpkin cheesecake from a recipe her mother had always used.

She was ticking off the menu items on her fingers, making sure she wouldn't forget something, when the doorbell made her jump. Taking off the shapeless apron, she stowed it out of sight in the broom closet. Her father got to the door first.

"Laurie, nice to meet you," he said in his best hearty-host voice. "Mindy talks about you a lot."

Her friend was a hugger, and Dad didn't seem to mind in the least when she gave him a friendly squeeze. Laurie was a tall, willowy blonde, genetically thin with no worries about weight gain, but Mindy loved her anyway. Her short hair was bobbed around a face more classical than beautiful. She deplored the Romanesque shape of her nose and talked of having cosmetic surgery, but Mindy didn't encourage her. She liked a nose with character, a nose like Eric's.

Why did her every thought turn to him? Disgusted with herself, she walked around the kitchen counter to the front door to meet the tall, bony man in black pants and black turtleneck standing behind Laurie.

"This is Gary Snell," Laurie said. "Mr. Ryder..."

"Just call me Wayne." Her dad offered his hand, but the pinch-faced man didn't seem to see it.

"And this is my best friend, Mindy," Laurie said.

"Hi, Gary. Make yourself at home. We'll have appetizers as soon as Eric gets here."

He was, of course, fifteen minutes late and counting.

"I was just checking out the football game," her father said. "Have a seat, Gary. What team do you like?"

"I don't follow professional gladiators," Laurie's friend said.

"Oh, what is your sport?" Her father said, turning off the TV.

"I'm into meditation, the more esoteric disciplines. You've probably never heard of them."

"Peaches needs to go out," Wayne said, playing the good host. "Come out back with me, Gary. I can't get enough of this great weather. Back home they've already had some snow."

Peaches stubbornly dug her paws into her rug at the end of the couch, obviously not interested in leaving her private refuge. She and Laurie's boyfriend weren't going to be pals. She dragged her rear when Dad hooked on her leash and tried to lead her outside.

"Bad dog. Go outside," Mindy said, feeling unfair because Peaches was obviously wary of the tall stranger with slicked-down black hair and muddy, expressionless eyes.

When they were alone, Laurie asked the question Mindy had been hoping to avoid.

"What do you think of Gary?"

"How long have you been seeing him?" Nothing like a question to avoid an answer.

"Three weeks, but we met a few months ago. He was installing a new computer system for our branch.

That's his specialty, putting in systems for insurance companies."

"He must be smart. And he's certainly tall."

"Six-four. He makes me feel downright dainty."

"So you really like him?"

"I'm not sure. He is a little unusual, slow to warm up to people. But he can be nice when he wants to. He'll grow on you when you get to know him."

Like a wart, Mindy thought, a little disconcerted because she was reacting to Gary the way Dad usually reacted to her male friends. Was she the helpless pawn of genetics, becoming more like her father? It was terribly unsettling that he liked Eric—and she couldn't get him out of her mind. She and her father rarely agreed on anything.

"You know tall men are hard to find," Laurie said leading the way to the kitchen. "You're lucky to be short."

"I guess."

Being short meant friends were always trying to fix her up with dinky dates. She hadn't dared accept a blind date since her first one in college when the hulking, manly wrestler she was expecting turned out to be an emaciated shrimp who spent the evening trying to teach her choke holds.

"There is one little problem with Gary," Laurie said.

No surprise there. Laurie's luck with men was arguably worse than her own.

"He's on a special diet."

"We're having all kinds of things. I hope he can make a good meal on what we have."

"Well, today is orange day."

"I have orange juice, but no whole oranges," Mindy said.

"No, I don't mean the fruit. The color."

"You've lost me." Mindy took the shrimp, which she'd artfully arranged on a glass plate with a dish of cocktail sauce, out of the fridge.

"He only eats certain colors on certain days. You know, all green one day, all white another. This is orange day."

"Why does he do that?"

"He got the idea from a trendy new nutritional guide he found through the Internet, 'Colors for Health' by B. B. Bent. It's not widely known but—" Laurie lowered her voice to a whisper "—the author is actually in prison. Gary says they always try to silence the voice of truth."

"Who are *they?*"

"You know, authorities, society, the powers that be," Laurie said. "Anyway, it's an interesting idea. I tried it a little myself."

Was it love that was making her friend so goofy? She was actually trying to follow this weird diet herself?

"Another conspiracy theory?"

"No, nothing like that. Anyway, what do you have that's orange?"

"Besides juice? I guess the shrimp might qualify. They have orange tails. Candied yams, pumpkin cheesecake."

"Wonderful! I was afraid I wouldn't be able to eat anything. Gary, either."

"I was hoping you'd sample the dressing," Mindy said, shamelessly testing her friend's commitment to Gary's dopey diet. "Make sure I seasoned it enough."

"Sure, I'll be glad to, but don't mention it to Gary."

The bell rang again, and Mindy left her friend sampling everything that was ready—and some bake-and-serve rolls that weren't.

Mindy smoothed her dress, pressed her lips together to blot them, and opened the door with her heart beating double-time, which was absolutely moronic since Eric was only here to fulfill his part of their agreement.

"Hi. Wow, you look terrific," he said.

He handed her a bottle of wine with a fancy French label and looked her over from head to feet. It was such an openly sexual appraisal, she momentarily lost the power of speech.

"Ah, thank you. So do you."

He was casually dressed in chinos and a long-sleeved royal blue knit shirt that brought out the sapphire in his eyes. His hair looked newly styled, cut above his ears and shortened on top. She wanted to comb it with her fingers and feel the soft locks tickling her nose, her throat, her...

He glanced toward the kitchen and saw Laurie standing in front of the oven trying to hack a piece of turkey from the huge bird without making it noticeable.

"I like your dress." He closed the door behind him. "Not many people look as good as you do in lavender."

He leaned over and kissed her cheek softly, but oh so sweetly.

"I can't thank you enough for doing all the auction stuff for me," he whispered.

Her cheek still tingled, but her happiness faded. There was nothing romantic about a thank-you kiss.

"Where's your dad?"

"Out in back with Laurie's friend."

No point in calling him a boyfriend. She had to believe Laurie's good sense would reassert itself soon.

"Laurie, this is Eric Kincaid."

"Oh...hot...just a sec." She dropped a slice of turkey onto the spoon holder on the stove, rinsed her fingers and stopped munching to walk over to Eric.

"Laurie Davis. Nice to meet you." She thrust out her hand. "You're the vet, right?"

"Correct."

He held her hand several seconds longer than necessary. Mindy hated herself for the raw, inexcusable jealousy that unexpectedly hit her, never mind that Eric was only a couple of inches taller than her friend who never dated men under six-two. Anyway they'd just met, and Laurie had turkey grease on her chin. Mindy stood thumping the thick bottom of the wine bottle on her palm while they exchanged pleasantries.

"I'll go out and say hello to your dad," he said releasing Laurie's hand and looking into Mindy's eyes. "That is, if you don't need my help with the dinner."

"No, go out and check in with him."

He was here for her father's benefit, at her father's invitation. Why think he might want to hang in the kitchen with her? It was the natural order of parties for the men to sneak off somewhere and talk boy-talk.

For a few brief minutes, she'd had hope, but she'd just been dunked in the icy sea of reality. A smile, a kiss on the cheek and a bottle of wine were all she could expect from Eric, his way of thanking her for hours of drudgery gathering gift certificates and assigning committee members to get others. The ones she'd collected were in a folder in her bedroom. She had to remember to hand them over when the opportunity presented itself.

"I'll see you in a few minutes then," he said.

She went back to work, and the men soon wandered inside. Her father and Eric settled down to watch football on her small TV. Laurie's friend stood by the window using a nasal inhaler and sniffing loudly.

"You should know," Gary said to the other two, "the negative vibes coming from the players can actually radiate out of the television and affect the energy of anyone within range."

"There's a new theory."

It was the first time she'd heard sarcasm from Eric.

"People are too casual about the electronic medium," Gary went on, talking to her dad and ignoring Eric. "When you see static on the screen, you're looking at energy radiated by the big bang."

"Big bang as in Fourth of July celebration?" her father baited him.

"Big bang as in the creation of the universe," Gary said sounding disgusted.

Mindy carried out the shrimp platter and scowled at the two of them. She thought Gary was a pseudo-intellectual and a weirdo, but he must have some good qualities only Laurie could see. Even though he was an idiot, she didn't want her friend's feelings hurt.

The other men got her message. Eric winked at her father, who tried to look contrite.

"We'll behave," he mouthed.

We? When had Eric and her father become *we?* She was vaguely uncomfortable about the notion, but wasn't sure why.

Shrimp, Gary solemnly announced, did not qualify as an orange food just because their tails were that color. Laurie didn't touch them, either, although she was probably too full after all her sampling. Eric put two on a small plastic plate and slowly nibbled them. Apparently shrimp weren't a favorite of his. Her father enjoyed most food but was by nature a light eater. Her big Thanksgiving dinner was bombing, and they were only on the appetizers.

When, at last, everything was ready for the big feast, her guests sat at the table. Her father gave a heartfelt blessing that made her remember why she loved him. He was a sweetheart when he wasn't trying to run her life. Then he carved the golden brown turkey with an electric knife he'd bought especially for that purpose, doing it with the finesse of a master chef. He'd spent an afternoon researching the craft on the Internet, and his study paid off.

"Good job, Wayne," Eric said.

"Guess I'm immune to negative vibes," Dad said.

He and Eric exchanged maddening buddy-smiles.

What was going on here? The two of them were bonding the same way her father and brother did.

She'd set all the serving dishes on the kitchen counter since the table was too small. Everyone got up to fill a plate, first Laurie who took a miniscule portion of candied yams and a few carrots past their prime that Mindy had found in the fridge. She wasn't worried about her friend's food intake. She was probably full after three slices of turkey and bites of dressing, mashed potato and green-bean casserole. But it wasn't like Laurie to play silly games with a date.

Gary filled his plate with candied yams and carrots leaving almost none for everyone else. Her father took his usual moderate helpings, and, oddly, Eric was smearing food on his plate as though trying to make the portions look larger than they were. In the interest of not eating leftovers for a week, she heaped her plate. Unfortunately, eating the picture-perfect dinner she'd slaved to prepare seemed more like a chore than pleasure.

ERIC FOUND himself feeling sorry for Mindy. She'd worked hard on the dinner, but her father was the only one appreciating it. Well, her father and Peaches. As a vet he deplored letting pets stuff themselves on table scraps, but he couldn't handle any more Thanksgiving dinner. Sure, it was dumb to eat two holiday dinners, but he was becoming less and less rational when it came to spending time with Mindy. This afternoon his mother had pulled out all the stops for her visiting Iowa cousins, not to mention the applesauce nut bread she made especially for him. So he passed bites of his turkey down to Peaches, who had the good sense to wait quietly under the table for treats. Mindy was either too tired or too distracted to shoo her away.

"I don't know about you," Wayne said after putting up with a ludicrous explanation of the color-coded diet from Gary, "but I'll enjoy dessert a lot more when my stomach has settled a little."

Eric would enjoy food again sometime next week. For the moment, he wasn't even sure he could haul his butt off the chair. He had a bowling ball in his stomach, and Mindy on his mind. At the moment it was a toss-up which was harder to handle. By tomorrow his two dinners would be history, but her micromanaging would not. Ever since she'd fallen asleep on his bed, he'd had a hard time thinking of anything else. He'd made a big mistake with Cass. Was Mindy only a softer, gentler version of his demanding ex-fiancée? He didn't want to think so, but he wasn't sure.

"I'll help clean up," he offered with the best of intentions—well, not bad intentions anyway.

"Nice of you, Eric," Wayne said. "I think Peaches and I need to walk off some dinner. What about you, Gary? Is an evening constitutional on your agenda?"

"That sounds like a wonderful idea, if you don't mind, Mindy," Laurie said.

Laurie had too much class for the jerk she'd brought to dinner, Eric thought, but she could dance naked on the table and he still wouldn't stop thinking about Mindy. This was bad, very bad. How could he be attracted to another woman who wanted to mold him into her idea of the perfect man? Sure, she was a wonder, so efficient even Della was impressed, but he had a managing mother and a receptionist who thought she was in charge of his practice. After his close call with Cass, he definitely didn't want another woman who thought he needed improving.

Mindy stood and started clearing plates as the others left. He sat and lusted. What was she wearing under that soft, clinging dress? He had a yen for lacy black panties and see-through bras, but she could wear white cotton and be the sexiest woman he'd ever met. Something about her sweetness and innocence had a hold on him.

"Well, are you going to help?" she asked.

The two of them were alone. Wayne had engineered it, of course, but if the other guys Mindy had hooked up with were anything like Gary, he couldn't blame him too much.

"Where did Laurie meet that jerk?" he asked to make conversation.

"She explained that pretty thoroughly at dinner."

"Yeah, I guess she did."

He hadn't heard a word, maybe because he'd been

fascinated by Mindy's arm. It was slender with the golden hue made possible by year-round desert sun. She used it like a dancer, reaching, touching and resting it on her lap with uncommon grace. He'd wanted to cup her elbow and run his fingers down the length of it. He'd hungered all the way through dinner, but not for more rich food.

"I'm really ashamed of you," she said.

"Of me?" He felt like a cartoon dog caught with his paw in the treat box.

"You, a vet of all people, feeding turkey scraps to Peaches."

"You saw."

"Yep."

"I was bad."

"Very, very bad. If she gets sick, I'm calling you in the middle of the night."

"Just what I deserve."

"If the turkey was so bad you couldn't eat it..."

"No, it was delicious." There came a time in every man's life when only the truth would suffice. "Unfortunately, so was the Thanksgiving dinner I ate at my parents' a few hours ago."

"Oh."

"I am sorry. Your dinner didn't deserve to be dog food."

"At least you ate all colors."

"Can you believe..."

They both laughed, a spontaneous outburst that left his side aching and his spirit soaring.

"Laurie seems like a sweet kid," he said.

"She'll dump Gary. His poetry got to her, is all."

"He writes poetry?"

"Boring, maudlin stuff, Laurie admitted. He wants to move in with her, but the blue-food day opened her eyes. Can you imagine eating only blueberries, artificially colored juice and Popsicles for a whole day?''

''Please, don't tell me any more.''

He stood and started gathering tableware, then followed Mindy to the kitchen area. She tossed the plastic plates into a black garbage bag and gave him a guilty grin.

''I know, I should recycle.''

''That's not what I was thinking.''

The last time they'd been alone in this kitchen, he'd forgotten all the reasons not to get involved with the wrong woman again. Unfortunately, he couldn't remember any of them now, either.

He rinsed his hands in cold water, holding them under the faucet until they felt numb. It was the safest thing he could think of doing with them.

She sighed, and he turned to see her slumped against the counter by the stove.

''Cleaning up the mess afterward is the worst part,'' she said.

He met her eyes, something he'd avoided since coming to the house. They were darkly shadowed, and he felt guilty for adding to her heavy holiday workload.

''You look beat.''

She didn't answer.

''I shouldn't have let you handle the auction certificates all by yourself.''

Did her silence mean she agreed? He felt compelled to keep talking.

''But I'm grateful, very grateful.''

Words were puny little things. He stepped up to her and brushed aside a lock of hair on her forehead.

''Your hand is cold,'' she said.

She covered his cold fingers with her warm, soft hand.

He'd intended to be Mr. Cool, eat the dinner, pal with her dad and get the hell out of there before he did something he'd regret.

Regret was the last thing on his mind at the moment.

He took her in his arms and covered her mouth with his. Her lips parted as the tip of his tongue slid between them. Their mouths melded, and he didn't think anymore.

"Eric..."

Her voice was muffled by unmistakable passion. He pulled her hard against him, cupping her bottom and parting her thighs with his knee.

She locked her wonderful, smooth, sexy arms around his neck, the feel of her fingers electrifying on his skin. He explored her face with his lips, tasting the salty-sweetness of her skin after hours spent preparing the dinner, and it was delicious beyond comprehension.

Her breasts were crushed against him, but he couldn't feel the hardness of her nipples with so much cloth between them. He fumbled with a top button on her dress, but manual dexterity had deserted him. Although his fingers were slow and clumsy, he found the edge of her neckline and plunged his hand under it. Her breasts were fuller than they looked and were satiny under his touch. She shivered when his frigid fingers gently teased her nipple, rolling it between his thumb and forefinger, but she pressed closer. That was all the encouragement he needed.

Her thighs locked around him, and he wanted much, much more. He was so aroused he ached, but his mind was fogged by the intensity of what he was feeling for her.

"They'll be back." Her voice was husky and regretful.

"Come to my place. We can leave before they get here."

He pressed his lips against her throat, delaying her answer.

Then they heard Wayne's voice as he noisily opened the front door. He released Peaches from the leash. The other two were right behind him.

Eric straightened as she struggled to put on a normal face and adjusted her stretched-out neckline before they were busted.

He cursed to himself, wondering what her answer would have been.

"Looks like you two aren't quite through cleaning up," Gary said, ambling uninvited and unwanted into the kitchen. "Wonder what you've been up to?"

Eric went back to the sink and ran more cold water on his hands. That wasn't where he really needed it, but at least it kept him from stuffing the color-kook's head into the garbage disposal.

8

PEACHES SCAMPERED around her feet, her toenails clicking on the floor tiles. Mindy had to play hopscotch to avoid being knocked off her black spike heels. It was the night of Eric's charity auction and the last thing she needed was to break a leg.

Her father hovered and tried to play his favorite game, twenty questions.

"Why haven't you seen Eric since Thanksgiving? It's been two weeks!" he asked.

"I did. Remember, he came over the next day."

She'd forgotten to give him the gift certificates for the auction, no wonder since he'd practically sprinted out of the house as soon as the others returned from their walk.

Dad snorted. "I don't count a two-minute visit. Hardly worth the gas to drive here."

"You know how busy I've been. Eric, too."

"Well, anyway, you look nice."

"Thanks. Answer the door when Eric comes, would you, Dad? I think I'll get a coat. Nights have been pretty cool lately."

She escaped to her bedroom with Peaches right behind her and checked the clock on the nightstand. Eric was twelve minutes late. It was prom night all over again. She was dressed to the max and worried stiff her date would change his mind and not show up. Only this time her father actually liked her escort, which was downright scary. Dad's seal of approval guaranteed Eric was totally wrong for her.

Sadly, he wasn't coming because he wanted to be with her. She had to keep reminding herself they were playacting, putting on a performance until her father went home.

The kitchen kisses hadn't been in the script. She closed her eyes and imagined the taste of his mouth, the pressure of his lips, and the excitement of his hands on her body. The daydreams had to stop!

Taking a look in the mirror, she straightened the jacket of her best evening outfit. The wide portrait collar of the black crepe de chine suit framed too much cleavage to allow her to wear a bra. The skirt under the short jacket clung enough to make her decide to go with stockings and nothing else. She hoped the lining of the suit would disguise her lack of underwear—or did she? Part of her wanted Eric to see what he was missing, but was her look classy enough for the silent auction and gala being held at a posh hotel?

She checked the hem that ended high on her thighs and smoothed her new "Mysterious Mist" stockings. With a name like that, they promised a more interesting life than hers. Her dangling earrings resembled tiny gold Christmas balls, and her hair was fluffy and curly, not too bad considering she still hadn't had time for a cut.

The doorbell sounded, Peaches bounded off the bed, and Mindy wondered if December seventh was a momentous day on her horoscope. At least her father thought she was having a real date.

She slowly counted to fifty to avoid looking too eager, then sashayed out to greet Eric putting a little exaggerated oomph into her walk as she dangled her fuzzy pink coat from one hand. She forgot about making an impression the instant she saw him.

He was breathtaking in a charcoal suit, a dazzling white shirt and a sophisticated burgundy-and-gray striped tie which she definitely would not straighten for any reason whatsoever.

She stood silent while the two men performed the greeting ritual which, predictably, included an exchange of basketball scores and comments about the weather. The atmosphere might not be so cordial if the two of them said what they were really thinking. Dad would probably caution Eric about his driving, then warn him not to think of having sex with his daughter before they were legally man and wife. But what would Eric say? Would he confess that being there was only part of a charade?

At last he looked at her. Did his jaw drop just a little? Did his eyes glow like the blue lights on a Christmas tree?

He moistened his lips, a good sign. He smiled, and a tiny dimple at the corner of his mouth punctuated it.

She straightened her spine and thrust out her breasts, poised to receive his compliments with haughty grace.

"We have a small problem." He was talking to her, not her father, who discreetly retreated to his spot on the couch.

"Oh, am I overdressed?"

She was fishing for a compliment and not ashamed of it. A woman deserved some return for hours invested in the body beautiful. All the women's magazines said so, or at least they should. Recreational reading was only one of the things she'd sacrificed to keep her business booming.

"No." His smile radiated heat. "You're perfect."

"Thank you." Perfect for what? Did perfect mean spectacular or adequate?

"Maybe I should change..." Self-doubt spoke, not her.

"Don't be silly. You're..."

She held her breath anticipating a *G* word or even a *B* word.

"Fine," he said.

The pot holder she'd made in Girl Scouts had been fine. So had the turkey burgers she'd grilled for her father. Fine didn't cut it for her very best outfit.

"I want to take Peaches with us," he said.

The Corgi was nosing around Eric's black loafers and nudging his leg with her nose. He acknowledged her by stooping down and petting the attention-hungry mutt.

"Take Peaches?"

Her dad was pretending to read the newspaper he'd devoured page by page with breakfast.

"To the party?" She couldn't believe what he was saying. Her father was skeptical enough about their relationship without them taking a dog on their date.

"Part of the entertainment is a doggie fashion show, a way to display some of the great animals available for adoption."

"I plan to keep Peaches, I think."

The shameless hussy was literally slobbering over Eric. Weren't dogs supposed to hate their vets?

He detached himself from Peaches and straightened.

"One of the dogs got adopted and isn't available, so the entertainment committee needs a substitute. They called me because I'm a vet and see lots of canines. They need a short-legged breed, thirty to thirty-five pounds, well-trained with class."

"Why the weight requirement?"

Whatever she'd expected this evening, it wasn't a furry, four-footed chaperone.

"To fit the costume."

"You're going to a fashion show for dogs?" her father asked, dropping the paper.

"A fund-raiser to expedite pet adoptions," Eric explained.

"I guess a vet has to do some public relations," her father conceded gruffly.

"I'm not sure about taking her to a nice hotel," Mindy said. "She's pretty rambunctious."

"She can stay in her carrier when she's not doing her part in the show. I brought some doggie treats to keep her happy."

"Can't they just eliminate one dog from the program?"

"Unfortunately, no. All the costumes have sponsors who've made considerable donations. Their names will be announced when each dog struts its stuff."

He grinned sheepishly, and she put her reservations on hold.

"I guess we're taking Peaches."

ERIC LUGGED the dog carrier into the lobby of the Morgan Suites Hotel and put it down beside an impressive man-made waterfall.

"There's a sign," Mindy said, pointing at an easel that directed Maricopa County Animal Friends to the main ballroom.

She hadn't said much on the way, and he didn't know if she was mad or just uncomfortable with their situation. He could think of a lot of things he'd like to do with her, but none of them involved a dog or his mother's charity event.

He switched hands to pick up the heavy carrier again. They walked past a huge tree decorated with red lights and gold balls and followed signs to the ballroom.

"Wow," Mindy said when they'd found the room and made their way through patrons milling around the wide doorway. "It looks like someone's bad dream exploded."

"The decorating committee did get carried away," he agreed, staring with something less than awe at giant cardboard saguaros leaning against walls and support pillars.

Peaches was playing rollover games inside her temporary prison. The carrier thumped against Eric's leg, and he put it down, pretending interest in the bizarre cacti decorated with Southwestern style ornaments like chili peppers, coyotes with bandanas and roadrunners.

"Why blue lights?" Mindy asked, sounding more puzzled than critical.

He had to admit the blue lights on green cardboard created surreal turquoise cacti. At least his mother hadn't been on the decorating committee.

"Beats me. We need to go up there," he said, pointing at a raised platform at the far end of the ballroom beyond the rows of tables set up for the silent auction.

He hefted Peaches one more time and carried her to the rear of the burgundy-and-gray carpeted room wishing he'd worn a tie that didn't match the rug. So much for impressing the little organizer, and damn it, he was trying to do just that.

They passed between chairs set up for the doggie fashion show and went behind a series of temporary screens setting aside an area to serve as backstage and dressing area for the canine models.

He didn't see his mother, but he did see trouble, five feet ten inches of it. Cassandra was sipping champagne from a disposable plastic goblet and talking a blue streak to a gray-haired man who didn't quite come up to her shoulder. Unlike most tall women he'd met, she didn't pay any attention to a man's height. She was looking for the convenience of a horse-doctor husband. It didn't matter to him that she looked glamorous in a floor-length brown dress. Now that the blinders were off his eyes, he didn't much care for the way Cass always looked down on people.

Unfortunately his mother was likely to make a big deal of Cassandra being here. Since she'd struck out trying to fix him up with one of her committee members, she'd be sure he was still smitten with Cass. She might even think Cass was there because of him or vice versa.

He and Mindy stepped into the screened-off area backstage, and Eric was sure he'd landed in never-never land.

"Oh, look," Mindy said. "That Scottie-poo is wearing a Christmas tree sweater."

He looked with a jaundiced eye at a Scottie-poodle mix biting and clawing in a futile attempt to get out of a wooly red sweater with green trees woven into the pattern.

"What kind of a dog is that?" she asked, giggling at a bored mutt dressed like a clown.

"A cosmopolitan mix, I'd say."

In spite of serious reservations about dressing dogs

in clothing, he was enjoying her pleasure in the spectacle.

"What do we do now?" Mindy asked.

He didn't have a clue, but a stout woman in a camel hair jacket and dark trousers spotted them and hurried over.

"A Corgi! I love the breed," she said expansively. "This must be our substitute. No one would ever give up such a gorgeous dog." She poked her finger into the latticework front of the carrier for Peaches to sniff it. "You have his leash, don't you?"

"Her leash," Mindy corrected, taking the leather strap out of her purse. "Her name is Peaches. She's been to obedience school, so if you're really firm with her, she should do okay."

"I'm sure you'll both do just fine. You're number seven on the program, right after the big spotted dog in the rhinestone sweater and the charcoal dog with the Christmas tree motif. Don't you love that adorable faux fur muff on the Spaniel mix?"

The organizer darted over to a pug-faced dog who was refusing to wear a stiff pink ruff.

"We'll both do fine? You didn't say anything about me being in the show," Mindy protested.

She had green lightning flashing in her eyes, and he expected to see fire erupting from her nostrils. He'd wanted to tell her earlier, but had been afraid she'd back out of their agreement entirely.

"I'm sure there's nothing to it," he said lamely. "Just walk across the stage with Peaches, pirouette a few times and..."

"Pirouette! I'm not a runway model!"

"Neither is Peaches." He was treading on dangerous ground here. "You can't send her out there by herself."

"Then you take her!"

"I have a job—talking up the auction and encouraging people to bid."

"I can't do it. I'd rather watch professional wrestling on TV and stick needles under my fingernails. It's a stage. I don't do stages!"

"It's only a makeshift platform. You look so gorgeous tonight...."

"Now you use the *G* word," she groused. "I never would've come if I'd known..."

"Please, I'll make it up to you."

"Oh, sure, how will you do that? Tell my father we're engaged?"

"You're engaged?" a familiar voice trilled.

"Cass, what are you doing here?" he asked, even though he already knew the answer. His ex-fiancée reveled in playing Lady Bountiful at charity events.

"Actually, I agreed to walk down the runway with an adorable sheltie mix. There he is, the one in the tasteful black doggie sweater."

He knew her tricks. She was deliberately snubbing Mindy, her way of pointing out his bad taste in choosing her replacement.

"Mindy, this is Cassandra Wills. We used to be friends."

"Not just friends." Cass said, "We were engaged. And you are, Miss..."

"Mindy Ryder," he said quickly.

"Mindy." Cassandra made it sound like the name of a social disease.

"You left several things at my place. A green nylon jacket, a pair of sunglasses and a tennis racket that I remember. You never could keep track of your possessions. Please come by tomorrow afternoon between two and three to collect them. I have plans for later in the day, so don't be late for a change."

She tuned away from him and spoke to Mindy. "I don't know why he bothers to wear a watch. Time means absolutely nothing to him."

"Dispose of anything I left at your house," Eric said curtly.

"It's not a half-bad tennis racket."

"Then give it to someone."

"Really, Eric," Cass said with disgust, "I have better things to do than clean up after you. The least you could do is send someone to remove your things from my space."

"Yes, well, I need to see if my mother needs any help, Mindy. Why don't you wait for me over there?" He took her elbow and gently guided her away from Cass and her sharp tongue.

MINDY LET ERIC lead her away then watched him head off for his duties, realizing she was stuck with the job of runway escort for her dog. First she had to coax, entice or wrestle Peaches into a costume.

Without saying goodbye, Cassandra left her and began giving orders to one of the show's workers. This was the ex-fiancée who'd rocked Eric's world and left him brokenhearted? She was the reason he couldn't recognize the right woman when she was right under his nose? No way!

Mindy ran into enough social climbers in her business to recognize a genuine dyed-in-the-wool snob. Eric was too genuine, too sweet and natural for that woman.

She went in search of the keeper of the costumes as the show was about to start.

There was a reason why Peaches had to weigh a

certain amount. The costume was a red-and-green plaid jacket and kilt tailored to fit a dog Peaches's size, and it fit her admirably. A sprig of mistletoe on a little bonnet was the perfect Christmas touch. She looked adorable when Mindy finally cajoled her into wearing all the parts.

Mindy checked her black silk suit for dog hairs, brushed her hair away from her moist forehead and rubbed a spot off her shoe. She wished for a mirror to check on the state of her bralessness, but none was in sight. The dogs were the stars of this production, which was clear from the applause she heard when the first dog went out.

Peaches was much more interested in a leggy greyhound who'd been abandoned at an animal shelter when he became too lame to race. Mindy knew the breed made wonderful pets when their racing days were over, but her house was too small and her schedule too full to let Peaches take him home.

"What am I going to do with you?" she whispered to her pet. "You're a lady, and a lady doesn't sniff strange behinds."

For this she'd worn her favorite black suit and dared to venture out sans undergarments.

She'd seen a demolition derby that was better organized, but at last her turn came. They followed the Scottie-poo who'd finally managed to unravel part of his costume and wanted to sit and have a good chew.

Mindy walked across the platform, arms tight to her sides trying to minimize her breasts. She made the mistake of scanning the sizable audience and saw Eric standing behind the rows of chairs. He could have done this himself!

Peaches took advantage of Mindy's momentary lapse of attention by dragging her rear to do some recreational scratching. Mindy managed to prod her forward and prevent her from bounding off the front of the low platform. Applause for her performance was halfhearted. She took it personally, but Peaches was more interested in resuming her friendship with the greyhound.

After the show Eric found her while she was still wrestling Peaches out of her costume.

"Let me help," he said.

"You'll get dog hair on your suit."

You look so great it makes my throat ache, she wanted to say but didn't.

"Occupational hazard. My mother would like to meet you," he said, finishing the undressing and lifting Peaches into her carrier.

"Is your father here, too?"

"No, he's too cagey to get roped into these affairs."

"What should I do with Peaches?"

"Leave her here in the carrier for now."

She caught a glimpse of the muddy brown dress Cassandra was wearing, presumably to match her hair which was cut to resemble a horse's mane. Thankfully Eric took Mindy's hand and led her in the opposite direction. Either he was totally disinterested in his former fiancée or he had a great future as an actor in Hollywood.

They didn't have to find Felicia Kincaid. She found them and beamed at Mindy from under an elaborate pile of curls. Her cheeks were bright red, whether from heat, excitement or makeup it wasn't clear. Like most guests, Mindy included, she hadn't dressed to hang out with dogs. She was wearing a floor-length electric blue dress that made it obvious where Eric got his astonishing eyes. Although she was comfortably plump, she had enough self-confidence not to disguise it with boxy black clothes.

"I'm so excited about the auction," Felicia said after they'd exchanged pleasantries. "Eric did a spectacular job gathering the donations. Some businesses can be a real pain. They say they'll donate, then try to substitute a cheaper prize or don't come through at all. Thanks to all his work, we collected every single certificate that was promised. I don't know how he found the time...."

"Mom, you should know Mindy..." Eric began.

Mindy stepped close and came down with a spike heel on top of his foot hard enough to get his attention without crippling.

"Oh, sorry," she lied, warning him with her eyes not to confess. Why spoil his mother's pleasure in her son's good performance?

"Can you believe," Felicia went on, "some people who watched the fashion show have agreed to adopt one of the participants? In fact, the greyhound got two offers. Unfortunately, no one has spoken for the pudgy Corgi you were leading, Mindy."

"Actually, Peaches belongs to Mindy," Eric said. "The show committee asked me to find a substitute at the last minute for a dog that was adopted. I decided not to take a chance and get a dog I didn't know well. Mindy saved the day."

"Peaches did a very nice job," his mother said. "You just need to make sure she doesn't get table scraps and exercises every day. But Eric is the vet, and I'm trying to do his job, aren't I?"

Eric had the grace to look sheepish, but his mother was distracted by a loudspeaker announcing the end of bidding in two minutes.

"Do you need me to help close the auction?" he asked.

"No, you've done your share. You can enjoy yourself now. It was lovely meeting you, Mindy."

"My pleasure," she responded truthfully.

Felicia hurried toward a podium on the far side of the room.

"Why didn't you let me give you credit for all the work you did?" Eric asked.

"You're making my father happy. It seems only fair not to burst your mother's bubble. She's really proud of the way you helped."

"She should've had six kids," Eric said without rancor. "Then she wouldn't have time to worry about every detail of my life."

A busty blonde in a red sequin dress sidled up to Eric and offered him a goblet of champagne. She was obviously one of his mother's dating candidates. Mindy noticed there was a lipstick smear on the rim and quietly pointed it out. He refused the drink but not without a little chitchat about what a smashing success the event was.

"More kids wouldn't help," Mindy said, resuming the conversation when the *Baywatch* babe tottered off. "Once an interfering parent gets one offspring settled down, it's on to the next. I speak from my brother's and my experience."

"Maybe so," he agreed absentmindedly as a flashy brunette ambled over, hips swaying, to flirt with him.

Why on earth was his mother worried about his love life? He attracted woman like pins to a magnet. She only wished she were a contender. She fervently regretted fussing with his tie, poking her nose into his closet and any other little thing she'd done to make him think she was a management freak.

They wandered off together, filled plates at the buffet, and listened to the auction results until he learned his bid hadn't won a massage and steam room visit.

"It was worth a shot," he said, giving her a high-powered smile that made her spine tingle.

She imagined him lying flat on his tummy, only a tiny towel covering his adorable buns. Would the masseuse be a man or a woman? She didn't like the possibility of another female in this fantasy, so she moved to the steam room where he sat naked and glistening on a redwood bench. She stepped into the misty room and dropped her towel as he gazed awestruck....

"Mindy!"

"Oh, did you say something?"

"I asked if you're ready to go."

"Oh, sure, fine." She started moving toward the exit.

"Aren't you forgetting someone?" he asked.

"Should I say goodbye to your mother?"

"I don't know where she is, but Peaches might like a ride home."

"Oh, I wasn't thinking!" At least not about her faithful canine companion, but how often were her dates a threesome with a dog? "I'm a terrible pet owner! But I'm sure I would've remembered before we left the parking lot."

"I'll get her."

After Eric loaded the carrier into the back of his SUV and opened the passenger door for her, he didn't have much to say. He drove her home with only a few comments about the evening.

Had he been bored? Was she a dull date? Would she have to moon him to get more than a bland, nice-guy response?

She slipped her aching feet out of the punishingly high heels, wiggled her toes under cover of darkness, and resented the seat belt and gear shift that kept her from snuggling up to him as he drove.

"Here we are," he said as though she couldn't recognize her own house.

Her father had shut the blind on the front window, but lights were still blazing in her little hacienda. He, undoubtedly, was waiting up for a little friendly interrogation.

Eric walked around to her side of the vehicle. He was good at chivalrous acts like holding coats and opening doors. His mama had trained him well.

She unbuckled, poised to slide out, but wasn't prepared for the way he blocked her way, then backed up just enough to let her wedge herself between the car and him.

"I really enjoyed the evening," he said.

The way he said it made her nerve ends vibrate.

"I guess Peaches did pretty well." She strung the words together as she were a child arranging alphabet blocks in the hopes they meant something.

"Forget Peaches. The part I liked was being with you."

"Oh."

She wanted to say something witty, clever, cautiously semiapproving, but his lips got in the way.

He was undisputedly the best kisser ever. She kissed him back and melted against him, giddy with the joy of being in his arms. Her steam-room fantasy paled in comparison to the way it felt when he ran his hands all the way down her back.

"No panty line," he whispered. "I was pretty sure."

She started to explain, but lost her thought when he slid his hands under the back of her jacket.

"I was sure you weren't wearing a bra."

He caressed her back, his hands warm on her skin, and pressed feathery kisses on her closed lids.

"Was it terribly obvious?" she gasped. "I didn't expect to be in a fashion show."

"Only to me." He found a sensitive spot under her left earlobe and hot-wired her whole response system. "I'm more observant than most—and much more interested."

Peaches yelped from the rear of the car, awake now and indignant at the long confinement.

"I wish your father wasn't in your house," Eric said.

He reached behind her to close the door and click off the dome light. The night had turned desert-cold, and his hands were cool. She shivered when he slid his fingers under the silky fabric of her jacket. They warmed up fast, and she felt heat rise to her cheeks.

He kissed her, teasing the nub of her nipple with his thumb at the same time. His tongue slid between her teeth and teased her tongue. She fumbled to find his free hand, wanting to press it against her, but he anticipated her move, inching up her skirt and…

They both jumped as Peaches let out a howl that made her sound like first cousin to a coyote.

"Peaches, hush, quiet!" she called out with an urgency that had nothing to do with dog training.

"Uh-oh," Eric said,

He dropped his hands and stepped back as the outdoor light beside her front door went on.

"My father!" How could he, how could he, how could he? This is high school all over again, she thought unhappily.

"I'd better not walk you to the door," Eric said apologetically. "I'm not in any shape to see your father."

No, this wasn't a replay of high school dates with her dad as self-appointed chaperone and policeman. It was much, much worse. Now that she had a glimmer of hope that Eric might be interested in her, Dad had barged out and interrupted.

9

"YOU CERTAINLY don't have the Christmas spirit, Doc," Della said as she locked the door behind the last patient on Friday.

When she called him "Doc," Eric knew she was going to give him motherly advice—as if he didn't get enough from his own mother.

"Cats don't like me," he grumbled by way of excuse.

"You poke 'em, prod 'em and stick 'em with a needle. What's to like?" she asked, patrolling the waiting room for items to put in the lost and found box. "You're grouchy, and it has nothing to do with the Frankenheimer cat."

"Go home, Della. I'll finish closing up."

The fact that she was right didn't improve his mood.

"I'm in no hurry. I left a casserole for Larry to stick in the oven, so dinner will be ready when I get there."

"Go anyway."

She was the best receptionist any vet could want except when she tried to analyze him.

"We had a cancellation at ten-fifteen on Monday. I thought I'd try to fill it before I leave."

"Forget it. Maybe I wouldn't get so far behind if there was more slack in the schedule."

Where did that thought come from? He never worried about falling a little behind on appointments. Mindy was the one who liked precision timing.

Mindy.

He hadn't talked to her all week even though he thought about her constantly. He'd called several times, but she always seemed to be out, hopefully because it was her busy season. He didn't have any right to be jealous if she went out with some other guy, but he didn't like the possibility at all. Trouble was, if he did reach her, he didn't know what he'd say.

"Okay," Della said thoughtfully.

Now she was pouting. He couldn't win with women. They played by a different set of rules than men. Maybe he should try to be more like his father, just do his own thing and let life ebb and flow around him.

Della gathered her baggage. She always arrived for work with a collection of woven and canvas bags, but he didn't have a clue what they all contained.

"If you ask me, you should call that nice Ryder girl and have some fun this weekend. You're always working, never any time for play. No wonder you're grouchy."

He didn't like hearing it, but she was right. He was a crab, and he should do something for recreation. But he wasn't so sure about calling Mindy.

"Well, good night, Dr. Kincaid."

Della flounced off to the rear exit where she parked her yellow VW, the love of her life after family, friends and advice-giving.

He finished up and turned off the overhead lights. He'd never noticed how lonely the place was after everyone left.

What he needed was a long, grueling run and then

a cold shower, which he hated. It was getting harder and harder to deny himself the pleasure of being with Mindy. Any way he rationalized it, he was hot for her sweet little body. Life was dull and frustrating without her.

How would his life change if he gave in to his growing need for someone to share it? He was glad he'd seen Cassandra at the charity event to confirm that he was right about avoiding manipulative women. She was a walking mistake. He had a hard time remembering why he'd been—however briefly—in love with her.

Or maybe he should be sorry he'd seen her. She was a reminder of his bad judgment when it came to picking a potential partner. That was something he had in common with Mindy. She hadn't said a lot about her last serious boyfriend, but he'd pieced together a picture of a selfish egotist. Her adult history with men was as bad as his with women, but this didn't mean they were meant for each other. He wasn't up for an alliance of losers.

Mindy a loser? Not exactly. He went upstairs to his living area remembering the too-brief moments they'd shared after the fund-raiser. He'd been delighted when he realized she was naked under her silky jacket. She'd dressed for him, not a dog show, which explained her reluctance to trot across the stage with Peaches. But she'd pulled it off admirably, and he was pretty sure only he noticed the gentle sway of her braless breasts, thanks to Peaches's scene-stealing.

He put his lab coat in the bathroom hamper and stripped to his briefs to change into running clothes. It was nearly dark and cooling down rapidly. He went to his bedroom closet and found some sweats between his terrycloth robe and a ski jacket he hadn't worn in ages.

Pulling on the sweatshirt, he froze. Mindy had had to wait an hour or more in his bedroom. Could he blame her for being put off by zebra-striped sheets? Was it so terrible to look for a blanket? Was he being an all-around jerk? Or did he just have a sensible handle on her personality, something he'd failed to do when he was engaged to Cass?

He tossed the sweatpants on his bed and sat down to use the bedside phone.

Wayne answered. No surprise there. He was probably bored out of his skin hanging around waiting for his daughter to land a husband.

"Is Mindy there?" Eric asked.

"She's getting ready to go out. Hold on. I'll see if she's out of the shower."

"Thanks."

Mindy stepping out of the shower, water droplets falling from her taut nipples, her whole body slippery and glistening. The image went beyond torture.

"Hello, Eric," she said after a long two-minute wait.

Was she standing there wrapped in a bath towel, damp hair curling in a triangle above her shapely thighs? Or was she dressed for a date, a date with someone besides him?

"Hi, how are you?"

He wasn't even sure why he'd called, only that he couldn't get her out of his system by keeping his distance.

"Fine. And you?"

"Fine."

When it came to inane conversations, this one was a classic. He plunged in.

"I wondered if you'd like to go to a movie tonight. Assure your father we're still an item."

Would she admit she had another date? Would she, impossible scenario, break it for him?

"Sorry, I have plans. But thanks for asking."

She wasn't going to tell him! Damn! He wanted to know what she was doing even if he didn't have any right to know.

"I tried to call, but always got your machine. If I had reached you, what would your answer have been?"

"No."

"No?" That stung.

"Laurie dumped that idiot she brought to Thanksgiving dinner. Black food finally did it. She'll never eat another black olive. We're going out to celebrate."

He slumped with relief. A girls' night out. He could live with that.

"Have you finished your Christmas shopping?" he asked, trying to come up with another plan to see her soon.

She laughed, a delightful, inviting sound.

"This week I had to find gifts for all the employees in a real estate office—twenty-seven gifts that made it look as if the head honcho had personally selected them. I figure I'll get my own bought by Valentine's Day."

"Let me help you tomorrow, if you're free."

"Really? You wouldn't be bored to tears? I have my niece and nephew, Kim and Sam, my brother, Dwight, and his wife, Carly. Laurie and I usually exchange, and, of course, Dad. What on earth do you get a man who doesn't want anything?"

"A son-in-law?" It slipped out. He bit his lower lip.

"Yeah, right, there's a suggestion."

"I'll help you find something for him."

"Sure, why not? It'll be fun."

"Great! I'll pick you up around ten if that's okay," he said, grinning.

"How about I pick you up? I have to deliver a stack of addressed invitations for a New Year's party to a client who lives out your way."

"See you then," he replied.

He hung up, horny but happy. Her soft, breathy voice had that effect on him.

MINDY WOKE UP Saturday morning before her alarm rang and wondered why she felt extraordinarily lighthearted. It only took a second to remember she had a date. Well, not a *date* date, but Eric was going shopping with her. Didn't most men hate shopping for the kinds of gifts her relatives would want—clothes, toys and stuff? It was his idea, so it must mean he wanted to be with her enough to endure Christmas crowds.

She hoped.

Or could he be doing this for her father's benefit? Technically Eric still owed her. Trotting Peaches through a doggie show hadn't been part of their deal. Still, she felt too content to dwell on her doubts. She'd play it cool and enjoy the day without worrying about her job or her father, who, thankfully, had connected with several other men through his college friend.

She wanted to look good without being obvious, so she went with stretchy jeans that hung low on her hips and a fairly new turquoise cotton sweater that was cropped and showed a bit of her midriff. The outfit was perfect, hot but not obvious.

When she arrived at his place five minutes early, he was waiting in the parking lot wearing stone-washed jeans, cowboy boots and a waist-hugging navy denim jacket. He bore little resemblance to a hardworking vet in a lab coat. The day was off to a good start.

It got better. They drove to a big suburban mall where parking was already scarce this close to Christmas. Inside the pale brick complex, they found a holiday wonderland. Beautiful garlands hung from the high ceiling and festooned support pillars. There was a huge tree in the main commons decorated with thousands of red-velvet bows and white lights. Another one, nearly as large, was near the food court, and stores had gone all out in their individual displays. It was a carnival atmosphere with a school group singing in one area and a band performing in another. Workers in elf costumes passed out cookie samples, and people seemed good-natured and playful.

Eric didn't shop her way, which was to make an orderly survey of favorite stores and decide quickly what to purchase. Instead he liked to see everything, then backtrack with lots of detours. They watched kids talk to Santa, sipped sodas and played games in the video arcade. By the time they had steak salads at Caulfields, the best restaurant in the mall, she still had more than half of her list to do. But she'd never had more fun shopping.

By midafternoon she'd finished her list with lots of help from Eric, who had more fun in the toy store than most kids. But there was a problem. Now that her father was retired, he was rekindling his interest in golf. She bought him a new bag to replace the twenty-year-old one she and her mother had given him when Mindy was only eight. Eric talked her into a green-and-red plaid one. At first she thought it was too flashy for her conservative father, but the more she saw it, the better she liked it. He'd look downright dapper with it, but she wanted it to be a surprise. Nothing much got past her long-term houseguest!

"How am I going to hide it from him until Christmas?" she wondered aloud.

"No problem. You can leave it at my place."

They left the mall under a warm winter sun, the weather splendidly mild. The light had a clarity that made colors outside sharper and the sky dazzling blue. She loved the holiday season in the Southwest. The only place she wanted to see snow was on a Christmas card.

They talked and laughed all the way to Chandler as she drove him home. It was the best time she'd had in ages, and her Christmas shopping was nearly done with ten days to spare. Dad could wrap her presents for Dwight's family and get them ready to mail. It would give him something to do.

"This was really fun," she said when they arrived at his place. "Thank you for helping me shop."

"Was I helpful?" He grinned broadly. "If I was, will you do one tiny thing for me?"

Were they back to swapping favors? His request took some of the luster away from their time together.

"What?"

"Come up and help me throw some ornaments on my Christmas tree."

"I'll be happy to."

It was true. She didn't want their day to end.

He shouldered the golf bag and led the way to his

living quarters. Since he was keeping her father's gift, she'd be sure to see him at least once more before Christmas. Would she see him after the holiday when her father went home? She pushed aside this depressing doubt and followed him to his living room.

If his cleaning service had come the day before, they hadn't left much of a mark on the big cluttered room. He put the golf bag in his bedroom while she looked at the artificial tree parts scattered on the floor.

"I had good intentions," he said with a sheepish grin, "but I didn't have time to assemble it."

A plastic storage box full of ornaments and tangled strings of lights was sitting on the coffee table. Bits of tinsel were dangling over the edges as though he'd started to untangle it from the jumble in the box.

"This will be fun," she said.

She meant it. Quirky as it was, she loved sorting through a big mess and making something of it. She picked up an ornament, a plastic dog with a red wool scarf around its neck riding on a wooden sled.

"I thought I'd take it down to the office when it's decorated," he said. "Della thinks I have no Christmas spirit."

He pouted a little. She did like his pucker, a boyish expression on a thoroughly masculine face.

"You'll probably want to leave the tinsel off if it will be in the reception room where animals wait. I know Peaches will chew on it if she gets a chance. I never put it on my tree."

He didn't answer. She turned and saw him staring at her with an impish grin.

"I can think of something better to do with it."

He extracted a long strand from the edge of the box and held it over her.

"A halo for an angel," he said, dropping it on her head.

"I'm hardly that," she replied, giggling as he ran his fingers through the hair at the back of her neck.

"I sincerely hope not."

He leaned toward her and pressed his lips against hers in a kiss so soft and sweet she felt teary.

"It must be mistletoe, not tinsel," she said a little breathlessly.

"Or magic."

He held her in his arms, her cheek pressed against his chest.

"Definitely magic."

He released her, but only to slip out of his denim jacket. Letting it drop to the floor, he reached into the box and grabbed some torn strands of tinsel.

"Earrings," he teased, dangling a strand over one of her ears then the other.

He nuzzled her throat below one ear then softly touched the lobe with his lips. His breath was whispery warm, and she giggled.

"Ticklish?"

He locked her in the circle of his arms and rubbed her lips with his. She tensed with anticipation and deliciously erotic tremors made her whole body hum.

"The nicest tinsel earrings I've ever had," she said—or thought she said. The buzzing in her ears made it hard to know if she was thinking or talking.

He nuzzled her throat, his lips tracing a mysterious pattern on the supersensitive skin. Her lips parted, waiting, and his leisurely progression to her cheek, her forehead, and then her mouth heightened her anticipation. When he did kiss her, she was weak-kneed with pleasure. She parted his lips with her tongue and was rewarded by a hard, urgent kiss that held nothing back.

Breathless but more than willing for more, she could only gasp, "Oh."

"Silly to let all that tinsel go to waste," he murmured, not sounding all that steady himself.

He reached toward the box, grabbed a handful of the trim and dangled a silvery ribbon in the hollow between her breasts.

"I thought we were decorating a tree, not me," she said, but her voice was softly encouraging.

"You're more fun."

He dropped what felt like a crushed ball of the stuff under the back of her sweater as though it would distract her from the hand he was inching downward over the slight swell of her tummy, down the length of her front zipper.

"It itches." She giggled and tried to remove the tinsel by reaching behind her. She wanted his hand just where it was.

"Didn't mean to be mean. I'll get it out."

He carefully peeled off her sweater and tossed it in the direction of the ornament box. He stood so close to her the scent of his aftershave was making her light-headed.

Uh-oh. She forgot. She was wearing a plain cotton bra, about as unglamorous as lingerie could get.

"I didn't dress for this."

"Um."

He held one breast in his hand and slowly, deeply, covered her mouth with his as he caressed her through the cloth.

"Tell me," he said between vigorous kisses that utterly siphoned away her breath, "when you want me to stop."

Stop? As in red lights and no more kissing? She dropped her hands to his butt and dared herself to squeeze. His muscular bottom tightened under her grip.

"I'll take that as a go," he said with a strangled laugh.

He unsnapped her bra and slid it off her shoulders, trapping it between her bare breasts and the white T-shirt he was still wearing. It was incredible, being naked to the waist while he was still dressed, even more exciting than dropping her towel in a steam room. But this was no fantasy, and she loved the way he cupped her breast and moistened her nipple with the tip of his tongue. She was tight with arousal and hugged him to keep her balance.

"Would you like to see my leopard sheets?" he asked in a voice so husky it was barely recognizable.

"Spots, not stripes?"

She parted her thighs to lock his knee between them. She was out of control. Some wild woman had taken over. She wasn't into spontaneous sex orgies, but leopard spots danced in front of her eyes as she imagined the two of them spending hours of ecstasy in his king-size bed.

"Are you prepared..." That was her real self talking.

"Oh, yeah."

His phone screeched on the other side of the room. He tensed, and she wrapped her arms around his back as though she could restrain him from answering.

"Are you going to..." she dared ask.

"No way."

Thank you, thank you, thank you, she silently mouthed.

The answering machine clicked on, but that couldn't matter, could it? He wasn't going to…

"Eric, this is Mom."

As if he wouldn't recognize her voice.

"I'm at your door. I saw your SUV, so I know you're home. I got your dad one of those game consoles he likes. Why, I'll never know. I want you to keep it for me until Christmas. Come let me in."

"She'll go away," he said.

"I don't think so," Mindy said. "She knows you're here."

"Eric, if you're taking a nap, wake up! I can't carry this thing another inch, let alone load it back in the car."

He shrugged and looked even sexier, his hair so rumpled she couldn't help wondering how he'd look with bed-head.

"You have to go," Mindy said, managing to catch the bra trapped between them as he stepped back.

He walked over to the phone stiff-legged with disappointment.

"I'm on my way, Mom. Don't try to lift it again by yourself."

"I knew you were home," she said triumphantly.

He cut the connection.

"I'd better…"

She knew what he meant. He dashed into his bedroom and came out wearing a plaid flannel shirt hanging over the telltale crotch of his tight jeans.

"Can you…"

He didn't need to ask. She was scrambling into her clothes, pulling off tinsel and deciding what needed to be done in the few short moments before his mother got there.

While Eric went to let his mom in, Mindy tried to

finger comb her hair and make the room look as if they were actually decorating a tree. She stuffed Eric's jacket under a couch cushion and found the stand and trunk of the artificial tree. She had just enough time to stick a few branches into the holes, but she didn't have any illusions about fooling his mother. Even if her lips weren't swollen from kissing and her face hot and flushed with arousal, she had to look as guilty as Eric did.

"Good grief, we're not teenagers caught making out," she scolded herself.

They were on the steps. She had tinsel trapped in her bra irritating her breast and threatening to make her crazy, but there wasn't time to dig it out. She had to stop being Santa's little hottie and get respectable.

Felicia's head popped into sight as she climbed the stairs. Mindy didn't miss the flicker of surprise when she saw her son had company.

"You should've told me you had a visitor," she scolded Eric, who was right behind her carrying a large corrugated cardboard box. "I could've come another time."

"What you should have done," he said, "was leave Dad's gift in the car instead of carrying it to the door yourself."

He set it down with a grunt.

"After thirty-two years in the furniture business, I can carry a box."

"Mom, you remember Mindy. She was..."

"Of course! We met at the fund-raiser. Hello, Mindy."

"Nice to see you, Mrs. Kincaid." Mindy smiled and tried to sound cordial. "Was the event as successful as you'd hoped?"

"More than successful. We raised twenty-seven percent more than last year."

She looked at the tree clutter with a jaundiced eye, but didn't comment on it.

"Great," Mindy said.

"Want something to drink, Mom?"

"No, I'm not staying." She sat down on the end of the couch, negating her words. "I can't tell you how much everyone on the committee appreciated your help, Eric. And you were very sweet to participate in the dog show, Mindy."

"Mom, Mindy did more than lead her dog across the stage."

Mindy tried to frown him into silence, but he ignored her.

"In fact, she did most of the work. She organized the pickups and did a lot of them herself."

"How nice of you, Mindy. Why did you take credit for her work?" she accused her son.

"We weren't ready...that is, we weren't sure where our friendship was going, so..."

He shrugged. Mindy knew that goofy smile. It meant he was busted and was trying to charm his way out of it. Unfortunately, she found it enchanting.

"We've kind of been seeing each other," he went on.

Oh, boy! That kind of comment had gotten her in trouble with her father. Had Eric learned nothing from her mistakes? Did he want to be tangled in a web of deception? Couldn't he be more careful about what he said?

"Where have you been hiding such a lovely girl?" Felicia asked, beaming with what seemed like genuine pleasure.

In the bedroom asleep on zebra-striped sheets,

Mindy was tempted to say. Instead she smiled weakly and kept quiet.

"We've been pretty busy," he answered vaguely. "Sure you wouldn't like a cup of tea or something?"

"You have tea? You are becoming more civilized," his mother said. "Do I have you to thank for that, too, Mindy?"

"No, I'm a coffee drinker. Love the stuff. Hot, black coffee."

As far as she knew, Eric drank coffee himself. Was the tea left over from Cassandra days? Jealousy was an ugly emotion. She wished she'd never laid eyes on the supercilious snob.

"I'll have tea another time," Felicia said. "I really have to go. But I have a wonderful idea, Mindy. Why don't you spend Christmas Day with us? There'll just be the three of us and my cousin and her husband from Council Bluffs."

Eric visibly flinched.

"Not Harold and Nadine?" Eric looked a little frustrated, maybe because he was trying to force a tree limb into the wrong hole. Or maybe not.

"I know Nadine is a little talkative, but she dotes on you," Felicia reprimanded her son.

"It's sweet of you to ask, but I really can't accept," Mindy said. "My father is here from Pittsburgh."

"Perfect! Bring him, too. I love big family dinners. Makes cooking seem more worthwhile."

"Mindy's father is pretty much housebound," Eric said. "He came for a short visit and had an accident."

He was as bad about stretching the truth as she was! Her dad had played nine holes of golf yesterday.

"Is he in a wheelchair? Eric, his father and I could come help you get him into the van we use for small deliveries."

"Oh, no, that's too much trouble," Mindy said.

"He may not want to come, Mom," Eric added.

"Well, I'll have a talk with him. Is your phone number in the book, Mindy? Do you spell your name *R-Y-D-E-R?*"

"Yes, but..."

"I'll take a rain check on the tea, Eric. You help Mindy convince her father to come. I'll give him a call, too. So nice seeing you again, Mindy."

She bustled energetically down the stairs. Mindy glared at Eric hoping he'd get the message and talk his mother out of the Christmas invitation, even if it meant saying her father had leprosy. He followed with a hangdog expression.

He was gone long enough for her to slap the tree together and untangle the snake's nest of lights in the box. She could tell by looking at him when he returned that his mother was unstoppable. She probably had visions of a pre-wedding conference between families, a pre-rehearsal-dinner feast so they could size each other up.

He shook his head when he stepped into the living room.

"She's stubborn when she gets an idea in her head," he said apologetically.

"Now what are we going to do? Why didn't you let her think I'm just here to organize your home?"

"Doubt she'd believe it. She knows I like my clutter. What are you doing?"

She was scratching at the lump of tinsel lodged under her right breast, but this made it even more irritating. She lifted her sweater, fished under the edge of her bra, and extracted the wad of silvery glitter.

"I hate tinsel!"

"It has its uses."

"*Now* what are we going to do?" She tossed a string of lights back into the box not caring if his scrawny tree ever got decorated.

"We'll think of something."

"Embellish our story some more? I'll tell Dad you're a space alien who only wants to eat my brain."

"I had another part in mind."

"Be serious!"

"Your cannibal-alien story is serious?"

"We cannot let your mother and my father get together for Christmas. Nitro and glycerin are a safer combination."

"We could tell them the truth," he suggested.

"Merry Christmas, Dad. I invented a doctor-boyfriend because you make me crazy meddling in my personal life. What's your version of the truth? You pretended to be interested in me so I'd do your mother's committee work?"

"It wasn't quite that way."

"Well, no amount of spin can whitewash our deception. And now your mother thinks you're, you're..."

"Hot for you?"

"How eloquent!"

"Sorry, but I thought we should try the unvarnished truth."

"Like you tried it with your mother?"

"I'll think of some way to keep them apart."

"What?"

"I don't know." He stuffed his hands in the pockets of his jeans, a pretty good trick considering how tight they were. "I'll handle it."

"Like you handled explaining why I'm here?"

"She wouldn't have believed you were a plumber or an exterminator. I only told her we'd been 'seeing each other.' That's the story you used on your father, remember?''

''Yeah, and look where it got me.''

She picked up a handful of tinsel and threw it in his general direction, but none stuck to him. Her heart ached more than a bra stuffed full of it.

''I'll make excuses to my mother. Just don't let your father answer the phone for a while in case she calls him.''

''Do you think I have nothing better to do than stand guard by the phone? Never mind that I'm organizing three different New Year's Eve parties.''

''You don't have to be mad.''

''I want to be mad.'' She should shout more often; it was liberating.

''I suppose next you'll storm out of here.''

At least he sounded nearly as unhappy as she felt.

''I'm going home and plan a wonderful Christmas dinner just for Dad and me.''

''Fine.''

''Yes, fine.''

She was out in the parking lot before she realized they'd had their first and probably their last fight because the relationship they'd never had was over.

10

ERIC FINISHED trimming his tree Sunday morning and carried it down to the reception area. Della wanted Christmas spirit? Now she had it.

He plopped the three-foot excuse for a Christmas tree on the counter where she registered patients, then tried to turn it so the best side was in front. The trunk could serve as a model for curvature of the spine. The branches drooped under the weight of ornaments. There were too many lights on top and not enough on the bottom, but at least the job was done. He wanted the mess out of his living space. He had bigger problems, namely how to sabotage his mother's plans for Christmas with the Ryders.

At noon he showed up at his parents' Mesa home, a tasteful stucco house sitting in a showplace cacti garden. His father had spent long hours experimenting with commercially available desert flora when he first moved to Arizona, and now it was his pride and joy.

Inside the house his mother's taste had prevailed. She'd tried to create an Iowa farmhouse in the Southwestern community and had largely succeeded. Her collection of heritage quilts was displayed on the walls and rotated frequently to avoid overexposure to the light. The furnishings were mostly oak replicas of antique pieces, a specialty at their furniture store.

He was invited for lunch, but had a promise to keep. He had to figure out how to keep his mother from inviting Mindy and her father to share Christmas with them. It would be a disaster. Felicia and Wayne would have their children's wedding planned in the first fifteen minutes. If—when—they found out the relationship was a hoax, they'd feel much more betrayed after a cozy two-family dinner.

Ironically, he'd like nothing better than to spend the day—and the night—with Mindy, but her dippy idea to make him her boyfriend had landed them both in an awkward situation. He was honest enough to accept his share of blame, since he could have refused to go along with it, but that didn't solve the problem. Her father thought he was a hot prospect. His mother was planning a joint family get-together and raving about what a sweet girl Mindy was.

"Remember the Christmas you got Prince?" his mother asked as she dished out bowls of chili in her cozy kitchen and set them on a round oak pedestal table. "You were so excited you didn't sleep all night."

"I remember."

He'd wanted a Golden Lab puppy with all the urgency a six-year-old could muster.

"Christmas Eve your dad read you the riot act about ten times, but still you kept sneaking out of bed. Remember, Ray, you had the puppy hidden in the basement."

"I remember, Felicia." He didn't look up from the Sunday *Monitor* spread out among place mats decorated with frolicking black-and-white cows.

"Finally your dad gave up around four in the morning and brought Prince upstairs."

"Then I had to shampoo the carpet where the little scamp wet it," his father grumbled.

Eric listened to his mother ramble down memory

lane while they ate spicy chili and hot sourdough bread. Afterwards his father settled down in front of the TV, but he volunteered to clear the table.

"I'm going over to Mindy's this afternoon," Eric said, wanting to talk to her about an idea that had just come to him. "While I'm there, I'll ask about Christmas."

"You might mention it," his mother conceded. "Then I'll call later in the week to firm up the details. We'll be glad to bring Mindy's father here in the van."

"I think he's getting around on his own now."

It was past time to cut through the tangle of lies and half-truths. He'd never wanted this charade to go as far as it had.

"We're picking up Nadine and Harold at the airport at eleven. They got a good break on the tickets for traveling Christmas Day."

He stifled a groan. His mother had a vast number of siblings, cousins and assorted other relatives, most of whom he liked, but Nadine was a scientific curiosity. She could talk nonstop for hours without pausing for oxygen intake.

"Why invite Mindy and her father when you're already having company for dinner?" he asked.

"So Mindy's family can meet our family." She looked genuinely astonished that her son was so clueless.

"You're being premature. She's just a friend."

Felicia smiled slyly. "But Mindy seems like such a nice girl."

He left before his mother got sentimental about her hopes for grandchildren, lots and lots of grandchildren.

THE TRACKER was on autopilot, or so it seemed. Going to Mindy's was a bad idea, but he was headed in that direction even though he had no intention of mentioning Christmas to Wayne. One more lie wouldn't weigh that heavily on his conscience. He could tell his mother he'd asked, and they'd said no. He didn't have to see Mindy to know her answer would be negative.

Would she still be mad? He'd grown used to Cassandra's tirades, her big scenes staged to bend him to her will. He'd been surprised when Mindy shouted, and amused when she threw tinsel at him, but that didn't mean she wasn't stubborn and unreasonable...and sexy and adorable and...

"Enough!" he said aloud to himself.

Sure, he had a lot of sympathy for her. Laurie had told him Mindy's last serious boyfriend had badly undermined her confidence, and her father's pushiness compounded the problem. She hadn't met the right man yet, but that didn't mean she had an affinity for bad guys, only for ones that were wrong for her.

Like him.

She'd meet the right person someday, but not while he was hanging around complicating her life. She'd find a man who wanted to be organized, or maybe one who really needed her to shape him up. There was someone for everyone, except maybe for him. Call him altar-shy, but he couldn't see himself as the one for her.

Or could he?

He spent his days missing her and his nights reaching for her in his sleep. Could he possibly be...

He didn't know whether it was a good idea to see her, but he started driving to her house anyway.

Her van was in the carport. He was relieved even though seeing her was probably a bad idea.

He parked, thought about it and went to the front door.

She was wearing low-slung, faded jeans and a little red top that didn't quite meet the waistband. He imagined her navel winking at him and forgot the speech he'd prepared.

"Why are you here?" she asked.

"That's direct. Are you going to let me in?"

"Whatever." She shrugged and stepped aside.

"I came to see your father." Not true, but it seemed like a good time to tread lightly and see what developed.

"How lovely of you."

Ah, sarcasm, a sure mood spoiler. Thank you, Mindy.

"Isn't he here?"

He looked at the spot Wayne had staked out for himself on the couch. His father had a creaky old recliner that nothing in his furniture store could replace. Eric wondered if he himself would get so set in his ways even his butt had opinions. Or would he always live alone and have the choice of any seat in the house?

"He went to see some war movie with his friend, Jack."

"I could wait."

"Or you could not wait."

"You're still mad."

"You're not?"

He was, but that wasn't the point. All he'd done was try to help, well, almost all.

"We're mature adults. We have a little problem, one of our own making, I admit. We can work it out," he reasoned, suddenly realizing he was there because he hated having her angry with him.

"We? There is no 'we.'"

"I see you're decorating your tree," he said to change the subject.

She had a big bushy one, artificial, but so well made it looked real. The lights were on, precisely spaced from top to bottom, and she was hanging ornaments in that order. It would probably look spectacular when it was done.

She looked spectacular herself. Her hair a curly dark crown, and her cheeks were rosy pink as she walked over to the tree. She bent over a storage bin of ornaments, each one individually wrapped in tissue on a layer of cardboard. Her round, provocative backside made him want to get close—very close—even though he was miserable not knowing for sure how he felt about her.

"Like some help?" he asked with misgivings.

"Look where tinsel got us last time." She blushed, and it was wonderful to see.

"About that..."

How could he tell her she was more woman than any man deserved—delectable, delightful and desirable—then encourage her to look for some other man?

How could he get rid of the nagging suspicion that maybe that man was him?

"You have everything going for you," he said. "You have to stop worrying about what your father wants and find a guy who deserves you."

"You're breaking up with me, aren't you?"

She clipped a bird's nest on a clothespin on the tree and didn't look at him.

"No, I only..."

"Which is silly because we're not a couple. We can't split up if we're not together."

"Let's leave things the way they are until your father goes home."

"I guess there's no need to spoil his Christmas." She sounded glum, extremely glum.

"All we have to do is keep our parents apart until after Christmas. Once your dad is home, you can leak hints of trouble between us, then give him the bad news later."

"Losing his future son-in-law will go over better when he's home," she admitted, hanging a tear-shaped bulb on the tree. "Have you had a brilliant idea about keeping our parents apart on Christmas yet?"

"I'm supposed to invite your father for dinner today. I'll tell Mom you can't come for some reason."

"Without actually asking him?"

"Of course."

"Your mother will believe you since her son is always upright and honest."

"Like your father's daughter."

She stopped fiddling with the tree and faced him, feet spread and hands on hips.

"I hate this! I wish I'd never started it! So what if good ol' Jack Webster wants me to go out with his loser nephew. Nose hair isn't hereditary. I could handle it."

Eric caught a glimpse of a vehicle through the front window.

"Your father's home."

"Fine, have a nice visit with him. Peaches!" She walked to the door of her bedroom, opened it and called to the dog sleeping on the end of the bed. "Peaches! Walk!"

The dog scampered to her feet and wiggled with enthusiasm.

"Let's get your leash."

She found it under the kitchen sink, attached it to Peaches's collar and led her to the front door.

"I'll go with you." He wanted to walk with her more than Peaches did.

"You came to see my father, so see him."

She stood in the doorway as Wayne came up the walk.

"I'm taking Peaches for a walk, Dad," she said, even though it was obvious. "Eric came over to see you."

"Wait," Eric whispered urgently, but she ignored him.

Was she so fed up with their pretend dating she wanted him to make up some reason why he wanted to talk to Wayne? He'd rather sit on a cactus than invent any more fabrications.

"Eric, good to see you," Wayne said, coming into the house. "Don't you want to walk the dog with Mindy?"

"I can't stay long. I have a patient in my infirmary. Have to check on him because my hospital assistant is out of town on a family emergency."

The lies began again. The man probably thought he was staying behind to ask for his daughter's hand in marriage. Did his generation still expect that?

"Whadda' you say we have a beer," Wayne said, walking into the kitchen and ignoring the fact that Eric was hovering by the door poised for flight.

"I really can't stay long." He was tired of the game and didn't have a phony excuse to offer.

"I'll split a can with you, then." He went about dividing beer into two glasses without waiting for

Eric to agree. "I've got big news. Mindy doesn't even know it yet."

Eric perked up. If Wayne was leaving early, the whole Christmas hassle was resolved.

"Good news?" he asked, joining Wayne at the kitchen table.

"The best." He took a sip of beer. "Even the brew tastes better out here. I've decided to stay."

"It's a great place for a winter vacation," Eric said, trying to force some enthusiasm into his voice.

"No, I'm not talking vacation. I'm relocating, moving here permanently. Year-round sunshine, golf every day. There's nothing for me to do in Pittsburgh but baby-sit, and I'm hoping for a new litter out here."

Permanently! Eric downed half of the beer in one gulp.

"You haven't told Mindy?"

"No, and you're not to tell her, either. It's my surprise, and I want to break the news to her. I've made an offer on a nice condo right next to a golf course. Didn't want to bother her with house-hunting."

"This is..." Words failed him.

"A little sudden?" Wayne laughed. "I've had it in the back of my mind a long time. Always did like hot weather."

"Summers here are sizzling hot."

If her father ever learned their relationship had been bogus from the start, he'd make Mindy's life miserable. There was no way to let him down easily now.

Eric opened his mouth without an idea about what to say.

"I'm afraid I won't be seeing you anymore," he said impulsively.

Wayne looked stunned as if he were the one being dumped. Eric wanted to take back the words, but her father jumped on them.

"What does that mean, you won't be seeing me?"

"I should've have said Mindy."

"You two had a fight. I thought it was odd she flounced off without you. Well, I'm sure it's nothing that can't be patched up."

"I don't think so, sir."

"Now, don't start with that 'sir' business. I'm not giving up on your relationship."

"There is no relationship."

He was skirting perilously close to the truth. He felt terrible, but he didn't want Mindy's father to learn that she'd deceived him, however well-intentioned she'd been.

"I'm married."

It was the granddaddy of all whoppers, a colossal untruth that dwarfed all the little fibs in their web of deceit.

"You're what?"

Wayne bounded out of the kitchen chair. Eric expected him to scramble across the table and throttle him.

"We've been separated, but my wife and I are going to give it another try."

"Mindy has been seeing a married man?"

"No, absolutely not, not knowingly."

"I think you'd better get out of my house," Wayne said in a tight-lipped, harsh voice.

It wasn't the time to point out it was Mindy's house.

"I don't want you anywhere near my daughter. Is that understood?"

Wayne wasn't a big man, but now Eric knew how

he'd intimidated a whole string of Mindy's former boyfriends. In a past life, he could've been a judge, cold-eyed and unrelenting, presiding over the Salem witch trials.

"I don't want Mindy to know," he said, matching Wayne's outrage with his own stubbornness. "I'll exit her life permanently if you don't say a word to her about my marital state."

Apparently the older man wasn't used to back talk. He visibly sagged.

"Think about her feelings for once," Eric said, on a roll now and resentful of the pain this man had caused Mindy. "Your approval means a lot to her, but she never really gets it. She's perfectly capable of picking her own friends."

"You're a fine example of that."

"I'm a lousy example, but she's an adult. Cut her some slack. She'll find the right man someday without any help from you."

Wayne's face was mottled, his lips trembling, and his fists clenched. Eric sincerely hoped he wouldn't have to call 9-1-1.

"Get out," Mindy's father said.

"I will, but I want your promise not to hold me against Mindy—and not to mention my marriage."

"You have it."

Wayne was furious, but he wasn't a bad loser.

Eric left. His mother's chili and Wayne's beer were at war in his stomach, and he wasn't sure he could contain them. Despite Wayne's meddling, he'd grown to like the man, and he wanted to take back everything he'd said. A wife! Why did he conjure up that mythical creature?

He sat in his car breathing deeply and half hoping Mindy would come back with Peaches. He wanted to explain why he'd invented a marriage and precipitated their breakup.

He wanted to see her.

Finally, the truth. He hadn't made up the story about being married solely for Wayne's benefit. He was beginning to care too much for his daughter, but he still didn't want a woman to manage him, reorganize him or try to make him something he wasn't.

He started the engine but still sat there in front of her house. Wayne's plan to stay permanently changed everything. What choice had Eric had? He had to cancel the bargain and make sure her father wouldn't blame her. He'd done it for her own good. She deserved a nice guy who was ready to commit. There were plenty of men who'd love to hook up with her, but she wouldn't be able to find them with him hanging around all the time.

Some noble gesture. He felt rotten.

MINDY WAS TIRED of walking Peaches. She wanted to be with Eric and was mad at herself for not letting him come along. When she saw him outside in his SUV, she jogged toward him with Peaches trotting at her heels.

He lowered the driver's side window on his car when she approached.

"Leaving?" she asked.

"Looks that way."

"Did you and Dad have a good talk?"

Peaches jumped up, paws on the side of his vehicle threatening to scratch the shiny red paint.

"Sit, Peaches."

After three commands and some firm nudging, she did.

"We're officially broken up," he said in a tone that assured her he wasn't joking.

"I thought we were going to be a couple until he went home." She tried to keep her voice steady.

"The moment was right. I took care of telling him about our breakup."

"You could've talked to me first."

Her throat ached. She couldn't think of a single argument against what he'd done except that it was wrong, wrong, wrong.

"Trust me, it wouldn't have changed anything," he said.

When a man said "trust me," it usually meant he was hiding something. But the only thing that mattered was not having a reason to see him anymore. She grasped at the last tenuous link between them.

"You will still take care of Peaches, won't you?"

"Whenever she needs me." He smiled wanly, not looking at all like himself.

"Well, goodbye," she said reluctantly.

"Bye."

"And thanks for everything."

"I'm the one who should thank you."

She stepped back and gripped the dog leash so hard her fingers hurt. He drove away, and she listlessly decided to walk a little longer. She needed time to stifle the sobs welling up in her throat before she faced her father.

11

MINDY COULD HEAR familiar music even before she unlocked her front door and opened it. Stepping inside she was bombarded by a song she'd loved when she was ten years old. Now it only irritated her. A person couldn't go to the supermarket without suffering seasonal audio-overload. It would take a lot more than "Jingle Bells" to make her jolly this year.

At least her father had company to occupy him this Christmas Eve. He and Jack Webster were hooting over a gin rummy score and hardly noticed her return.

"Having fun?" she asked, putting a sack of last-minute items for their dinner tomorrow on the kitchen table.

"Just trying to win back what this coyote trickster took from me playing golf today," her father said, leaning over the coffee table where they were playing and watching a wrestling match on muted TV.

Since her father had decided to move to the Phoenix area, he'd started sprinkling his conversation with what he thought were Southwestern phrases. She wished he'd stop.

"Have a chocolate ball, Mindy," Jack said. "They're the real thing, not brown imitation candy."

"Thank you, but I don't think so."

"You girls, always watching your figures." He unwrapped a foil-covered ball and popped it in his mouth. "Sure was nice of you to invite me and Brad for Christmas dinner."

"Our pleasure," she said, feeling like a hypocrite. The invitation had come from her father. Now that Eric was out of the picture, he'd fixated on Jack's nephew, absolutely insisting she meet him. She didn't know if including him for Christmas dinner was better or worse than a blind date. Either way, her father was in top form, manipulating and matchmaking.

He didn't really like wrestling, and he'd never been much of a card player. What would happen to the friendship of the two old buddies when nothing developed between her and the nephew?

She was getting used to Jack's bombastic personality, but why didn't he have his barber trim his nose and ear hairs? If nephew Brad was the hairy gorilla she was expecting, she was moving to Alaska. Let Dad see how he liked the weather there. She'd had it with his meddling.

She went to work making two pumpkin pies, using frozen pie shells. At least it wouldn't be just the two of them for Christmas dinner. Laurie was coming, alone this time, and Jack would be there with the nephew. Whenever Mindy was alone with her father, the strain of not talking about Eric made her doubly depressed.

She couldn't blame Eric for bailing. Initially he'd only agreed to a single date. When her father sprained his ankle, he'd been a good sport and gone along with the arrangement for longer than she'd had any right to expect. Their bogus relationship had to end sometime.

She checked the turkey to make sure it was thawed and returned it to the fridge. Dad had urged her to plan an easier meal, ham or something, but she opted for an elaborate turkey dinner with all the trimmings. She wanted an excuse to spend as much time as possible in the kitchen.

By ten o'clock she was tired of puttering in the kitchen. The men had given up on cards and carols and were glued to the TV.

"Would you mind taking Peaches out before you go to bed, Dad?"

"No problem. Good night, honey."

"Brad and I are really looking forward to tomorrow," Jack said.

"I'll see you then. Good night."

Easy to say but hard to accomplish, Mindy thought an hour later. If this was insomnia, its name was Eric. She could push him to the back of her mind when she was busy doing things, but he took over her thoughts the minute her head hit the pillow.

She missed him. They'd had wonderful chemistry. If his mother hadn't interrupted their tree-trimming party…

There was no solace in what might have happened. She thumped her pillow, pulled a sheet over her head, and burrowed under the covers.

She woke up suddenly and bolted upright. Surprised that she'd fallen asleep at all, she was instantly alert. There was an odd noise in the living room, not the mechanical drone of the television or the muted voices of her father and his friend.

Dismissing every explanation from sneak thieves to Santa, she realized Peaches wasn't zonked out on her usual spot at the end of the bed.

"Peaches!"

Mindy dashed out to the living room turning on overhead lights as she ran.

"Oh, no!"

Cards were scattered on the floor, the Corgi was making odd noises, and there wasn't a chocolate ball in sight.

Unless her dad and Jack had gorged on the candy after she went to bed, Peaches had gobbled them up, foil and all. The mangled bag and scattered remnants told the whole story.

"Bad doggie. Oh, Peaches, oh, sweetheart. Dr. Eric will know what to do."

He said he'd still be her vet, never mind that it was past 2:00 a.m. on Christmas morning.

Eric answered on the second ring and didn't hesitate to help when he heard what had happened.

"Bring her right over."

She left a note for her father, frantically loaded Peaches into her carrier and rushed through deserted streets to the sparse traffic of the freeway.

Eric was waiting and came out to help unload her sick pup. He was one-hundred percent the professional.

"Wait out here," he said, carrying Peaches to his examining room. "This won't be pleasant."

She wanted to go with her dog and would have insisted with any other vet. But she wouldn't inflict her presence on a man who'd been humiliatingly eager to end their relationship.

Instead she waited and paced, her ears attuned for any sound that would tell her Peaches was okay. She didn't hear anything, but maybe his examining room was soundproof.

She tried sitting, even picked up a magazine and held it in front of her for several minutes before realizing it was upside down.

Peaches might by dying. She should've warned her father about the foil-wrapped chocolate. He probably never gave it a thought, but Peaches was her responsibility. She should've put them up on a shelf before she went to bed.

Facing Eric was hard enough without her terrible guilt. He probably thought she was a negligent pet owner, an uncaring canine caregiver.

Her glance fell on the lopsided Christmas tree on the counter. The ornaments needed to be spaced better. The wire branches could be bent for a nicer shape, especially the ones on the left. She'd just tweak it a little. She went to work on it.

"It's a pretty pathetic tree," Eric said, coming out of the examining room a few minutes later.

Mindy spun around, angry at herself for interfering again. "I'm sorry, really sorry. There's nothing wrong with it. I just had to do something to keep busy."

"I understand."

"You do? Is Peaches..."

"She's one sick pup, but she'll be okay. I think I'd better keep her for a day or two."

"Whatever you think. Can I see her?"

"She's sedated and bedded down, so it's probably better if you don't get her excited. I have a vet student working nights in the hospital when I need him. We're pretty empty. No one schedules elective surgery the day before Christmas."

"Well, thank you." Now that the crisis was over, she felt horribly awkward. "I didn't know who else to call."

"I'm glad you called me."

"My dad is the one who's really mad at you."

He shrugged.

"He's moving here permanently to keep an eye on me."

"I think he likes the weather."

"You know? You must have known before I did!"

"He told me. We couldn't go on deceiving him, making him think..."

"Of course not, but you could have warned me. Maybe I could've talked him out of it before you broke up with me. Without even telling me! Now he's convinced I'm not to be trusted choosing any man by myself."

"It seemed like the thing to do at the time."

He was wearing a rumpled, soiled lab jacket, no doubt trashed by Peaches, and running shoes with no socks. He had a severe case of bed-head and dark shadows under his eyes, but looking at him made her heart ache with longing. She did have terrible taste in men. The one she really wanted was a hopeless cause.

"Whatever you said to him," she said petulantly, "he's hopping mad. He mentioned kicking your sorry butt from here to the Grand Canyon if he ever sets eyes on you again."

"I just told him I was breaking up with you. His mind was made up about moving. You couldn't have changed it no matter what I did or didn't do," he said.

"Now you're an expert on parent psychology?"

She reminded herself that the vet had come through for Peaches, but gratitude only went so far.

"I have parents of my own," he said stiffly.

"Yes, and they must have spoiled you rotten because you barge ahead and do whatever you like without thinking of the consequences to other people."

"Don't blame me because you can't stand up to your own father."

"I can. I just don't want to hurt him. He's been terribly lonely since Mom died."

"Then tell him to do some matchmaking for himself."

"My father wouldn't..."

"Well, maybe he should get a life of his own. Either that, or tell him to mind his own business. I'm not the cause of your problems, and I'm not the solution. It's not very flattering to be used...."

"Used? I didn't see any resistance when you tried to decorate me with tree tinsel."

"Am I supposed to apologize for that, too?"

"Don't apologize for anything! I'll send someone else to pick up Peaches when she can go home. Thank you for treating her, Dr. Kincaid."

"I like Peaches."

He had to have the last word. Well, let him, she decided furiously as she left. This was the last time she'd have anything whatsoever to do with Dr. Eric Kincaid.

Outside in the parking lot she was forced to change her mind. Eric had Dad's Christmas gift. She ran back and banged on the door until he came and opened it.

"What's wrong?"

For a moment she forgot what she wanted. He'd taken off the lab coat and anything he'd been wearing under it. She found herself staring at a gorgeous chest sprinkled with golden brown hair. She'd known he was lean and fit, but even in her best fantasies she hadn't imagined the way her fingers ached to touch him.

"Is something wrong?" he asked.

Yes, something was horribly wrong. She desperately wanted him to put his arms around her and hold her tight. One word from him, and she wouldn't go home tonight or any other night. Why couldn't he see that they belonged together?

"You still have the golf bag."

"The what? oh, yeah, I do. Wait here. I'll run up and get it."

"Please do," she mumbled.

He came back with the gaudy plaid bag slung over one bare shoulder. Too bad there wasn't time to exchange it for sensible brown or navy. She'd offer to make the switch after Dad saw it.

"Thank you," she said in a somber voice.

"You're welcome."

Again with the last word. She hurried away from him before she did something she'd regret.

When she got home, she slapped a sticky gift tag on the plaid side of the bag, kicked off her shoes, and fell onto the bed without bothering to undress.

A few hours later she heard the grating noise of her father's newest toy. Why was he grinding coffee beans at this ungodly hour?

She checked her clock and rolled out of bed with alarm. It was nearly 10:00 a.m., and she had a turkey to cook and a turkey to meet, Jack's conveniently available nephew. Later she'd have time to cry her eyes out, but she was determined not to let her misery spoil her father's Christmas.

She slipped on a long yellow robe, wished Peaches was home where she belonged, and went out to begin the Christmas festivities.

Three hours later she had the day, if not her life, under control. Her father had been so contrite about leaving the chocolate balls where Peaches could get them she couldn't be mad at him. They exchanged gifts, and he raved about the golf bag, refusing her offer to exchange it. He gave her a pile of new clothes, all the perfect size, style and colors. How could her dad know her taste in clothes so well and be totally clueless about her taste in men?

To please him, she decided she would wear one of his gifts, a silk chiffon floral dress in shades of red, deep red and pink. It had long sleeves that hugged her arms, a deep vee neckline and a swirly skirt that didn't quite reach her knees. Never mind that it wasn't a turkey-dinner kind of dress.

She showered, dried the wild mop her untrimmed hair had become and opened the underwear drawer of her dresser. Back in her deluded days when she'd still had hope, she'd bought a bra and panty set like nothing she'd ever owned, bold see-through zebra stripes to match Eric's wild sheets. Now they had all the appeal of burlap undies, but she put them on anyway.

"Eat your heart out, Dr. Kincaid," she said, substituting defiance for despair, at least for her Christmas party.

Laurie was the first to arrive. She was wearing a long red skirt and a green cutaway tank top with horizontal white pinstripes. With her blond hair and slender figure, it was a smashing outfit.

"I am so glad to see you," Mindy said when her father ducked into the spare bedroom he now called his. "Dad's friend is coming with his bozo nephew."

"Will Eric be here?"

"'Fraid not. We'll talk later."

The turkey was browning beautifully in its special cooking bag, and the dinner was totally under control. Mindy lit her gift from Laurie, an aromatic mood candle. Laurie raved about the exotic tea sampler from Mindy, and the holiday was off to a festive start.

Then the doorbell rang.

Her father sprinted to answer it, reminding her of the miraculous way his ankle had recovered. She pushed aside an ugly suspicion and braced herself for Jack and jerk.

Oh boy, was she wrong!

"My nephew, Brad Webster," Jack said. "If you ever need a tax lawyer, Brad's your man."

Not only did he not have nose hair, Brad was tall—supertall—a full head taller than his uncle, who was probably six foot himself. He had big brown eyes, dark ringlets, classically handsome features and a smile that lit up his face when Dad introduced him to Laurie.

Laurie looked up at him, gave him a radiant smile and forgot about helping with the wine.

"Mindy runs her own business," her father said.

He tried hard to draw Brad's attention to his daughter, but the lanky tax lawyer scarcely noticed her. After a reasonably courteous interval, Laurie offered to show him the sunlit patio in back of the house. He nearly tripped himself rushing to follow her.

Dad's holiday spirit fizzled. He glumly turned on the TV so Jack could watch some football game.

Mindy felt almost happy. She'd heard of love at first sight, but this was the quickest love connection she'd ever seen. She busied herself in the kitchen and decided to wait an extra half hour before serving dinner. She guessed Laurie and Brad would find a lot to see on her little four-by-four patio.

Her father was rereading yesterday's *Monitor,* Jack was shouting coaching advice at the football players on TV and she was taking the turkey out of the oven when the doorbell unexpectedly rang.

No one dropped in on Christmas Day. She thought of Eric. She was always thinking of him, so it was no stretch.

Her dad opened the door.

"You're Mindy's father, aren't you? Poor man, I hope you're feeling better. I'm Eric's mother, Felicia, and this is my husband, Ray."

She sidestepped Wayne before he could say anything and put a huge woven picnic basket on the kitchen counter. Her husband followed lugging a cooler the size of a minivan. He dumped it on the floor with a sigh of relief.

"My cousin and her husband are stuck at the Denver airport. Bad weather. I couldn't help thinking about how you've been laid up, Mr. Ryder, and here I have this huge dinner with no company to eat it. So what is Christmas if it's not about sharing?"

"Her idea," Ray said, gravitating toward the TV where he introduced himself to Jack.

It was the first time Mindy had seen her father speechless. She didn't know what to say, either, except to introduce Laurie and Brad who'd just returned pink-cheeked and dewy-eyed from their tour of the patio.

One member of the Kincaid family was conspicuously missing.

ERIC WAS LATE for dinner, and his mother was going to be ticked. He didn't even have a good excuse, not one he wanted to mention.

After Mindy left the night before, he'd given up on sleep and plunked down in front of TV, eventually dozing off sometime after dawn. He'd botched any chance he'd ever had with her, and regret didn't cover the way he felt.

She'd been worried about Peaches, scared even, but when he went out to tell her the Corgi would be all right, she'd been fussing with his tree. How could he have been do dumb? Organizing things was her way of dealing with stress. It wasn't much different from his need to run when he was tense. She was nothing like Cass, never had been.

He was the one with the problem. He'd screwed up with the sweetest, sexiest, most special woman he'd ever met, and he didn't know how to make things right between them. Mindy had every reason in the world to be hurt and angry. He'd pretty much done everything wrong and nothing right since their first fake date. He should've told her then that only professional concerns had kept him from asking her out. Deep down, he knew that everything he'd done since then had only been an excuse to see more of her.

Damn it, he thought glumly as he drove up to his parents' house. He'd let his pride get in the way, and now he was paying big time. She'd originally gone out with him to please her father, but that didn't mean she was using him the way Cass had. If his brain had been this mushy in vet school, he'd be mowing lawns for a living instead of operating his own practice.

He steeled himself for an afternoon with Nadine's incessant chatter and walked up to the front door of his parents' house.

There was a note taped on the Spanish-style green plank door. He pulled it off, frowning.

Dear Eric,

Cousin Nadine and Harold had to change planes in Denver. Now they're stuck at the airport there until the weather clears.

Had so much food it seemed a shame not to share. Found your friend Mindy's address in the phone book. So we've gone to surprise her poor father with a nice big Christmas dinner.

Love,
Mom

"Oh, no!"

He crumpled the note into a ball as he ran to his SUV. Jumping in, he tossed it on the passenger seat as he hurriedly started the engine.

He didn't know if he was madder at his mother or himself. Self-loathing won out. He'd brought this on himself by misleading his mother. He'd wanted to quell her matchmaking mania, and now she was on her way for a confrontation with a man who thought he was married.

What had he told her about Wayne? Oh, yeah, his injury was acting up, and he wanted to spend the day on the couch. His dad had agreed it was a sensible decision, so why had he gone along with hauling Christmas dinner to people they'd never met?

Sometimes Dad took the path of least resistance, and it was always easier to go along with Mom than thwart her plans. Eric was guilty of doing the same thing. He didn't have to work on her committee. He could've said no. He was as bad as Mindy at not standing up to a parent.

Mindy! He drove faster, thankful for the sparse Christmas Day traffic. With luck he'd get there only minutes behind his parents. Mindy was at the epicenter of a potentially huge explosion. If Wayne and his mother started unraveling their tangle of lies and half-truths, both parents were going to be very angry. He couldn't let Mindy take the heat alone.

Then there was the part about being married and getting back with his wife. Her father believed it. What if Mindy did, too? How would his mother react?

It was a balmy December day in the desert community, but he broke out in a cold sweat. He might lose Mindy forever, and suddenly that was his worst fear.

When he got to her subdivision, he had to park in front of a neighbor's house. The spot behind Mindy's van in the carport was taken, and his parents' Lincoln occupied the space in front of her house.

The place looked deceptively peaceful. He walked to the front door and rang the bell.

Mindy answered.

"We have a problem," she whispered urgently.

She was beautiful in a flowery red dress. He'd been an absolute idiot to let her leave after he treated Peaches.

"Let's get out of here!" he said.

He reached for her hand, but she backed away, forcing him to follow her into chaos. The TV was blaring, and his father was staring glassy-eyed at the screen while Wayne's friend shouted instructions to a coach half a continent away. Laurie was putting dishes on the counter, and the almost overwhelming scent of roasted turkey suggested dinner was ready. Mindy's friend waved, but kept her focus on the task at hand. A tall guy with Shirley Temple curls was hovering.

"Who's that?" Eric asked, feeling prickles of jealousy in spite of the situation.

"Oh, that's Brad."

The guy ambled over to the foyer where they were standing.

"Brad, this is Eric."

"Hi."

"Where's my mother? Your father?" Eric asked Mindy.

"I think they're out on the patio," Brad said. "Want me to tell them you're here?"

"That would be nice, Brad." Mindy gave him a winning if somewhat wan smile.

"Who is Brad?" Eric asked more urgently when the guy left them.

"Jack's nephew. My date supposedly."

"Your date?" This was getting worse and worse.

"He took one look at Laurie and was smitten. Did you know your parents were coming here?"

Eric closed his eyes for a second, grateful she wasn't interested in Brad. "No, of course not. I was a little late for Christmas dinner, and she left a note stuck on the front door."

"You're always late. It's rude, Eric."

She was so right he wasn't even tempted to argue. He'd been hopelessly slow to realize how he felt about her. Now he was scared silly he was too late to do anything about it.

His mother erupted into the room resplendent in a purple pantsuit. Wayne trailed in her wake. He hadn't seen an angrier looking pair since…well, never.

"How could you tell Mr. Ryder you're married?" she demanded.

The room went silent except for the drone of a television commercial.

"You're what?" Mindy's face went stark white, and he was afraid she'd keel over.

"I'm not married!" He only cared that Mindy registered the truth.

"You told me you were married," Wayne said angrily. "Said you were dumping Mindy to go back to your wife."

Wayne made *wife* sound like a four-letter cuss word. In another age Eric would have oiled up his dueling pistols for a dawn encounter.

"You can't dump me!" Mindy protested vehemently. "There has to be a relationship to break up!"

"I *told* you my son isn't married," Felicia said triumphantly. "He would never deprive me of his wedding. I would know if my own son was married."

Eric saw Brad motion to Laurie, and the two of them slipped away. He envied them. Their parents weren't there.

"Maybe we'd better start at the beginning," Eric said.

Mindy wouldn't look at him.

"Maybe you should turn off your turkey, Mindy," his mother suggested.

"I'll worry about my turkey, Mrs. Kincaid."

She'd talked back to his mother. He was crazy about her!

"You two." Mindy pointed at Wayne and Felicia. "Sit at the kitchen table. We have to talk."

She gave Eric a look that invited him to head for the county line, but he followed her to the table anyway.

"Your turkey will dry out." His mother was nothing if not single-minded, but she sat docilely at one end of the small table.

Wayne sat at the other end with Mindy between them. Eric turned the fourth chair and straddled it. This didn't feel like a peace conference.

"Dad, you've been interfering in my love life or lack thereof since Tommy Garfield asked me on an eighth grade Halloween hayride."

"I just don't want you to make a serious mistake."

"Well, Tommy Garfield was a serious mistake. He put slimy pumpkin seeds down my back and tried to... Well, never mind. But he was my mistake, and I learned from it."

"That was eighth grade," Wayne mumbled.

"I could just take the turkey out for you," his mother said.

"I don't care if the bird turns to leather!"

Mindy sounded borderline hysterical, but his mother froze on the chair. Eric had never before seen her intimidated.

Taking a deep breath, Mindy continued talking to his mom.

"Eric didn't want to be on your committee. You don't know how busy he is. He's probably the best vet in the state of Arizona if not the whole United States of America, and Peaches might be dead if it weren't for him."

"I told you how sorry I am about the chocolate balls," her father grumbled.

"Peaches is your fat little dog?" His mother liked every detail clear.

Mindy ignored her.

"I told you I was seeing a doctor so you wouldn't sic some friend's nephew on me," she said, turning to her father.

"Brad seems like a nice young man," Wayne said.

"I'm sure Laurie will thank you if things work out, but I *want to pick my own man.*"

"That's why I agreed to pretend to be Mindy's boyfriend," Eric said. "It started as a harmless deception to keep you off her back. Obviously it had to end when you decided to live here permanently."

"Why tell me you're married?" Wayne snarled. "I'm assuming you aren't."

"He most certainly is not," Felicia said.

"We couldn't go on pretending if you were going to live here. It was the only idea I came up with on the spur of the moment."

"It was a really, really dumb one," Mindy said.

"Almost as dumb as pretending we were in love!" he shouted.

There, he'd said the word. Her color was back, her cheeks flaming red.

"If you two really don't care for each other, maybe we can have a civilized dinner and go home," his mother suggested.

"I didn't say anything about not caring." Eric kept his eyes riveted on Mindy's face.

"You never said anything about caring." Her voice was a shaky whisper.

"I've been an idiot."

"At last something we can all agree on," Wayne said.

A team must have scored. Jack hooted and howled as crowd noise blasted out of the TV.

"I don't know how my daughter hooked up with a horse's ass like you," Wayne said.

"My son is not..." Felicia began.

"Quiet, Mom. Please. Wayne is right. I thought Mindy was only using me to keep him from interfering in her life. It's not much of an ego builder to be a pawn in someone else's game, but I should have had more faith in her."

"I never intended to use you!" Mindy protested. "After our first date, I only wanted to keep seeing you any way I could. All the stuff about Dad was only an excuse."

"You didn't need an excuse. I needed a brain transplant. I compared you to Cass not realizing you didn't have a hidden agenda like she did. All she wanted was a resident vet for her horses. You're the most genuine, sincere person I've ever met."

"About time you told her that," Wayne groused.

"If we're going to be in-laws, you've got to learn to keep your opinions to yourself," his mother warned Wayne.

"Mom, let me do the talking," Eric protested.

"I'm not the one who barged in uninvited with enough food to feed all the homeless people in Phoenix. As if my daughter can't cook a holiday dinner," Wayne said.

"Dad!"

"Her turkey is going to be dry as a bone." His mother sniffed indignantly, but smiled at Mindy. "But since you're smart enough to use a baking bag, I'm sure it will be all right. Besides all I brought was some ham, rolls, gelatin salad..."

Eric stood, knocking the chair against the table.

"I think we should check on Peaches."

Even Mindy looked blank.

"She's in my hospital. She'll be missing Mindy."

"We're about to eat dinner." His mother's protest was weak, and he ignored it.

"Peaches needs me," Mindy said.

"I knew he was the right one," Wayne said with satisfaction.

"Why wouldn't my son be the right one? He's a very nice boy, not to mention he has his own practice."

Eric glanced at his father and exchanged grins, then he linked hands with Mindy. They ran out the door and into his vehicle.

"They'll never forgive us for missing dinner." She was laughing so hard her eyes were tearing.

"Teach them not to meddle."

He leaned over ignoring the gear handle that jabbed his stomach and kissed her with so much love he felt dizzy.

"I'm crazy about you," he said.

"Or maybe just crazy."

"I love you, Mindy. Now I know why Peaches was my favorite patient. She gave me a chance to see you."

"I love you." She said it so softly he had to strain to hear. "But we'd better leave before your mother brings out plates of Christmas dinner."

"Or before your father thinks of reasons why I'll make a lousy son-in-law."

"A what?"

Whoops! He'd skipped a step.

"Marry me, Mindy."

"Make us all one happy family?"

"No, make me the happiest man in the world."

"When you put it that way, I would love to marry you."

"I love you, Mindy. Only one thing makes me unhappy."

"Our parents?"

"No." He grinned broadly. "We'll have some interesting family holidays to look forward to. I'm only sorry I don't have a Christmas present for you. Will you take a rain check for something small and sparkly?"

"Gladly."

She touched his cheek with so much tenderness and love he melted inside.

"I, on the other hand, am the organizer, no detail overlooked. I have a little gift for you if you can stand me the way I am."

"I adore the way you are. And I'll try to be on time from now on."

He reached for her even though the separate seats in the SUV didn't make it easy to hold her close.

"But you probably won't be."

"Afraid not." He grinned and kissed the tips of her fingers and the soft skin of her inner wrist.

"Eric?"

"Um?"

"Don't you want to see your gift?"

"Sure, but I don't see how I can be any happier than I am now."

"Then put your hands on the steering wheel and close you eyes."

He raised his brows in a silent question but did as she asked even though he didn't know how she could possibly have a gift concealed on her person.

"Now look."

She's shifted onto one hip and raised the skirt of her dress to reveal one round, luscious buttock covered in skimpy, semitransparent, zebra-striped panties.

He reached over to skim his hand over her enticing bottom, totally wowed until he remembered something.

"You didn't know I was coming. You put them on for a blind date with Brad."

"Oh, don't be silly." She dropped her skirt and settled back on both cheeks. "I just didn't see any point in saving an expensive set I'd bought just for you when I didn't know if I'd ever see you again."

"Set?"

"Matching bra."

"They match my sheets."

"Do you think so? Maybe we should compare patterns," she said.

"Best idea I've heard in a long time. Did I mention I love you?" he asked.

"Not nearly often enough."

He reached under her skirt and stroked silky cloth warmed by her body heat.

"Drive," she whispered.

He shifted into gear, wondering why he'd ever thought he could get along without her.

"I love you so much, I feel like crying," she said, leaning over and caressing his ear and the side of his face with the back of her fingers.

He drove away in a haze of happiness. The only woman he'd ever loved was beside him.

A Groom in Her Stocking

Barbara Dunlop

TORONTO • NEW YORK • LONDON
AMSTERDAM • PARIS • SYDNEY • HAMBURG
STOCKHOLM • ATHENS • TOKYO • MILAN • MADRID
PRAGUE • WARSAW • BUDAPEST • AUCKLAND

Dear Reader,

A good friend of mine, Maureen Martin Osland, once told me a story from her childhood about a teenage boy whose nickname had become so ingrained in his family and his community that his mother had to stop and think before she could remember his real first name.

After hearing the story, I wondered what might happen if a grown man still used his nickname. And then I wondered what might happen if it mattered....

I hope you enjoy meeting RJ—that's the nickname for the hero in *A Groom in Her Stocking*. I love writing stories set in my home, the Yukon Territory. And I had a terrific time writing this one!

All the best,

Barbara Dunlop

Books by Barbara Dunlop

HARLEQUIN DUETS
54—THE MOUNTIE STEALS A WIFE

HARLEQUIN TEMPTATION
848—FOREVER JAKE
901—NEXT TO NOTHING!

For Richard Lawrence and Rachel Grantham,
and the people of the Yukon Territory

1

"AND WHAT can Santa bring for little Lindsey Parker this year?" Resplendent in a top-of-the-line Santa suit, Sommerton Hartwig had grandfatherly eyes that twinkled with the reflection of a hundred tiny Christmas bulbs. His silky beard bobbed up and down as he spoke.

Lindsey grinned self-consciously, standing in the decorated reception area in front of thirty co-workers and spouses. She wore a basic black cocktail dress and higher-than-usual heels in honor of the staff Christmas party. Sommerton, the managing partner, leaned over from his festooned executive chair to peer in the red velvet Santa sack. A flashbulb went off, and Lindsey blinked. Heather Hallihan waved from the crowd.

"How 'bout old man Herrington's signature on a million-dollar check?" Dick Johnson, Progressive Dynamics comptroller, called from the far side of the office. Dick knew exactly how many overtime hours Lindsey had logged on the Herrington proposal.

She rolled her eyes good-naturedly in Dick's direction. He held up his glass of eggnog in a mock toast and winked. Not that Herrington's signature wouldn't be one heck of a Christmas gift.

''What about a date?'' Annabelle Martin, the mail room clerk, giggled then hiccuped as she leaned her head against her husband's broad shoulder. The spacious reception area erupted in laugher, thirty-odd people sharing the joke at Lindsey's expense.

Her grin faltered slightly. Okay, so it had been a while. But she was a busy woman. The Herrington proposal was only one of a dozen different investment packages she was putting together for Progressive Dynamics, the Vancouver venture capital firm. Who had time to date?

''How about a laptop computer?'' asked Sommerton.

''Sure,'' Lindsey agreed in a bright voice, more to distract the crowd of co-workers from her ten-month dateless streak than from any burning desire to get a laptop computer for Christmas. She shifted to relieve the pressure on her baby toe.

She hated to admit it, but a date sounded more appealing. Although the million-dollar signature would probably be a darn sight easier to come by than the date. The odds of finding the man of her dreams *and* a free Saturday night were pretty remote.

''Ho, ho, ho,'' intoned Sommerton, bending a little further, reaching into the recesses of the bag. Gold and red silk balls swayed from the padded arms of his leather chair. The administrative staff had definitely outdone themselves decorating this year.

"What does Santa have here?" he asked, fumbling with both hands.

The sack fell away, revealing a state-of-the-art laptop computer. A gasp went up from the assembled crowd, and he stretched forward to place the computer in Lindsey's hands.

It was slim and light and sleek. She stared at the manufacturer's logo, blinking in astonishment and confusion. Everyone else had received personalized coffee mugs and gift certificates for a local restaurant. Lovely coffee mugs to be sure, but…

"Aside from being a *very* good girl this year—" Sommerton's voice boomed above the sudden buzz of the crowd "—it's my pleasure to announce that Lindsey has just achieved Gold Merit Certification."

Gold Merit Certification? Lindsey's eyes widened, and her glance flew from the laptop to Sommerton. The words echoed incredulously through her brain. She couldn't have heard him right.

Her co-workers burst into instantaneous applause.

It had been fifteen years since anyone in the Vancouver office made Gold Merit Certification. The laptop suddenly felt heavy. She'd known her portfolio was growing, but to make the top one percent in the country? It was a professional dream come true.

"All right, Lindsey!" somebody shouted.

"Is it true?" she asked Sommerton, her voice little more than a squeak.

"It's true." He beamed with obvious pride. "We got the results last week. Congratulations." He stood up and shook her hand.

"All right, Linds." Heather rushed forward.

As soon as Sommerton drew away, Heather pulled Lindsey into an exuberant hug. Lindsey clutched the computer, but she was beginning to lose the feeling in her fingers. As a matter of fact, she was beginning to lose feeling everywhere.

"Let me set that down for you," offered Sommerton, relieving her of the laptop. Lindsey's was the last name called, so his Santa duties were done for the evening.

She muttered a grateful thanks then hugged her friend and fellow investment portfolio manager.

"Can you believe it?" she whispered in Heather's ear, amazement coloring her tone. The implications of the achievement were just beginning to sink in.

"Of course I can believe it," said Heather, drawing away. "You're incredible,"

"I'm not incredible. I'm stunned," said Lindsey. She stepped back, running a palm over her dark French braid, blowing out a small breath.

Heather's sequined dress flickered in the blinking white lights of the ten-foot balsam tree. "Nobody deserves it more." She reached out and squeezed Lindsey's hand.

"I guess my coaching finally paid off." Dick Johnson sauntered up, coming to a halt beside Heather.

"Give me a break." Heather slanted him an irritated look. "It was Lindsey's brains and hard work that paid off."

"Don't forget," said Dick with a wave of his eggnog glass. "I was the one who showed her the ropes."

"You are such an egomaniac," said Heather.

"It's called self-confidence, young lady." Dick straightened his tie and squared his shoulders. "Well earned self-confidence, as you're well aware."

Lindsey was quite sure Dick's tongue was planted firmly in his cheek on the "young lady" remark. He might have more than his fair share of the world's ego quotient, but he wasn't a chauvinist. He also loved to yank Heather's chain.

"Must come with age," Heather returned smoothly. Her perfectly made-up eyes narrowed contemplatively, and she made a show of peering around the side of his head. "I've been meaning to ask you. Is that a bald spot you're developing?"

Dick's hand flew to his hair. He was more than a little proud of his thick mane of Gentlemen Only, Number Five Bronze.

Lindsey couldn't help smiling at his momentarily stunned expression. When Dick and Heather started in, the prudent thing to do was to simply get out of the way.

"Congratulations, Lindsey." Another co-worker offered her hand, pulling Lindsey's attention away from the argument. Then another hand was offered, and another.

Lindsey accepted the good wishes as gracefully as she could, but the outpouring of accolades quickly made her uncomfortable. Sure, she'd worked hard, but the very people congratulating her were the ones whose support made it possible for her to do her job.

She thanked them all sincerely. But she was grateful twenty minutes later when the attention shifted away from her and the party started to break up.

"You'll get that corner office yet," said Heather with a delighted laugh once they were left alone.

"And my very own secretary," Lindsey added in an answering teasing tone, much more comfortable making light of the accomplishment than accepting praise.

"And a limo. Don't forget to ask for a limo before you sign your next employment contract. You can pick me up in the mornings." Heather perched herself on the edge of the reception desk with a graceful little shimmy.

"You've got it. Do you think we can call the driver Jeeves?" Following Heather's example, Lindsey lowered herself into the Santa chair. Her feet practically sighed with relief. The three-inch party heels might look good, but they were murder on her arches.

"Of course. You'll be paying him, we can call him whatever we want. And don't forget the free champagne. I just love free champagne."

"With breakfast?" asked Lindsey.

Heather sighed. "Okay. If you insist, we can dilute it with orange juice."

Lindsey chuckled at Heather's patented long-suffering sigh. Six years ago, after graduating with economics degrees from the University of British

Columbia, they'd both joined Progressive Dynamics and had quickly become friends.

"So, when does your plane leave?" Heather kicked her strappy sandals halfway off and swung her legs beneath the desk. The gold-threaded embroidery on her black stockings winked in and out of view as she spoke.

Where Lindsey's tastes ran to classic, Heather's ran to flamboyant. Where Lindsey was conservative, Heather was impulsive. Nevertheless, they both took their careers very seriously, and their friendship had bloomed over the years.

"Seven tomorrow morning. I'm meeting Mom at the airport." Lindsey stifled a small yawn. "I've just got a couple of hours to put in tonight before I head home to pack."

"You're working *tonight?*"

"Not for long. I need to get the Group Twelve proposal in shape for a meeting in the new year." She'd thought it would be easy to spare a week and take her mother away for Christmas, but now the deadlines were beginning to stack up. Even with the invention of microwave food and home dry-cleaning systems, there were simply never enough hours in the day.

Lindsey often wondered how other people coped.

Heather shook her head. "Why do you think these things were invented?" She tapped her polished fingernail against the laptop. "It's so women like you can go home at night."

Lindsey's eyebrows flexed as she watched Heather's tapping finger. What a great idea.

If she took the laptop home tonight, she wouldn't have to stay late. And... Oh... A broad smile parted her lips. If she took the laptop on the trip, she'd have eight whole days to develop a really bang-up presentation for the Group Twelve account. Eight whole days for the ideas to flow freely. She could play with that new graphics program, maybe even animate a slide show.

"What a great idea," she said to Heather. She could make sure her mother had a great Christmas and still use her time profitably—talk about the best of both worlds.

Heather hopped off the reception desk, sliding her small feet into her sandals. "Personally, I'm heading straight home to Roger, my stone fireplace and grilled salmon. I'm not even going to *think* about this place until after the holidays."

Heather's words invoked a cozy, sensual image. The animation project suddenly paled a notch, and Lindsey was forced to squelch a jealous twinge. She shook herself. Where had that come from?

Steady boyfriends and a career track were a recipe for trouble. Lindsey was under no illusion that she could have made Gold Merit with other distractions in her life. Like men.

Heather was constantly pulled in two directions.

Not that she ever complained, and Lindsey was thrilled that her friend had found love. But love wasn't for Lindsey. Not if she wanted a successful career. And she *definitely* wanted a successful career.

She grimaced a little as she stood on her sore feet. "You go home to your gorgeous boyfriend. And I'll go home with my gorgeous laptop." Wait a minute. That sounded a little pathetic.

"I don't know, Lindsey," Heather's eyes lit up. "Maybe Annabelle was right. We should get you a date."

"Oh, *please.*" Lindsey scooped up the laptop. She wasn't pathetic. A simple personal life was a deliberate choice. "Harry the hard drive and I will have a marvelous week together."

"You're taking it with you?"

"Him," corrected Lindsey. "Don't make him feel bad."

"Well, I suppose..." Heather waggled her eyebrows. "It does have possibilities. Depending on the pictures you download..."

Lindsey grimaced. "Ick!"

"Try hot firemen dot com."

"I don't think so."

"Hey, every woman needs some kind of a sex life."

Lindsey pursed her lips and eyed Heather disapprovingly. She had no desire to ogle nameless firemen. She affected a prissy tone. "Harry and I have a platonic relationship."

"You sure you don't want to meet some of Roger's friends?"

"No, thanks." Lindsey patted the laptop. She had

everything she needed in life. "It's just me, Harry and the Gold Merit ladder to success from here on in."

Heather's teasing demeanor disappeared, and she squeezed Lindsey's hand. "I am so *thrilled.* I know how much this means to you."

"Thanks. Now you go see Roger." Lindsey might not have a boyfriend, but she had freedom. And freedom was exactly what a woman needed to pursue a career in the financial world.

"Have a wonderful Christmas, Lindsey."

"You, too." Lindsey gave Heather a final hug.

She was truly looking forward to Christmas this year.

Her father had passed away in early December three years ago. Since then, Christmas had been a particularly difficult time for her mother. But this year, she and her mother, Janet, had been invited to a big, old-fashioned Webster family reunion at a luxury fly-in lodge in the Yukon Territory.

Lindsey and her parents had lived in the Yukon until the year Lindsey turned sixteen. Since they hadn't had extended family in the territory, the Websters had pretty much adopted them. The Webster families and the Parkers had all lived within a few miles of each other. Lindsey's mother and Celia Webster had traded baby-sitting while sharing a job at the local post office.

Her mother seemed genuinely excited about the trip. There was a sparkle in her eye when she talked about leaving gray, drizzly Vancouver for mountains of pristine snow and wide-open spaces. Lindsey hadn't seen that sparkle for a long time.

As Heather made her way toward the exit, Lindsey shrugged into her coat. She'd play around with the laptop tonight and make sure she knew how to use everything. Then she'd be ready to take her proposal writing on the road.

There'd be plenty of downtime between visiting long-lost friends, and there was absolutely no sense in wasting it. She couldn't help but feel a tiny thrill at the thought of all those hours to devote to devising the perfect Group Twelve proposal. People at the office were going to expect big things from her after tonight. She had no intention of disappointing the partners.

As she made her way toward the exit, her gaze caught Annabelle Martin on her handsome husband's arm. Annabelle stood on tiptoe and whispered something in his ear. He grinned, hugged her close and placed a quick kiss on the top of her head.

The funny jealous twinge echoed again. Lindsey shook herself. She'd just made Gold Merit Certification. It was the professional milestone of a lifetime. And she was thrilled to her toes.

ON THE THICK ICE of Wolverton Lake, RJ Webster hoisted a heavy Christmas package out of the passenger seat of his Beaver ski plane. A welcoming plume of smoke rose from the chimney of the cabin on shore, spiraling into the thin, frigid air.

The northern lights shimmered on the horizon as

he adjusted the baggy pants of his rental costume. He started across the ice toward the building. The boys back at the Fifty-Below Tavern would have loved this—a night landing with nothing but the moon and the aurora for illumination. Of course the story would be a whole lot more exciting if he'd hit some overflow or had to avoid a pressure ridge or two.

He guessed a guy couldn't have everything. He was a twelve-year veteran pilot, and the young guys expected a certain level of excitement in his trips. Or at least a decent amount of exaggeration over a Budweiser.

Not that he normally exaggerated. Didn't have to. In his younger years...

Good grief, he hated that phrase.

The door of the cabin opened briefly, and a cloud of steam rose as the warm inside air met the frigid winter wind. Cameron Phillips emerged from his cabin.

Thirty wasn't old. It was really only a day over twenty-nine. Well, three days over twenty-nine now, he supposed. He was sure he'd battle plenty of pressure ridges in the years to come.

"Hey, RJ." Dressed in oversize boots and a down parka, his friend Cameron strode down the worn snow path. "What are you doing here?"

"RJ? Who's RJ?" RJ called, banishing his unaccustomed moodiness. "Santa Claus is here with a special delivery."

When Cameron made his monthly trip to town last

week, he'd been profoundly disappointed to find that his kids' Christmas packages hadn't arrived.

"Aren't you supposed to be at your sister's by now?" asked Cameron. "We're way outta the... *What* are you wearing?"

RJ shifted the pillow that he'd stuffed under his red velvet suit. Watching Cameron's expression, he wondered if dressing up had been such a great idea, after all. "I didn't want the kids to think Uncle RJ had mugged Santa for their presents."

Cameron stared at RJ's fake beard and red cap, apparently speechless. Well, heck, it had seemed like a good idea at the time. Exactly how tacky did he look?

"If you take this box," he prompted, "I'll go get the other one."

"Sure. Of course." Cameron held out his gloved hands, a sudden smile splitting his face. "The kids are gonna bust something when they see you."

RJ grinned in relief, handing off the heavy box to Cameron. "Just don't give me away."

"Not on your life," said Cameron.

RJ trotted to the plane. Happy anticipation hummed through his system as he secured the pillow in his waistband. He really hoped the kids were fooled by the cheap Santa suit. Three days before Christmas was a tough time to find a decent costume.

At the plane he grabbed a second, smaller box. Then he balanced the poinsettia plant he'd wrapped in a protective plastic cover. The plant was an impulse purchase made after Cameron's packages had shown up at the hangar, after RJ had decided to make a detour on the way to his sister Susan's lodge.

He'd figured Cameron's wife, Marianne, would appreciate fresh flowers.

Then an exuberant Saint Nicholas mood had kicked in, and he'd picked out a fancy box of chocolates. After that it was a warm wool sweater and a pair of new mitts for Marianne, then the same for Cameron. He knew how carefully they budgeted and guessed any spare cash would go to presents for the children rather than the adults.

Just before hitting the checkout line, two plush husky dogs had caught his eye. He'd grabbed them for the kids, figuring a couple of extra presents wouldn't hurt them at all. Then he'd wrapped the gifts, put a bow on the chocolates and stuffed everything in a paper sack, which now dangled from his wrist below the poinsettia plant.

"Ho, ho, ho," he bellowed as he met up with Cameron. He wasn't sure if his voice would carry into the thickly insulated log cabin. But two little faces were pressed firmly against the yellow windowpane, and he wanted to make their fantasy as convincing as possible.

Cameron shook his head, falling into step next to RJ. "This is above and beyond the call of duty," he said. But the pleasure in his voice was clear.

"Merry Christmas," RJ called heartily as they mounted the steps.

The door flew open. Seven-year-old Ian and his

little sister, Katie, stared at RJ with wide, unblinking eyes.

Marianne's mouth dropped open in astonishment as she dried her hands in the small kitchen.

"Santa?" asked Katie in a reverent whisper, eyes shining in the lamplight.

"Merry Christmas, Katie. Merry Christmas, Ian." RJ shifted the big poinsettia plant so the children could get a good look at his outfit.

Katie's smile grew and grew.

Ian's eyebrows furrowed as he scanned RJ. "You're early, Santa."

RJ gave another hearty ho ho ho as he moved into the cabin so that Cameron could close the door.

"Why are you early?" Ian persisted.

"Well, kids." RJ placed the packages and the flower on the kitchen table, mind racing for a decent explanation. He should have planned something beforehand. But it never occurred to him that kids would look a gift Santa in the mouth.

"It's like this," he continued. "There's a storm. Yeah, a *big* snowstorm forecast for the whole Yukon on Christmas Eve. So I'm delivering to you folks a little early this year." There. That was pretty good. He stepped back from the table, rather proud of himself.

"Can we open the presents early?" asked Katie with an eager smile.

"No, you can't," said Cameron, ruffling her blond hair.

"But we can put them under the tree." Marianne

moved smoothly toward RJ, ineffectually pressing at the wrinkles in her plain flannel shirt. "R—I mean, Santa." She placed a quick kiss on RJ's cheek. "Thank you *so* much," she whispered, giving his shoulder a squeeze.

"Just doing my job," said RJ. The family's joy felt embarrassingly gratifying. In return for a mere fifty air miles, his heart was puffing up like a balloon.

"Where are the reindeer?" asked Ian, peering out the window again. The kid was way too astute for his tender years.

"Rudolph has a cold." There. Another good on-the-fly story. RJ was getting better at this. "He's resting up for Christmas Eve, so I brought my plane." Thankfully it was too dark for Ian to make out the distinctive blue swirls on the fuselage of RJ's Beaver.

"Who wants to help open the boxes?" asked Marianne, drawing Ian away from the window.

"Do reindeer get colds?" asked Ian.

"I do. I do," Katie sang. Her moccasin-covered feet scuffed against the raw wood floor as she headed toward the packing boxes and paper sack.

"Sure they get colds," said Cameron. "Just like kids. Now go help your mother."

"Candy, Ian. Lots of *candy!*" Katie's voice drove the skepticism right out of Ian's posture.

He immediately darted to the table. Apparently, exact explanations weren't required when there was candy involved.

Marianne held up the box of chocolates, a questioning expression directed at Cameron.

Cameron raised his eyebrows at RJ.

"I grabbed a couple of little things on the way out of tow—the *workshop,*" said RJ.

"This one's for you, Mommy."

Marianne gently took the small parcel from her daughter's outstretched hand. When she looked at RJ her eyes were shimmering.

Shoot, it was only a pair of mittens.

"This one's for me," said Ian, pulling a wrapped package out of the big carton in a hail of foam chips and packing paper. He shook the wrapped box against his ear. RJ smiled. The kid was fully into the spirit of Christmas come early.

Cameron cleared his throat. "Put it under the tree, son."

The children began unloading packages and running back and forth from the tree to the table, squealing with each new discovery. Homemade decorations jiggled on the tiny spruce tree as its base became buried in gaily wrapped packages.

"Can you stay, Santa?" asked Marianne, surreptitiously wiping her eyes with the back of her hand.

"I'm afraid not. I'm already late for Susan's."

She bit her lower lip. "I don't know what to—"

"Don't." RJ shook his head, smiling gently at Marianne. "The excitement in their eyes was worth ten times the effort I put out."

"But how can we ever—"

"Just have a wonderful Christmas," said RJ.

"Thank you, Santa." Cameron reached out to

shake RJ's hand. "I don't have to tell you the kids are thrilled."

RJ chuckled, glancing over to where Ian and Katie were arranging then rearranging each and every package. "Believe me, you don't have to say a word."

RJ shifted toward the door.

"Merry Christmas, Santa," Katie called, rushing across the floor to fling herself into RJ's arms. He crouched and hugged her tight.

"I love you, Santa," she whispered.

RJ was forced to blink rapidly. "I love you, too, Katie. You have a very merry Christmas." As he released her, Ian stepped forward.

"Merry Christmas, Santa." He held out his hand.

RJ solemnly shook it. "Merry Christmas, Ian."

Ian stood frozen for a few seconds. Then suddenly his chin wobbled and he threw himself into RJ's arms. "I hope Rudolph feels better."

"Rudolph will be just fine. He's already getting excited about all those cookies on Christmas Eve."

Ian pulled back. "Do the reindeer eat cookies?"

"The reindeer love cookies," said RJ.

Ian turned to Marianne. "Can we send a cookie for Rudolph, Mommy?"

"Sure," she said with a bright smile.

Ian pushed away from RJ and headed for the cookie jar.

"I'll make sure Rudolph gets it," RJ promised.

"Have fun at Susan's," said Cameron in an undertone.

"Huge crowd this year," said RJ. "Nearly every relative for a two-thousand-mile radius."

Cameron shuddered. "Too busy for me."

"Me, too," said RJ. But, strangely, after watching Cameron's children, he was looking forward to seeing all those little nieces and nephews on Christmas morning.

He'd only be able to stand the noise for a short time, of course. But still, that initial excitement in the little ones' eyes would be worth the decibel level.

THE HOMEMADE COOKIES were long gone before the lights of his sister's lodge came into view. The huge log building was also located in the middle of the wilderness, but it was a world apart from Cameron's place. Susan and Seth's lodge was as luxurious as any four-star hotel.

RJ adjusted the flaps and pushed forward on the stick.

His sister and brother-in-law had spent four years on construction alone. They'd opened last spring and were already booked solid through next summer and beyond because a couple of international tour companies had discovered them. Apparently, overseas customers were clamoring for a rustic wilderness experience that came complete with a French chef.

RJ had ferried countless wealthy Europeans in from the airport in Whitehorse. It wasn't exactly thrilling flying, but the tourists paid very well. And the steady income made up for the…well, *settled* feel of the job.

At the lodge, guests lacked for nothing. Generators

supplied them with electricity, and a deep well and propane heaters gave ample hot water to rooms equipped with oversize tubs.

RJ banked the Cessna to line up parallel with three high-wattage lights that shone on the snow-covered runway out front. No pressure ridges here, either. He'd flown his mother and great-aunt Camellia in yesterday and was very familiar with the ice conditions.

Most of the other guests had come in this morning in Graham Marshall's Otter.

His skis touched down smoothly, and he taxied to a sheltered spot in the frozen bay. No one rushed out the front door to meet him. The Christmas carols and the party chatter must have masked his arrival. That was okay. He hadn't expected a big welcome, anyway.

After doffing the beard and Santa suit in favor of jeans, a ski jacket and a cap, he secured the plane. Then he swung his backpack over one shoulder, hooked his garment bag on a couple of gloved fingers and headed for the wide front deck.

Strains of jingle bells greeted him as he mounted the stairs. He drew closer to the glass doors and could see buffet tables, a punch bowl and a bright wood fire in the central stone fireplace. His mother, his sister, Susan, various nieces and nephews of assorted shapes and sizes, plus a good number of other friends and relatives, were clustered in the high-ceilinged great room.

He couldn't immediately identify all the adults, and

he wondered if he'd missed some weddings over the past few years.

Hand on the doorknob, he hesitated, savoring the last moments of peace. Susan was handing her youngest daughter, Rose-Marie, a glass of red punch. Then she turned to speak to her twin sons, Jeffry and Aidan, who were racing their fire engines across the buffet table. A person had to wonder just what Chef Henri thought of tire tracks in his canapés.

RJ's glance strayed to Rose-Marie's white lacy dress and that brimming cup of red punch. He cringed when she began to bounce up and down in place. Without missing a beat while reprimanding her boys, Susan deftly scooped the punch out of her daughter's hand.

RJ shook his head, thinking about his quiet cabin on the shores of Lake Lebarge. This week was going to be total bedlam.

Across the room, he spotted his cousin Bobby beside the fireplace, cola and something in his ring-bedecked hand. RJ tried to get along with self-absorbed Bobby, he really did. They were the same age and often played together while they were growing up.

But, during their teenage years, Bobby had changed. He ran a bar now, favored loud clothes and even louder parties and surrounded himself with so many brainless, adoring women he couldn't hope to keep his ego in check.

In fact, Bobby was chatting up a couple of attractive women right now. RJ didn't recognize them. At least he didn't recognize their profiles. They must be new wives or girlfriends brought to the party.

He hoped, for their sakes, neither was dating Bobby.

His attention was snagged by the woman on his cousin's right. His gaze started at her deep brown French braid and made a leisurely trail down her shimmering, midnight-purple cocktail dress, along shapely calves to high-heeled sandals right out of a man's deepest fantasy. He glanced at the other woman. She was attractive enough, but his eyes insisted on revisiting the midnight purple.

He caught Bobby checking out the woman's cleavage. Then his cousin shifted closer to her.

She couldn't be with Bobby. Surely fate wouldn't waste a classy lady like that on his cousin.

RJ's ears started to burn from the cold wind, and he turned the doorknob to slip inside.

Just as he shut the door, the seasonal music came to an abrupt halt. Great-Aunt Camellia turned from the stereo system to survey the room with faded blue eyes. Her jewel-bright dress fell in gentle folds against her rounded hips, and her cane dangled from one forearm.

She tapped her wineglass with a spoon handle. The tinkling sound hushed voices as she glanced myopically around. Her expression was a study in concentration.

Her gaze came to rest on RJ, although he knew she couldn't really see him from this distance. "I have a prediction." She addressed the entire room without preamble, smoothing the riotous curls of her henna-colored hair.

Her announcement guaranteed everyone's attention. Aunt Camellia's predictions were the very foundation of Webster family folklore.

She'd predicted the rise of several prominent stocks—making herself and other family members tidy sums of money. She routinely predicted the weather and sports scores. Though RJ privately noted she only hit the mark on those about half the time. And, of course, she always had colorful, convoluted explanations when she missed.

But it was the armed insurrection in a small Latin American country that still had RJ scratching his head. That one had to be the longest shot of the century, yet Aunt Camellia had been right on the nose.

She soaked up every second of the extended family's attention. Her gaze moved across the room, and RJ followed it. It settled on the midnight-purple woman standing next to Bobby.

The woman must have felt Aunt Camellia's regard, because she made a half turn so she was looking directly at her.

RJ felt his stomach hit a low-pressure pocket.

Lindsey Parker?

The gorgeous midnight-purple woman was Skinny Linny from high school?

This was how the strait-laced, prissy girl had turned out? The one he'd spent years trying to get to chill out and crack a smile for him. One smile. Any smile.

He knew he'd gone overboard teasing her in the

end. Nobody would have smiled at some of the stunts he'd pulled. But it was such fun to see her mouth purse into that little moue of anger and watch her green eyes flash fire as she tried to repress her baser emotions and keep herself from killing him.

"I predict," said Aunt Camellia, pressing her weathered fingertips into her temple and scrunching up her forehead with all the pizzazz of a one-nine-hundred commercial psychic. "Lindsey Parker is going to marry our Robert."

Lindsey's face blanched.

Bobby's eyes lit up, and his lascivious grin stretched a mile wide.

Though RJ stood by his opinion that the grown-up Skinny Linny was *way* too classy for Bobby, he felt a latent shot of mischief hit his system. Lindsey's confounded expression took him back in time.

He was far too old to tease her now, but he couldn't suppress a small grin as Great-Aunt Camellia went one better than he'd ever dreamed.

2

LINDSEY nearly choked on her Bordeaux. Marry Bobby Webster? Her gaze shot sideways to his salon-tanned face, fashion-chasing goatee and that ostentatious gold-nugget earring. Age must have finally caught up with Camellia. The woman had lost her mind.

Pronouncement made, the elderly Camellia returned to her seat and let the effect of her words ripple through the crowd. A buzz of conversation started immediately. And Lindsey became the object of thirty sets of eyes.

She took an involuntary step backward. Oh, no, no, no. Camellia's predictions were all well and good for entertaining the children, but they tended to induce a sort of mass hysteria, and Lindsey was not about to get caught in the middle of it.

Bobby's mother, Connie, swept across the room. The spindly woman pulled Lindsey into a claustrophobic, perfume-sweet embrace. She kissed the air on either side of Lindsey's cheeks. "Welcome to the family, honey," she said in a voice loud enough for onlookers.

''Connie,'' Lindsey frantically whispered. ''This isn't—''

But Connie abruptly released Lindsey and turned her attention to her son. She swatted Bobby playfully on the arm, her voice tinkling with laughter. ''Why didn't you say something?''

An inarticulate exclamation worked its way through Lindsey's throat. Thankfully, the Christmas music swelled to life before it could escape.

Susan's children and some of her nieces and nephews started dashing between the tables, drawing a bit of attention away from Lindsey. Thank goodness. The floor couldn't open up and swallow her fast enough.

''We wanted to surprise you.'' Bobby's arm encircled Lindsey's bare shoulders, fingertips brushing familiarly against her spaghetti strap as he engulfed her in a wave of industrial-grade cologne—musk, and very nearly fatal.

She shrugged him off with a shudder and took a step away. This was ridiculous. She wasn't letting the lounge lizard use his eccentric aunt as an excuse to grope her or incapacitate her with toxic fumes.

''I'm overwhelmed,'' said Connie. ''Pleasantly overwhelmed,'' she added.

''This isn't funny,'' Lindsey pointed out. ''Bobby and I haven't seen each other in over a decade. I didn't even recognize him tonight.'' Lindsey had been sixteen years old and Bobby seventeen when she and her mother moved out of the Yukon.

Connie's hand fluttered to her breast. ''Then this is

where it's all going to happen. Love is going to bloom this Christmas.'' She looked frighteningly serious.

Lindsey stared at the model-thin, perfectly made-up, apparently *thrilled* Connie, searching desperately for a glint of humor. There wasn't one. A wave of anxiety crept into Lindsey's chest.

A few coincidental stock purchases aside, Connie couldn't really believe that Camellia actually predicted the future. That was just for the children. Just for entertainment. Right?

''Congratulations, you two lovebirds.'' Susan's father, Henry, slapped Bobby on the back. ''You sly dog.'' He winked outrageously.

Lindsey glanced frantically around the room, hoping against hope for a collective burst of laughter that would end the joke. She could be a good sport about this.

Really.

She swallowed.

Well, for a few minutes, anyway.

She scanned the faces of the onlookers, but all she saw were curious gazes and speculative smiles. Connie's was the most curious and speculative of all.

Lindsey searched for her mother, hoping for a little support to head off the fiasco. Her gaze moved from the buffet to the fireplace to the door. There it stopped as she focused on a tall stranger. The man's lips were curved in a wry, knowing smile, and she could almost feel his mirth from across the room.

She relaxed in relief. His expression was exactly

what she'd hoped for. This guy was definitely enjoying a great big joke. And he couldn't be the only one.

Nobody thought she was going to marry Bobby.

Everyone was just playing along.

Thank goodness.

Without breaking eye contact, he shrugged out of his jacket and hung it on one of the pine coat hooks near the entrance. For a second Lindsey thought she recognized him. But then she decided it was either wishful thinking or a trick of the bouncing oil-lamp shadows on the planes and angles of his face.

A waiter offered the man some wine. He accepted a glass of red. As his lips closed on the rim of the glass, Lindsey felt a shimmer of awareness skitter through her chest. He took a long, slow sip.

Annabelle's teasing at the office party last night flashed through her mind. This guy was definitely date material. He was by far the most attractive man she'd come across in the past ten months, and it *was* Saturday night. Perhaps fate was giving her a hand, after all.

He had to be six foot two. Broad-shouldered and slim-hipped, he had a strong, square chin and a killer smile that lit up his dark, intelligent eyes.

Lindsey let her gaze linger speculatively, not even minding that he might read her interest. She was on a holiday, after all. And if a gorgeous guy dropped right into her lap, there was no harm in looking. It wasn't like she'd compromise her career simply by looking.

He raised his glass in a mock toast, regarding her

just as openly as she him. A shiver tripped along her spine, raising goose bumps on her bare shoulders.

"What do you say, sugar?" Bobby nudged her, nearly spilling her remaining wine.

"What?" She glanced at Bobby, annoyed at being forced to give up the flirty eye contact with the guy across the room. It had been years since she'd flirted.

"New Year's," said Bobby.

"It would be perfect," said Connie. "Fireworks and champagne."

"Perfect," agreed Henry with a sage nod.

"What do you think?" asked Bobby.

"Do whatever you want for New Year's." Lindsey didn't plan to be anywhere near Bobby when the clock struck midnight. She shuddered at the very thought of a slack-lipped kiss. "Can you excuse..." She turned back, but the mystery man was gone. There was nothing left but an empty doorway.

So much for fate and a helping hand.

She suppressed a wave of disappointment. If he was here for the week, she was sure to run into him again.

"Lindsey Parker?" asked a voice directly behind her. It was deep, dark and delicious. She let her lips curve into a seductive smile.

It had to be him.

She turned, deciding then and there to throw caution to the wind. Maybe Heather was right, and Harry the hard drive wasn't the be-all and end-all of a woman's romantic life.

As she focused on the mystery man, shock made

her facial muscles go lax. Her jaw dropped open in a completely undignified manner.

"You?" she gasped.

His wry smile suddenly seemed mocking. The tilt of his square chin reminded her of the thousand times he'd plotted pranks against her.

Of *course* he was enjoying Camellia's joke. He'd probably set it up. He'd probably bribed Camellia with that sickly, witty charm that seemed to work on every female on the planet except Lindsey.

The rat. She snapped her jaw shut.

"Skinny Linny," he drawled, blue eyes glowing with private amusement. "We meet again."

"Don't call me that," she automatically replied, then wished she hadn't given her emotions away quite so readily. It was amazing how a single phrase could zap a woman right back to her awkward teenage years.

She wished she'd remembered that he was going to be here. She could have prepared herself. She could have been ready with a cool, sophisticated comeback, which showed how little his opinion meant to her.

Instead, she had to stand here under his mocking gaze knowing he knew just how much power he still had over her. Tactical error.

One she never should have made.

She could handle being teased, for goodness sake. There was a long line of Webster boys who teased every girl in school. Gary was the oldest, then RJ, then Sam and finally Curtis. Plus there were the cousins, Bobby and Thomas. When necessary, Lindsey could give back as good as she got. But, for some reason, no matter how snappy her retort, RJ always got in the last word. He was the one Webster who had the power to get under her skin.

His gaze moved insolently along the length of her dress. "You're right," he said, taking the scenic route, lingering on her breasts. "The name doesn't fit anymore."

Lindsey forced herself to count to three. She was not going to let him get to her. "Why, thank you," she said, forcing herself to smile. Pretending he'd complimented her dress instead of her breasts.

She could handle RJ for a single week. And she'd find a way to diffuse this silly Bobby prediction, too.

Fortunately for her, Gary, Sam and Thomas were married with small children to look after. And Curtis had brought along a gorgeous supermodel girlfriend. Lindsey suspected his attention was fully occupied for the duration of the week.

Lindsey only needed to worry about Bobby the suitor and RJ the juvenile.

"You've filled out." RJ nudged her a little harder, obviously disappointed by her mild reaction.

"RJ Webster, you apologize this instant." Connie's words rapped a staccato rhythm beside Lindsey's ear.

Thank you, Connie.

"I'm not sorry she filled out." The cocky drawl was vintage RJ.

"You are *not* to speak that way to Bobby's fiancée."

On second thought, maybe she didn't want Connie's help. Lindsey sighed. "I am not—"

Bobby's arm snaked around her shoulders again, choking off the sentence.

"Don't get your knickers in a knot, Aunt Connie. I didn't mean to upset anyone." RJ grinned, his dark blue eyes lighting up in that ingenuous way that had always made teachers and parents alike question facts that were staring them right in the face.

Connie glared, and RJ grinned, and Bobby squeezed affectionately. Lindsey decided retreat was her very best option. She stepped none too gracefully from under Bobby's arm.

"Excuse me," she said to Connie.

"Excuse me," she said to Bobby.

"Excuse me," she said to RJ's chin.

Without giving any of them a chance to respond, she broke free of the group and crossed the great room. Happily, she spotted her mother on the far side.

Avoidance might be the coward's way out, but it was the best thing she could come up with. She'd simply try to stay away from RJ and Bobby for the rest of the week. The wedding prediction should die its own death once everybody realized she wasn't interested. And she was really looking forward to spending time with RJ's sister, Susan.

She and Susan were the same age, and they'd been pretty good friends in high school. Susan might be married with three children and living in the wilderness, but Lindsey was sure they'd still have plenty of things in common.

Besides, the primary point of this trip was to make sure her mother had a great time this Christmas. And *Lindsey* was going to have a great time. She wasn't an insecure teenager anymore. She was a grown woman, a successful woman, a *Gold Medal Certified* woman.

RJ could take his best shot.

She was up to the challenge.

Finding herself in front of her mother sooner than she'd expected, Lindsey came to an abrupt halt.

"You okay, honey?" Concern clouded her mother's eyes as she took in Lindsey's expression.

"Fine." Lindsey nodded, smiling with her new-found determination. "I take it you heard?"

Since Lindsey had never let on to her mother how much RJ's teasing got to her, she knew her mother had to be talking about the wedding prediction.

"Camellia's voice does carry," said Janet, confirming Lindsey's suspicions.

Lindsey shook her head. "I must admit, she's got me feeling extremely self-conscious." She glanced around the room, catching a few covert looks and speculative grins.

"I'm sorry you're uncomfortable about this," said Janet.

Uncomfortable seemed like a mild word, considering she'd just been publicly linked with a preening lounge lizard.

"How do we put a stop to it?" she asked.

The sooner Bobby was off her list of things to worry about this week, the better.

''The excitement will die down before you know it. Don't you worry.'' Her mother took her arm and guided her to a comfortable sofa in one corner of the room, where they were a little away from the main crowd.

Lindsey sat down, giving her feet a grateful rest. She was seriously considering giving up her ultra high-heeled party shoes, no matter what Heather said they did for her calves.

''Do you want to talk about it?'' asked Janet.

''I'd rather forget about it.'' Lindsey didn't want to ruin the party for her mother by complaining. ''Can I get you a glass of wine or something?''

''No, thanks. I've just finished one. And I'm stuffed with Henri's canapés.''

One of Susan's sons zipped by—Jeffry, or maybe it was Aidan—a handful of tinsel trailing from his fingers. He was followed closely by his father, Seth, who was carrying a pair of pajamas.

The mood in the room seemed to be getting back to normal. Her mother was right. The best thing to do was let the silly prediction blow over of its own accord.

''It happens to all of us eventually, you know?'' said Janet. She patted Lindsey's hand.

''Being embarrassed in front of friends and strangers?'' *And in front of your nemesis,* Lindsey added with a silent shudder. Even after ten years, it still rankled when RJ got the last laugh.

''No, honey. Love.''

''Love?''

''You and Bobby. I admit he's not my first—''

"Huh?" The sharp exclamation was the closest Lindsey could come to an actual word. "I am *not* in love with Bobby."

What had happened to letting the whole thing blow over? Lindsey thought they had a plan.

"Of course you're not, dear. It's been years since you've even seen him."

Lindsey sighed in relief. Okay. They still had a plan.

"But you will be," Janet added, smiling benevolently as she nodded.

Yikes! "Are you craz—"

"You know, your father—God rest his soul—and I got off to a very rocky start, too."

"Mom—"

"It takes a while sometimes before the heart knows."

"Moth—"

"I'd go so far as to say I thought your father was the last person in the world I'd marry."

"Bobby *is* the last person in the world I'd marry."

"See what I mean?" Janet smiled again. "You don't have to worry. And you don't have to do a thing. It'll just happen all on its own."

"Mother." Lindsey stared directly into Janet's eyes. "Read my lips. I am *not* marrying Bobby or anyone else."

"I know just how you feel." Janet nodded sympathetically. "But maybe you shouldn't be so emphatic about it in front of Camellia. You know how easily she gets her feelings hurt."

Was Lindsey misunderstanding her mother? *Was*

Janet just going along with this to humor Camellia? "So you believe me?"

"Of course I believe you. Isn't that what I just finished saying?"

"So you're not going to try to throw me and Bobby together?"

"Of course not, dear."

"Thank goodness." Maybe Lindsey hadn't just walked through the looking glass.

"Do you suppose there are any jobs for you in Whitehorse?"

"What?"

"Well, Bobby is part owner of the bar now. I doubt he'd be in a position to—"

"I thought you said you believed me?" Lindsey tried to keep her voice below a shriek. Her mother had gone crazy, too.

"I'm not saying we should force anything. But when it happens—"

"It's not going to happen, Mother. It is *so* not going to happen."

"Of course, dear." Her mother might as well have patted her on the head. It sure wasn't Camellia who was being humored here. "I understand perfectly."

"MERRY CHRISTMAS, Aunt Camellia." RJ leaned down to give her a kiss on the cheek, settling next to her on the couch. He kept one eye on the byplay between Lindsey and her mother across the room. They were head-to-head in conversation. By the looks of things, Lindsey was having quite a struggle.

RJ knew what she was doing. It was exactly what

he'd be doing if Aunt Camellia had made a prediction about him. He'd be telling everyone who would listen that Aunt Camellia had gone dotty in her old age.

Aunt Camellia cocked her head, motioning to Lindsey with a weathered hand. "Well, what do you think?"

"I think you've embarrassed her." And it was going to get much worse. Aunt Camellia's word was pretty much gospel in this family. Poor Lindsey didn't have a prayer.

RJ suppressed a wayward chuckle. He hadn't looked forward to spending a week with this many people, but it would definitely be entertaining to see how unflappable Skinny Linny coped with *this*. She was captive here for the next eight days, and the aunts could probably organize a credible invasion of Normandy in that amount of time. He was in for quite a show.

"But she is pretty, isn't she?" Aunt Camellia watched him through narrow, assessing eyes.

"Who?"

"Don't play coy with me, young man."

RJ sighed. "Yes, she's pretty. She's very pretty." Read sexy, hot, desirable, gorgeous. Too bad about that unbending caustic streak that tended to emasculate anyone who got within range.

Aunt Camellia nodded. "I knew it. These eyes might be old, but they see plenty. You watch your step before the wedding, young man. I don't want any shenanigans from you."

"Me?" Could Aunt Camellia sense that he was

physically attracted to Lindsey? He hadn't said or done anything about it. And he certainly wouldn't.

So she was pretty. His gaze strayed to her again.

Really pretty.

Drop-dead pretty.

So what? There were plenty of drop-dead pretty women in the world. And none of the others could cut him to ribbons with a mere look. Nor were they quasi-engaged to his cousin.

Lindsey was dangerous, and RJ was way past the age where he considered himself invincible. He was taking the safe road here. He was going to sit back, keep his hands to himself, maybe get an eyeful once in a while and watch her squirm under the ludicrous prediction that she would marry Bobby.

He loved watching Lindsey while she was off balance. Always had.

"I mean it, RJ," said Camellia. She gave him a stern look that he remembered well from his teenage years.

"Don't worry about me." He held up his hands in mock surrender. "I have no intention of engaging in *shenanigans* or anything else with Lindsey Parker."

Camellia harrumphed as his gaze strayed to where Lindsey sat with her mother. He was only going to watch. He wouldn't touch.

He gritted his teeth as she leaned over to settle her foot into that sexy high heel.

No matter how tempting it became.

3

LINDSEY HAD BEEN assigned one of four bedrooms on the second floor of the lodge's south wing. Camellia was across the hall.

Like the great room, the north and south wings were built of peeled logs that Susan and Seth had cut from the surrounding forest. The lodge had sixteen guest bedrooms, plus the family living quarters in a separate building connected to the kitchen by a heated passageway.

Lindsey had fully expected to share a room with her mother. But since the children were having a giant slumber party in the basement recreation room, there were plenty of private rooms for the adults.

Hers was gorgeous. It had an en suite bathroom, a king-size bed, couch, table and a private hot tub tucked into a little plant-dotted alcove. The sliding glass doors that opened to a balcony overlooked the frozen lake and the craggy mountain range beyond. Lindsey wondered if all the rooms were this lavish or if she'd just lucked out.

While she unpacked her suitcase, she debated cranking up the laptop immediately or taking a soak in the deep tub. Her creativity was always at its peak late at night, and she had plenty to do. But she also thought she deserved a chance to switch gears after that odd welcome party.

Tonight had been one unsettling experience after another. And she really did deserve an hour to relax.

Having convinced herself, she left her suitcase to turn on the taps and start filling the tub. There was a selection of soaps and bath oils arranged in a seashell next to the tub. She chose citrus and broke the seal on the mini bottle.

When she returned to her unpacking, the room was filling with a wonderful combination of orange blossom and lemon. She shook out a pair of blue jeans, then folded them on the bed. This felt more like a vacation.

Marry Bobby? Not a snowball's chance. But it was too bad the prediction alone had the power to put such a damper on the atmosphere this week.

She pulled out her nightgown. She was going to be battling sidelong looks and suggestive comments every day unless she could get Camellia to retract the prediction.

Lindsey paused with the white satin dangling from her fingertips. Camellia retracting the prediction... That would work.

If Camellia called it off, Bobby and Connie would both leave her alone, and RJ would have nothing to tease her about.

Then she could spend the week focusing on her mother, the business proposal and citrus-scented bath products.

Perfect.

All she had to do was convince Camellia to change her prediction. She could do that. After all, she routinely convinced cynical investors to part with thousands upon thousands of dollars for high-risk business ventures. One elderly woman couldn't be that difficult.

She loved Camellia dearly, but enough was enough. Lindsey cringed at the memory of Bobby's hands on her bare shoulders. They'd been soft and warm and vaguely repulsive. She had absolutely no desire to spend the rest of the week fending him off.

She dropped her negligee on the bed, shut off the tub faucet and headed out to the second floor hallway.

Her stocking feet left footprints in the thick, cream-colored carpet, and silence buffeted her passage. The building logs were solid and well chinked. Though there were nearly forty people in the lodge, she might have been completely alone.

"Camellia?" she called softly, rapping on the bedroom door. "Camellia?"

"She won't hear you."

Lindsey jumped at the sound of RJ's voice.

"Once she takes her hearing aids out, she's deaf as a doorpost."

"Don't sneak up on me like that." Lindsey turned to confront him. Her loose hair tickled her cheek as she moved, and she brushed it behind her ear.

"I didn't sneak." Dressed in faded jeans and a black T-shirt, he was less than two feet away. His gaze had followed the movement of her hand. It lingered on the mass of dark curls brushing her neck.

"Then what are you doing?" She wished he wouldn't stare at her so intently. Her loose hair and stocking feet put her at a distinct disadvantage.

"I'm going to bed," he drawled. "What are you doing?"

"I'm going to talk some sense into your aunt." She turned to knock again. Maybe Camellia was just in the bathroom.

A muffled snore rumbled through the closed door.

"Not tonight you aren't." RJ shifted a bit closer.

Darn. She should have come over here earlier. She tipped her head to glare at RJ, still half convinced he'd put his aunt up to this. Her expression faltered when their height difference registered. When had he grown so tall?

"This is absurd," she said, trying to unobtrusively retreat from his solid form.

"You think it's absurd that an old lady is sleeping at—" RJ raised his wrist to look at his watch "—midnight?" His eyebrows shot upward.

Lindsey didn't answer. Trading quips with RJ was risky at the best of times. She wasn't about to try it at midnight in her stocking feet.

His callused hand returned to his side, and her gaze involuntarily followed. Some wayward part of her brain began speculating on its strength and texture. RJ's hand was so different from Bobby's.

"Why can't you just leave me alone?" She

dragged her gaze to his face. She was *not* interested in RJ's hand.

He leaned in, pointing to the door next to hers, voice dropping to a husky whisper. "Because you're between me and my bed."

The timbre of his voice made the words evocative, and she swore she felt his body heat swirl out in the cool hallway. The temperature of her skin took a sudden spike. "I'm not the least bit interested in where your bed is."

"Want to know where Bobby's is?"

"No!"

"Saving yourself for the wedding night?" His chuckle was knowing, reminding her that while he might be insufferable, he was also quite possibly the only other person who realized this wedding prediction was silly.

"Keep this up and you won't *live* till the wedding night," she countered.

"Ah." RJ shifted to lean indolently against the log wall. He crossed his arms. The posture made his biceps stand out in relief. "So you admit there *is* going to be a wedding night."

"I most certainly do not." Her voice was tart as an early apple.

"Bobby not your type?"

She shook her head, voice low and definite. "Not in this lifetime."

"So where do you suppose Aunt Camellia got her inspiration?" He tilted his head reproachfully, as if

Lindsey was somehow responsible for Camellia's outrageous prediction.

"I don't know, RJ." Lindsey leaned against the wall on the other side of Camellia's door, crossing her arms defiantly, matching his posture. "Where do *you* suppose she got her inspiration?"

She watched him carefully, waiting for the sign that he was the one who had put Camellia up to this.

"New age channeling?" he suggested. "Astrological signs? Dreams?"

"What about great-nephews?" Lindsey refused to respond to the impish grin that had carried him so easily through life.

"Bobby?" he asked, face a picture of innocence.

"You, RJ."

"What?" he looked genuinely confused.

"Don't tell me you don't think this is the greatest prank of the decade. Set Skinny Linny up and watch her squirm."

RJ shook his head. "Much as I'd like to, I can't take credit for it."

She scoffed.

"Honest." He held up his hands in a gesture of surrender. "I wish I could." His gaze traveled the length of her body once again. "Though the Skinny Linny I remember sure has changed."

"RJ, stop." His silly ogling game was having a ridiculous effect on her body.

"Sorry." His gaze returned to her face, all traces of cockiness gone.

"You think Camellia actually believes this stuff?" she asked.

"I'm sure she does," said RJ.

"What about the rest of them? What about you?"

He paused. And for a second there, he actually looked like he was having a reflective thought. "She sure nailed the Bochesky Revolution. I never did figure that one out."

"The Bochesky Revolution?" Lindsey frowned.

He got a faraway look in his eyes. "Maybe if this clairvoyance gig doesn't work out she can get a job with the CIA."

"What are you talking about?" Was he setting her up for another joke?

RJ didn't look like he was joking. But when had that ever meant anything?

"Camellia predicted the revolution weeks before CNN. And I have to tell you, that one made even cynical me sit up and take notice."

"You believe she can tell the future?" Lindsey choked out a disbelieving laugh. Just how gullible did he think she was?

He shrugged his broad shoulders. The ones Lindsey *wasn't* noticing.

"Let's just say I hope she never predicts me ditching my plane."

"Would that scare you?"

"Out of my mind."

Lindsey bit her lower lip. "Would you play the stock market based on her say-so?"

"In a New York minute."

"You're putting me on, aren't you?"

"Believe what you want. Her dividends speak for themselves."

Lindsey drew in a breath. If even RJ wasn't sure about Camellia, everyone else must be picking out china patterns by now. A sinking feeling gripped her stomach, and she groaned.

"You okay?" he asked, looking for all the world like he truly cared.

"Do you think she would..." Lindsey cleared her throat as wonder warred with curiosity. RJ was the last person she should be looking to for answers.

She pressed her lips together.

"What?" he asked, leaning in a bit closer.

Okay. Pride be darned. He was here, and he sure seemed to know a lot more than she did.

"I mean..." Lindsey continued. "Just how bad is this likely to get for me before it blows over?"

"Depends," he replied, mouth curving into a small grin.

Why, oh, why was she doing this to herself? This was RJ, for goodness sake. That concerned expression was a fleeting illusion. How many times had he led her down the garden path to humiliation by trailing tantalizing bits of information like bread crumbs?

Despite herself, she gritted her teeth and took the bait. "On what?"

"On how you feel about baby-name books."

Lindsey groaned again, letting her head drop forward. "This is ludicrous. Why would anybody *believe* her?"

"She's got a pretty good track record."

The hallway was suddenly pitched into darkness.

"What happened?" Lindsey glanced around, the total black throwing her off balance.

"Generator." RJ's deep, disembodied voice seemed unnaturally close. "Hold on, I'll just—"

"Ouch!" She lost her balance. Her hands automatically flailed out, one of them stabilizing against RJ's shoulder.

"Sorry." His hands closed around her waist.

"That was my foot." Big hands, warm hands, secure hands. Her hormones leaped instantly to attention, and she sizzled with the brush of his fingertips on her spine.

His scent surrounded her. His body heat enticed her. This was crazy. She was no more interested in RJ than she was in Bobby.

Her eyes adjusted to the faint moonlight from the window at the end of the hall.

A flashlight beam rounded the corner.

"Oh," said Connie's voice. Bobby's father, Jackson, was with her. She shone the flashlight from RJ's face to Lindsey's and back again. "RJ? And... *Lindsey?*"

Lindsey cringed and took a step backward, yanking her hand away from RJ's shoulder.

RJ took a second longer to let go of her waist.

Perfect. Now she'd betrayed the fiancé she didn't even have. She scrambled to think of something to do or say that wouldn't make this look even worse.

RJ moved across the hall, struck a match and put

it to the wick of an oil lamp. As the flame swelled to life and lit up the hallway, he replaced the glass chimney.

"So, I guess you two were..." Connie's voice trailed away as her pupils ping-ponged between RJ and Lindsey.

"Talking," supplied RJ.

"About?" asked Connie.

"Nothing much," said RJ with an innocent smile that fairly screamed guilt.

Lindsey gritted her teeth. He was looking like that on purpose. He knew perfectly well how to look innocent innocent, not guilty innocent. Lindsey had seen him do it a thousand times.

"I see." Connie drew back her shoulders.

"I'm quite sure you do." RJ didn't elaborate.

Silent seconds ticked off.

"Good night," Connie finally said, drawing out the words, obviously reluctant to leave.

"Night," said RJ.

"Good night," added Lindsey, moving toward her bedroom door, deciding a simple, hasty exit was probably her best course of action.

"I thought she was marrying Bobby," whispered Jackson as they moved down the hall.

Connie elbowed him in the ribs.

RJ grinned.

Lindsey tried to twist her doorknob.

The other bedroom door swung firmly closed on an accusing look from Connie.

Lindsey jiggled the stuck knob ineffectually. "You

did that on purpose,'' she whispered with a glare in RJ's direction. The knob didn't budge.

''What did I do?''

Oh, yeah. *Now* he looked innocent innocent. Why did the stupid door have to lock automatically? Why now?

She gave up trying to turn the knob, dropping her voice to a whisper, easily picturing Connie with her ear pressed up against the inside of her bedroom door. ''You let them think....''

''What?'' he asked, sauntering slowly toward her, matching his low tone to hers.

''That...'' She pointed from him to her and back again. All the while he closed in, and her pulse started to react. As if his proximity mattered. As if his proximity had the power to do things to her circulatory system.

She held her breath and tried to slow her pounding heart. ''That you and me in the hall were...well...*you* and *me* in the hall.''

He shoved his hands into his jeans pockets and glanced around. ''This *is* the hall. And we *are* you and me.''

''You know what I mean.'' She hated it when he twisted her words, deliberately misunderstanding her.

''Would you rather we got out of the hall? We could go into my room.''

''No!'' She modulated her voice. ''Jeez, Connie's probably got her eye pressed up against the peephole as it is.'' She tried the doorknob one more time. She needed to get out of Connie's viewfinder. She needed to get away from the totally unconscionable reaction she was having to RJ.

"Problem?" he asked, crowding even closer, making her skin itch.

"No problem." She ground the words out.

"Locked?"

"No."

He shook his head and chuckled. "It's locked, Lindsey."

"I'll get another key from Susan."

"Susan's in bed."

"Then I'll..." What could she do? Wake Susan? Sleep on the couch?

"Our balconies are joined."

"What?"

"Our balconies. Come in through my room, and you can cut across the balcony."

"Are you crazy?" she whispered. "Connie will see us."

"Worried she'll tell Bobby?"

"Of course not." Lindsey hesitated, trying to figure out why she cared what the heck Connie saw. Worst-case scenario, she'd tell Bobby that Lindsey was having a screaming affair with RJ, and Bobby would call off the wedding. Actually that was probably a best-case scenario. But Connie would also tell everyone else.

"I don't care what Bobby thinks," she clarified.

"Then why not come in through my room?" His gaze dropped to her lips in the soft lamplight.

Lindsey's chest constricted. No, no, no. She was

not reacting to him. Now that she knew he was him and not some stranger with whom she was destined to have a Christmas fling, she was completely immune to any physical attraction.

"I may not care about Bobby's opinion." She quickly filled the silence between them. "But I care about my mother's opinion. And I care about Susan's opinion. And I care about Camellia's opinion. She may be a dotty old woman, but she's an honorable dotty old woman, and I love her dearly. It would be worse than tacky to trot into your bedroom after midnight."

"I was only suggesting you cut through." But his eyes smoldered. Then he blinked, and he looked innocent innocent again. Was he flirting?

That was ridiculous. He just wanted to get a rise out of her.

"Tell you what," she hurriedly suggested. "You go into your room, cut across the balcony and open my door from the inside. I'll pretend to open it from out here. Just stay hidden behind the door while you let me in."

"You're joking."

"Why would I be joking?"

"Isn't that a lot of trouble to keep your non-fiancé's mother from getting suspicious?"

"I told you I didn't care about Bobby."

"You sure about that?"

"I am absolutely and completely positive about that."

"But you still want me to crouch behind your door

like a criminal?'' He cocked his head to one side, an amused expression covering his face.

''Yeah.''

''Whatever you say, Skinny Linny,'' he drawled, turning to saunter away. Lindsey wished she could afford to toss out a sarcastic remark.

As he inserted the key into his door, he turned back to wink at her. ''See you in the morning,'' he stage-whispered. Something thumped against the inside of Connie's door.

RJ LIT the battery lamp on the table beside Lindsey's king-size bed. Seth often shut down the main generator for a few hours in the middle of the night. Interruption to the guests was minimal, since the water pump was on a separate power source, and all the rooms were equipped with battery lamps.

As RJ straightened, his gaze was caught by a white negligee lying on the bed beside the open suitcase. He froze, staring at it for a moment as his wayward mind conjured up a vision of her draped in satin and lace. His hand made an involuntary move toward the garment before he snapped it back, clenching his fingers into a fist.

Skinny Linny, he reminded himself, turning sharply for the door, leaving the negligee undisturbed. She was the girl he'd fought with for years. She was prim and proper and sarcastic, and she hated him.

He stiffly marched across the floor, forcing his thoughts away from her creamy skin and the killer body that moved with such fluid grace beneath her form-fitting dress.

He reached out, fingers tightening around the metal doorknob. He heaved a sigh. She might be the girl who hated him, but unfortunately, she was also a woman on the verge of blowing his mind.

He cursed under his breath and yanked the door open.

She had a tight grasp on the doorknob, and her arm stretched straight out. She stumbled toward him.

"Hey," she gasped.

At the last second, he remembered she wanted him to hide behind the door. He stepped quickly to one side, feeling like an adulterer.

"You did that on purpose." She glared at him in the dim light, swiftly shutting the door behind her.

"What did I do this time?"

"Why do you have to be so...so...*you?*"

How could he possibly be attracted to someone who was so downright ornery? "All I did was sneak across a freezing balcony to help you out of a jam."

"Oh." Her glare faltered. "Right. Thanks."

"Never mind." He hadn't hidden quickly enough, and he *had* opened the door too fast. "It's just..." He struggled to explain.

Just that he was upset?

Just that he was attracted?

Just that he was totally, inappropriately and frustratingly aroused?

As she gazed at him, every hormone and nerve ending stood at attention and begged him to *do* something. They were only inches apart. She was against the door. He was facing her.

They were alone.

Completely alone.

Probably for the first time in their lives.

Nobody knew he was in here, some crazy part of his mind pointed out. He swayed forward an extra inch and inhaled her dusky floral scent. He studied her jewel green eyes. A strand of her dark hair had fallen over one brow, and he reached out to touch it.

Neither of them breathed as he brushed it across her temple, barely touching her skin, barely testing its heat.

"Lindsey," he whispered, letting his fingertips linger in the soft strands mere millimeters from her scalp.

Her eyes widened, and her lips parted. "Oh, no," she breathed.

It was either an acknowledgment of their cataclysmic attraction or a denial of the inevitable. He couldn't tell which. He wasn't sure he cared.

Every particle of his being screamed at him to kiss her mouth. He longed for it, ached for it. Despite his better judgment, he dipped toward her.

"RJ?" Her voice seemed miles away and nearly indecipherable through the roaring in his ears.

Her sweet breath fanned his face. His fingers contacted her scalp. They curled and anchored in her thick hair.

She didn't move, simply stared at him as he drew closer, her breath coming faster.

What had happened to the girl whose sharp tongue could slice him to ribbons? Where was his feisty rival? Why wasn't she killing him for daring to make a move on her?

He gave her one final second to take him out before he boldly crossed the last inch and his lips captured hers.

She was sweet.

She was hot.

She was soft and supple and malleable beneath his kiss.

Liquid fire rushed through his veins. He opened wider, coaxing a response as his free hand moved to encircle her waist. He pulled her tight against him. There was no mistaking his body's reaction.

She tipped her head back with a soft moan, and he took. He took everything she had to offer, some dim part of his brain noting that something this good couldn't possibly be real.

"RJ?" Her voice trembled against his mouth.

"Yeah?" His moved to kiss her neck.

"This…"

He kissed her earlobe.

"Is…"

He kissed her temple.

"Really…"

He kissed her mouth once more.

She mumbled something against his lips.

It sounded vaguely like, "We can't," but he wasn't in the mood to give his hearing the benefit of the doubt.

"RJ." Her voice was stronger this time, with an edge of desperation. There was a definite intonation of *no* in it that a lifetime of principles wouldn't let him ignore.

He pulled back just far enough to break contact with her mouth. "Yeah?"

"Does the word *insane* mean anything to you?"

"Yeah." Oh, yeah. The word insane was invented for this very moment. He fought a mental war between dragging himself farther away or kissing her again and having himself committed. Instinct pulled him forward. Logic held him back.

Logic finally won. He loosened his grip on her waist and disentangled his fingers from her hair.

"I'm sorry," he whispered, lying through his teeth. The only thing he was sorry about was that she wasn't the kind of woman who could throw caution to the wind, dive into bed with him and explore this avalanche of unexpected chemistry between them.

"You should leave now." She stared directly at the floor, chest rising and falling rapidly beneath her tight purple dress.

"I know." He willed his feet to move, but they were stuck fast to the carpet.

Seconds ticked by.

"RJ."

"I'm going." He raked a hand across his hair and sucked in a deep breath. The log walls creaked, wood fibers contracting with the ravages of the outside temperature. His body empathized.

"I hate to point out the obvious...." She tipped her head far enough to focus on his chest.

He forced himself to take a step back. "See? I'm almost gone."

"Almost," she muttered, still not making eye contact.

"Lindsey?" He wasn't sure what he was going to say. He only knew he couldn't walk out onto that cold balcony, go back to his own room and pretend the universe hadn't shifted.

"Please, RJ." She raised her lashes to look pleadingly into his eyes. "This never happened."

He stared at her in stony silence, frustration obliterating what he was sure should be softer emotions. "How could anything have happened?" He choked the words out. "I was never here."

4

NOTHING had happened, Lindsey reminded herself for the hundredth time since RJ left her room last night. It was a simple kiss.

So he'd made her heart beat faster. So he'd made her lungs work harder. That was only natural. He was a good-looking guy, and she hadn't been kissed like that in…

Well, okay, in forever. But it really didn't mean a thing. It was over and done with.

She peeked through the doorway into the lodge's dining room, surreptitiously checking out the people helping themselves to a continental breakfast buffet. No Bobby, no Connie, no RJ.

Luck was with her. She let out the breath she'd been holding, adjusting the waistband of her multi-hued red and green sweater as she stepped into the room. The coffee smelled heavenly, and she quickly headed to the silver urn and poured herself a cup. Her plan was to blend in with the crowd and hope that by some miracle nobody mentioned Camellia's prediction.

Thankfully, the dining room was already a bustle of activity. People were filling their plates then heading into a separate section dotted with table groupings. Some had obviously finished breakfast and were getting a head start on decorating the lodge for Christmas Day. Long tables at one end of the room were covered in tinsel, greenery and boxes of Christmas balls.

The room hadn't fallen silent when she entered. And nobody pointed at her and gasped. So far, so good. She wandered down the length of the buffet.

It looked sumptuous—fresh fruit, pastries, eggs and bacon. Krista and Helen, RJ's sisters-in-law, crossed her line of vision and uncoiled a roll of fluffy silver garland. They chatted vigorously while sizing up various spots on the log wall.

Lindsey spotted her mother on a step stool. Her mother had a big grin on her face and a length of string in one hand.

Coffee cup in hand, Lindsey headed toward her. Breakfast could wait a few more minutes. It warmed her heart to see her mother so happy, particularly at Christmastime.

"Can you hand me some mistletoe, Lindsey?" her mother called.

"You be careful up there, Mom." Following her mother's pointing finger, she located a sprig of silk mistletoe on a table covered in holly, pine boughs and poinsettia plants.

Just as a precaution, she glanced around for Bobby before even touching the stuff. Maybe she was paranoid, but she wouldn't put it past him to come leaping out of the woodwork, puckered up and aiming for her lips.

"Don't worry about me." Her mother accepted the mistletoe. "I'm surefooted as an antelope." Then she giggled—actually giggled like a schoolgirl.

Lindsey sniffed the coffee, checking it for signs of liquor. Nothing but pure Colombian beans. She took a deep drink.

"Now that you know where it is—" her mother secured the mistletoe to the top of a doorframe leading to an outside deck "—you can bring Bobby around later."

"Mom, *please,*" Lindsey hissed, glancing around to see if anyone was listening. "Can we just let that alone?"

"Sure, honey." Janet stepped down off the stool and stood back to admire her decoration. "I won't be a busybody mother. We'll just let things progress naturally. Have you had breakfast yet?"

"Not yet." Lindsey took a bracing swig of coffee, more than delighted to change the subject.

"Try the chocolate croissants. They are absolutely divine. In fact, I think I'm going to propose to Chef Henri after breakfast."

Lindsey choked on her coffee, certain she must have misheard. "What?" she sputtered.

In three years, her mother had never once talked about another romantic relationship. Not even as a joke. Lindsey knew several of her mother's friends had tried to introduce her to men. But she'd never seemed interested.

"Don't look so shocked, dear." She patted Lindsey on the shoulder. "I loved your father dearly, but a woman has needs."

Needs? Lindsey sniffed the coffee again.

"Morning, Lindsey." Susan breezed past them. "How's the blushing bride?"

Lindsey cringed. A couple of the people around her smiled warmly in her direction.

"Better grab yourself some breakfast," said Susan without breaking her stride. "It's decorating day." She hustled through to the kitchen, where a couple of her employees were carrying armloads up from the basement. "Careful of the white boxes," she called to them. "They're fragile."

Lindsey wanted to beg Susan to stop talking about the wedding prediction, but calling after her would only make things worse.

She deliberately turned her attention to her mother.

"Needs?" she asked her mother. She *must* have misunderstood that twinkle in her mother's eye. "What do you mean by *needs?*"

"Oh, you know. A man."

Nope. No misunderstanding there. "A *man?*"

"Yeah. The kind who cooks, does dishes and knows just the right wine to bring to the hot tub." A slight flush rose to her mother's cheeks.

Lindsey was getting that through-the-looking-glass feeling again. "What hot tub?"

Her mother waved her fingers in the general direction of the deck. "The one around the corner overlooking the lake."

Had she missed something last night? Like a geriatric orgy in the hot tub? Okay, so her mother was only forty-nine, hardly ready for hearing aids and orthopedic shoes, but her widowed mother in a hot tub with the French chef? It positively boggled the mind.

Jeffry and Aidan raced by, followed closely by Gary's sons, Frank and David. They were all trailing garland and making airplane noises.

Lindsey quickly lifted her coffee cup out of harm's way.

Sam's oldest, Ricky, was sure to show up any second now. A whole new crop of Webster boys on the loose. Poor Rose-Marie was hopelessly outnumbered. Although Sam's wife, Helen, was six months pregnant and swearing this one was a girl.

"Better grab a croissant while you can," Janet advised above the noise. "They're going fast."

Before Lindsey could ask any more questions about whether or not widows wore black bathing suits in private hot tubs and exactly how much of the right wine had been consumed, her mother headed for Susan and the new boxes of decorations.

Gary and Krista and cutely pregnant Helen had joined Susan to retrieve the Christmas treasures. The dining room was beginning to look like Santa's workshop meets the Chinese New Year.

Later, she'd talk to her mother about... What? The pitfalls of holiday romances? Safe sex? The truth of it was, given Lindsey's focus on her career, her mother probably had more experience on both counts.

Shaking her head in amazement, Lindsey snagged

a warm blueberry bagel from the buffet. She bit into it, and after a moment moaned in appreciation. It was crispy outside, tender inside—scrumptious. She took another bite. On second thought, if it kept her supplied with bagels like this, her mother and Chef Henri could do whatever they wanted in the hot tub.

Her momentary euphoria vanished as Bobby appeared in the room. Swallowing, she quickly ducked out of sight into the dining room next door. She glanced around and spotted Camellia alone at a corner table.

Leaning through the doorway, she checked for Bobby. He was engaged in a conversation. Thank goodness.

The opportunity to talk to Camellia was too good to pass up. Number one on her to-do list today was stopping this marrying Bobby nonsense in its tracks. If she could just get Camellia to recant her prediction, there'd be no more reason to skulk around the lodge.

She made her way to Camellia's table.

The older woman was dressed in a brightly colored caftan. From her flaming hair and liberal makeup to her rhinestone slippers, it was obvious how much she adored attention.

Lindsey smiled. She'd always admired Camellia's willingness to defy convention. The woman might be strong-willed and opinionated, but she was also intelligent and honest. She'd been a role model for Lindsey when she was young.

"Sit down, Lindsey." Camellia rapped an empty chair with her cane.

Lindsey sat down, and Camellia peered into her eyes. ''You didn't get enough sleep,'' she pronounced in a gravelly voice with her characteristic conviction.

''I slept fine,'' Lindsey lied, blinking quickly and taking another sip of the strong coffee.

Though she'd tried valiantly to focus on the Group Twelve proposal last night, images of RJ had hijacked her brain, making her toss and turn. The images would have been bad enough, but they'd been augmented by tactile memories and some kind of imprint of his scent.

Camellia harrumphed. ''I warned him to stay out of your room.''

''*What?*'' A swallow of coffee burned its way down Lindsey's windpipe. Had Camellia been awake last night, after all? Had she seen them through the peephole?

''He's a young reprobate, that one. Always was.'' Camellia lifted her teacup.

Lindsey swallowed, reminding herself that she wasn't here to discuss RJ. If Camellia had seen RJ last night, there was nothing they could do about it now.

But Lindsey *was* going to accomplish her primary objective. And she *was* going to take control of this conversation. ''Camellia.'' She set the bagel down on a small side plate. ''About your prediction last night—''

''Just don't you go anticipating the wedding night, young lady.'' Camellia actually shook a finger in Lindsey's direction.

Lindsey's eyes widened. There wasn't a chance in a million of her anticipating the wedding night. A trillion. Make that a gazillion.

Camellia leaned forward conspiratorially, her eyes softened. "They always blame the boys, don't they?"

"Huh?"

She cackled. "Always blame the boys for the pre-wedding shenanigans—"

The bagel felt like lead in Lindsey's stomach. "Believe me when I tell you there will be absolutely no shenanigans, prewedding or otherwise, between me and—"

"We women have needs, too." Camellia patted Lindsey's hand.

What was with women and needs today? It was only ten in the morning for goodness sake.

The hard, cold fact was that Lindsey didn't have a single need Bobby could fulfill. Nothing, nada, zero, zilch.

She took a deep breath and tried again. "Camellia, you have to tell everybody you made a mistake."

"What mistake?"

"The engagement. You can't let people think—"

"I don't tell people what to think."

Lindsey tried to be diplomatic. Maybe senility was setting in, and Camellia truly didn't remember what she'd predicted. "You told them last night."

Camellia's chin tipped up a notch. "I did no such thing."

"But you did. You said, and I quote, 'Lindsey's going to marry our Robert.'"

"And you are."

"No, I'm not."

Camellia smiled knowingly. "Give an old woman a little credit. My eyes might be failing, but I can see the way you look at him."

"The way I *look* at him?"

"Your face lights up with affection."

That wasn't affection. That was aversion. Lindsey leaned forward, her voice dropping to an earnest whisper. "Camellia, you have got to listen—"

"You are going to be a beautiful bride." Camellia closed her wrinkled eyelids and sighed. "I can see it all so clearly—"

"No! You can't." Lindsey grabbed Camellia's papery hand. "Please tell them you were wrong. Right now. Before this goes any further."

Camellia opened her pale blue eyes and blinked. "Now why would I want—"

"Hello, Aunt Camellia." Bobby slithered into the chair next to Lindsey. "Good morning, sweetheart."

Lindsey clenched her jaw and sat back, letting go of Camellia's hand. Then she discovered Bobby's hand resting on the back of her chair, and she bounced forward again.

Camellia's gaze narrowed in Bobby's direction. "Didn't your mother tell you to fill the wood box?"

"Later," said Bobby. "How can I leave two such beautiful women sitting all alone?" His gaze traveled down the length of Lindsey's snug blue jeans. When it returned to her face, he had the audacity to wink.

Lindsey hopped up.

"No," commanded Camellia imperiously. "Lindsey, sit. Bobby, firewood."

Why had she ever thought one little old lady was going to be easy to handle?

A muscle ticked in Bobby's cheek.

"Now," said Camellia.

Lindsey sat.

Bobby hesitated. It was the first time Lindsey had seen the man exhibit actual courage.

But nobody disobeyed Camellia for long. Particularly not people who'd spent their formative years under her watchful eye. Mumbling something under his breath, Bobby stood up and headed for the door.

Lindsey forced herself to relax and take stock. Okay, so she hadn't made any real progress with Camellia. But she had not yet begun to fight. Camellia might be tough, but Lindsey hadn't made Gold Merit Certification without determination and courage. She still had a few tricks up her sleeve.

"RJ," Camellia called, going from censorious to cheerful in the blink of an eye. She motioned to him with her hand.

Lindsey's stomach clenched. She hadn't counted on trying her remaining tricks in front of a critical audience—a critical audience who now knew how her lips tasted and how his name sounded on her moan.

Camellia grinned. His footsteps grew closer. Lindsey's hand tightened on her coffee cup.

Okay. She could do this. Better to get the first meeting over with, anyway.

She'd made a fool of herself last night, practically

swooning in his arms. It was a stupid mistake, but she'd have to live with it. She squared her shoulders.

"Good morning."

Just the sound of his voice sent butterflies spiraling through Lindsey's stomach.

"Sit," said Camellia.

The chair legs scraped along the wooden floor, but Lindsey didn't dare look in his direction. He'd held her in his arms. He'd whispered her name. He'd plundered her mouth. And, Lord help her, she wanted him to do it again.

A loud clatter echoed through the dining room. Out of the corner of her eye, she saw Bobby dump an armload of wood in the box beside the fireplace. Frank, David, Ricky and Brian trailed behind him with a couple of logs each. The boys ranged in age from four to seven.

Trust Bobby to enlist child slave labor.

"Susan needs a Christmas tree," said Camellia without preamble.

"I slept very well, thank you," said RJ. "And you, Aunt Camellia?"

Camellia made a face. "I'm an old lady. I don't sleep."

"And you, Lindsey?" he asked.

She heard him shift in his chair and felt his gaze on her face.

"Lindsey didn't sleep well," said Camellia.

"I slept fine," Lindsey quickly said. "What about the Christmas tree?" If Camellia mentioned RJ having been in her room last night, she would absolutely die.

"I told her you'd get one." Camellia directed her remark to RJ.

"No problem," said RJ.

Lindsey dared a glance in his direction. He caught her gaze, but his expression wasn't mocking. He looked almost wary, as if he was as uncomfortable as she with the morning after. Not that there'd actually been a night before.

"A big one," said Camellia.

"Sure," said RJ, still looking at Lindsey.

"Lindsey will help you," Camellia pronounced.

"No." Lindsey's attention flew to Camellia. "I can't. Really, I have—"

"Nonsense." Camellia's cane rapped on the floor. Another load of wood clattered into the box. Bobby wasn't going to take long at this rate.

"I..." Lindsey glanced from Bobby to Camellia to RJ.

Well, this was a daunting choice—outside, Christmas tree hunting with RJ, or inside dodging Bobby while she decorated.

Lesser of two evils, she told herself. "I'd love to help find a Christmas tree."

"Off you go," said Camellia with a satisfied smile.

LINDSEY STARED at a fifteen-foot pine tree, which was liberally covered in sugar snow. Her head was tipped back, red lips pursed. "I don't know, RJ..." She paced around to the back, hands going to her hips as she sized the tree up from all angles.

The gold scarf wrapped around her neck picked up flashes of the weak sun rays, reflecting in her eyes, showing off little golden flecks within the forest green. Not that her eyes were relevant or anything.

"What's not to know?" asked RJ, spreading his feet to anchor himself more firmly on the slippery snowpack, determinedly moving his attention from Lindsey to the tree. He didn't even attempt to mask his frustration. "It's a tree."

She clicked her tongue. "It's not...quite..." She spread her arms wide. "It's kind of scrawny."

"It's the fiftieth one we've checked out." His embarrassment over having kissed her last night had been replaced by exasperation. For the past hour, the woman had been selecting, then rejecting, tree after tree.

They'd climbed a random zigzag pattern from one potential candidate to the next, taking them halfway up the mountainside.

"They always look better from a distance." She sighed, stepping away from the tree onto the trail. On one side of the trail, a forest grew up the mountain. On the other, a snow-covered meadow swept away toward a cliff, which fell to the lakeshore. Lindsey glanced around.

"What about those?" She pointed to a stand of pines a hundred yards farther up the hill. "They look fatter."

"That's what you said about these ones."

"It's Christmas. Don't be a spoilsport." Squaring her shoulders with an air of renewed purpose, she headed for the next potential candidates.

RJ hoisted the backpack containing the handsaw higher on his shoulders and put one snow-booted foot in front of the other, knowing she was doomed to disappointment. This was a natural forest, not a Christmas tree farm.

"Are you by any chance a perfectionist?" he called to her retreating back. "An overachiever?"

"Are you by any chance an underachiever?" she retorted, turning to take a few backward steps up the hill.

"I have better things to do with my life than hunt for mythical Christmas trees."

"We're surrounded by *real* Christmas trees."

"Not the kind you want."

"Grinch."

"Dreamer."

"Me? Are you kidding? I'm the most down-to-earth, practical woman you are ever going to meet."

"She says, from a doomed Christmas tree quest halfway up a mountain."

"It's not doomed."

"We're not going to find what you want," he warned, as the distance between them closed. "Yukon trees are skinny and spindly."

"You need to set your sights higher in life, RJ." She kept walking backward. "I'm not willing to settle for half measures."

"I'm not asking anyone to settle for half measures. I fully intend to bring them an *entire* tree."

"We've been entrusted with a sacred responsibility."

"It's a tree, Lindsey." He caught up to her, and they paused beside the next candidates, breathing deeply in the cold, thin air. "We'll decorate it, toss a bunch of presents underneath. I can guaran-damn-tee you that nobody will be counting the needles and lauding us for our heroic defiance of frostbite—"

"It's for the children. We need to make sure we get just the right one."

"Are you always like this?"

"Like what?"

He leaned forward. "Are you always so blindly single-minded?"

Her eyes narrowed for a split second. He waited for the comeback, but it never came.

She blinked and turned her attention to the tree. "Hmm."

Hmm? That was it? Maybe she was slipping.

"It's a great tree, Lindsey." He filled the silence, not even bothering to look at it. It was exactly the same as every other one they'd considered.

"Hmm," she repeated, sounding frighteningly uncertain again.

"I'm cutting it down." He shrugged out of the backpack.

"It's a little—"

"You are not going to find a Norman Rockwell

Christmas tree in the middle of the Yukon bush.'' He unzipped the pack.

''But the lower branches—''

''You are holding this poor tree to an impossible standard.''

''There's a big hole back here.''

''It's a bitter cold desert here for most of the year. You should just be thankful it grew at all.''

She made an unladylike exclamation.

He pulled out the handsaw, flexing the blade and moving toward the tree trunk. ''Can't you see it *wants* to become a Christmas tree?''

''RJ—''

Before RJ could make the first cut, a faraway voice drifted from behind them. ''*Lindsey?* You up here?''

It was Bobby.

Lindsey froze. Her eyes went comically wide, and she pressed a gloved finger across her lips, giving her head a little shake.

''Lindsey?'' Bobby called again.

RJ cursed under his breath and stowed the saw. Sure, last night he'd thought it might be fun to watch Lindsey cope with Bobby. But today…

Maybe it was the glimpse of her vulnerability, or maybe it was the kiss, or maybe he'd just grown up a bit since high school. Today Bobby pursuing her didn't seem like such a good joke.

He grabbed her hand and quickly pulled her into the stand of pines.

''Lindsey?'' Bobby's voice grew louder as he emerged into the bottom of the meadow. Though they were concealed by branches, if Bobby looked closely enough, he'd spot Lindsey's red parka.

"Back here," RJ whispered, angling his forearm across her back and coaxing her along a nearly invisible pathway through the sparse stand of trees. Their boots squeaked against the snowpack, and he didn't dare walk too far in case Bobby heard them.

A dozen yards from the main path, he tucked her into the nook of a large boulder. Then he used his body to shield her. His green and brown clothing would blend with the surrounding forest. He pressed against her, hands on either side, against the vertical rock face. He told himself he was hiding, not trying to get up close and personal again.

He almost believed it.

"Lindsey?" They could hear Bobby's footsteps squeaking on the dry snow.

The squeaks grew louder. Then they paused. Thank goodness the wind-packed snow wouldn't show their footprints.

Lindsey bit her bottom lip. RJ held his breath. He tightened against her, pinning Lindsey to the rock.

She bit down on a nervous giggle, and he cupped his gloved hand over her mouth. Her eyes danced, but she stayed quiet. He felt himself smiling in return.

Bobby's footsteps started squeaking again as he continued up the path.

"Feels like we're kids again," RJ whispered against her ear, relaxing the hand over her mouth. Then he inhaled deeply. She smelled of cold air and citrus.

"I don't remember doing this when we were kids." Her voice was wry, her awareness of their proximity crystal clear in her tone.

He knew he should back off, but he didn't. If he'd known it felt this good to hold her in his arms, he might have tried it back when they were teenagers.

"Hide-and-seek," he whispered, giving in and letting his cheek brush against hers, feeling anything but childlike. Her skin was cold, but he knew he could warm it with just a little friction from his own. He was tempted to try.

"Oh." Her voice trembled a little.

He wondered if it was anger, desire or just plain cold.

"Lindsey?" Bobby's voice was well down the pathway, drifting farther away.

RJ had to back off before he tried something stupid—like warming her skin or kissing her again. He knew that if he shifted just a little to the right, their lips would meet, and he'd feel that staggering rush of desire.

How would she react?

Had she lain awake last night like he had, puzzling over their cataclysmic reaction to one another? Had she forgotten about it already? He wished he could guess.

"I know another way down," he said, dropping his hands, clenching his fists under his gloves. He took a step back, forcing himself to put a little airspace between them.

But even as he backed off, he couldn't help staring

into those forest green eyes, trying to figure out what was going on inside her head.

She didn't look angry, but she didn't look happy, either. She looked…unsettled.

And unsettled was exactly how he felt.

5

LINDSEY RUBBED her gloved hands together in an effort to keep them warm as she followed RJ down the new trail. She stretched her legs, stepping from one of his big footprints to the next on the sheltered, deep-powder trail. Her mind was doing mental gymnastics—part tree spotter, part hormone damper.

RJ's brief touch was burned into her cheek like a permanent brand, and she could still feel his deep voice rumbling through her. Combine that with his mind-expanding kiss from last night, and she was fighting to keep her perspective.

When he turned to look back and check her progress, she shivered with the insistent memories.

"Cold?" he asked.

"No," she lied, not ready to give up the Christmas tree hunt and not nearly ready to go back to the lodge and play the blushing bride. At least out here she could force her mind to concentrate on tree hunting. Better that than to be at the lodge dodging Bobby with plenty of time to ponder her reaction to RJ.

Trees, she told herself with a mental shake. *Think trees.*

"Let me show you something," said RJ.

"Did you find a good tree?" she asked hopefully, picking up the pace to keep up with his longer strides, blanking her mind to everything but the Christmas tree hunt.

The kids were going to be so excited. It was easy to picture the look on Jeffry and Aidan's faces when they returned victorious. Along with Ricky and Brian, the boys had been stringing colored popcorn when RJ and Lindsey had left. Rose-Marie had wrapped herself in silver garland as the anticipation built to a fever pitch.

"We'll wait until we're a bit closer to the lodge to cut a tree," RJ said dryly, veering onto a narrower path that took them into a sparse, miniature forest of ten-foot, snow-laden pine trees.

He turned to look at her again, raising his eyebrows. "Unless *you're* planning to carry it down the mountain."

"I'm just the quality control analyst." She tossed the words out, falling easily into their usual teasing conversation as the path turned to a steep uphill climb. The snow was deeper off the main trail, and her boots scuffed through it, kicking up waves of tiny crystals.

"What does that make me?" he asked. "The mindless muscle?"

"Your words, not mine." She inhaled deeply with the increased exertion, clouds of steam billowing around her face as she breathed out.

"The master of the unspoken implication."

"You can't tell what I'm thinking."

"I can always tell what you're thinking."

Lindsey stumbled on a buried branch. He was bluffing. Of course he was bluffing. But what an unsettling thought.

"So, what am I thinking now?" she challenged.

He glanced over his shoulder and chuckled. "Nothing I can repeat in the presence of a lady."

"Cop-out," she sang, as they emerged on a rocky precipice overlooking the lake. Set back against the hillside was a tiny, picture-perfect log cabin. Deep snow was stacked on its roof, and icicles overhung a wide porch, generously appointed with willow furniture. The view would be gorgeous in the summer.

"Wow," Lindsey whispered.

"You're thinking it's beautiful," said RJ.

"You're right," she admitted.

"Susan calls them the wilderness cabins." RJ took the stairs two at a time to the wide porch. "I usually stay in one of them if I'm going to be at the lodge for more than a day or so."

"How many are there?" Lindsey followed him up, turning to gaze across the frozen, windswept lake and the snow-covered mountains beyond. The view was spectacular in the winter, too.

The sun had passed its low zenith on the southern horizon and was fading toward the west. The shortest day was December twenty-first, but it would be a long time yet before the region had more than six hours of daylight.

"This and three others are hike-in only," said RJ,

pushing open the front door. "They're for clients who don't mind roughing it and want more privacy."

He gave her a wink and a patented RJ half grin. "Right now, you're thinking you'd like to go inside and warm up," he drawled.

"Does that line ever work?" She crossed the threshold into the little cabin.

"Like a charm. All I need is a little thirty-below weather, and women are putty in my hands."

"I'm not putty in anyone's hands." She felt compelled to assert herself. Though, privately, she admitted the jury was still out on RJ.

"I'm crushed." RJ clicked the door shut behind them.

"You'll live." She squinted around the interior. Long rays from the low-hanging sun supplied little light.

He struck a match and lit an oil lamp that sat on a pine table in one end of the room.

Rectangular in shape, the cabin had a large bed on one side and a kitchen cum living room clustered around the woodstove. The floor was hardwood with rugs scattered around, and the walls were natural logs.

"That's what I always liked about you, Lindsey."

"What's that?" She gazed at him expectantly. She couldn't imagine that he actually liked anything about her—particularly not on an ongoing basis.

"You keep a guy humble."

"Well." She chuckled. "Somebody sure has to give you a reality check. Putty in your hands," she scoffed.

She stripped off her gloves and strode toward the airtight fireplace. "Give me the matches."

"You never did like me much, did you?" He tossed her a small square box.

She caught it in midair. "You never really made yourself easy to like."

"Touché." He chuckled. "But what about now?"

Now? There was a minefield. He still teased, but the biting edge was gone. In fact, sometimes she felt like he was lobbing her a soft one so that she could tease him right back.

And he could kiss.

Boy could he kiss.

But did she like him? Did she dislike him? Was she attracted? Fascinated?

She glanced into his dark blue eyes and couldn't answer any of those questions.

"I don't really know you anymore," she finally said judiciously.

"That's right." He took a step forward, holding eye contact, his snow boots rustling on the wooden floor. The teasing note completely gone from his voice. "You don't know me at all."

"I wouldn't go that far." She sure knew him well enough to be wary.

His full lips curved in a knowing grin as he took another step toward her, glancing at the box of matches she held in her hand. "Need some help with that?"

"No, thanks." She shook off the unsettling sensations mounting within her. "I'm a former

Yukoner.'' She forced herself to look away from his compelling expression and crouched to pick up a few sheets of newspaper from the tinder box. She deliberately crumpled them into balls.

''But I like playing with fire.'' His voice was bedroom husky as he crouched beside her.

She glanced sideways at his profile, waiting for the punch line.

''You...'' He took a deep breath, wadding a couple of sheets of newspaper, keeping his focus on the small glass door. ''Are fire.'' He shifted the handle and opened the door wide, then tossed the newspaper onto the layer of cold ash inside.

Her mouth went dry and her chest constricted as she tried to come up with a retort that would get the conversation back on track. He needed to still be teasing her. She wasn't ready for anything else.

He gently lifted the newspaper ball from her hands and tossed it into the fireplace. Then he laid some kindling sticks on top. Finally, still silent, he caught her gaze for several heartbeats as he took the matches out of her hand. He removed one and struck the red and white head against the side of the box.

''You can warm me up,'' he continued, almost as if he was talking to himself. He touched the match to a flimsy corner of the newspaper. ''I'm sure you can light up my life.'' The orange flame caught and climbed upward, consuming the paper in a rush. ''Or I can get very badly burned.''

''RJ, what are you...'' Was he saying what she thought he was saying? He'd teased her for so many years, she couldn't quite believe he was serious. And yet…

He added a couple of larger pieces of wood to the fire. It started to crackle and give off heat.

While she watched his profile in the orange light, a myriad of fleeting emotions crossed over it.

He closed and latched the glass door, dusting his hands together.

"Here's where I have to decide," he said, pivoting on the balls of his feet so that he was facing her, still crouching. "I can backpedal now and tell you that you're fire because of your devious brain and that razor-sharp tongue that takes me down a peg every time we have a conversation."

He inhaled and seemed to steady himself. "Or I can admit that I'm dying to kiss you again and risk having you turn me down flat."

Lindsey tried to swallow. She couldn't believe what he was saying—couldn't believe they were here, what she was feeling, or what she wanted.

She wanted RJ. She wanted RJ a lot.

"So, which are you going to say?" she whispered.

He took her hand, slowly standing and drawing her to her feet. The muscles in her thighs protested as they stretched out.

"That I am dying to kiss you," he whispered.

"What does that mean?" This was so confusing. Where were they going? What were they doing?

"It means I've just stuck my ego *way* out there for you to tromp on."

"I should be able to come up with a scathing retort here, shouldn't I?"

"Oh, yeah." He nodded.

"Words fail me."

He started to grin, looking more like his old self. "Now that's a first."

"And you complain about the danger of *my* rapier sharp wit."

"I believe I said razor sharp." His grin faded, and he inched closer.

"Right. If I'm so razor sharp, why do you always get the last word?" She tipped her head sideways. *Here we go.* For better or worse, she was having another try at kissing RJ.

"Not this time," he said. He dipped toward her. It was last night all over again.

He had the same expression on his face, and she had the same tingle in her chest. Only this time, she knew what was coming. This time she was privy to the powerful memory of his lips on hers and the incredible hormone rush that invaded her system.

"You just did," she whispered, closing her eyes and waiting for the burst of sensation.

"No, I didn't." There was a thread of laughter in his voice.

"Give up and kiss me."

"You got it."

She opened her mouth to get in the last word, but he swooped down. He was still laughing as his lips pressed against hers.

His lips were cool from the chilly air, and the feeling was strangely erotic. Before she had a chance to savor the sensation, his laughter died, and his mouth opened.

Heat. Pure heat singed her, drawing her in, coaxing her lips apart. His hand tangled in her hair, both an anchor and a caress. His other arm wound around her waist, pulling, tightening.

A spark pinged against the cast-iron fireplace, and the heat wafted through the glass to caress them.

Lindsey tried to lift her arms to wrap them around his neck, but her bulky coat made moving difficult. His coat got in the way, too, and she was frustrated by the stiff layers of clothing between them.

She thought of the big bed in the corner, with its fluffy quilts and plump pillows. They'd be warm in there. They could get seriously up close and personal under the covers without risking frostbite.

RJ sucked in a deep breath, running his thumb along the soft skin of her neck, following it with a trail of kisses.

"RJ," she gasped, battling the stupid coat, trying to fight her way closer to him. "I can't... This isn't—"

"I know." His voice sounded strained. He stopped kissing and rested his forehead against hers, breathing deeply. "We are in such big trouble."

Trouble? It wouldn't be any trouble at all to hop into the bed in the corner.

"We need to slow it down." He took a step back, raking a hand through his hair. "This thing between us... It's like some kind of freak winter storm."

He sure had the storm part right.

"You're big city," he continued. "I'm small town. We're former rivals, family friends. We've got no business acting like it could be simple."

Lindsey stepped back, pressing cool fingers against her swollen lips. He was making excellent sense.

She couldn't jump into any kind of a relationship at this point in her life. Especially not with RJ. And a fling was probably a really bad idea, anyway. Funny, it had seemed like such a good idea a few minutes ago.

She glanced into his deep blue eyes. They glowed in the reflected firelight, sending a shiver of sensation down her spine.

Okay, so it still seemed like a good idea. But she could see where it would be complicated. And they really should slow this down a notch and decide what they both wanted.

"You're right." She nodded.

His mouth curled up at the corners. "I think this is the first time you've ever said that to me."

Lindsey managed to pull a smile out of the confused jumble of her emotions. "Don't let it go to your head."

"I think we better go back out and find that tree." He adjusted the zipper on his coat.

"Right." Besides, she was plenty warm now.

OFF IN THE DISTANCE, smoke rolled from the lodge's chimney. The sun set against the jagged peaks, turning clusters of clouds into pink cotton candy.

RJ came to a halt on the trail, quickly sticking his

arm back to keep Lindsey from coming too close to the edge of the cliff.

"This way down's a bit tricky," he warned, gazing at the narrow, switchback path that wove its way through large boulders and small poplar groves. "We can take the long way around if you'd rather."

Lindsey pressed against his arm, and he had a fleeting desire to wrap it around her and pull her close.

Okay, so the desire wasn't very fleeting. In fact, those glorious seconds when he'd held her at the cabin had been circling his brain in a continual loop. He was dying to do it again.

"I'm up for a little risk," she said. There was the usual teasing quality to her voice as she leaned against him, peering over the edge. He wished he was brave enough to look into her eyes and see if there was any sexual innuendo there, or if she was really just talking about the trail.

"I'm not much of a risk taker anymore." He decided to assume she was only talking about the trail. After all, when push came to shove, she'd backed off at the cabin. She backed off last night in the lodge, too. Despite her current claim of bravery, the woman obviously wasn't one to jump into a physical relationship.

Which was okay. He could respect that.

"A non-risk-taking arctic bush pilot?" she asked.

"It's more of a small airline," he admitted. The days of bush camps and drop-offs in inclement weather had given way to wealthy tourists willing to wait.

He pointed to the first steep hairpin turn in the trail.

"That's the start. And it gets worse. You sure you don't want to take the long way around? We'd probably still make it before dark."

"Come on, RJ. Be a man about it." She ducked behind him, heading for the steep trail.

"Whoa." He blocked her path. "I think the man gets to go first here."

"Oh, thank you. You're such a hero," she crooned.

"I just don't want you to fall." He reached back and grasped her gloved hand, holding it tight in his.

"Hey," she protested. "I'm tough. I risk millions of dollars every day," she said, following close as he guided her along the narrow pathway. "I think I can make it down one tiny trail."

"Good for you. But if you slip, grab me around the waist." He carefully gauged his first few steps. The snow was fresh, and it wasn't too icy, but the path fell away to the right over numerous large boulders.

"So, if I go over, I pull us both to our deaths?" she asked.

"I'll cushion your fall."

"I thought you just said you were getting cautious."

"Guess there's still a bit of the old me left inside."

"The *old* you?"

"You should have seen me when I was young." He anchored a hand against a small pine tree and wrapped an arm around her waist as they traversed a particularly steep section.

"I did," she said. "I believe you were two when we first met."

He smiled to himself. ''I mean as a pilot. In my late teens and early twenties.''

''You were a wild boy?'' she asked, close to his ear, the timbre of her voice tickling the sensual embers inside him.

''No landing too tricky, no takeoff too short.'' He shook his head when he remembered some of the stunts he pulled. By rights, he should have died on several occasions.

''But not anymore?'' she asked.

''I'm mortal now.''

''That's disappointing.''

''Sorry.'' He couldn't feel her body heat through their thick coats, but he liked having her tight against him all the same. ''At one time, I started studying for a jet license.''

''Why did you stop?''

''I was too bold a pilot.'' The trail evened out, and he reluctantly let her go. ''I'm sure you've heard the saying there are no old, bold pilots?''

''I have.''

He took her hand again. It wasn't necessary, he simply wanted to. ''In one of my rare lucid moments back then, I realized I was way too bold to go seven hundred miles an hour.''

''Was it a good decision?'' she asked. ''Are you glad?''

''I'm still alive.'' Was he glad? That was hard to say. He wasn't sure he wanted to ponder that question too closely. ''Why don't you tell me about your million-dollar risks?''

The clouds had closed in above them, and a few flakes of snow started to fall.

"It's never life and limb," she said, slipping on an ice patch and groping him for balance. "Except now, of course."

He chuckled.

"But my reputation is on the line every time I sign a deal. And, believe me, that counts for a lot in my world."

RJ nodded. "You've got a good reputation, I take it."

"I just achieved..." Her voice was a bit of a singsong. Then she paused. "You mind if I brag?"

"Brag away."

"I just made the top one percent at Progressive Dynamics for capital and investment return figures right across the entire country."

"Really?"

"And you don't get there without taking a few risks, baby."

RJ smiled at her pride and enthusiasm. He came to a halt near the bottom of the steep trail, checking out the pine forest in front of them. "Well, well, well. Will you take a look at that, my intrepid financial adviser."

"Portfolio manager."

"Sorry."

"It's okay. What do you see?"

"Our tree."

6

BY CHRISTMAS morning the tree looked every inch the dignified centerpiece Lindsey had hoped for.

RJ's mother, Celia, had sewn Christmas nightwear for all of the grandchildren. So Gary's sons, Frank and David, Sam's two, Ricky and Brian, and Susan's children, Jeffry, Aidan and Rose-Marie, all scampered around the great room in flannel Santa pajamas and nightgown.

Connie, the supermodel, sat cuddled up beside Curtis in a big armchair in the corner. Susan had told everyone to stay in their loungewear for Christmas morning, and Connie looked stunning in violet satin.

Curtis had given her a pair of diamond earrings, and her long, whispered thank-you was actually making him blush.

Lindsey smiled and shifted her attention as her mother sat down on the couch beside her and placed a small package in her hand.

"Thanks, Mom." She smiled. Dressed in tights and an oversize T-shirt, Lindsey carefully removed the tiny, green bow and peeled off the silver paper.

Inside, there was a flat, white box, which contained a pair of gold and emerald earrings. The emeralds were delicate, square-cut and surrounded by thin loops of gold.

"Oh, Mom." Lindsey leaned over to hug her mother. "They're gorgeous."

"I was thinking about your green dress and that little jacket when I bought them," said Janet, squeezing her.

"They'll go with so many things." Lindsey sat back, smiling. The earrings were just the right size, small and flat. She didn't like anything too ostentatious or dangly. Her mother had such good taste.

After a long look, Lindsey slipped the earring box into her purse for safekeeping.

"And for you." She used both hands to lift a large box from beside her feet and place it on her mother's lap.

"It's so heavy. What did you go and do?" her mother asked, leaning sideways and playfully bumping shoulders with Lindsey. "I thought we agreed to keep it simple this year."

"I don't see how you can consider emeralds simple," Lindsey arched her eyebrows. "Besides, I couldn't resist."

She'd been in a little antique shop in the Quayside Market way back in September when she'd come across the china serving pieces—a tureen, a pitcher and a salad bowl. They matched her great-grandmother's china pattern.

Lindsey wasn't about to pass up an opportunity to buy her mother some of the rare pieces, no matter what the price. She'd painstakingly packaged them for the plane ride in order to give them to her mother on Christmas morning.

Her mother opened the box and worked her way through the foam packing material.

"Oh, Lindsey." She lifted the pitcher, turning her head, her eyes suspiciously bright. "Where on earth did you..."

"Botachimi?" asked Chef Henri, moving closer.

"Yes," said Janet, smile widening. "Isn't my daughter just a doll?" She reached out with one arm to give Lindsey a hug.

Lindsey's chest tightened. She'd hoped it would be the perfect gift.

"They're in mint condition." Henri lifted the tureen. "You must have paid..." He cleared his throat. "I mean, what a lovely gift."

"I'm so glad you like it." Lindsey gave her mother a squeeze. "I was thinking we could add another section to the built-in china cabinet."

"You know, honey..." Her mother got a faraway look in her eyes.

"Yes, Mom?"

"Since your father passed away." She ran her fingertips over the smooth china.

Lindsey's mother rarely mentioned her father's death. So Lindsey sat very still, waiting to see what she'd say.

After a moment, she took a deep breath and continued. "That house is awfully big for one person."

"You want to move?" Lindsey was amazed. Her

parents had built that house together the first year they were married.

"It has three great big bedrooms," her mother said with a little apologetic half smile.

"I think you should live wherever you want." Lindsey's forehead tightened. "If you move somewhere smaller, will the china be too bulky?"

"No," her mother hastily assured her. "It'll go with me wherever I live. And I'll save it for you and your daughters some day."

Daughters? Children were far, far away on the horizon of Lindsey's life. If ever. She didn't even have time for a date. Never mind a boyfriend. Never mind a husband. Never mind doing justice to the job of being a mother.

"Dishes?" asked Bobby, suddenly wedging in next to Henri, frowning at the gold floral pattern on the pitcher.

"Yeah," said Lindsey, with short laugh and a nod to Bobby. "I bought her some dishes."

Henri scowled in Bobby's direction.

"*I* have a gift for Lindsey," Bobby announced, waving a small package in the air.

"Ah," said Gary's wife, Krista, moving into view. "A ring perhaps?"

Bobby's lips curved into a secretive smile, and his eyes sparkled with mischief. He perched on the thin section of couch beside Lindsey, pressing his thigh against hers. "Open it," he prompted, holding out the package.

Celia and Connie also moved closer.

Lindsey's heart slid to her stomach.

Oh, no. Please, not a ring. There was no way in the world she could put a ring from Bobby on her third finger. It would seem positively sacrilegious.

"Go on," Connie urged, as Bobby pressed the packet into Lindsey's hands.

It couldn't be a ring, Lindsey told herself, as she gently pulled up the tape and unfolded the holly leaf paper. There was no way in the world Bobby could have bought a ring on such short notice.

Even when the paper parted to reveal a velvet box, she told herself not to panic.

Taking a deep breath, she snapped open the lid.

A collective gasp went up from the women around her.

"It looks very valuable," Lindsey's mother whispered in her ear.

"It was the most expensive one at the gift shop," said Bobby, pride obvious in his voice.

Gift shop? Susan had a gift shop?

Lindsey blinked at the giant gold nugget balanced on a wide band. It probably weighed an entire pound. She'd sure never be able to type the letters *s*, *w* and *x* with that thing on her finger.

While she sat there trying to make her mouth form some kind of words, Bobby leaned over and kissed her on the cheek. She would have recoiled, but his hand was clamped firmly around her shoulders. His soft lips left a damp spot below her eye, making her shudder.

"Try it on," said Connie.

Lindsey whimpered.

SUSAN CHUCKLED. She stood next to RJ in one corner of the great room. "I remember that feeling." She sighed as she watched Lindsey, Bobby and the small crowd around them.

"What feeling?" All RJ could feel was his hands beginning to cramp with the need to hoist Bobby up against the nearest wall. How dare he kiss Lindsey?

RJ had seen the size of the package, heard the collective murmur of appreciation from the women and had seen Lindsey's horrified expression for a second or two before Connie shifted and blocked her from his view. It didn't take a rocket scientist to figure out Bobby had snagged a ring from somewhere.

"Me and Seth," said Susan.

"What about you and Seth?" That kiss had made his stomach clench. Bobby had no *right* to kiss Lindsey.

Not that RJ did, either, but at least he'd asked permission first.

"You remember," said Susan.

Asked and *received* permission, as a matter of fact.

RJ glanced at his sister. "Remember what?"

"The year Aunt Camellia predicted I'd fall in love with Seth."

RJ forced his mind to shift gears and focus on his sister. He was pretty sure Bobby wouldn't try anything else in front of Janet. And if RJ kept on watching them, he'd probably scandalize everyone by throwing Bobby into the nearest snowbank.

He focused on Susan instead.

"Lindsey and Bobby take me back to when I started dating Seth," said Susan.

"Oh, please." *Do not make that comparison.* Seth was a perfectly nice guy.

"I would have sworn Camellia was wrong back then," continued Susan. "I remember Seth dogging me all that summer. I just wanted him to go away."

"What happened?" asked RJ, fighting a feeling of unease. He knew his sister had fallen in love, but for the first time he wondered about Camellia's role.

Not that he was in any way willing to entertain the notion that Lindsey might fall for Bobby. His glance strayed to them again, but he couldn't see past Connie and Jackson.

"One day I looked past his smart, sarcastic mouth and saw the man inside," said Susan.

"What did you see?"

"A man of principles and morals who loved me so strong. Plus we got stranded on the island overnight and I discovered he was...uh, never mind."

"Never mind is right." That went *way* past any detail RJ needed to know.

"Well, there must be something to it." Susan blew out a breath and fluffed her damp bangs. "I know from experience that Camellia doesn't predict these things lightly."

"She's been wrong before," said RJ.

"Only about sports scores. Shoot. Rose-Marie's eating the wrapping paper again. Talk to you later." Susan headed across the room to her daughter.

"SUSAN!" When Lindsey saw RJ's sister heading across the great room toward her daughter, she seized on the opportunity to escape.

She pressed the ring box into Bobby's hand. "Sorry. But it's way too big."

"But you didn't even try it on," he whined.

"Later." Much later. She glanced at her mother.

"Go on and see Susan." Her mother smiled. "Henri will help me repack the dishes."

"Of course." Henri nodded. "Glad to assist."

Lindsey didn't wait another second. She jumped from the couch and squeezed past Celia.

"Need some help in the kitchen?" She gave Susan a say-yes-or-die stare.

"Sure. I'd love some help," Susan said brightly. She was no slouch. She relieved Rose-Marie of a handful of soggy wrapping paper, scooped her off the floor and headed toward the dining room to the kitchen.

"Thank you," said Lindsey in relief as the double, kitchen doors swung shut behind them. "I could not have tried on that ring to save my life."

"It was a two-ounce nugget," said Susan, setting Rose-Marie on a stool at the counter. "I sold it to him myself."

The room was empty. The four turkey roasting pans lined up side by side behind the glass oven doors were just beginning to fill the air with delicious smells.

"You should have warned me," said Lindsey.

"And spoil the surprise?" Susan laughed. "I was

just telling RJ that I remember when it happened to me.''

Lindsey felt a small hormone surge at the mention of RJ's name. She'd lain awake last night wondering, half hoping he'd cross the balcony again and talk her into throwing caution to the wind.

Sure, a physical thing between them would be unwise. It would be short-term and complicate their lives even more than their teenage history, but still…

She shook herself, determined to forget about RJ. She had bigger problems right now.

''When what happened to you?'' she asked Susan.

''That summer Camellia predicted that Seth and I would fall in love.''

''She predicted you and Seth?'' Lindsey blinked. Then her body went still. This had happened multiple times? First her mother and now Susan?

''Oh, yeah,'' Susan continued. ''And I felt exactly like you do.''

''I don't think so,'' said Lindsey, shaking her head, quite certain Susan had *never* felt about Seth the way she felt about Bobby.

''Couldn't stand him,'' continued Susan. While she spoke, she pulled a coloring book and a plastic container of crayons out of a cupboard and set them in front of her daughter.

''I don't think it's quite the same thing,'' said Lindsey.

''Why not? Back then I would have bet large sums of money that I wouldn't marry Seth.''

''Bobby makes my skin crawl,'' said Lindsey.

"I thought Seth was a conceited jerk."

"Seth?" Seth was one of the nicest, most down-to-earth men Lindsey had ever met.

"You should have seen him back then. A legend in his own mind." Susan laughed. "I sent him packing more times than I can count. Don't know why he kept coming back. I was a shrew."

"He loved you," said Lindsey.

"Dog, *purple,*" said Rose-Marie with a toothy grin, holding up the coloring book for her mother to see. The dog picture had a scribble of purple across the middle.

"It's beautiful, honey." Susan stroked her daughter's hair. "Maybe Bobby loves you."

Maybe pigs flew. "Bobby loves himself."

"That's what I thought about Seth. You might want to give the guy a chance." Susan's eyes lit up, and she smiled secretively. She was obviously remembering the highlights of her courtship with Seth.

"Bobby and I are a totally different circumstance than you and Seth."

"How so?"

"I can't stand the man."

Susan just smiled knowingly.

"I don't even like to be in the same room with him," Lindsey continued, pressing her point.

Susan's smile widened, and her eyebrows rose.

"It ain't happening," said Lindsey. "It *so* ain't happening here."

"I think you should relax," said Susan in a voice filled with compassion and understanding.

''Relax?'' Lindsey's voice, on the other hand, was nearly a shriek. ''How am I supposed to relax when there's a lounge lizard out there with a gold ring in his hand?''

''You should stop analyzing this to death. There are times in a woman's life—''

''Analyzing?'' It sure didn't take any actual analysis to know Bobby was wrong for her.

''There are times in a woman's life when she should trust her instincts.''

''My instincts?'' Lindsey's instincts were screaming loud and clear. But they sure weren't telling her to go anywhere near Bobby Webster.

Susan leaned forward. ''Turn off your analytical brain for a few hours, and just let nature take its course.''

Nature?

Lindsey stared directly into Susan's eyes. ''If I were to let *nature* take its course, I'd be having a screaming affair with your brother.''

Susan's eyes widened. ''Come again?''

Lindsey couldn't believe she'd actually said the words. She bit her lower lip. ''Never mind.''

Susan shook her head. ''Uh-uh. You don't get a *do over* on that statement.'' She grinned, and her eyes lit up. ''RJ?''

Lindsey closed her eyes. ''Yeah. Okay. I'll admit it. I'm attracted to RJ.''

Susan slapped her hand over her mouth. Her voice turned to a mumble. ''But the two of you…''

"Have been fighting since we started walking. I know."

"So, what's the..."

Lindsey cocked her head sideways. "I don't know. I just don't know. But there's definitely something..."

"What kind of thing? Like a physical thing?"

"It's *no* thing at the moment."

"But in your dreams?"

"There, we're definitely talking a physical thing." Lindsey shook her head and covered her eyes with her palm. "I can't even believe I'm saying this."

It was bad enough to be thinking it, never mind saying it out loud.

"Come on, it's not the nineteenth century. Women are allowed to have desires, you know," said Susan.

"I know." Lindsey dropped her hand.

"So, it's not romantic?"

"No. I'm not the romantic type. It's pure, unadulterated lust."

A grin split Susan's face. "Go for it."

"Are you nuts?"

One of the cooks pushed through the doorway. Susan and Lindsey went quiet.

"Dog, *yellow,*" said Rose-Marie, holding up the coloring book again.

"Wonderful," said Susan.

"Dog, black?" Rose-Marie held up a black crayon, pink lips pursed questioningly.

"Sure. Do a black one now." Susan slid her gaze to the cook on the other side of the room.

"I said let nature take its course," she whispered to Lindsey. "I'm not changing my advice just because nature isn't quite what I expected."

Lindsey shook her head. "I don't think he's interested in—"

"Not *interested?*"

"Well...no..."

"Have you looked in the mirror lately? Proposition the man. He'll jump at it."

"Actually..."

The cook crossed toward the doors.

Lindsey waited for them to swing shut. Still, she whispered. "I already did."

"What?"

Lindsey nodded. "I think he turned me down." He'd made it sound logical and rational. But, bottom line, while she was thinking about getting naked in that big bed in the wilderness cabin, RJ had called a halt to their kiss.

"You *think* he turned you down?"

"Well, he did kiss me—"

Susan let out a little squeal. "Sit." She swung around the end of the counter and plunked down on one of the stools. Then she rested her elbows on the counter and her chin on her hands. "Dish."

Lindsey sat down. "We were up in one of the cabins."

"My cabins?"

"Yeah. You mind?"

"Of course not. So, yeah, he kissed you, and..."

Lindsey sighed. ''He, uh, well, we started getting a little—''

''Naked?''

''*No.*''

''Oh.'' Susan looked disappointed.

Lindsey tapped her fingertips on the countertop for a second. ''Carried away.''

''So far so good.''

''Then he stopped.''

''Stopped?''

''Just like that.'' Lindsey snapped her fingers. ''He stopped. Then he said it was too complicated, and we needed to slow down.''

''So, what did you do?''

''I agreed. Sort of. I didn't know what else to do. And then he said it was time to head back to the lodge.''

Susan sat up straight. ''And that's it?''

''Well, we did cut down a tree.''

Susan let out a snort of derision. ''I can't believe my brother.'' She held up flat palms, moving them up and down like a balance scale. Then she put on a comically contemplative expression. ''Gorgeous woman? Complications? Gorgeous woman? Complications? What to do? How to choose?''

Lindsey laughed.

''Is RJ out of his *mind?*''

''I hoped he might sneak over to my room last night.''

''And?''

This was more than just mildly embarrassing. "He never showed."

"Well, I think you should—"

The double doors burst open. "*There* you are." Bobby made a beeline for the counter.

Lindsey stifled a groan.

"HAVE YOU LOST what little is left of your *mind?*" Susan's whispered question took RJ by surprise.

He glanced at the tiny train rails in his hands, wondering what was so crazy about helping Frank and David set up their new toys. Sure, the train would be noisy and it would take up part of the floor space, but he didn't think the other guests would mind. He didn't begrudge the boys their fun.

"I don't think so," he said.

"I just talked to Lindsey." Susan jerked her head sideways, motioning to a corner of the room.

Uh-oh. RJ shook his head. He really wasn't in the mood to get reamed out by his sister over a kiss. She might think Bobby was about to turn from a toad into Prince Charming and sweep Lindsey off her feet, but RJ sure knew better.

He reluctantly rolled to his feet. No point in delaying the inevitable. His sister never had learned the art of butting out.

"Keep putting these together," he told his nephews. "I'll be right back."

He followed Susan to the little alcove next to the fireplace, composing arguments inside his head as they walked. If he wanted to kiss Lindsey, he'd kiss

Lindsey. They were both adults, and it was none of Susan's business.

He put a hand against the stone face, bracing himself. He was putting a stop to her interference here and now. "It's really none of your business—"

"RJ—"

"—what happened between Lindsey and me."

"Listen—"

"She's not interested in—"

"RJ—"

"—Bobby, so you can just forget—"

"RJ!"

"What?" He pasted his sister with an exasperated expression.

"She meant it."

"Meant *what?*"

"When she kissed you...she *meant* it."

RJ's heart lurched in his chest. What did Susan mean? How much detail did she have on that kiss?

"It was an invitation, you moron," said Susan, socking him in the shoulder.

Had she bugged the cabins? "How did you know what we..."

"I told you, I just talked to her. She's attracted to you."

"I *know* that." She kissed him, for goodness sake. Kissed him like a maniac, if the truth be known. "You think I'm stupid?" But being attracted to a man and taking that kiss to its natural conclusion were two totally different things.

"I'll take the fifth on that one, if you don't mind," said Susan.

"There's a difference between being attracted to someone and...well..." RJ paused.

Amusement rose in his sister's eyes as he tried to figure out how to end that sentence.

Forthrightness was sure never a problem for her. He, on the other hand, couldn't bring himself to be quite so blunt.

"*Doing* something about it," he finally finished.

"Listen to me, RJ," she whispered, leaning forward, glancing around the room to make sure nobody would overhear. "Lindsey *wants* you to do something about it."

RJ's heart rate doubled as the possible implications of Susan's words penetrated. Not that he was ready to believe her. Lindsey had backed off. Twice.

"How can you know that?" he asked.

"What part of I just talked to her are you struggling with? Quite frankly, she thinks *you're* the one who's not interested."

RJ drew back. Him not interested? Not bloody likely. "Where is she?" he demanded.

Susan grinned.

7

HIS SIBLINGS, his cousins and the rest of the family were already assembling for dinner by the time RJ found Lindsey two hours later. Admittedly, he'd lost some time shaving and changing into his suit.

She'd changed, too—into a slinky little spaghetti-strapped black dress and his fantasy heels. He gazed at her from across the dining room for an indulgent moment, boldly planning the demise of that little black dress.

She'd put up her hair, revealing her graceful neck and smooth shoulders. Pretty little emerald earrings highlighted her spectacular eyes.

Lose the dress. Keep the earrings. Maybe keep the heels, too.

He crossed the room to sidle up to her.

"I talked to Susan," he whispered low next to her ear, inhaling her sweet perfume. He couldn't wait to hold her in his arms once again. Seriously hold her. Full frontal holding.

She stilled, and a gratifying blush broke out on her cheeks. She didn't look like the bold and brave million-dollar-risking Lindsey at the moment. In fact, she looked embarrassed—like she'd put some very personal cards on the table.

Encouraged by her reaction, he reached down and surreptitiously took her hand, angling his body so that nobody else could see what he'd done. He stroked his thumb across her warm, smooth palm, reveling in the electricity that flowed between them.

She sucked in a quick breath, obviously feeling some of the same.

"Is Susan right?" he asked huskily, putting his sensual hopes and dreams into his voice.

"About what?" she asked, but her wide, green eyes and the breathless quality of her voice had already answered.

A wave of satisfaction pushed through him. "I backed off last night because I thought you wanted me to."

She stilled.

"It was the hardest thing I've ever done."

Her fingers convulsed around his hand.

"I'm putting my ego way out there again," he stated baldly, lips just touching the shell of her ear. "Truth is, I'm yours. Anytime, anywhere, any way you want."

Her blush deepened, and he had to fight to keep from kissing her, fight to keep from pulling the pins from her hair and wrapping his arms around her. He couldn't wait another second.

"What do you say we ditch this crowd?" He gave a tug on her hand and started edging toward the door.

"Ditch Christmas *dinner?*" she asked incredulously.

Her words stopped him.

"Yeah. Okay. Good point." He forced himself to concentrate on slowing his pulse and lowering his blood pressure. He gazed at his parents and brothers and everyone else getting ready to enjoy a leisurely meal and sighed in exasperation.

He sure had a big family.

This sure was going to take a long time.

"Sit next to me," he demanded. If he couldn't get her out of this room, he was taking the next best thing. The tablecloths were long, and her skirt was short. He surreptitiously stroked the bare skin near her shoulder blade.

"Right next to me," he said.

A breath hissed between her teeth. But she nodded in agreement.

RJ smiled, and his blood heated. Maybe this wouldn't be so bad. If the anticipation didn't kill him, it would probably make him stronger. In the meantime, if he had anything to say about it, Lindsey was going to have a long and torturous dinner.

The giant table was rapidly filling. RJ spotted two empty chairs and guided her toward them.

As she sat down, he pushed in her chair, and his body began humming in anticipation. Just then, Bobby appeared out of nowhere and took the seat next to her, and RJ's hum abruptly halted.

His jaw tightened. He reached out to clap his hand

on Bobby's shoulder. No way. No how. Not a chance in…

"RJ?" Susan touched his tight arm, forestalling the manly challenge.

"Yeah?"

"I need your help."

"Why?" This was not a good time. This was definitely not a good time for his family to need his assistance. He needed to evict Bobby so that he could stay close to Lindsey. He wanted to hear her voice, smell her perfume, touch her skin and reassure himself that this wasn't all a dream.

"Seth's carving at one end of the table. Would you do the other turkey down there?" She pointed to the far end of the table.

"Are you sure somebody else can't…"

Bobby picked up his glass of water and took a swig. Great-Aunt Eileen, sitting on the other side of Lindsey, struck up a conversation. RJ's hands tightened on the back of the chair. He could feel his evening spinning out of control.

He wanted Lindsey. He wanted her now.

Susan leaned close. "No offense, big brother, but if I don't separate the two of you, I have a feeling I'll have to get out the hose."

RJ glared at her, but she just smiled complacently. A twenty-eight-year veteran of teasing him, she wasn't about to scare easily.

"I really do need you to carve for me." Her expression shifted, and she looked apologetic. "I have to take care of Rose-Marie and the boys."

A lead weight of guilt sank through RJ.

"Of course." He straightened, instantly feeling like a jerk.

It was Christmas dinner. Susan had worked for weeks to make this a spectacular family occasion. And here he was putting his libido ahead of helping out.

It was only dinner. He forced himself to curb his impatience. It would be over soon. And he and Lindsey had the whole night ahead of them. He'd make sure of that.

He swallowed his disappointment.

"I'm sorry," he said to his sister.

Susan smiled and patted his arm. "Thanks."

He bent over to whisper in Lindsey's ear. "I'm sorry. But I have to go help Susan."

Lindsey turned, her eyes widening. She looked for all the world like a deer trapped in the headlights of an oncoming truck. He didn't blame her.

He hated to leave her sitting alone between Bobby and Aunt Eileen.

"AND WHAT SIZE is your bust, dear?" Eileen's sweetly solicitous voice belied the ridiculously personal nature of the question.

"Excuse me?" Lindsey nearly choked on her turkey. Eileen was Camellia's sister, the more reserved sister. Or so Lindsey had always thought.

"If somebody wanted to pick up a little something for your trousseau, what size should it be?"

"I'm not getting married," Lindsey assured her,

deciding she'd been beating around the bush long enough. No more making polite excuses. She wasn't marrying Bobby, and that was that.

She was sleeping with RJ instead.

Of course, she wasn't about to announce that over cranberry jelly.

Eileen smiled. "But just in case."

"I am not..." Lindsey clamped her jaw and blinked slowly, torn between pressing the issue and just answering the silly question.

Resigned, she leaned over so that Bobby wouldn't overhear. "Thirty-four B."

Connie piped up from across the table, waving her fork in a small circle above her green beans. "Do you attend church regularly, Lindsey?"

Lindsey looked up. "Regularly?" She was a little embarrassed to admit she spent most of her Sunday mornings buried in financial reports. Monday always arrived so fast, and she had to keep up with her accounts.

"Is there a particular minister you'd like for the ceremony?" asked Connie.

"No!"

"I'm flexible," Bobby stated, patting her hand.

She quickly jerked it away, clattering her knife into the side of her china plate.

"Listen," she said, glancing around to include the ten or so people in her section of the table. "I know you all mean well, and I know Camellia has been right in the past. And I love Camellia as much as anybody, but she's mistaken this time."

Lindsey turned to Bobby. ‘‘I’m sorry if this disappoints you, but I can’t marry a man I don’t love.’’

Bobby just smiled and brushed a wisp of hair from her forehead. She tried not to shrink back.

‘‘You’re so sweet,’’ he said.

A few of the women sighed.

Lindsey stifled a groan.

‘‘I’m not sweet,’’ she assured him, setting down her silverware. ‘‘I’m cold-hearted and calculating. I work long hours, don’t cook and I can be a real shrew in the morning.’’

Bobby’s eyes heated, and the corners of his mouth turned up in a serpentine sort of way.

‘‘In the morning’’ was definitely a bad choice of words.

‘‘The fact is—’’ she began.

Bobby chuckled and captured her hand.

She yanked it into her lap. If he went after it there she was going to deck him.

‘‘The feeling will overwhelm you when you least expect it,’’ said Bobby. ‘‘That’s how it happened for me.’’

Lindsey caught a few nods in her peripheral vision. Her dinner settled hard in the pit of her stomach.

‘‘I suddenly knew you were the one,’’ Bobby continued.

His romantic words would have been a whole lot more effective if his gaze hadn’t strayed to her cleavage.

‘‘I’m not the one, Bobby.’’ She wasn’t anybody’s *one.* She had her career to think about and her mother to take care of. Marriage was not on her agenda now and probably never would be.

But announcing that wouldn't do her a bit of good in this particular company. In the absence of a reversal from Camellia, everyone would simply chalk her protests up to a lack of enlightenment.

In fact, the more she protested, the more eagerly they'd await her eventual capitulation.

"Be patient, sweetheart," said Bobby, sawing into a slice of turkey. "I'm going to make you a very happy woman."

Lindsey glared at him, wondering briefly if jabbing him with her salad fork would deflate his ego.

"With her hair and complexion, we should consider yellow roses," said Connie.

"I had yellow roses," said Eileen.

"You're not married," said Connie.

"In my hothouse." Eileen reached for a roll. "I had yellow roses in my hothouse. Maybe if they get married in the summer we could use my roses."

Lindsey bit back the protest that tried to leap from her mouth. She glanced down the length of the table to where RJ was dishing out seconds on the turkey. He said something to Aidan, and the young boy's mouth curved up in a delighted laugh.

Lindsey relaxed a little. She couldn't help but smile at RJ's way with the kids.

"May I have your attention?" Seth stood up, holding his wineglass aloft. "I'd like to propose a toast."

Lindsey quickly reached for her glass, as did the rest of the guests.

"Thank you all so much for coming," said Seth. "I know you've made Susan very happy." He smiled across the table at his wife. "Here's to family, and to friends, and to Christmas memories."

At the words "Christmas memories," Lindsey's gaze traveled to RJ. His eyes smoldered blue fire, and he lifted his crystal glass in her direction. She could almost feel him reaching out to caress her from all that distance away.

Her hand convulsed in her lap.

Next to her, Bobby jostled her arm as he pushed back his chair. He crumpled his napkin onto the white tablecloth and stood, clearing his throat. "I also have a toast," he announced, gazing around the room.

He glanced meaningfully at Lindsey, and she cringed. It was all she could do to keep from squirming against the padded chair. Her gaze moved to RJ again, silently begging him to help her.

"To new beginnings," said Bobby, putting a hand on Lindsey's shoulder.

After the second where everybody put their glasses to their lips, the guests burst into spontaneous applause.

RJ's jaw clenched. His shoulders squared, and he straightened out of his chair. Lindsey's eyes widened as he strode determinedly around the table toward them, an irritated glare pasted on the unsuspecting Bobby.

Her chest tightened as she slipped away from Bobby's touch. She silently shook her head in RJ's direction, but he didn't stop.

"You have a toast, RJ?" asked Seth, watching RJ's progress.

Aunt Camellia piped up. "He just wants to dance with Lindsey. The young reprobate," she grumbled.

A titter of laughter rolled through the room.

The object of many sets of eyes, RJ finally stopped. His shoulders relaxed, and he curved his lips into a credible smile. "Camellia is right." He held out a hand to Lindsey. "When does the music start, Seth?"

"Henri?" called Seth. "Let's have the music, please."

Lindsey reached gratefully for RJ's hand. She was glad he hadn't confronted Bobby. And she was doubly glad to get away.

RJ drew her against his body as the taped orchestra music swelled to life from several speakers. Some of the other guests decided to join them on the wooden floor of the great room.

"What were you going to do?" Lindsey asked against his suit jacket, settling into RJ's arms, relaxing for the first time in over an hour. Although she was glad Seth had stopped RJ, a small part of her couldn't help but feel gratified by RJ's interference. She'd never had a knight in shining armor before.

"I have no idea," he admitted, smoothly spinning her. "But it wouldn't have been pretty."

Lindsey laughed in relief, her steps matching his as they settled into the rhythm.

Someone dimmed the lights, and the glow of a hundred candles seemed to intensify. Soft, flickering light bounced off polished wood, and an orange fire danced in the big fireplace.

"You're mine," RJ whispered, voice vehement, arms tightening around her. "Not his."

"RJ," Lindsey warned. His words were disconcerting. Lindsey was no more RJ's than she was Bobby's. No matter how neatly she fit in his arms. No matter how much she wanted to close her eyes and let the dance go on forever.

"Sorry," he said, taking a breath. "I didn't mean that the way it sounded." He sighed and rested his chin against the top of her head. "But I do want you. Very, very much."

"Me, too," she admitted in a small voice, and a low sound rumbled through his chest.

The music slowed to a stop, and Lindsey took a reluctant pace back.

"Dance with me, RJ," Connie commanded, placing a manicured hand on his jacket sleeve.

A pained expression crossed RJ's face, but he couldn't very well say no to his aunt.

"I believe this is our dance." Bobby clasped Lindsey's hand and turned her against his chest.

She caught a fleeting glimpse of her mother and Henri swaying in the corner and a vague impression of the children at the table tugging on colorful Christmas crackers before her vision was obliterated by Bobby's white shirt and paisley tie.

And then the cologne. The horrible musk that seemed to permeate every inch of his clothing and ooze from his pores.

She pulled back with a gasp.

"I'm fifty percent owner in the Iceberg Tavern now," he said.

"That's nice." She choked the words out, scanning the dance floor, looking for a way out. Maybe Henri would…

No. It wasn't fair to stick her mother with Bobby.

"I don't want you to think I can't take care of you financially," said Bobby.

"Bobby, we're not going—"

He tightened his hand on her back, pulling her close again. "Let's not argue," he crooned.

"As long as you insist on talking about marriage, we're going to argue." She pressed against his hand, gaining a precious inch of airspace, taking shallow breaths through her mouth.

"Okay. I won't talk about it."

"Really? I mean good." She nodded.

"We grossed over a quarter million last year." He sounded inordinately proud, but Lindsey knew that a quarter million gross was pretty small for a bar or restaurant.

"What about net?" she asked, tipping her chin to look at his face, trying valiantly to keep up with his erratic dance steps.

"Net?" He blinked, like he couldn't believe she knew the difference between gross and net.

She was a venture capitalist, for goodness sake. "I'd be interested in knowing your asset-to-debt ratio and finding out if you've considered any alternative valuation approaches. I assume you own the building?''

''Uh, yeah, we...''

''Good. Then we can talk about equity financing options.''

The music stopped, and Lindsey smiled at Bobby. ''Thanks for the dance.''

She turned away, somehow knowing that RJ would be there waiting for her.

''You okay?'' he asked, pulling her firmly into his arms and twirling her away from a stunned Bobby.

''I feel like a bath,'' she said. Buffalo musk was definitely not her preferred perfume.

''A bath we can do,'' he murmured, waltzing her toward the door. ''Your tub or mine?''

''Won't they miss us?'' She glanced worriedly around the dim room.

''They're going to put the kids to bed in a few minutes. Everyone will be distracted. Hold tight.''

They turned a quick circle, and the next thing Lindsey knew, she was out in the hall.

''Quick.'' RJ gave her a shove toward the staircase. ''I don't think anyone saw us leave.''

Fueled by twin shots of adrenaline and passion, Lindsey scooted up the stairs.

''Your tub's closer,'' RJ whispered over her shoulder.

''You sure nobody will try to track us down?''

''Who cares? Susan's the only one with a passkey.''

Lindsey stopped in front of her door and slipped

the key into the lock. She couldn't help the smile that formed on her face or the goose bumps that popped out on her skin at the thought of having RJ alone for the next few hours.

When the door clicked shut behind them, he put a hand on her waist and turned her to face him. His thumb tightened beneath her breast, and his gaze traveled hotly along the length of her body.

"I have been waiting all night for this moment." His voice was hoarse. He shifted forward and slid the flat of his fingernails across her bare shoulder. "First time I saw you—"

"I was still in diapers."

He chuckled low, his fingertips continuing down her arm, the inside of his wrist grazing her breast. "First night here," he corrected. "When I walked into the lodge and saw you standing next to Bobby, all I could think was that you were going to be wasted on a guy like him."

"Not if I have anything to say about it," she asserted.

"Knew you'd see it my way." RJ pressed a light kiss on the curve of her neck. His hands slid up and down her bare arms. "I love a woman who thinks the way I do."

She tipped her head back and closed her eyes, inhaling deeply and reveling in the sensation of RJ. "I suppose you can tell what I'm thinking right now?"

"Haven't got a clue." He kissed her shoulder, pushing the thin spaghetti strap out of the way.

"Too bad," she sighed. Her hands crept along his

arms, and she steadied herself on his shoulders. The fabric of his suit was cool and rough to her touch.

"Why?" He drew back and gave a little half smile that made her shiver. "Is it something good?"

She moved her palm to his chest and wrapped her fist around his tie. She stood on tiptoe and touched the tip of her tongue to his earlobe. "What about now?" she whispered. "Can you tell what I'm thinking now?"

"It's becoming clearer," he teased.

She released his tie and slipped her fingertips between the buttons of his dress shirt, popping one and then another and then another. "And now?"

He sucked in a breath. His hand clamped over hers. "Hold that thought."

"*Hold* it?" She faltered. They were finally alone. Admittedly, she wasn't very experienced at this fling thing. But wasn't this the part where they let loose and got naked together?

"I have something for you."

She grinned at him. "That's exactly what I was hoping for."

"No fair tempting me."

Lindsey glanced pointedly to where her hand had worked its way into his shirt. She looked at the shoulder he'd bared. Then she shifted her gaze to the big bed on the other side of the room. "You probably should have mentioned that sooner."

RJ chuckled deep in his chest. "I brought you a Christmas present."

"You *did?*" Lindsey drew back. "But I didn't get you anything."

"That's okay. It's nothing special." He reached into his jacket pocket, drawing out a colorful beaded necklace.

The beads were cardboard, painstakingly cut and rolled out of old Christmas cards and strung together on colorful string. Lindsey put a hand to her mouth and giggled.

The kids had been making them this morning in the lodge kitchen. Back in high school, Lindsey and her friends used to craft them all the time, and sometimes the boys made them for their girlfriends.

RJ gently drew the beads over her head, lifting her hair so that the necklace rested against her chest. "I think this means we're going steady," he said.

She reached up to finger the small, conical beads, imagining his blunt fingers working with the glue and cardboard. It was the sweetest present she'd ever received.

She looked into his dark eyes. "Thank you."

He smiled, and her chest tightened, her heart constricting.

Good thing this was only physical. Good thing it was only temporary. Good thing they lived so far apart.

Because she could feel herself falling hard and fast. Nobody had ever asked her to go steady before.

Not in high school and certainly not recently.

For the last three years, she'd been nothing but strong for her mother. She'd kept her chin up and her mind focused. She'd forgotten what it felt like to lean on someone else.

Not that RJ was here for her to lean on. But, just this once, just for a few minutes, she was going to let herself pretend that he was.

"I wish they thought it was you instead of Bobby," she confessed, the words out before she thought them through.

"Me, too." He settled his arms around her, and she sighed against his broad chest.

"We'll fix it," he said, kissing the top of her head. "This thing with Bobby. We'll fix it."

"How?"

"I don't know yet. But we'll do it together."

Something broke free inside her, flooding her with warmth, and she wrapped her arms around him, squeezing tight. She knew she wasn't going steady with RJ, and she knew he wasn't here for her to lean on. Still, she felt an overwhelming sense of relief at the thought of having someone on her side.

"Okay." She nodded against his shoulder. It was okay to let him help her.

He smoothed her loose hair from her temples, tipping her head up, bending low, lips parting. This was it. Arousal shimmered to life inside her.

He kissed her mouth. "Oh, Lindsey," he breathed. "I want you so bad."

Throwing caution to the wind, wanting to make him feel as loved as she did, she shifted. She held his gaze as she slowly pushed the other strap of her dress over her shoulder. Then, with a wiggle and a shimmy, the black fabric pooled at her feet.

RJ froze and sucked in a breath.

"Was that daring?" she asked.

"Absolutely," he answered.

"Good." She smiled.

His gaze took in her wispy black panties and lacy bra. "You are the most beautiful thing I have seen in a decade."

"Yeah?"

"Oh, yeah. Make that two decades." He cupped his hand around the back of her neck and drew her forward. "Make that three." His lips met hers in an openmouthed kiss full of pent-up heat and simmering passion.

Yes. Oh, yes. This was definitely, definitely where she wanted to go.

She pressed against him, her sensitized skin brushing the smooth cotton of his dress shirt, her legs entwining with the rough fabric of his suit pants. His scent surrounded her. The sound of his heartbeat filled her ears while everything else faded into the background.

The pressure of his lips mounted as his hands swiftly explored her hair. Then they toyed with the beaded necklace before moving down her body. Each spot they caressed was more sensitive than the last.

And all the while he kissed her, kissed her in a way that made her blood boil and her skin burn.

Her heart was pounding, and her lungs felt as if they would burst. She plucked at his suit jacket, dragging it over his arms. Then she popped the rest of the buttons on his shirt and pushed it off his shoulders.

She kissed his bare chest, suckling, nipping and leaving dampened circles all over his pecs.

He gasped her name and lifted her, crossing the room to the king-size bed where he laid her gently on the down-filled comforter.

"Did I mention you were beautiful?" he breathed.

She smiled. "Did I mention you were gorgeous?"

"You haven't seen all of me yet," he said with a rakish grin.

"What are you waiting for?"

He stood and shucked the last of his clothes. He *was* gorgeous—every square inch of him.

When she caught his warm gaze, she felt gorgeous, too.

"Now?" he asked, levering himself down.

"Now," she answered.

"Here?" he asked, kissing her swollen lips and letting his fingertips trail along her stomach.

"Here," she breathed.

"Like this?" he asked, dipping lower, pressing into her.

"Like that," she groaned.

"Whatever you say." He shifted on top of her and took her to the stars.

8

It was 7:00 a.m., and RJ was in heaven with an angel in his arms.

He'd put off going to his room as long as he dared. But his time was up, and he had to leave her. The last thing he needed was to be in her room when the rest of the guests woke up.

"Sweetheart?" He propped himself on one elbow, smoothed Lindsey's hair away from her neck and gave her a tender kiss.

"Mmm," she moaned, still half asleep.

"I have to go."

"You sure?"

Oh, man, he liked that.

"'Fraid so. I've already stayed too long." In fact, the night had flown by. Despite the fact that RJ hadn't slept a wink, not wanting to waste a moment.

She shifted onto her back and blinked at him. Her thick, dark hair contrasted with the stark pillowcase. She was very tough to leave.

Then she smiled, and he decided ten more minutes wouldn't hurt.

"Does this seem a little surrealistic to you?" she asked.

"What do you mean?" But he was pretty sure he knew. The two teenagers who'd been at each other's throats had been wrapped in each other's arms all night long. The strangest part, for RJ, was that it didn't seem strange at all.

She was an incredible woman, an exciting woman, a hardworking, successful woman. He couldn't remember why he'd ever teased her. In retrospect, every cutting line she'd ever delivered had revealed her intelligence and wit. He wondered why it had taken him so long to realize that.

Or maybe on a subconscious level he always had. Maybe that was why he'd baited her. Truth was, sparring with Lindsey was one hell of a lot more fun than agreeing with anyone else.

"Do you think that when we get back to our real lives, this will all seem like a dream?" She reached up and ran her fingertips across his chin, testing the night's growth of beard.

"Best dream I ever had," he said sincerely and captured her finger in his mouth.

"Me, too." Her smile turned wry. "Well, except for the Bobby part."

"I told you not to worry about that."

"I know."

"We'll fix it today."

She nodded but looked unconvinced.

"I'll talk to Camellia," he promised.

The nod turned into a shake. "I tried that already."

"What did she say?"

"That she wouldn't retract her prediction and that

she wasn't responsible for what other people thought."

"She said that with a straight face?"

"Yes."

RJ chuckled and waggled his eyebrows. "Perhaps you just didn't use the right brand of charm."

"And here I thought you'd changed."

"I have."

"You're going to flash those blue eyes and that killer smile to manipulate a little old lady, aren't you?"

"Killer smile?" He liked that, too.

"Manipulate, RJ. The operative word here is *manipulate.* The same way you always did. The only way you passed economics."

"The dog really did eat my homework." He put on a mock hurt expression.

"Oh, sure it did. This is me, RJ. Go tell that to someone who's actually susceptible to your charm."

Was that a challenge? A slow smile grew across his face. "You're saying that you're *not* susceptible to my charm?"

"Never was, never will be."

"You sure about that?" He leaned in just a little bit.

"Positive." But her bravado was marred by her slight withdrawal into her pillow.

"Not even a tiny little bit?" He leaned in further and placed a kiss on her neck. She was delicious.

"RJ—"

"I can be very charming." He traced a damp circle

with his tongue, sucking slightly on her delicate skin. He was rewarded with a shudder. His body answered it in a split second.

"R—"

He moved to her lips then, cutting off further words of denial.

Her mouth instantly softened, and her arms wound around his neck. She arched against him, and he felt desire rush to life. When he finally broke contact, he was breathing heavily.

"Uncle," she whispered softly.

He smiled. "I like the sound of that."

"I guess you can be very charming when you put your mind...and body to it."

He chuckled low. "You *guess?*"

"Okay. I know."

"This is a pretty hollow victory," he said, glancing at the clock.

"You really do have to leave," she agreed.

"I hate it when you're right."

"Me, too."

He stayed still for the space of a couple heartbeats. "But I'll be back tonight," he promised.

"I know that, too."

Intelligent woman. He quickly kissed her one more time.

Brilliant woman. Then hoisted himself into a standing position.

Unforgettable woman. He grabbed his slacks before he could change his mind.

She cuddled into the comforter.

He focused on the door to keep himself from bailing back in with her. "I'll talk to Aunt Camellia today," he said as he pulled on the pants.

"Good luck," she muttered.

He zipped his fly. "Thanks. But just in case my charm's not at its peak—"

"That can happen?" She grinned, and he almost lost his resolve to get dressed.

"Well, I used quite a bit of it last night."

She tossed a pillow at him.

He ducked. "Maybe you should try talking to your mother, too. She was always pretty logical. Maybe she could help us beat some sense into the others."

Lindsey nodded. "I suppose it can't hurt."

"Right." He buttoned his shirt. Every instinct he had told him to crawl back into bed with her and block out the rest of the world. He didn't want it to be morning yet. He didn't want to share her.

He didn't want Bobby anywhere near her.

"Here's the plan." He determinedly pulled on his shoes. If he just kept dressing, he'd be out of here before he could stop himself.

"We have a plan?" she asked, pushing up on one elbow. The comforter slipped, revealing the tops of her breasts.

He could feel his arousal strengthening. "Of course we have a plan. Every mission needs a good plan."

"Will anything self-destruct?"

Only his rapidly hardening body. He really had to get away from her, and quick.

"I'm going to take a shower," he said. A cold

shower. "Then we'll go out there and mingle casually, manipulate little old ladies, gather intelligence."

She shifted into a sitting position, bringing the comforter with her, eyes alight. "Do I get a decoder ring?"

He gave her a mock-stern frown, but he was glad she found some humor in the situation.

"We'll meet back here at..." He glanced at his watch. "Twenty-three hundred hours to compare notes." Among other things.

"Aye, aye, sir." She gave him a snappy salute.

"I like that even better than uncle." Unable to resist, he leaned down to give her a final, hard kiss.

RJ WAS LUCKY. Camellia was an early riser, and he found her alone, sitting on one of the sofas studying the screen on a laptop computer. When he approached, she closed it and looked guilelessly at him.

"Aunt Camellia," he greeted her, wondering what she was up to. Seth had a satellite link, and Camellia was plugged into the wall socket. RJ could only hope she wasn't ordering a wedding cake.

"Good morning." She chirped the words. "Sleep well?" She squinted and peered into his eyes.

"Great." He looked away, ostensibly concentrating on sitting down. Truth was, he'd been sitting down most of his life and could do it without much focus at all. But he didn't want Camellia to see the lines under his eyes and come to some silly conclusion.

Like, maybe, the truth.

He cleared his throat. "I was talking to Lindsey this morning—"

"Talking?" The demand came on the heels of an arched eyebrow.

"Yes, *talking.*" He looked directly at Camellia, doing his very best to appear innocent.

She harrumphed, looking for all the world as if she'd witnessed every caress, overheard every throaty endearment that passed between him and Lindsey overnight.

She couldn't know, he reminded himself. It was not humanly possible for her to know that he'd spent the night in Lindsey's arms.

"Aunt Camellia." He tried again. "This thing with Lindsey getting married. It's gone way too far. She's—"

"Well satisfied, judging by the look on your face." Camellia planted her cane firmly on the hardwood floor and shifted herself forward on the soft sofa.

RJ forced himself to ignore her penetrating look. "This thing with Bobby is—"

"I don't think it's Bobby we need to be worrying about right now, young man."

"But—"

"I think we need to worry about you despoiling the bride."

"I didn't *despoil* anyone," said RJ, telling the truth but also knowing he was using a technicality.

Sure, he and Lindsey were both adults. And they'd obviously both had relationships before. But Camellia wasn't referring to that. She was referring to the fact that he'd just slept with the woman she considered Bobby's fiancée.

"You're not too old for me to box your ears." Camellia looked for all the world as though she meant it.

"Camellia." This was ridiculous. RJ was not going to be bullied by his aunt. Indomitable though Camellia was, Lindsey's happiness was at stake. "You don't know the trouble you're causing. You have to take back your prediction."

"You're suggesting I tell people she's not getting married."

"Yes. Exactly. Because she's not."

Camellia slowly drew herself up to a standing position, squaring her shoulders. "My lying won't change a thing."

RJ paused, guilt creeping in. He knew the prediction was ridiculous. Lindsey knew the prediction was ridiculous. And, deep down inside, even Bobby knew it was ridiculous.

But Camellia didn't.

Camellia believed she could predict the future.

"You'd do well to get used to the idea," she said, with a sniff. "When you come to your senses, you'll thank me."

She picked up her laptop and strode stiffly away, head held high, muttering the words "stubborn" and "kids."

RJ buried his head in his hands. He could only hope Lindsey had better luck.

"MOM?" Lindsey rapped on her mother's door, anxious to speak with her privately before they went down to breakfast. She shifted her weight from one foot to the other on the hallway carpet, feeling electrified, excited, unsettled. She knew she needed to put a stop to the confusion with Bobby.

Then she knew she'd have to consider her feelings for RJ. He was sweet and funny and sexy, and she was half afraid of what was happening between them. When he was in the room with her, it was all so simple. She wanted to hold him and laugh with him and talk to him.

It was when he left that doubts started to hit her. So far she'd shied away from putting him into the context of her real life. But she knew she couldn't do that forever.

She knocked again.

"Lindsey?" Her mother's voice came from the other side of the door. "Is everything okay, honey?"

"It's fine," Lindsey called.

Well, fine if you didn't mind being engaged to a lounge lizard and purring in the ear of your archenemy. She caught herself smiling again as she remembered waking up in RJ's arm.

"Mom?" she called, wondering why her mother hadn't opened the door.

"Just a..."

"Mom?"

The door opened, and her mother appeared. She was dressed in a casual fleece suit and stocking feet, and her hair was slightly mussed.

Lindsey glanced at her watch. Nearly nine. "Did I wake you up?"

Her mother smoothed her hair. "Of course not, honey. Come on in."

As she stepped out of the way, Lindsey caught sight of Chef Henri pouring water into the coffeemaker. He was dressed in formal pants and a white shirt. But he wasn't wearing a jacket or tie, and there was a wrinkle across the back of his shirt.

The meaning of the scene hit Lindsey full force. "Uh, I, uh..."

"You remember Henri," said her mother, her voice only slightly high-pitched. "Would you care for some coffee?"

"Right. Sure. Love some," Lindsey stuttered. Good grief, she wasn't the only one who'd spent the night wrapped in the arms of a man. Her mother was sleeping with the chef.

"Nice to see you again, Lindsey," said Henri, turning to face her.

Lindsey took a step into the room. "Thank you. I'm... I—I loved your blueberry bagels." She cringed at the inane observation.

"What do you take in your coffee?" asked Henri. His voice was nothing but courteous. They could have been seated in his restaurant on a Saturday evening.

Lindsey realized she should take a lesson.

"Just black." Strong, unadulterated coffee seemed like a very good idea.

She sank down on the couch, glancing from her mother to Henri, then back again. Everything had seemed so normal when they left Vancouver three days ago.

"What can we do for you?" asked her mother, sitting on the sofa across from Lindsey as Henri placed a cup of hot coffee in each of their hands.

Lindsey blinked. *Wake me up?*

"I'll step out and let the two of you talk." Henri patted her mother's shoulder.

"That's not necessary." Lindsey quickly shook her head.

"Not at all," her mother echoed.

"You talk to your daughter," Henri said to Janet. "She looks like she needs your attention."

Janet gave Henri's hand a quick squeeze, then he headed to the door. "I'll see you later."

As he left, Janet turned to Lindsey. "Is everything all right, dear?"

Lindsey took in the sparkle in her mother's eyes and the flush on her cheeks. She hadn't seen her mother this animated in years, and she didn't have the heart to detract from her joy. She'd solve the Bobby problem on her own. And she'd figure out RJ, too.

"Everything's just fine, Mom. I'm having a great Christmas." Seeing her mother this happy was worth everything.

"Isn't it all perfectly lovely?"

Judging by the grin on her mother's face, the entire universe was perfectly lovely at the moment.

"I love the earrings," said Lindsey, flipping her hair out of the way to model them for her mother.

"They look very good on you."

''You have excellent taste.''

''So do you. Henri and I were just talking about Grandma's china.''

''He likes it?'' asked Lindsey.

''He loves it. We were trying to decide how best to display it.''

''The two of you are making *china* plans together?''

''He has some great ideas.'' The smile grew on her mother's face. ''I think I'll have a cabinetmaker look at how best to showcase all the pieces.''

''That makes sense.''

''No matter where I decide to live, I think I'll entertain more. Henri says the greatest gift you can give is hospitality.''

''Henri says that?''

Her mother nodded. ''What about you, dear?''

''I'm not planning to entertain more often.'' In fact, she was going to have to consider becoming a hermit to get the Group Twelve proposal done on time. RJ might be the most fun she'd had in months, but he was also the biggest distraction.

Her mother smiled at the small joke. ''Are you sure everything's all right?''

''No problems,'' said Lindsey, with a wave of her hand. At least nothing she couldn't handle on her own.

''The little thing with Bobby?''

''Will work itself out.'' She put as much conviction into the statement as she could muster. New Year's at the latest, she told herself. Bobby was hardly in a position to bother her once she was in Vancouver.

Her mother beamed. "Good. That's good."

"So, tell me about Henri."

"Isn't he wonderful?" Her mother's chest expanded. "And such a gentleman."

"I'm glad."

Her mother sighed happily. "We need to be discreet, of course. But, I swear, I feel like a teenager again."

"I'm very happy for you, Mom." And she was somewhat amazed at her mother's serenity. A physical relationship with a man was a huge step.

Her mother leaned forward and whispered, "Henri knows *French.*"

"Really." Lindsey nodded.

After all, Lindsey had also embarked on a physical relationship last night, and she was feeling anything but serene about it. There were so many questions. So many complications.

"And Frenchmen. Well, I swear they are born knowing certain *things.*" Her mother nodded sagely.

Lindsey felt her eyes widen. "That's nice." She was pretty sure she didn't want any more details on the things her mother's Frenchman was born knowing.

"Ooh, la, la," said her mother with a giggle.

Oh, my goodness. Lindsey set down her coffee cup and started to stand. Forget serenity, Henri had created a monster.

"Did you know there's a way of kissing—"

"Want to meet for lunch today?" Lindsey squeaked.

"Sure, honey. But do you have to leave so soon?"

"I'm afraid so." She backed toward the door.

"I wish you'd had a chance to talk to Henri."

"I'm sure I'll have a chance to chat with him later on."

"He'll be working most of the afternoon. He's making his special crêpe suzette for dessert, and if there's any whipping cream left over—"

Good grief. Her mother, a Frenchman and whipping cream? "See you at breakfast." Lindsey groped for the doorknob.

HER MOTHER was having an affair. Lindsey tried to assimilate the fact that both she and her mother were having holiday flings while she sipped a cup of hot chocolate in front of a big bonfire on the lake ice.

The fire snapped and crackled, burning hot enough to evaporate the top layer of ice, rather than liquefy it. The lone adult left outside, she watched a group of well-bundled children shriek in delight, careening down the steep slope next to the lodge on brightly colored plastic sleighs.

RJ's boots squeaked on the snow as he strode toward the fire. He perched himself on the rough-hewn chair next to hers.

"Well?" he asked. His deep voice was somehow comforting, despite the fact that he was partially responsible for her confusing swirl of emotions. "How'd it go with your mom?"

"She's having wild sex with the French chef." Lindsey half laughed, half moaned.

She scrunched her eyes shut and rubbed her forehead with her mitt. Maybe she was just jealous. All she could do was worry about her and RJ, and her mother was behaving like a happy, carefree teenager.

"Henri?" asked RJ, his eyebrows knitting together.

Lindsey nodded.

"You sure?"

"Yes, I'm sure." There wasn't much room for interpretation. "Henri was in her room this morning in a wrinkled shirt. My mother was talking about Frenchmen and ooh, la, la." Lindsey waved her mittened hand in the air for emphasis.

"Ooh, la, la?" RJ grinned, leaning toward her, expression open and expectant.

"I didn't ask for details," she told him. Though her mother had seemed surprisingly willing to give them.

"So, is she going to help us out with Bobby in between—" his voice dropped to a conspiratorial level "—the ooh, la, la?"

"RJ," Lindsey admonished. "Have a little respect. We're talking about my mother."

"So?"

"She's my *mother.*"

He chuckled, putting a hand on her shoulder. "They're both adults."

That small touch felt wonderful. Suddenly, the world didn't feel quite so off balance. "I know," she sighed.

"Besides, we're hardly in a position to judge," he said.

"We're different."

"Different how?" He picked up a small branch and tossed it into the fire. "I distinctly remember a few ooh, la, las last night."

"But we're both..."

"Adults?" he asked.

"Worldly," she said. Maybe her mother just hadn't thought about how much a holiday fling could complicate her life.

"You think you're more worldly than Henri? He grew up in Paris."

"I'm more worldly than my mother."

"How so?"

"She was in a relationship with the same man her whole life." Where Lindsey hadn't had a relationship with any man. Unless she counted RJ. Which she didn't. Because it wasn't.

Okay. Bad example.

"So?" he asked.

"Well..." Lindsey tried again. "I...have a very responsible job." But she knew her argument was going nowhere. Her mother had a perfect right to do whatever she wanted with Henri.

"She's twenty years older than you," RJ pointed out.

"Okay, fine. If my mother and Henri want to talk French, sleep together and play around with leftover whipped cream, it's perfectly fine by me."

RJ's grin widened. "There's leftover whipped cream?"

"RJ."

"You know the possibilities are—"

"No." She couldn't believe he was even suggesting they raid the kitchen along with her mother's lover.

"But we could—"

"Not a chance."

"Have you ever—"

"We won't be getting any help from my mother on the Bobby front," Lindsey told RJ. She didn't even want to imagine RJ and firelight and whipped cream. The picture was too compelling, too addictive. "Tell me how it went with Camellia."

"Spoilsport," he whispered.

"Is she going to retract her prediction?"

He sighed. "Afraid not."

"What happened to your boyish charm?"

"Guess it doesn't work on women over eighty. She's one tough old bird."

Lindsey leaned back in the wooden chair, squelching her disappointment. "I knew it was a long shot. But with Mom out of the picture, I'd really hoped..."

"I'm afraid Camellia really believes you're marrying Bobby."

A shudder ran through Lindsey. "You don't suppose..."

RJ turned to look hard in her eyes. "Don't even *think* it. Can you imagine any circumstances under which you'd marry him?"

Lindsey shook her head. ‘‘No. But it’s a bit creepy. What with Mom and Susan.’’

‘‘Camellia predicted your mom and Henri?’’

‘‘My dad.’’

‘‘Oh.’’

‘‘Yeah. She’s probably got a better track record than Madam Rosa on cable.’’

‘‘You watch a cable psychic?’’

‘‘Only the commercials. And I think she’s a fortune-teller. Magnificent-looking woman. Wears a psychedelic turban.’’

‘‘Nice touch.’’

‘‘It’s all fake.’’

‘‘Of course it is. And you’re not going to marry Bobby. They can’t very well march you shotgun down the aisle.’’

‘‘Connie might try.’’

RJ chuckled. ‘‘My gun’s bigger than hers. I’ll save you.’’

‘‘My hero.’’

‘‘Seriously, Lindsey—’’

‘‘I’ll ride it out,’’ she sighed. ‘‘I suppose I can stand it for a couple more days.’’

‘‘Anybody who thinks you’re a good match for Bobby is either blind or foolish. You shouldn’t give two hoots about their opinion.’’

‘‘I know.’’

His voice dropped. ‘‘I miss you.’’

Lindsey played dumb. ‘‘I’m right here.’’

‘‘Yeah. But you’re wearing way too many clothes.’’

"It's twenty below."

"There are ways." His tone made her shiver, not with cold but with desire. She missed him, too.

"Want to go for a snowmobile ride?" he asked, waggling his eyebrows.

"On a *snowmobile?*" She didn't know why he said he'd outgrown risk taking. He was much wilder than she'd ever be.

"It's been done."

"I don't want to know about this."

"I thought you were adventurous. We've really got to work on that."

"Uncle RJ?" Frank called, waving madly from the sleigh hill. He was wearing snow pants, a long scarf and colorful mittens, and he, David, Ricky and Brian were struggling to drag a giant toboggan up the slope.

RJ turned toward the group.

"Yeah?" he called.

"We're all goin' to the very top." Frank slipped and fell, losing a few feet on the hillside, dragging the wooden toboggan with him. He came to a stop and lifted his head. "Want to drive?"

RJ chuckled as he stood. "Duty calls," he whispered to Lindsey. "Be right there," he yelled to the children.

She watched while he crossed the short distance to the hillside and took the toboggan rope from his adoring nephews and began towing it up the steep hill. The kids fell into step behind him, and he turned every once in a while to check on them.

When Brian, the smallest of the group, fell behind,

RJ waited. Then scooped him into his arms and continued up the hill. Lindsey smiled at the picture they made.

At the top, they all piled onto the sleigh. RJ settled himself on the back, took up the rope and pushed off. They looked like a colorful train against the glaring white snow—toque pom-poms bouncing, scarves flying behind.

Lindsey shaded her eyes as a chorus of delighted shouts echoed through the valley. They rocketed down the steep slope and far out onto the snowy ice.

Her chest tightened. RJ was a caretaker. He was deep-down kind and compassionate. While Bobby only paid attention to the children when he wanted free labor, RJ assembled their toys, told them stories and never once brushed off their questions.

"Want to come for a ride?" RJ called to Lindsey as the toboggan came to a halt.

Lindsey shook her head. She hadn't been sleigh riding in years.

"Come on," he insisted, straightening, turning the toboggan and walking toward her.

The kids raced toward the hill. "Again, Uncle RJ! Come on!" called David.

"Kick back," RJ said to Lindsey. "Have a little fun. I thought you said you were a risk taker." He winked, and she could see the challenge in his eyes.

He reached out and took her mittened hand in his, tugging gently. Though there were several layers of insulation and fabric between them, she could feel an electric connection.

"Come with me," he whispered. "Let me take you for a ride." And suddenly, she was willing to follow him halfway up a mountain just for the heck of it, just to slide screaming down again at breakneck speed.

She nodded.

He grinned.

They started walking, her footsteps light.

Maybe her mother had it right. Maybe whipped cream and sex wasn't such a bad idea. And maybe she could make love on a snowmobile.

For the rest of the afternoon, she clambered up the hillside, then zoomed down—wind in her face, RJ's arms tight around her—forgetting she had a single care in the world.

9

AFTER DINNER, Lindsey climbed into a bath to take away the chill. Then she dressed in a comfortable pair of sweatpants and a fleece pullover.

RJ had promised to join her. But there was a games marathon in full swing in the great room. He was partnered with Frank playing hearts, and she didn't know when he'd get away.

Just as well. Between tobogganing and helping Susan with dinner, Lindsey had gone yet another day without getting any work done on the Group Twelve proposal. The new year was creeping up fast, and she hadn't made any significant progress. Instead of going downstairs, she decided to settle in and get some real work done.

She fired up her laptop and was quickly immersed in learning the graphics program. She imported the company logo and some pictures, then she started developing graphs.

This was going to be her most exciting presentation ever.

"EARTH TO LINDSEY." She felt the brush of RJ's lips as he kissed the back of her neck.

She hadn't even heard the balcony door open.

"Hi," she breathed, glancing at her watch. It was after eleven.

"Busy?" he asked.

"Can I..." She clicked the mouse, adjusting the scale of the current graph. "Just..."

She'd made serious progress on the proposal—twenty slides finished, only five or so to go.

RJ rubbed her shoulders. "You need a couple of minutes to finish up?"

She held up one hand, signaling five minutes, while clicking the mouse with the other. A blue background might look better against the red company logo.

"I'll wait," RJ whispered in her ear.

She smiled without turning away from the screen.

The next time Lindsey glanced at her watch, it was two o'clock in the morning. She gasped and whirled to check on RJ, wondering why he hadn't said something, wondering if he'd fallen asleep on her bed.

He hadn't fallen asleep.

He'd left her bed altogether.

He'd left her room altogether.

While Lindsey was absorbed in her work, RJ had grown impatient and walked out.

She cringed in regret, all the buoyant emotions from the afternoon evaporating in a rush. Forget about a full-blown relationship, she couldn't even balance her workload properly with a quick fling.

She turned to the computer and saved her work. She was tempted to flash through the slides one more time, to check for errors. But she forced herself to shut it down.

She owed RJ an apology. He might be asleep already, but he might be sitting over there fuming, too. She wasn't completely sure she wanted to find out which, but she wasn't about to let herself take the easy way out. She slipped her feet into a pair of oversize snow boots, wrapped herself in her parka and opened the sliding glass door.

The temperature had dropped since afternoon, and the frigid wind took her breath away. Her face stung where blowing snow brushed against it as she scooted across the balcony. The northern lights swirled on the horizon, teasing the nearby mountains. They were gorgeous shades of green and yellow, but it was way too cold to stop and get a good look.

She tested RJ's door. Unlocked, thank goodness.

His room was dark. The only illumination was from the greenish northern lights flickering through the windows. RJ was a still shape under the covers.

Lindsey closed the door behind her and stepped out of her snowy boots. She tiptoed across the carpet.

"RJ?" she whispered. Part of her acknowledged that he was most certainly sound asleep, and she should wait until morning. But another part of her needed to know if he was upset. Plus, okay, she could be honest with herself, she didn't want to wait another full day before being held in his arms again.

She sure hoped she hadn't blown their entire relationship by standing him up.

"RJ?" She tried again, crouching, speaking a little louder this time.

"Yeah?" He didn't sound very happy to see her.

"I'm sorry."

"What time is it?"

"Around two."

"You finished?"

She nodded. Then, realizing he probably couldn't see her, she whispered guiltily. "Yes. You awake?"

"I am now."

"You upset?"

"I'll get over it." He didn't proposition her or invite her into his bed.

She hesitated. Now would be a really good time to walk away. Walking away would prove she could do it. It would be good practice for New Year's Day when she'd have to leave him for good.

She tried to straighten up, but for some reason her legs didn't get the message. She licked her dry lips. "You want to go back to sleep now or..."

He reached for her, touching the parka sleeve, then groping his way across her back. "What is with you and too many clothes today?"

Despite the fact that she'd just failed a very important walking-away test, Lindsey smiled in the dark. "It's cold out on the balcony."

"Tell me about it," he grunted. "You going to stay awhile or what?"

It wasn't exactly the most gracious invitation, and he did seem at little annoyed with her. But she wanted to stay anyway. She wanted to stay so badly it scared her.

"If that's okay with you." Her voice trembled a little.

His hand found her neck, and his fingertips brushed her skin. "I did say anytime, anywhere, any way you want." There was an inflection in his voice that she couldn't quite put her finger on.

"RJ. I'm..." She bit her lip to stop herself from apologizing again. She had obligations. Her work was important, and she couldn't, *wouldn't* change that for any man.

"Take off your coat," he whispered, tugging at her parka, nothing but pure passion in his voice this time.

Good.

Pure passion. That's what she needed. Pure, uncomplicated passion.

The sound of her zipper echoed through the silent room. She shrugged out of the coat, and the green and yellow northern lights danced against the fabric of her fleece shirt.

RJ shifted to make room and flipped open the covers.

She dropped the coat on the floor and slid into the warm bed.

"I missed you so damn much." He was wide awake now, his eyes like flints in the darkened room.

He bent his head and captured her lips. He splayed his hand over the small of her back, pulling her tight against his heated body.

Lindsey groaned. Lying wrapped in his arms felt so good. She pressed her body against him, returning his kisses, running her hands over his skin.

How could she have forgotten, even for a few

hours, what this felt like? Why had she taken so long to get here tonight? Now she never wanted to leave.

She never, *ever* wanted to leave him.

She knew her thoughts were dangerous. Her work was important. She lived for it. It couldn't be replaced by RJ's hot breath, his tender kisses, his…oh!

She groaned.

He whispered her name.

Okay, so maybe it could. Just for a little while.

Somewhere deep inside her an alarm bell sounded. It was a false alarm, she assured herself. This was simply a stolen interlude. She didn't actually love RJ. She wouldn't let herself love RJ.

Okay, so maybe she would, but only for a few minutes. She'd love him here in the dark and then stop before morning.

She could easily stop before morning. After all, a woman didn't achieve Gold Medal Certification without a whole lot of self-discipline.

"THEY'RE PLANNING a *what?*" RJ stared incredulously at Susan. She balanced Rose-Marie on her knee at the empty dining room table while filling out next week's grocery order.

"A wedding shower. New Year's Eve. Near as I can tell, Connie is spearheading it, but Camellia isn't doing a thing to stop her."

RJ took a couple of paces, then turned and paced back. "Lindsey is *not* going to take this well."

Susan looked up. "You think we should tell her?"

"Of course we have to tell…" RJ paused. Or did

they? What was the point in ruining the rest of her holiday? And that's exactly what would happen if she spent it worrying about New Year's Eve.

He didn't want her to worry.

He wanted to spend some more time with the wonderful carefree woman who'd raced down the hill with him yesterday. He wanted to hold her, relaxed and satiated in his arms again—like he had last night. Like he wanted to again tonight.

Tonight and as many other nights as he could get away with.

"RJ?" Susan snapped her fingers in front of his face.

"Huh?"

His sister grinned. "The mere mention of her name sends you off into la-la land."

"Don't be ridiculous."

Rose-Marie made a sound in the back of her throat and reached toward him with her chubby little arms. He turned his attention to her, picking her up so that she curled against him, all warm and soft and smiling.

Lindsey didn't send him into la-la land. She just…

A warm feeling suffused his body. Okay, so it was la-la land. Too bad. He liked it there.

"Nose-ah, nose-ah, nose-ah." Rose-Marie tapped the end of his nose with her sticky index finger.

"Nothing says we have to tell her right away," Susan ventured.

RJ shook his head. "We have to figure out a way to stop them."

"Well, I'm open to suggestions."

"It's your lodge. You're in charge."

Susan choked back a laugh. "Uh, you might want to try pointing that out to Camellia and Connie. They've bribed half the kitchen staff."

"Chef Henri?"

"No. I don't know what's going on with Henri lately. Half the time he's humming, the other half I don't even know where he is."

RJ nodded, but didn't offer any insider information on Henri. Rose-Marie tugged on his ear.

"Connie's got the morning shift making canapés and petit fours."

"Terrific."

"At least we've got a couple of days to play with," said Susan. "Maybe we can stop it."

"You're more optimistic than I am." If they had an outright confrontation with the aunts, it would only drive their efforts further underground. And there wasn't a hope of getting Camellia to change her mind.

RJ was willing to simply fly Lindsey out of here, but there was her mother to consider. He didn't think Lindsey would be willing to compromise her mother's holiday.

Besides, if he flew Lindsey out of here, she'd probably hop the first plane to Vancouver.

He wasn't ready for Lindsey to go back to Vancouver yet. In fact, the thought of her leaving made it difficult for him to breathe.

It wasn't that he was thinking long term. Well, not exactly. He just knew he had to do *something*.

He couldn't let her fly to Vancouver and end it. He

had to convince her to come back or let him visit her there or take up phone sex. Something. *Anything* to keep her in his life.

Susan stood up and lifted Rose-Marie from RJ's arms. "If worse comes to worst, we can always warn her at the last minute."

"Yeah." RJ nodded. They could warn her about the wedding shower at the last minute. And if she wanted to bail, he'd fly her out on a moment's notice.

But, as far as his relationship with her was concerned, he was in big trouble. If the tightness in his chest was anything to go by, phone sex wasn't going to cut it.

RJ SQUEEZED a sponge full of warm water over Lindsey's bare breasts, tickling her skin. She squirmed against him in the oversize tub, deciding this was the memory she'd hold on to. RJ naked, satiated, making her feel like a treasure.

They'd lain awake all night long in her big bed, trying to make their last day into forever but knowing they never could. Once again, morning was creeping up on them, and tomorrow Lindsey would leave.

He kissed the back of her neck, his lips cool against her wet, heated skin. The kiss intensified, and she reached to caress the hair at the nape of his neck, feeling as though her bones were going to melt.

"I guess we worried for nothing," she sighed. Even without Camellia or her mother's help, Lindsey had managed to keep Bobby at bay for the past few days. She'd found that if she gave him polite, noncommittal answers to his questions about the future, he went away happy.

''Nothing?'' RJ asked between kisses.

''I half expected Connie to dig up some copies of *Modern Bride* or start baking a twelve-tiered cake. But we're almost in the home stretch.''

''Bobby did convince you to give him your ring size.''

''But I'll be long gone before he gets anywhere near a jeweler. I'm sure he'll catch on that I'm not coming back.''

''Are you ever coming back?'' asked RJ. He let his hand and the sponge come to rest against her chest. He tucked her wet hair behind one ear.

Lindsey swallowed. ''Not in the foreseeable future.''

The admission made her stomach clench. Much as she hated to leave, she had a mountain of work to do in Vancouver. Gold Merit Certification was only the beginning.

She felt his chin move against her scalp as he nodded.

''I see.'' The words were clipped.

''RJ...'' What was she supposed to do? What was she supposed to say? They'd both known this was temporary.

''We've still got twenty-four hours,'' she offered.

''Don't you want to see me again?'' he asked, sounding heart-wrenchingly vulnerable.

''Of course—''

''Good.''

"It's just—"

"What about this weekend?"

"This weekend?" She tipped her head to stare at him.

What was he talking about? How could she possibly see him this weekend? They'd be two thousand miles apart.

He'd be flying over the tundra somewhere. She'd be at the office finishing up the Group Twelve proposal. Which, by the way, she had yet to spend any decent amount of time on.

"I was thinking...." He focused on the faucet at the far end of the tub instead of her face. "I might pop down to Vancouver on the weekend."

"What?" Oh, no, no, no. Cold turkey was her only hope.

"I just want to see you again." He made it sound so simple.

"RJ. We promised."

"I didn't promise."

"Well, you definitely understood." It wasn't fair for him to suddenly change the rules.

"We can change our minds, you know."

"No. We can't. It's impossible." Why was he putting this all on her? Why did she have to be the heavy?

"Nothing is impossible." He stared into her eyes, and for a second she wanted desperately to believe that the fantasy could go on forever. Leaving him was going to be more painful than she'd ever imagined.

But she couldn't let herself believe. She hadn't

even been able to finish a single financial proposal with him around. He distracted her. He got mad when she worked late. She could never balance a career around him.

She didn't want their relationship to end badly, but it definitely had to end here.

"I can honestly say you're one of the best things that ever happened to me," she said, voice trembling.

"*One* of them?" He stiffened, letting go of her, moving his elbows to the edges of the tub. He sucked in a breath. "You are the best damn thing that has ever walked into my life. And I want you. Period."

"RJ, don't—"

"But I guess I'm just *one* of the nice things on your extensive list. Thanks so much, sweetheart," he drawled, drawing further away.

She immediately felt cold. "RJ, please. Don't—"

"Don't what?"

"We've still got today." She wanted today. She needed today. If she was going to go the rest of her life without him, she needed to hold him close and imprint him on her brain.

"And that's enough for you?" He stood and stepped abruptly out of the tub. Water cascaded from his body onto the wooden floor. "I can't believe..."

"It has to be enough," she said, wrapping her arms around her wet body and starting to shake.

"I can't believe you're just going to walk away." He grabbed a white terry robe.

"I have no choice." Was she supposed to drop her

clients? Drop her career? Her dreams? Move away from her mother?

How could she simply give up everything she'd ever worked for?

"You always have a choice."

She shook her head. "Don't make me, RJ."

"Oh, I'm going to make you, all right," he said, stuffing his arms into the sleeves of the robe. "I'm going to make you choose big time." He tightened the belt.

She raised her wet fingers to her lips and whimpered.

"I love you, Lindsey Parker." He headed to the door and flung it open. "Choose that."

With the sound of the slamming door ringing in her ears, Lindsey slumped against the side of the tube.

He loved her.

Well, she loved him. She hadn't even admitted it to him, and they were already tearing each other apart.

What had she imagined? She asked herself ruthlessly. That they would shake hands? Say thanks for the memories? Each go their own way without a backward glance?

This was all her fault. She never should have propositioned him. She should have stayed far, far away from their attraction to one another.

That's what she should have done.

And that's what she would do, if she could go back and fix it.

Then RJ wouldn't hate her. And she wouldn't be cradling her broken heart in a room full of memories where the candlelight and citrus bath oil mocked what could have been. And her future at Progressive Dynamics would look bright and exciting instead of bleak and lonely.

She never should have let this happen.

RJ STAGGERED against the log wall in the hallway, not caring if anyone found him there.

What had he done?

He'd come on like a high-pressure salesman, trying to force Lindsey into the future he wanted—clearly not the future she wanted.

If she didn't love him, she didn't love him. Now he'd made sure she hated him.

This week was supposed to be her beautiful Christmas memory. And he'd destroyed that, too.

If he loved her… And he definitely loved her. He had to do what was best for her. He had to help her remember the good things about the past week. And then he had to let her go.

He turned and raised his fist to her door, rapping twice with his knuckles.

A moment later, she cracked the door. There were tear trails down her cheeks, and he immediately felt worse.

"I'm sorry," he whispered.

She nodded silently.

"Can I come back in?"

She shrugged but stepped back to open the door.

He slipped inside. She'd pulled on a robe, and the moisture from her skin had soaked through it.

"I want you to be happy," he whispered, reaching out to brush her hair from her forehead. He'd give anything to turn back the clock and spend the next twenty-four hours with her in blissful innocence.

But he couldn't. They'd both said what they'd said, and both knew what they knew.

She nodded again, not looking the least bit happy. "We both have busy and complicated lives," she whispered.

"I know," he said.

"We won't mean to hurt each other. We won't mean to make demands. We won't mean to distract each other from what's important. But we will."

"You're sure?" he asked, giving it one more shot, hoping against hope she would give him just a little room.

But all she did was nod. She was sure.

It didn't matter that *she* was what was important to him. He knew there was no point in repeating that. He'd said it all. He'd laid his soul bare. He'd told her he loved her, and she still didn't want him.

He drew in a deep breath. "I wouldn't trade one single second of what we shared. I hope you have a wonderful, successful life, Lindsey Parker."

Twin tears spilled over the edges of her lashes.

This time when he walked out the door, he went straight to his room and started packing.

LINDSEY DASHED at her cheeks, promising herself she was through crying. She cranked up her laptop again. No more wallowing in self-pity. She had done the right thing, the only logical thing. And it was time to get back to real life.

Luckily, she hadn't seen RJ since the morning. She suspected he might have planned it that way, but she didn't care. If he'd been around at lunchtime, she doubted she could have kept her composure in public.

The Group Twelve presentation wasn't ready yet. But she'd spent all morning on it, and by tomorrow it was going to knock the partners' socks off. A wayward tear trailed down Lindsey's cheek, and she ruthlessly scrubbed it away. Debt-to-asset ratio was what mattered to her now. Nothing but.

"LINDSEY?" Susan's voice accompanied a light knock on Lindsey's door.

Lindsey kept her focus on the proposal. She planned to sit right here and keep working until New Year's Eve was over. There was no way she could possibly face RJ again.

"Lindsey, open up."

Lindsey kept typing. Gold Medal Certification was only the beginning. Next she wanted to be a partner.

"I just saw RJ," said Susan through the door.

The words blurred on the screen, and her raw throat tightened. Lindsey closed her eyes. She was holding her emotions together by a thread.

"I have a key," said Susan. "I really need to talk to you."

Lindsey ignored her. She knew Susan. Susan wouldn't invade her privacy by using a passkey.

"Lindsey, you're scaring me."

Lindsey rubbed her eyes. She did not want to face Susan. She'd made a huge mistake with RJ, and she wanted to pay the price in privacy.

She heard the lock click open.

She clenched her jaw and turned toward the sound.

"He's leaving," Susan said without preamble as she strode into the room and closed the door.

"Good." RJ leaving was the best possible thing that could happen at this point. If he wasn't here, then she wasn't in danger of changing her mind and tossing her life out the window. Lindsey drew in a ragged breath.

"I saw him heading out to the plane. I take it you two had a fight?"

Lindsey nodded. Her throat was one big ache, and she was afraid of how her voice might sound.

"Want to talk?" asked Susan.

Lindsey shook her head. She bit the inside of her lip.

"Then let me guess." Susan plunked down on the edge of the bed, spreading her hands wide to balance herself. "You're in love, and he's not."

Lindsey shook again.

"He's in love, and you're not?"

Lindsey shook.

"Well, somebody's sure in love here. You're pale as a ghost, and he's mad as a hornet."

Lindsey blinked. Her eyes started to burn, and she blinked harder.

"You're both in love?" Susan whispered, comprehension dawning in her eyes as she leaned forward.

Lindsey closed her eyes and nodded miserably.

"That's great." Susan brightened.

Lindsey shook her head.

"What's the big problem?" Susan asked.

"It won't... We can't... There's no future for us," Lindsey whispered, trying valiantly to keep the sob out of her voice as Susan's genuine concern broke through her wall of determination.

Her chest tightened in pain, and her entire body felt raw and vulnerable.

"Why not?" asked Susan, standing, crossing the room to Lindsey. "Why the *heck* not?"

"I have a career."

"So?"

"I can't do a career and a man." Her voice strengthened with the support of her long-held conviction. "I know I can't do it. Just the other night..." She waved a hand in the air and took a moment to swallow.

"Just the other night," Lindsey continued, "I had to work when RJ...when we...would rather have been together."

"And what? He got *mad?*" Susan's voice rang with incredulity.

"Yes."

"That doesn't sound like RJ." Susan shook her head.

"I let work come first, and he didn't like it."

"Are you sure? I work a lot. Seth doesn't mind."

"You and Seth work together."

"True."

"He doesn't feel left out. He doesn't feel threatened by your work life."

"I guess…."

"You haven't seen what I've seen. I've watched women torn apart by conflicting loyalties. I can't do it. I just made Gold Medal Certification. It's now or never for me and the big time. I know I can't do both."

Susan sighed and leaned against the desktop. "I think you're wrong, but I'm not going to push you."

"Thank you." Lindsey slumped in the chair. She had to take it one day at a time for awhile.

Cold turkey was going to be tough. But she couldn't have RJ. The sooner she came to terms with that, the better.

"We've got another problem," said Susan.

"What?" There was nothing in the world that could possibly compare.

"The aunts. Your wedding shower is starting in five minutes. They sent me to get you."

"My *wedding shower?*" A buzzing started in Lindsey's ears.

"RJ and I had a plan," said Susan. "We were going to tell you. He was going to fly you out if you wanted to leave. But now…"

"RJ knew about this?"

Susan nodded.

"He knew about this and he didn't tell me?"

"He was going to tell you today."

"No way," said Lindsey, standing up. "Not a

chance. I am *not* doing this." Not even Connie, Eileen and Camellia could go this far.

"Want to hide? I could give you a snowmobile and a ten-minute head start."

It was tempting. And if Lindsey knew how to drive a snowmobile, it would be even more tempting. But she didn't. Besides, she'd had about enough. This was ending here and now.

She squared her shoulders. "Let's go."

"You sure?"

"I am tough as nails in negotiations. Did I ever mention that? It's one of the reasons I've been so successful." Lindsey twisted the doorknob and pulled open the door. "Connie has *so* met her match."

10

"WHAT DO YOU THINK you're doing, RJ?" Susan crossed her arms over her chest, looking as stern as was possible in a parka and a reindeer toque.

"Inspecting my plane," he answered tersely, running his hand along the front of the wing as he walked its length. The last thing he wanted right now was to explain himself to his sister.

"Going to miss the wedding shower?" She probed.

"What do you think?"

"I think Lindsey needs you right now."

RJ snorted. Yeah. Right. Lindsey Parker didn't need him. She'd made that abundantly clear.

"I know you're in love with her."

RJ stopped. He let his hand drop from the wing. "You don't know any such thing." He ground the words out.

She snorted. "I've been putting off saying this to you...."

He turned to face her and sucked in a lungful of frigid air. "I don't know where you got this idea that you and I needed to have little heart-to-heart chats. We didn't do it as kids, and we don't do it now. So just back off."

You would think a thirty-year-old guy would be entitled to a little privacy in his life. He loved Lindsey. Lindsey was leaving. Couldn't Susan just back off and let him bleed in peace?

"What happened to you, RJ?"

RJ shook his head and went back to the inspection.

"I used to admire you. My big brother, so bold, so brave, so larger than life." She paused again, giving him a chance to rebut.

Not this time. He was past the point in his life where he had to prove himself to anyone.

"Used to be you had guts," she said. "You took chances. You lived on the edge. If life didn't want to hand you something on a silver platter, all the better."

She waved an expansive arm behind her. "You're the reason we bought this land. You're the reason we mortgaged our souls and hacked a hotel out of the wilderness. You set the example, RJ. I can't stand to see you give up and take the safe road."

The *safe* road? RJ shot her a glare. "I'm a bush pilot." There was still plenty of action, adventure and danger in his life. It wasn't like he'd turned into a bank teller.

"Bush pilot? Ha. You ferry my tourists back and forth from Whitehorse."

There was a whole lot of truth to what she said. Which made him feel even worse. He wasn't good enough for Lindsey, and apparently he wasn't good enough for Susan anymore, either. So kind of her to tell him at this particular moment in his life.

He moved to the prop, checking it for nicks. ''Is there a point to this?''

''The big brother I knew and loved grabbed life by the throat and shook it until it gave him what he wanted.''

''The big brother you knew and loved grew up.''

''You didn't grow up, RJ. You got old.''

''Same difference.''

''There's a big difference.'' She stomped across the ice to stand in front of him. ''You're thirty years old, RJ, not sixty. Are you just going to fly around in a holding pattern until it's time to retire? For goodness sake, Seth is a year older than you. We've just started on a brand-new life.''

Each of Susan's words stung like barbs. Okay, so maybe he had grown a little complacent. So what? She didn't have to toss it in his face like it was a crime. Plenty of people led quieter lives. They probably lived longer, too.

Once more he tried to stare her down. ''Is there a reason you're trying to make me feel like pond scum?''

''Heck, yeah.''

''And that would be?''

''Lindsey.''

RJ turned to the prop. ''I'm not discussing Lindsey.'' Susan might as well take a dagger to his heart and finish the job.

''You love her.''

''Is this a circular conversation? Because I recall this part before.''

"She loves you."

"Yeah. Right." That would sure explain why she was kicking him out of her life.

"She does."

"What? You're clairvoyant like Aunt Camellia now?"

"I just talked to her."

"Aunt Camellia?"

"No, Lindsey."

That got RJ's attention. "Lindsey actually told you she loved me."

"Right."

RJ's jaw hardened. It wasn't like Susan to be deliberately cruel.

Her voice dropped. "What would you do, RJ? If you were eighteen years old again and you found out Lindsey loved you? And you loved her back?" She paused. "What would you do?"

That was an easy one. At eighteen years old, RJ had been young and impetuous and he hadn't yet learned that there were limits.

He wouldn't have cared less what Lindsey *said* she wanted. He would have moved heaven and earth to get her. Nothing would have stopped him. Nothing would have stood in his way for long.

"Because she does, RJ," said Susan. "And you know what?"

"What?" His heart rate jumped. If Lindsey loved him... If Lindsey *loved* him...

"The wedding shower? It's not a wedding shower

at all. When I left, Camellia and Connie were stuffing Lindsey into a white dress.''

''A *what?*'' RJ's stomach bottomed out.

''It's a wedding, RJ. Lindsey is about to be dragged down the aisle.''

''She wouldn't,'' RJ whispered.

''Connie looked pretty determined to me.''

''I know she wouldn't,'' said RJ, but he was already heading for the lodge. There was no way in the world Lindsey would stand up and say ''I do'' to Bobby. Not a chance.

RJ TOOK THE STAIRS two at a time. Blurry figures moved behind the frosted glass. He burst through the front door.

Then he saw her.

The white chiffon dress hung from her shoulders, only half zipped up. She had a veil in her hand, a livid expression on her face.

Bobby was at the front of the room dressed in a suit. Uncle Herbert, whose justice-of-the-peace license had probably expired around the end of the First World War, stood next to Bobby, Bible in his hand, squinting at a sheaf of papers.

There was nothing in this setup that could possibly be legal, but Lindsey standing in the white dress with Bobby grinning hungrily set off a little explosion in RJ's brain.

Eighteen be damned. Susan might think he'd lost his edge, but absolutely nothing was going to stand between him and Lindsey.

Not Camellia.

Not Bobby.

Not even Lindsey.

RJ strode toward her. The guests parted under his determined look, and Lindsey gazed gratefully into his eyes.

He lifted her into his arms and turned to head for the exit. He was going for a whole lot more than grateful here.

He was tossing her in his plane, taking off, then talking some sense into her. Exactly how he was going to talk sense into her was a little fuzzy. But he'd work it out somehow.

"Stop right there, young man." Camellia stood between RJ and the door. She rapped her cane on the floor. "The wedding hasn't taken place yet."

"And it's not going to." He moved to step around Camellia.

She blocked him with her cane.

Lindsey was silent, but her arms tightened around his neck. Good. They'd work it out between them later. Right now, he just needed to get her out of the lodge and into his plane.

"What did I tell you about anticipating the wedding vows?" asked Camellia, steel in her eyes.

"There aren't going to be any wedding vows. Lindsey is *not* marrying Bobby."

"Bobby?" Camellia's forehead furrowed.

"Read my lips," said RJ. "I am—"

"Where on earth did you get the idea Lindsey was marrying Bobby?" asked Camellia.

RJ paused.

"That would be because you *told* everybody she was marrying Bobby."

Camellia drew herself up to her full five feet two inches. "I said no such thing."

"Can we just go?" Lindsey whispered in his ear.

Without another word, RJ stepped around Camellia. He was at the door in three strides.

"Robert Jamison Webster, you stop right this minute."

"Robert?" Lindsey's whisper was hoarse in his ear.

RJ's heart did a free fall as Camellia's prediction slammed into his brain. She'd said "our Robert."

"RJ stands for *Robert* Jamison?" Lindsey pulled back from his shoulder and blinked incredulously.

"You didn't know that?" he asked, mentally kicking himself for being a fool. It had been years, decades since anyone had used his given name. He didn't even know Camellia remembered it.

"If I knew once, I forgot a long time ago," said Lindsey.

Camellia's cane tapped on the hardwood as she made her way toward them.

RJ turned to face her. She was grinning ear to ear. "Why on earth would I tell everybody Lindsey was marrying Bobby when it's perfectly obvious she's in love with you?"

Connie gasped.

Bobby yelled, "Wait a minute."

Most of the other guests sighed.

"Could Lindsey and I have a minute alone?" RJ asked Camellia. Without waiting for the answer, he changed direction and headed for the empty kitchen.

A chorus of voices rose behind them, Connie's strident, Bobby's whining. Uncle Herbert asked everyone if he should start the ceremony.

RJ set Lindsey on her feet.

"Do you love me?" he asked.

"RJ. This doesn't change—"

"Do you love me?

She stared at him in pained silence for a moment. Then she slowly nodded.

He cradled her face in both of his hands and placed a tender kiss on her lips. "Then we'll make it work."

She shook her head. "I can't choose. Please don't make me choose."

"Choose? Choose what?"

"Between you and my career." Teardrops started to gather on the corners of her lashes, tearing at RJ's soul.

"I would never make you choose," he said.

"We're two thousand miles apart."

"I'll move."

"You hate it when I work."

"What are you talking about?"

"The night I worked late. You hated it."

"I never said I hated it." He hadn't liked it, sure. But he'd understood.

He hadn't said or done anything to make her feel bad about working. In fact, he'd waited patiently. He'd even been willing to wait until the next day.

She dashed at her eyes with the back of her hand. "I've seen careers ruined, women torn apart over loyalties—"

"They're not us."

"The day will come. I know it will. I'll have to work late. You'll be at home, tapping your foot. I'll feel pressure, you'll get upset. I'll compromise at both ends."

"Tap my foot? I have never tapped my foot in my life. When you worked late last week, I waited patiently. I went to bed. I was perfectly willing to wait all night if that's what it took."

She eyed him doubtfully.

He took a breath. "Okay, sure, I was impatient."

"See?"

"Have you ever *looked* at yourself in the mirror? Of *course* I was impatient. And where do you get off assuming I'll be hanging around the house waiting for you, anyway? Maybe I'll be the one out late. Maybe you'll be the one waiting for me.

"I'm not just coming to Vancouver to be your househusband. I have plans. I have dreams. I'm going to finish my jet license and lead an exciting and action-packed life." As he said the words, the plans took shape inside his head. He could to this. *They* could do this.

His voice rose. "Maybe, just *maybe* I'll be home in time for dinner. If not, you'll be the one waiting for me."

When he stopped talking, he realized just how loud

he'd been shouting. He clamped his mouth shut, hoping he hadn't blown any chance he ever had with her.

A small smile broke through her tears. "You'd work late?"

"Sure. I'm a pilot. We do it all the time."

"We'd both work late?"

"Maybe. If we do, fine. If we don't, that's fine, too."

"You wouldn't tap your foot?"

"I *never* tap my foot."

She smiled then. "I love you, RJ."

He nodded sharply. "I know. And you should probably stop telling my sister everything. She can't keep her mouth shut."

The kitchen door opened, and Camellia poked her head in. "You two about done in here? Believe me, it'll be way more fun later when you're naked."

Lindsey bit her bottom lip.

RJ chuckled. "Who are we to argue with Madam Camellia?"

"Sees all, knows all, tells all," said Lindsey. She cocked her head toward the great room. "You sure you really want to..."

"I sincerely doubt there'll be anything remotely legal about this ceremony. Even if Uncle Herbert's still a justice of the peace, we don't have a marriage license. And I suspect posting the banns on Susan's fireplace wouldn't hold up in court. You'll have plenty of time to back out later."

"I'm not backing out," said Lindsey.

He finished zipping her dress. Then he tightened

his arm around her waist and whispered in her ear. ''Good. Marry me now, sweetheart? We can always take care of the legalities later.''

She nodded. ''Yes.''

''Move it along,'' said Camellia. ''We've got fireworks ready out on the lake.''

LINDSEY'S CHEST was tight with joy as Henri walked her down the aisle. Her mother sat at the front of the makeshift chapel, dabbing her cheeks with a white handkerchief. RJ's parents were seated next to her. Susan stood up as matron of honor. And Seth was the best man.

Bobby grumbled quietly in the back row.

Uncle Herbert did a credible job of the vows, and the room was filled to bursting with love and good wishes.

When RJ kissed her, the children tossed a storm of homemade confetti. It tickled her cheeks and got caught in her hair.

''You'd better stay away from the fireworks,'' advised Camellia brusquely, brushing some of the paper from the front of her dress.

Camellia turned to RJ with a satisfied grin. ''Didn't I tell you you'd thank me later?''

''That you did,'' said RJ, pulling his aunt into a quick hug.

Lindsey's mother wrapped her arms around her. ''You can have my house,'' she whispered.

''What?'' Lindsey pulled back in confusion.

"Your apartment's way too small, and Henri's invited me to stay here."

"You're staying in the Yukon?"

Her mother winked. "He has this hot fudge recipe—well, warm fudge, not hot fudge." Her mother grinned and gave a little shiver. "Hot would be—"

"Thank you, Mom," Lindsey interrupted. The hot fudge details could remain between Henri and her mother.

"Why did you stop her?" RJ whispered close to her ear. "I wanted to know the French hot fudge secret."

"Because I'm not adventurous, remember?" Lindsey elbowed him gently in the ribs.

"We're really going to have to work on that."

"Outside for the fireworks," ordered Camellia.

The crowd moved toward the door, grabbing coats and hats along the way.

"Well," said Lindsey once they were alone.

"Well," said RJ, gazing at her with a twinkle.

"That wasn't exactly what I expected."

"The ceremony?" he asked.

"The day. The week." She slipped her hand into his. "The lifetime."

"Maybe not." RJ pulled her into his arms in front of the window as the first firework display streaked across the sky and burst into brilliant colors. "But it's definitely going to be an adventure."

"Are you generally good at predicting these

things?'' Lindsey asked with a smile as she slipped her arms into a parka.

''No, but Camellia said something about three children.''

''Children?'' Lindsey froze.

''All healthy. All happy. And we love them very much.''

''Children,'' Lindsey repeated. A small glow started somewhere deep inside her at the thought of RJ's babies. ''Boys or girls?''

''I don't know,'' he said. ''Let's go ask.''

Epilogue

"RJ?" LINDSEY SET her briefcase on the table in the entry hall of her mother's old house and crossed to the kitchen. She and RJ had redecorated last summer, and he was busy building a new fence around the backyard.

She opened the glass sliding door and stepped onto the deck. The cherry tree was in full bloom, and a light wind wafted the blossom perfume her way.

"Lasagna's in the oven," RJ called, closing the lid of his toolbox and picking it up to head into the house.

"How was your day?" He took the stairs two at a time, pausing at the top to give her a kiss.

"Busy," she answered.

"Peterson account go okay?" He wrapped his free arm lightly around her as they headed into the house.

"It did." She nodded, picking up the mail from the counter and sorting through the envelopes.

"Great. We should celebrate."

"And that's not all," she said, smiling at RJ, butterflies forming in her stomach.

"Yeah?"

"Sommerton Hartwig offered me a partnership."

RJ quickly put down the toolbox and hoisted Lindsey into the air. ''Congratulations! Way to go, sweetheart.'' He planted a long kiss on her mouth.

''I said no.''

''What?'' He let her slowly slide down his body until her feet were on the floor.

She shook her head. ''I told them with the baby coming and all—''

''Baby?'' RJ blinked.

''Oh, didn't I mention that part?'' She grinned.

''Baby?'' RJ hoisted her up again.

Lindsey laughed. ''I told Sommerton I was planning to switch to part time.''

''What? Why? I'll help with the baby.'' A huge grin split RJ's face, and he reached between them to place his palm over her abdomen. ''I'd be delighted to help with the baby.''

''I know. But with your new job and all those free airline tickets, I want to have time to travel with you.''

''Part time? You sure? What did they say?'' He was talking to her stomach, rubbing his hand back and forth.

''I'm sure.'' She paused. ''They said they want me to be a partner anyway.''

''Yeah?'' He looked at her face.

''It's never been done. But they're willing to give me a shot.''

''You're amazing.'' He cupped her chin and kissed her mouth. ''I'm going to be a daddy. And you are absolutely amazing.''

"Camellia says it's a boy."

"How does Camellia know you're pregnant?"

"How does Camellia know anything? She called this morning and told me his name was Alex."

"Works for me." He kissed her again. "Grandma Janet and Grandpa Henri will be over the moon."